A CITY ON THE RIVER

A City on the River

By RODERICK MacLEISH

E. P. Dutton & Co., Inc. | New York | 1973

Published simultaneously in Canada by
Clarke, Irwin & Company Limited, Toronto and Vancouver

SBN: 0-525-08166-6
Library of Congress Catalog Card Number: 72-82703

For Eric and Cece with love.

Contents

ACKNOWLEDGMENTS

Because of the somewhat unconventional structure of *A City on the River* I owe a rather special debt to a great many people in Washington and the other places in which research was undertaken. This book is half fiction and half nonfiction. The special debt that entails is to the scores of people in and around government who were willing to accept the idea that the various functions of government could also be rationally illustrated by fiction and who were willing to translate their roles in the Process into the various plots and subplots of the fictional sections. They not only indulged a writer's notion of his book, but so many of them strengthened the fiction by their willingness to point out how, in reality, those imaginary situations would be handled. From the people of the foreign policy–national security apparatus who described their roles in a mythic Peruvian crisis to the members and staff of the U.S. Congress who projected themselves into the struggle to pass an imaginary Youth Resources Development Act, I have encountered extraordinary kindness and patience.

Since Henry Adams anonymously published his superb novel *Democracy* in 1880, fiction about Washington has had a model set for it that, in my view, no work since has approached. What Adams teaches us is that one does not need to create synthetic drama in a city and a political society naturally endowed with real drama. All the drama one needs is in the reality of Washington. The politicians, civil servants, diplomats, bureaucrats, journalists, experts, and veterans of Washington politics who tried to help me see things as they really are share none of the blame for whatever failures lie in the pages ahead. The fault is mine alone. It is impossible to list the names of all those in Washington who gave so generously of their knowl-

11

edge of and feelings about the federal government and its workings, and besides some of them must remain anonymous.

But a few must be mentioned. Ruth Daniloff, my friend and
colleague of many years, has been as always a constant and invaluable fellow voyager through the months of this book's shaping and writing. The crew of young researchers who worked
with her were also extraordinary in their diligence, knowledge
of government, and enthusiasm. Edward John Kennedy, Linda
Smith, Arthur Bushkin, Diane Reynolds, Kathy Fitchey, and
Henry Lesansky have given so much of themselves to this project
that no word of thanks seems adequate. I am also indebted to
my son, Eric, for his criticisms and suggestions.

It is hard for a writer to explain exactly how and why cer-
tain people were important to his final conclusions. Perhaps it
will suffice to say that the following friends and colleagues in
Washington and Cambridge contributed more than they them-
selves knew in their discussions, suggestions, and criticism:
Daniel I. Davidson, Nicholas Daniloff, D. B. Hardeman, James
P. Anderson, James McManus, and Richard Braisie; Howard
Simons, Philip Geylin, Joseph Y. Smith, and David Broder;
George Reedy, Ward Just, Joseph Kraft, Joseph C. Harsch,
Bill Small, Benjamin Welles, and Stephen Barber. In addition,
Robert Amory, Jr., Lester Hyman, Averell Harriman, Dan
Levitt, and Abe Fortas were more than generous with their
time and wisdom. Robert Lowe, former Congressman F. Brad-
ford Morse of Massachusetts, and Congressmen Thomas P.
O'Neill of Massachusetts and Abner Mikva of Illinois were of
inestimable help. Doris Kearns of the John F. Kennedy School
of Government at Harvard University provided some invaluable
insights into the presidency, as did White House staff members
of two administrations.

Candida Donadio and Jeff Brown of New York know how
much I owe them. Hal Scharlatt of E. P. Dutton was my editor.

My wife, Maude, was that essential person who is always
there, a patient recipient of ideas that needed talking out, a
constant of encouragement and understanding, a sharer more
willing than anyone had a right to expect in the deprivations.

isolation, and harried circumstances that go with writing a book.

I am also indebted to a man I have never met—Samuel Eliot Morison. Of the scores of histories, historical treatises, and specialized works on government that my researchers and I have read, his *Oxford History of the American People* is the general one most diverse and complete. If the writing of history is really the writing of commentary upon history, Professor Morison's prejudices are, it seems to me, on the side of decency and joy.

Finally, two of my cats, an orange one named Robertson and a black one named Minnie, produced kittens during the time of this writing. That provided diversion, which, God knows, was needed.

R. MacL.

A CITY ON THE RIVER

1: The Process

Still one thing more, fellow citizens—a wise and frugal government, which shall restrain men from injuring one another, which shall leave them otherwise free to regulate their own pursuits of industry and improvement, and shall not take from the mouth of labor the bread it has earned. This is the sum of good government, and this is necessary to close the circle of our felicities.

Thomas Jefferson, First Inaugural
Address, March 4, 1801

Myth is the cure for time. It fills in what memory has forgotten or never knew. Myth positions the believer in time, offering him an explanation of where he came from and who he is. In our dreams we create the archetypes of king, demon, and slayer. In myth we give them conscious life, persuading ourselves that the world is as simple as our achetypical stories and that we are glorious within it. Myth is a substitute for history.

Time is the problem of the United States of America, the reason why it is not one culture, not one people bound together by a commonly understood tradition. The country evolved across time and space, from its beginning at Jamestown in 1607 to its final geographic form in the 1950s, from east to west, from an Anglo-Saxon outpost to an unequal compendium of people as diverse as the Hausa speakers of West Africa and the victims of Cumberland's brutalities on the chilled uplands of Scotland. Indeed, time separates the United States from America because there were people of an original American nature living along the East Coast and in the Middle Atlantic back kingdom long before there was a United States. That United States is approaching its two hundredth birthday, but original American culture is approaching its four hundredth.

Thus for most of American history there has been no single American character. The differences between various sorts of Americans are more than the normal differences between the classes and epochs of other countries. Not only do Americans derive from a clutter of varied cultures and races; they are also shaped by different internal milieus and eras. In the westward expansion of the United States pockets of culture were deposited across the landscape. In their flowering these separate cultures gave their own meanings to the facts of American history and its institutions. Andrew Jackson's fight with Nicholas Biddle over the Bank of the United States was really a clash of two sectional visions. To Jackson the Westerner, the moneyed interests of the Eastern seaboard were the maximum evil. To Biddle the educated Philadelphian, crude people like Jackson and his colleagues weren't grown up enough to handle other people's money.

Yet Americans were American however differently they interpreted that fact. What bound a majority of them together during the nation's formative epochs was their common hold on a myth and their common obeisance to a single, federal government.

Myth is usually derided as a collection of fanciful, egocentric unrealities that men use to escape from their condition. That is unjust. Myth, like fantasy, is essential to the spirit's survival. It ennobles the premises of lives that would otherwise seem pointless; it presupposes a loftiness of human purpose without which conscious life would be unendurable. Nor is myth rooted completely in fictional rationalization; the most successful myths have their origins in some universal truth like the Homeric master myth of man as a wandering searcher—or in some abstraction of reality.

The American myth was rooted in a profound belief in American goodness and benevolence. Other cultures, especially the aged cultures of Europe, conceive of themselves as a mixture of great principle and promise and repeated disappointments of them. The American myth was unique in its encompassment of high purpose and the successful realization of that purpose. The myth held that the American place was good and so was its land, its principles, and all its people scattered across the vast interior that Bernard De Voto once called "an internal domestic empire."

It was logical that the American place should be considered good because most of the immigrants came to it motivated by their rejection of the badness of life elsewhere. The frightened optimism of the immigrant was defensive; it had to be codified into a belief that in coming to the New World the immigrant had made a choice of supreme rightness. For him, there was no going back upon the greatest adventure of his life. He had to keep on insisting that his original optimism was justified, and that meant that the American place had to be good.

That vision of general goodness was supported by the real benevolence of American geography. There was an awful lot of it and not too many people to occupy it until after the middle of the nineteenth century. A man failing or souring on his neighbors—or souring on all of civilization for that matter—could decamp and go west. In that poorly organized wilderness he took his chances with hostile Indians, a savage climate, and winds that blew the topsoil off new farms. But such trials, it was believed, hardened and purified the spirit. That blessing of a second chance was something unknown to the rest of the civilized world. Therefore, it was reasoned, America had been singularly and specially blessed by God, the proof of its innate goodness.

The goodness of American principles and the new American man were linked together in an eighteenth-century vision of God's intent for the whole world. Buried deeply in that eighteenth-century American intellect was the concept of natural law—truths inarguable and irreducible because they were demonstrably the intent of nature and the Creator. The political writings of the Revolution and the formative period after it are riddled with the absolutist arguments of natural law: "We hold these truths to be self-evident . . ."; "to assume among the powers of the earth, the separate and equal station to which the laws of nature and of nature's God entitle them. . . ." Under the blinding reality of natural law Jefferson pondered slavery and trembled for his country when he thought that God was just. Even doughty John Adams, in answering the complaints of M. Turgot against the Constitution, used the acceptable argument that "the moral government of God, and his vicegerent, Conscience, ought to be sufficient to restrain men to obedience. . . ." If the founders of the new order in the New World considered that they had worked out something that was the purest political expression of God's will, then those principles obviously were supremely good. The citizens who lived under the principles had to be viewed as creatures inherently good, or at the very least in the perpetual process of evolving toward goodness. The American constitution and the new American man were therefore natural parts of the greater American good.

In time that concept of the American man's goodness turned arrogant and truculent. In the second quarter of the nineteenth century a new "American Republican" party came into being. Its principal tenet held that immigrants should have to spend twenty-one years in residence here before qualifying for citizenship. This nativist concept of goodness led to a spasm of ugly racial and religious rioting. In 1843 a mob attacked the Roman Catholic quarter of Philadelphia. They burned thirty houses and two churches, killed thirty people, and wounded 150 before the militia could drive them off.

In the late nineteenth century that myth of goodness was extended to cover America's relations with the rest of the world. From the slightly pompous dictates of the Monroe Doctrine onward America began to describe itself as superior to the autocratic and weakening old monarchies of Europe. It set itself up as the protector of this hemisphere against the corrupting influence of the monarchies. Simón Bolívar was on the march when Monroe promulgated his doctrine at the urging of John Quincy Adams. The Latin American liberator was recognized in Washington as the embodiment of the same God-given political impulses that had inspired the American Revolution. Like the nativist concept of American man's goodness, the concept of America's international goodness turned arrogant later. America rammed its way into a war that Spain had tried with all reason and compromise to avoid. Teddy Roosevelt pronounced his strutting axiom about walking softly through the world while carrying a big stick. At the turn of the century Americans thought that that was hot stuff.

Because the supermyth of American goodness was so powerful and so bolstered by experience for nearly eighty-five years—until the Civil War cast the first traumatic doubts—it inevitably created a spurious unity of the different cultures existing upon the American land mass. The belief in their own goodness and their country's innate goodness made them all Americans, whatever else they were. The myth was constantly being challenged during the period of its greatest validity with logic as ruthless as Thoreau's or exposés as brutal as Upton Sinclair's. But America tended to dismiss the challengers as cranks. What were the croakings of aberrant men against the overwhelming evidence that God had embraced the Americans as he had embraced the children of Israel before them?

The myth was too fragile to endure. The twentieth century assaulted its foundations, tearing the myth apart for many while hardening the desperate resolve of others to go on believing in it. From the intellectuals of Boston writing in the early decades of the twentieth century to the anguished, angry citizens marching and battling for peace in the late 1960s and early 1970s, Americans launched savage attacks on their own myth, making it seem hollower and more worthless than it really was. The exquisite despair of *The Education of Henry Adams* was the disillusionment of a man standing upon the American place, using his own American life as evidence of the planet's approaching doom. George Edward Woodbury, the Harvard-trained poet and essayist, was less cosmic in his doubt than Adams. But Woodbury put the case for American disillusionment more precisely in a letter written in 1911:

> I have come to think of America as a backward nation, in all of those things that are in a region above the material and mechanical parts of life and civilizations. . . .

The Democracy in which I was bred was of the souls of
men; but the fruit here seems to be of their bodies—comfort and mechanical convenience—admirable but not what
we most believed in.

If the myth overstated America's uniqueness in history, the
denigration of it in the twentieth century overstated the illness
of the country. If pseudo-patriotic slop translated the real meaning of America into graceless, egocentric belligerence, the re-
visionist historians cast the past in shades too dark. America
was no more best symbolized by the wars in which it had blood-
ied others than it was the sum of the injustices it had heaped
upon its black and Indian minorities. But in a whipsaw between
the fashions of overstated patriotism and overstated negation, the
myth cracked and began to die.

That left government—federal government—as the major common force that held the differing cultures of America together.
Yet government was something of a myth itself, a set of institutions grown enormous and distant and not very well understood by the people it governed, who both despised it and sub-
jected it to unreasonable expectation. As government became
more and more important to American lives, it grew more and
more remote from their reality.

That was its paradox.

The day of the pause comes to its first light with gusts of
freezing wind out of the southwest. The temperature in Washington at dawn is 27 degrees Farenheit. It will rise into the 40s
at noon, which is the mesmeric moment. Herded by the wind,
a shoal of gray clouds trundles northeast toward Chesapeake
Bay, toward the Atlantic's mute oceanic wilderness and the
world beyond, which will harken—bemused, apprehensive, or
glad—to the supreme ritual of the Americans.

The day is January 20, a huddle of chilled hours in the reign
of Capricorn the goat serpent, tenth sign of the zodiac. Capricorn's children pursue life at a relentless stumble. They are

burdened by responsibility and hounded by ambition, and Washington is their natural setting. On this particular January 20 the Process will expel from itself a man who knows more than anybody should have to know, who has endured a reality so bloated that it has become surreal. He will take his hands off the symbolic levers, the real buttons, telephones, and for-your-eyes-only papers, will put on his overcoat and walk out into the inclemencies of history. Another man who is filled with triumph, concealed apprehension, and belief that the world is still malleable will put his hand on a Bible, promise to defend the United States against its various enemies, and become its President.

But that, the mesmeric moment, is still some hours away. It is now 7 A.M. The morning light breaking across Washington's wintery gloom touches two edifices nicely arranged on two of the city's highest hills as if to symbolize equal deference to Caesar and to God in all that is done here. However, Caesar's things, as represented by the huge, Victorian dome of the U.S. Capitol, are the only durable obsessions of Washington. Heraclitus and Aristotle would have understood politics as practiced here. It is the Process without end. It exists for its own sake and, as a game, is played mostly so that the player increases his capacity to play. The rules of Washington politics are incomprehensible to nonplayers. The players sense but rarely articulate them. The tangible result of the Process is the public business and is more virtuous than not.

God—whose Episcopal cathedral on Mount St. Alban four miles to the northwest of the Capitol is now catching the first glints of the ascending sun—is an abstraction in the capital of the United States. Officials take their oaths with one hand on His book. Trust in Him is proclaimed on coins and paper money. Winners thank Him for their victories in ways that suggest that He and they were personal friends. Old-style left-wingers hold it an article of agnostic faith that God doesn't exist. Liberals tend to be privately skeptical. Conservatives believe that there is an order in the universe and that He created it. Right-wingers are convinced that God was born in Akron, Ohio, and is pro-

American. But He has no real significance in the District of Columbia.

In the center of Washington policemen in pale blue helmets and heavy jackets are roaring up and down the roped-off parade route between the White House and the Capitol. Their motorcycles bark amplified orders in the dark, cold morning. Even at this early hour the crowds are beginning to gather. They post themselves behind the police barriers along the route but not in front of the White House. Grandstands have been erected in Lafayette Park and a seat in one costs four dollars.

One hundred thousand out-of-town visitors are expected today. Five thousand National Guard troops will be on duty. Riot-control soldiers of the 82nd Airborne Division patrol the streets or are hidden in reserve beneath the Executive Office Building. Police chiefs and detectives from other cities have been wangled Inauguration Day jobs by their Congressmen. All leaves have been canceled for Washington's metropolitan police and their shifts have been extended to twelve hours. They, the Capitol and park police, the FBI, and the Secret Service can use all the help they can get. Most of the quarter of a million spectators—local and from afar—have come simply to participate in the mysterious reassurance derived from being physically present at great events. But among them there will also be every disease of the human spirit. Left-wing radicals will be here, whetting their Wagnerian visions of collapsing the system by butting against it and taunting it; religious fanatics will tell the crowd to rise, exhort, and make unpredictable gestures; right-wing misanthropes will peer at the pomp and confusion of the day and deduce that it is all a further setting for conspiracy. And there will be men of no special affiliation or affliction except an all-engulfing sense of their own pointlessness. They will madly rejoice at the chance to murder a President and thereby secure a fingerhold on history.

The last dark of a winter night lingers behind the drawn shades of a bedroom on the second floor of the White House. A house man is carrying a breakfast tray through the hushed length of the carpetless, bare living quarters. The tray bears a silver pot of coffee that will be taken black, a glass of fruit juice, and two slices of whole wheat toast. The house man is followed by the President's appointments secretary, who is carrying two folders. They come to the door of the darkened bedroom. The house man shifts his tray to one hand and knocks.

Light suddenly floods the carpet at their feet through the crack at the bottom of the door. They wait, listening to the sighing, grunting sounds of an exhausted man getting up. After a few moments the door opens, its light bursting into the hall around the tousled silhouette of the President of the United States.

The house man sets the tray on a small table at the foot of the bed and goes away to get breakfast for the First Lady, who is still asleep in a bedroom next door. While the President is in the bathroom the appointments secretary uncovers the toast and pours two cups of coffee. He arranges two armchairs beside the breakfast tray and unties the ribbons that bind the folders.

The President emerges from the bathroom with his hair combed. He is now wearing his bathrobe and slippers. He opens one of the folders. "What've we got this morning?"

"The postmasters were typed up before the girls left last night."

The President leafs through the papers. "And the judge-ship too. Good." The President is about to perform his last political favor. A faithful Congressman who lost in the November election is being made a federal judge. "Got a pen?" the President asks.

The appointments secretary takes a gold pen from his inside coat pocket and hands it across the breakfast tray. The President begins signing the documents, his face intent on the papers in his lap.

"The intelligence report will be in at eight as usual," the appointments secretary says.

The President nods without looking up. "Make sure he gets the same report. Talk to his people."

"Yes, sir. Almost everybody will be in to say good-by, except Grace Martelli."

The President goes on signing. "What's wrong with Grace?"

"Home with the flu."

"Draft a note to her and I'll sign it when I come down."

"Yes, sir. He'll be here at about 11:15 to have coffee with you before you go to the Capitol."

"Okay." The President holds up one of the documents appointing a new postmaster in upper New York State. "This isn't right. It says the term expires on the twenty-first. It should be the twentieth." He hands the paper across the table. "Have it retyped and I'll sign it when I come down."

The aide takes the paper. "Yes, sir." The boss is edgy this morning but it doesn't worry the appointments secretary. This is the end. The President's moods are no longer presidential. They are just moods.

These two men have met in this bedroom every morning including Sundays for the last four years except when the President was abroad, touring the country, or at his own home. Then the bedrooms differed but the hour and the import of the papers never varied. Now, suddenly, on the last day the matters laid before the Chief Executive early in the morning have no real significance. The aide feels bound by the inarticulate awkwardness one experiences when confronted by the injured, the aggrieved, or the dying.

The last day is the worst and the best day of the presidency. The pressure is over; the occupant can now revel in the fact that he won and handled the hardest political job in the world and that history will never forget him. That timeless eminence is one of the aspects of love and approbation that he originally sought in entering politics.

But the power and the perks of the job are about to disappear too. That is hard. During his White House years he was the central mechanism of his private world's works. Airplanes waited for him, cars whisked him wherever he wanted to go, somebody was always at hand to track down whomever he wanted to speak to on the telephone. He could have meals whenever he wanted, command people who were delighted to be with him whenever he was lonely. He could order movies, football tickets, or a cello recital by Pablo Casals whenever he wanted diversion. Implicit in all this was his commanding presence for everyone whose life touched his. Not only was everyone he knew focused on him, but a good part of the rest of the world was too. Now he is suddenly reduced to semiequality and it is difficult to bear.

In retirement Presidents get $50,000 a year, an office and a small staff at government expense, Secret Service protection for a while, and endless requests to comment on the acts and decisions of their successors. The gentlemen's agreement of the presidency requires that they either keep silent or utter pietistic platitudes about the new President's knowing what's best.

The worst part of a President's last day, however, is the nagging uncertainty about his conduct of the office. The Process is more thorough, precise, and married to detail than the general public could ever imagine. Every medium or large decision is pored over, taken apart, and reassembled in the light of innumberable ramifications and results. But the art of the presidency is to maintain a perspective that is both singular and flexible, to seize upon no opinion as absolute, to have clearer vision than the expert visionaries who surround one as advisers.

His mind constantly, fretfully, flitters back across his presidential years, lighting upon this decision, that crisis, the soul-curdling showdown with his best friend in Congress. He regrets, inwardly aches and dwells upon, much that he wishes he could redo in the light of what he knows now. His appointments secretary doesn't intrude. Outgoing Presidents must be treated with the same solicitude one offers the dying.

Georgetown is upriver from the heart of Washington. Excoriated for its exclusivity by modern Populists and despised with rancorous envy by the uninvited, it is a tree-lined district of old houses, quiet charm, mod shops, street people, bars blasting hard rock like open-hearth furnaces, male prostitutes, wealth and social power. The last is an important increment of general political power in Washington. An aged, venerated power broker of this city says: "I'm the sort of man people don't turn down

invitations from. Even if you hate me you like to be able to say
that you put me down at my house last night. This means that
I can get all sorts of people to come and I can explain my views
or argue my causes over dinner. It's damned convenient."

In a tall house on one of Georgetown's expensive streets a
Washington columnist wakes up and rolls over. He looks at the
clock on his bedside table, remembers what day it is, and mutters, "Christ."

Political life in Washington—the Process—is a continuing series of dramatic chapters. As bills of great importance are reported out of congressional committees, as events churn up
hotly disputed public issues, as causists try to nail one controversial measure to another as amendments, as congressional
forces gather to battle the President or other congressional
forces on a given matter, coalitions are formed for the lifetime
of the disputes at hand. The coalitions are composed of Senators and Representatives to wage the floor battles, veteran
lawyers to plan strategy and give advice, a retired diplomat
with extensive establishment contacts, a New York banker to
bring pressure to bear upon the opposition, a major newspaper
or two to trumpet the cause on their editorial pages, a columnist
to explain the matter, and national television to bring it to the
attention of the general public.

The columnist who now sits on the edge of his bed putting
on his glasses has played roles in dozens of such coalitions.
Contrary to the popular conception of the men in his trade, this
columnist works hard, thinks hard, and like most successful
Process game players in Washington cares very deeply about
the public good. He and his wife are almost as well connected
in New York, London, Paris, and Boston as they are here.
Their Washington friendships intertwine with the coalitions that
the columnist has served in. Friendship is absolutely indispensable to successful participation in the Process. The number and
quality of a man's friendships regulate his capacity to know
what's going on, his access to other people, his lines of query
into the high and inaccessible realms of government and party,
and the degree of tough elective campaigning he can do (if
he's an elected official) and still be tolerated and forgiven.

The really effective Process player in Washington has friendships and contacts all along the ideological spectrum and in both parties. The columnist's closest associations tend to be with people identified with the outgoing President and his party. The editors across the country who buy his column know this as well as he does. They will read him carefully in the first few months of the new administration to see if his perception falters, if his sources dry up, or if his grasp of Washington's new inner logic begins to waver. He could lose fifty papers. During the next round of the Process the columnist will anger key men in the White House and his name will be stained among middle-level bureaucrats for a while. But he will surmount that and survive well.

East-southeast of the Capitol and north-northeast of the city's center, the demographic color of Washington is black and is approaching 80 percent of the city's population at this writing. This is a paradoxical fact to reflect upon if one is inclined to ask what, exactly, cities are for. Here the greatest number of residents have the least to do with Washington's principal *raison d'être*. At its highest echelons the U.S. government is almost totally white. The ratio of Negroes to Caucasians rises as one descends along the civil service grades, until at the level of janitors, drivers, mailmen, cleaning women, envelope stuffers, incinerator operators, and boys who push delivery carts through the corridors of the State Department, the U.S. government is predominantly black. Once this imbalance existed by design. Now it exists by result. Democracy's great philosophical flaw is that it ministers first to the majority, whether or not the majority is most in need of ministering. In America the majority is white. Only in this generation has the U.S. government worked out devices for focusing a lot of its domestic energy upon the problems of the poor minority—most of whom are black. But the government has yet to find a way to make its preoccupation with blacks politically attractive to the majority.

The most simplistic folklore of America, that bumper-sticker wisdom that reduces all problems and solutions to slogans, holds that black people could be just as prosperous as anybody else if they'd get off the welfare rolls and go to work. But

as far back as 1830 Alexis de Tocqueville knew that such
harsh, simple reasoning contained its own self-defeating illusions.
He wrote:

> It cannot be denied that democratic institutions have a
> very strong tendency to promote the feeling of envy in the
> human heart; not so much because they afford to every-
> one the means of rising to the level of his fellow citizens,
> as because they perpetually disappoint the persons who
> employ them.

Here in the Washington ghetto the disappointed envy of thousands of exiled hearts celebrates itself in the poetry of graffiti
laid by spray can and paintbrush upon the girders of over-
passes, upon the plywood sheets that cover the broken store
windows, upon fences, sidewalks, and even cars: "Soul Brother," "Off the Pigs," "Free Bobby Seale," and "All Politicans Is
Just Like a Whore." All poetry says more than its surface meanings. The rage and frustration that these lines bespeak exist
in souls so insanely remote from government's theories for curing them that some reasonable doubts about the Process are in
order. The new left's dotty contention that everything is irrelevant is as far off the mark as the right's truculent claim that
everything is fine. To be precise, part of the Process doesn't
work because of democracy's flaw, and that flaw is going to result in a continuing social explosion when the Process resumes
after this day's pause. The issue in the ghetto is how to get it
now. The U.S. government can't get it for you now.

The Process is too articulate. It talks too much, explains too
much, argues too much with the wrong words about the wrong
things. Official noise is one price paid for reasonably good domestic government and working relationships all over the world.
At the White House the mail room staff is sorting through thousands of letters and telegrams that have poured in during the
night. The messages to the new President congratulate, beseech,
and instruct. Embassies have been delivering their government's
official cables since the previous afternoon. The President of the

Soviet Union—an impotent figure who in the meaningless world of protocol is the American President's equal—declares that "both of our states must strive to strengthen relations between peoples." The British Prime Minister sends a message about the world being on a new threshold of hope. The Pope passes the word that there are prayers in the Vatican for the guidance and protection of the new President. The official messages display far less true feeling than the spray-can poetry of the ghetto and are of no importance.

Enemies are an indispensable part of the Process. "Men do not know how what is at variance agrees with itself," said Heraclitus. "It is an atunement of opposite tensions like the bow and the lyre." In order to keep moving, parts of the Process must move against something. In the name of the official enemies all vigilance in Washington is exercised, vast sums are raised for death machines. Great policies are justified by the argument that the enemy will find them bad. Patriotism is in part the business of comparing what you know about this country with what you imagine about the enemies' countries and counting your blessings. Visionaries dream of reconciliation with the enemies. Presidents must at least pay lip service to reconciliation. Enemies justify much—some of it plausible, some not—and no modern industrial democracy can operate without them.

In order to work, the Process must also be seen. As the columnist explains it, the television networks show it. The great square tube threatens to become the fourth branch of government, so obsessed have governments become with using it, courting it, and hating it. Godlike, government seeks to remake television in its own image and curses when television remains as insufficiently mortal as it has always been. Not all that much of the Process is good visual stuff. Dramatic congressional hearings come across well, so do presidential press conferences, the arrival of famous or gaudy world leaders for state visits, and the massive protest demonstrations that have become part of the Processs itself. The most telegenic spectacle in all the Process is its pause, the inauguration of a President.

To cover this particular inaugural, the Columbia Broadcasting System's bureau on M Street has been making plans for a year. It has taken three hundred Washington hotel rooms for extra personnel flown in from New York, has unreeled forty thousand feet of cable, and has installed thirty-one cameras for itself along the parade route and at the Capitol while plugging into twenty-six pool cameras for use by all three networks. A gigantic platform has been constructed facing the Capitol steps where the new President will take his oath. Walter Cronkite and Roger Mudd will anchor the CBS coverage from there. For two weeks technicians have been unraveling wire and installing lights and cameras in the freezing temperatures.

It is breakfast time in Washington.

In Georgetown a plump, dapper man in his late fifties sits down at the dining room table and opens *The New York Times*. His own name is on the front page in one of those tentative, analytical articles that newspapers run before important events take place. This particular article—called a "thumbsucker" in the trade—is about all the people in Washington who will rejoice at the coming of the new administration. "The Senate Majority Leader," says the piece, "will be operating in a Congress that is now controlled by the same party that controls the White House. Therefore . . ."

The Majority Leader lowers the newspaper and looks across the dining room at a portrait of his grandfather on the opposite wall. It isn't quite that simple. For the last two and a half months, ever since the election of a President of his party, he has been far from overjoyed. He has, in fact, been uneasy. The political party in America is not at all what a lot of people think it is.

The Majority Leader finishes his coffee and lights his pipe as he broods upon the coming season. He is a fuse box halfway between the President and the party's members in the Senate. He must try to persuade the President not to send up legislation that won't pass and try to persuade the Senate to pass what the President sends up. He knows both sides too well.

He queries memory. Years ago he served a couple of terms in the House with the man who will become President later this morning. Then—and very privately—the Majority Leader thought the fellow a little too nice for Washington politics. The years are now filled with great matters that if played wrong could splatter the United States all over itself.

He sits looking at the portrait of his grandfather while the gray of Inauguration Day gathers upon his windows. At times a man feels inadequate before the mysterious nature of men. The Senate Majority Leader is far from joyous.

The temperature has risen to 39 degrees. Flecks of snow are carried by the wind across the gloom of downtown Washington. The crowd along the parade route has grown to 15,000.

In a twelfth-floor suite at the Statler-Hilton the man who is about to become President of the United States has been up since 7:45. Still dressed in his bathrobe and pajamas, he stands with his back to the living room looking across Lafayette Park at the uneven roof of the White House framed by dark tree branches. His wife and one of his sons are still asleep elsewhere in the suite. His secretary, one aide, and a Secret Service man sit silently behind him, watching him. The secretary and the aide have known him for years, but now he is as removed from them as he is from history unmade. He has been stripped of his name and has been given the magisterial title "Mr. President," which he will wear for the rest of his life. His crochets, gifts, and inner mysteries are matters for great speculation abroad. By becoming this thing he has both lost himself and projected himself in huge relief upon the world. His image will never again completely fade from it. Men he will never know wish to murder and to worship him, and he will hold the power of gladness and doom in the hands clasped behind his back. But all that is so important about him waits yet a little while, a few hours and the taking of an oath.

The most successful governments are those that both constrain and embody the people they govern. If a government is wise and secure, it will survive and surmount the momentary fears and passions of the people; in the tumult of emergency that roars for quick answers and quick action, for vengeance or instant surcease, good government pauses, assesses, and then proceeds on that course of action that serves not only the moment but the time that will come after the moment and its tumult have passed. The old saw about that government "governing" best that governs least does not bear close examination. The government that by its vigor, guidance, and inspiration extracts from its people the best in their natures is the government that governs best.

When control of the House of Commons changes hands in a British general election, it is said that a new *government* has come to power. When one party wins the White House from an incumbent in an American election, it is the custom to say that a new *administration* has taken over in Washington. In the difference between the two observations lies the difference between British and American understandings of what constitutes government. In Britain government is regarded as the sum of its political leadership in the Commons. Therefore governments are of short life in the general flow of history. In America the concept is that of a single government that has endured from the beginning of our present political system. Within the generations of that government there have been episodic rhythms: good, bad, useful, and ineffectual Presidents have taken their turns at administering. Scandalous or great Congresses and their leaders have made law or prevented its passage during the living duration of our government. The history of that government is partly a history of the epochs and crises it has lived through and partly a history of the changes that have been wrought upon the basic parts of the government and the relationship of those parts to each other; above all, that government's history is really the history of the human characters who have occupied positions in Washington that, because of the durability of government itself, are always of greater importance than the men who borrow them for just a little while.

The splendid, controversial, or lesser figures who dominate the history of American government did not act out their roles at random. Since 1865 the game of being, achieving, and surviving in Washington has been governed by three rather immutable precepts. Government is a flow of energy coursing through the federal structure in Washington. That flow, the molecular essence of government, is called in this book the Process. The first precept describes the Process, what government and its people are really doing as they act out their roles: *Washington politics is basically the art of moving men, money, and ideas from one place to another.*

That may sound simple, but it isn't. When we consider that the men—or people—being moved are whole generations of children whose education and very lives are being tampered with, millions of the poor whom the Process is attempting to elevate to affluence and stability, whole races being moved together or apart within volatile chambers of prejudice and competition, vast armies whose collective misstep could wreck a nation, start the last war, or drain the country's veins of its best talent and energies for a decade; when we realize that the amounts of money moved run into the multiples of billions and that every nickle of it authorized, appropriated, or spent is welcomed, regretted, contested, or sought with great passion and advocacy by someone with power; when we reflect that among the ideas being moved from theory to practice are notions whose unforeseen consequences could murder or cure civilization—then the Process appears to be what it really is, a game requiring great nerve, skill, experience, dedication, incredibly hard work, and not a little grace of one sort or another. Against the immense implications of the Process and what its internal politics involve, the traditional Anglo-Saxon contempt for politicians seems a little overdone.

The doing of all this is made possible by power—that curious word that everyone uses but few people define. Power in Washington exists largely in the minds of the Process game players and the people who study them. Power can be felt—triumphantly or excruciatingly—but it can't be seen, touched, borrowed, or gotten rid of by any means except death, resignation, defeat, or incompetence. The source of Process power is human assumption; if I assume that you have the power to help or hurt me in whatever I'm trying to do in Washington and if you know I'm making that assumption, then you have power. Power in the Process is the capacity to move things, to get other people to help with the moving, or to make them get out of the way. Some Washington power derives from position— from the presidency, from the chairmanships of important congressional committees or subcommittees, from the directorships of key independent agencies like the Federal Reserve Board, from party leadership in the House and Senate, and so on. The positions, however, don't automatically vest their holders with all the power that can be extracted from them. The people who occupy the positions must have a talent for demonstrating power, for creating in the minds of other men the assumption that the position holder has power. The prophecy of Washington power is self-fulfilling: if everybody begins to assume that a man is powerful, then he is until he or events prove otherwise. *Power in Washington is psychosomatic,* reads the second Process precept, *but then so is lust. Treat the former with the same pleasure and prudence used in dealing with the latter.*

Obviously, power to be believable, must be displayed from time to time. But if it is displayed in too negative a fashion it self-destructs because its wielder becomes burdened with an insupportable number of enemies. If, on the other hand, power is displayed in an overly benevolent fashion, it diminishes through implausibility. A man who is never a son of a bitch to anybody is considered too nice to be a major Process operator.

While not borrowable, Washington power can reflect. The people it reflects upon receive a lesser commodity—authority. Vice Presidents, the staffs of congressional committees, expert advisers, White House aides, the assertive wives of powerful men, and departmental Undersecretaries all have authority. That authority is the assumption that its possessors can make powerful men do things.

The third Process precept has to do with the limits of possibility in Washington. *Time and affairs are relatively immutable,* it states. *Not all that much can be changed.* The great fallacy of the Americans as they watch their politics and politicians is the belief that with each change of administration in Washington, with each change of party control in Congress, a new era in history is beginning.

Sometimes history does change with the coming of a new administration. Jackson's election in 1828 signaled the end of rule by the gentries of Virginia and Massachusetts and resulted in the full emergence of egalitarianism in American politics. The ascent of Franklin Roosevelt in 1932 ushered in a whole new set of assumptions about the uses of government, but nobody, including Roosevelt, knew it at the time. The rule is pretty much as Heraclitus set it out: "You cannot step into the same river twice. Fresh waters are ever flowing in upon you." New Presidents and congressional leaderships alike adapt themselves to what they have inherited—otherwise time and events will drown them.

The Process is thus a very continuum, a series of episodic political efforts whose flow never ceases and only pauses on Inauguration Days. By "Process politics" here one does not mean elective politics, the means by which a politician gets to Washington and stays there. The flesh huckstering of elective politics, while profoundly influential in the Process, is crude compared to the exercise of Process politics.

The cast in the Process does not only include elected and appointed officials and members of Congress. It also embraces academics, journalists, advisers to the mighty, lawyers, representatives of foreign governments, and the families and secret loves of visible Process players; it includes old men who are relics of the past political epochs, Washington hostesses, infamous influence peddlers, impassioned causists, visionaries and agitators, diplomats and typists, receptionists and spies. The cast encompasses the huge and often despised bureaucracy that is a mosaic of specialties constantly being assembled and reassembled by political generalists. The specialists help to provide the ideas that are moved in the Process, and the politicians do the moving. Then the specialists administer the results.

At the apex of this huge pyramid of human endeavor stand the politicians, those men and women of a mysterious personal alchemy. They are traditionally and unjustly regarded with contempt as a class because of the public badness of some members of their trade and because of the humiliations that custom demands of them in the business of getting elected. The politician is the key corpuscle of the Process. Yet he is a creature largely inexplicable, even to himself.

The politician is someone with a greater capacity for political belief than most people. He is a man possessed of the idea that most problems can be solved by political action or, inversely, that those problems susceptible to political action are the ones in greatest need of solving. If the politician's capacity for political belief gets out of hand, he becomes a fanatic and therefore a useless bore. Very few of those get to Washington, or if they do they don't last long or don't exercise much power. They are too predictable. Fanatics are incapable of compromise. They are political believers who have disintegrated into a state of distraught apoliticality.

The Process has many of the elements of Elizabethan drama when watched up close. It has the tension inherent in great affairs played out with results that are unknown. It has an intimate connection with the lives of the spectators when practiced at its best. In Washington at any given season there will be destiny-driven Macbeths and numb, serving minor heroes like Horatio. Great men fall to base conditions down the same inevitable, screaming chute through which Othello fell, and ever present are the grotesque Calibans and Falstaffs who provide the unintended humor of the piece—the drama goes on forever.

And, at its best, it constrains and embodies the American people.

A visitor coming into the White House at this hour would be puzzled. The administration ends at noon today, but the full staff of typists, clerks, guards, and middle-level aides has reported for work—apparently as usual. True, the girls are slightly better dressed than they would be on an ordinary workday. Also no typewriters clack, few phones ring. The staff is in this morning to say good-by.

The President, the First Lady, and the press secretary have

been going from office to office, shaking hands, kissing cheeks here and there, patting shoulders that shake with sudden, uncontrollable sobbing. The President's surface charm, cultivated over the decades of political ascent, has never been more meant, more sincere than it is now. "Mary," he says to a receptionist outside the science adviser's office, "I'm counting on you to keep me in touch with how that third grader of yours is doing."

"Yes, Mr. President, I will.'"

"Good-by, Mary. Thank you."

"Good-by, Mr. President. God bless you."

He goes into the hall.

A Negro guard of the White House police stands. "You and I are both leaving today, Larry," the President says.

"Yes, sir, Mr. President."

The President smiles. "How long's it been for you?"

The guard smiles back. "Thirty-two years."

"Where are you going now? Back to Minnesota did somebody say?"

The guard nods. He is loose and familiar. The man makes you feel that way. "Yes, sir, Mr. President. I got my sister and her boy out there."

The President holds out his hand. "I'll want to see you if you're ever down my way."

The guard shakes hands. "You surely will, Mr. President."

Alone, the President goes down the hall, opens two doors, turns down another brief corridor, and stops before the room that was his office for so many years. Here the stolid Stuart portraits of George Washington, bad teeth and all, have been replaced by a smirking, rheumy-eyed picture of Benjamin Franklin. The President looks up at it. "That old bastard knew something," he says to himself. "I wonder what it was. I wish I knew, even now, after all this."

He opens the door to the Oval Office and goes inside, closing the door behind him.

The big, curved room is empty and rugless and echoes with the small sounds made by the solitary man who now contemplates it. If the day were sunny, the French doors would be bathed by light diffusing through their thin, gauzy curtains. The light would have recast itself from the white walls, off the fluted, scallop-shell arches above the windows, reflecting in the brass andirons before the fireplace. But now the room simply extends the cold, dead illumination of the gray morning beyond. The only furnishings left are the flags of the President of the United States and of the United States. They remain, as the office remains, outliving its occupants, bigger than them—as the nation remains, waiting to be picked up and shoved forward by a new mortal soon to come.

The man about to leave the White House stands for a moment in his empty office, thinking oddly enough of all the names he has been called in his career—Communist, Fascist, Populist, demogogue, and crook. The accusations really say more about the condition of the accusers than that of the accused. He wonders what to call himself. He thinks back on the initial idealism, the original instincts that propelled him onto the fringes of politics. Then he begins to think about the years of compromise, of paring down idealism so that it would fit into situations that really existed. That doesn't seem so bad. What burdens him now is the realization of how few of the great things a man wants to do can really be done.

The door behind him opens. The appointments secretary, press secretary, and First Lady come into the bare office. "I think you've said good-by to everyone," the appointments secretary says. "There are some pictures to autograph, for Assistant Secretaries and people like that. I have the letter for Grace. Do you want to sign them now?"

The President nods. He looks around the Oval Office for the last time. Stripped of his furniture, pictures, and mementos, the TV consoles, naval prints, sofa, chairs, his desk, which had belonged to William Howard Taft, it is no longer his room. It waits to assume the personality of a new President. The law allows an outgoing Chief Executive to keep his desk and chair. "I wonder if he would have wanted it?" the President says. He is fond of his successor, despite the fact that they come from different parties and have profound ideological disagreements.

"Wanted what, dear?" the First Lady asks.

"William Howard Taft's desk," the President answers. "I wonder if he would have liked to have had it?"

"He'll be here soon, dear," the First Lady answers. "You can ask him." Even she treats her husband as one afflicted.

Two hundred and five thousand people line Pennsylvania Avenue. They stand six deep; some have climbed onto the sides of buildings for a better view. People are scattered up the snow-streaked slopes of the Capitol. Thousands jam so tightly into the parking lot before the inaugural stand on the steps that a man literally can't wriggle his shoulders. Some people in the packed crowds along Pennsylvania Avenue carry little American flags. The networks have been live for an hour. From the stand at the Capitol Walter Cronkite announces that the members of the Joint Committee on Arrangements—the Majority Leaders of both houses and the Speaker—have arrived at the White House. They will escort the incoming and outgoing Presidents to the Capitol. Along Pennsylvania Avenue three sanitation department workers in orange coats have gotten into a shouting match with spectators who threw trash into the street. Motorcycle cops still gun up and down the avenue.

The President-elect has arrived at the White House from a prayer meeting at the State Department. He enters through the south portico, his wife, son, and aides behind him. His eyes unaccustomed to the dim light, he walks briskly up a corridor. A figure appears before him. The next President stops. The two men, bound together by so much, stand looking at each other for a moment, eons of hope and emotion apart. "Good morning, Mr. President," says the President-elect.

The President steps forward, smiles, and holds out his hand. "Mr. President," he says, "welcome to your house."

In another house, a large, elegant one on a quiet Cleveland Park Street, a small, middle-aged lawyer leads two friends into a paneled room overlooking the back garden. A fire crackles and hisses behind a brass-trimmed screen; the makings of drinks have been laid out on an oak table while a color television set carries the portrait of downtown Washington into this cozy room in the city's fashionable northwest section. Walter Cronkite has just told the world that the President-elect has arrived at the White House.

Coats are taken, drinks are made, the sound on the television is turned down, and the three men settle into chairs before the fire.

"So, an era ends," says one of the visitors.

The lawyer smiles. With one finger he stirs the ice cubes on the surface of his cocktail. He has never held elective office, has never run for office, and is one of the best Process game players in Washington. The press calls him a power broker and the phrase amuses him. He has been an intimate of the Presidents of his party for over thirty years. He is a veteran member of kitchen cabinets, a calm man in the middle of frenzied political battles; and because he has the gift of detachment and nerves like the workings of a brass clock, he is someone that Presidents like to have around when things are rough. He is a close friend of the incoming President, who as a matter of fact is due at his house for dinner before the inauguration ball this evening. The lawyer gave a good deal of money and exerted a great deal of energy four years ago in the effort to defeat the outgoing President.

He raises his head and looks at one of his visitors. "Well, we survived after all," he says.

"But when I think that the country was in the hands of that—"

"He did his best," the lawyer says as he raises a drink. "On balance, he didn't do badly." He sips and lowers his glass. "Besides," he smiles, "he was the only President we had for four years."

"He was totally unequipped. He knew nothing."

"Don't you believe it. He knew where the power was," says the broker of that strange commodity, "and that's what counts the most." Considering the source, that can be taken as a supreme compliment.

The time in Washington is 11:45.

There is movement behind the doors at the main entrance

to the White House. The President and the President-elect are preparing to come outside and get into the limousine that will take them to the Capitol. It is a long, sleek automobile, black with a bubble top. They will be seen and being seen will smile, be serene, and wave. They have schooled themselves over the years in relaxed and simple public manners that intrigue the people who watch them.

The White House doors swing open. Amid a swirl of Secret Service men and wives the two Presidents come outside. They pause for a moment beneath the immense porch chandelier, inhale the freezing air, and climb into the limousine. Down the curved drive the left-hand gates slowly swing open as the limousine, with Secret Service agents jogging at its sides, rolls out and turns right onto Pennsylvania Avenue. People seated in the grandstands opposite and standing on the far corners break into applause. At the main entrance to the White House the Vice President and Vice President-elect are getting into a second car. Another limousine waits in line to take the wives and children of the Presidents to the Capitol.

For the last forty minutes the sun has been trying hard to break through the thin patch in the clouds. It finally did so seven minutes ago, thus giving further credence to the theory that God is a kid from Akron who blesses His people with the gift of light at their ultimate moment. The new, weak rays of the sun cast the spidery shadows of tree branches upon the walls of the Riggs National Bank as the presidential limousine turns down past the Treasury with its expressionless guards trotting on either side, holding on to little handles welded into the car's sides. The crowds, alerted by the sounds of distant applause, break into loud clapping and cheers as the black limousine crawls slowly along the swept, barricaded boulevard. Inside, the two hatless men can be seen leaning toward each other, gesturing as they talk. The applause mounts in volume, becoming a wave break of clapping and shouts rising in the cold air. Startled by the sudden explosion of human noise, flocks of pigeons clatter upward, wheeling against the fragments of blue sky.

Now, like some rounded Parthenon gleaming against the dark sky to the east, the great Capitol dome dominates the view seen by the American millions on television, by the present thousands, and by the two great men who approach. The applause and roaring churn up behind the limousine, its wake of acclaim. This is one of the rare moments of human rhapsody left in a land gone dour with its anxiety and foreboding. It is good to clap wildly and shriek with joy even if one doesn't quite know why one is doing it. Thousands upon thousands along Pennsylvania Avenue are crying themselves hoarse with a reassuring noise as they behold their magistrates. The two Presidents are leaning together in the car again and the excited public imagination runs in little circles of speculation. Are they discussing the great burden one is now passing to the other? Is there something terrible, final, and immensely secret which a President knows that this President is now imparting to his successor? The nation gazes in awe at the limousine laden with greatness as it purrs its way toward the very repository of American democracy.

"Nice day you've got for it," the President says.

The limousine, still holding to its dignified speed, has gone in among the trees of lower Capitol Hill and emerges at the plaza before the Capitol steps.

Here the enthusiasm is largely limited to applause. Six and a half thousand people, admitted by invitation only, are crammed into the space between the television stand and the east front of the Capitol. Here at last the whole cast of the Process is gathered in one place. And here among them the journey of the two Presidents has come to an end. The time is 11:55.

The ceremonies begin in the cold noon air. The prayers roll forward, the ancient words of ritual are spoken. Breath steams and women huddle in their expensive fur coats. All attention is focused on the lectern and the men around it—the two Presidents, the two Vice Presidents, and the Chief Justice of the Supreme Court.

Whatever their roles in the Process, those who watch are also the chosen and appointed Americans gathered in from many states and sections of the country to this one spot for this high moment, for the purpose of attesting, as delegates of the people, that the Process still works.

They listen in respectful silence as the Chief Justice administers the oath of office to the President-elect. They listen with outward respect, but they know that the moment means nothing aside from its grant of authority. Fired by the Process, they are aware of its pause, its day when nothing moves.

Now the Bibles are taken away.

Now the new President stands alone at the lectern.

Now destiny dangles from something intangible, something felt, supposed but unseen. Everything flows for a moment upon the character of one man. The men who will contend with him or ally with him rinse their minds of all preoccupation to listen.

"Ladies and gentlemen," says Walter Cronkite to the believing, hoping millions, "the President of the United States."

Now the man at the lectern looks up, clears his throat, and frowns. "My fellow Americans," he says.

Now the Process resumes.

2: The Presidency

. . . the first thing that strikes our attention is that the Executive authority with few exceptions is to be vested in a single magistrate. This will scarcely, however, be considered as a point on which any comparison can be grounded, for if, in this particular, there be a resemblance to the King of Great Britain, there is not less resemblance to the Grand Seignor, the Khan of Tartary, to the Man of the Seven Mountains, or to the Governor of New York. . . .

Alexander Hamilton, *Federalist 69*

This Constitution is said to have beautiful features, but when I come to examine those features, sir, they appear to me horrible, frightful. Among other deformities, it has an awful squinting, it squints toward monarchy. . . . It is on a supposition that your American Governors shall be honest that all the good qualities of this government are founded. . . . Away with your President! !

Patrick Henry, Anti-ratification Speech

The principal genius of the men who worked out the U.S. Constitution was the fact that they didn't quite know what they were doing—and they knew it. They were the orphans of British history siring an American national child whose adulthood they could not possibly envision. The experience that armed them as they sat down in the broiling Philadelphia spring and summer of 1787 was largely negative. Because of the unpleasantness with Britain eleven years before, they couldn't *officially* desire a monarchy. In its initial period of independence the United States had been first disorderly, then slatternly, and finally a preposterous mess mismanaged by what George Washington gloomily called a "half-starved, limping government." The Constitution writers, who had had the hell scared out of them by Shays' Rebellion, didn't want any more of that either. What they did want and what history would ultimately require were unclear in May 1787.

The authors of the Constitution have been glorified as men enchanted with democracy, universal liberty, and civil rights. But they weren't. They were for the most part the wealthy sons of wealthy fathers, aristocrats and intellectuals (the two often went together in the eighteenth century) who were interested in moneymaking and protecting themselves from the rabble. The freedom uppermost in their minds was freedom from disorder, foreign competition, and trade chaos between the American states. Their aim was to work out the mechanical devices of a government, not primarily to insure the protection of citizens within or from it. The Bill of Rights had to be nailed to the Constitution by Congress two years later. Democracy—or what the Founding Fathers thought of as democracy—was something many of them viewed with horror while holding a perfumed hanky to the nose. William Livingstone set the mood nicely when he offered the opinion that "the people ever have been and ever will be unfit to retain the exercise of power in their own hands," and Roger Sherman of Connecticut added a little prayer that "the people . . . have as little to do as may be about the government." The Founding Fathers, as card-carrying aristocrats, had intuitive disdain for anyone who wasn't.

Yet they were also intelligent enough to know that the nation was going to be composed largely of nonaristocrats. They were intellectuals. And they weren't extremists. Alexander Hamilton's suggestion that the United States be administered by a Governor who would be elected for life by the state Governors didn't arouse much enthusiasm. The idea of a military dictatorship crossed a few minds, but George Washington didn't want the job.

Among the many other ideas, notions, concepts, and theories abounding in the eighteenth century was the intriguing work of Sir Isaac Newton, who along with proving that apples fall from

trees had demonstrated by physics that the universe was a bal-
ancing mechanism. To make a balanced government the Founding Fathers separated its basic parts and set the power of those
parts against each other.

The parts so balanced included the interests of the moneyed
classes and the impulses and needs swirling through the American population. Even though the rabble's potential for egalitarianism was regarded by many of the Founding Fathers as
one of the supreme tyrannies, there were the forces working on
the Philadelphia convention that demanded a popular role in
government in the name of political prudence as well as Sir
Isaac's balance. Jefferson and John Adams weren't present, but
their influence was felt—Adams, in particular, with his argument for some "democratical" branch of government. The interests of the larger states were satisfied by a House of Representatives based on population, and the smaller states were
mollified by a Senate composed of two members from every
state regardless of size. The convention then proceeded through
Franklin's Grand Compromise to the direct election of the
House and arrived in due course at the question of who was
actually to run the country.

The model for the office was easy enough—there were state
Governors, and the *office* of the President was obviously based
on them. But the *function* of the presidency, especially in relation to Congress, was difficult to work out. Congress had been
given the fearful power of making laws. Within itself, Congress was a balanced mechanism, but in the larger scheme of
the government it needed to be balanced against something
else. A good part of that something else was obviously to be
the presidency. Yet there was so much popular prejudice in the
country against one man having great power—Patrick Henry's
pessimistic fulminations about the Constitution "squinting toward monarchy" pretty well summed up the fears of a powerful Executive—that the Constitution writers skirted trouble by
creating a vague presidency.

The muscle of the Congress is specifically described in Article
I of the Constitution; its vast array of powers to do everything
from raising revenue to impeaching are laid out explicity, and

its function in the government is limited to the "the powers herein delegated." Aside from describing the President's few specific duties, Article II of the Constitution says only that he shall "take care that the laws shall be faithfully executed." There are only nine sections in Article I, which describes the Congress. There are only four in Article II, which outlines the presidency, and two-thirds of Article II is taken up with a rather windy description of qualifications and how the man is to be elected.

The constitutionally defined rights and functions of the President aren't much. He has veto power over the laws passed by the House and Senate (but they can override him), is commander in chief of the armed forces, and can require his Cabinet officers to report to him in writing. He can grant reprieves and pardons in everything except impeachment, make treaties with the concurrence of two-thirds of the Senate, and appoint ambassadors, judges, and other people with the approval of the majority of the Senate; he can fill vacancies when the Senate is in recess, make speeches to the Congress about how things are going, summon and dismiss the House and Senate (the latter action only if the two houses disagree with each other), and receive ambassadors. He has a Vice President; he can be impeached if he commits treason, takes bribes, or otherwise misbehaves. It is a rather sparse description of an office that over a period of two centuries was to gather some pretty awesome powers.

Writing forty-five years after the Constitution was completed, Count Alexis de Tocqueville said that the only real, tangible powers given the President were the conduct of foreign affairs and the command of the armed forces. But, observed the author of *Democracy in America,* neither of these powers amounted to much in an eighteenth-century context. In 1778, the armed forces included only 6,000 soldiers and a piddling Navy. The United States was isolated from the rest of the world by the great oceans and was more interested in trade than in political relations abroad. De Tocqueville concluded:

> This proves that the practical operation of the government must not be judged by the theory of its Constitution.

> The President of the United States possesses almost royal
> prerogatives which he has no opportunity of exercising,
> and the privileges which he can at present use are very
> circumscribed. The laws allow him to be strong, but cir-
> cumscribed. The laws allow him to be strong, but cir-
> cumstances keep him weak.

Despite the fact that he missed the significance of the veto,
Count de Tocqueville had the original design of the American
presidency about right.

Most historians agree with Lord Bryce that everyone at the
Philadelphia convention assumed that George Washington would
be the first President. Pierce Butler said that the Founders
"shaped their ideas of powers to be given a President by their
opinions of [Washington's] virtue." Because of Washington,
the office would have great prestige and a good deal of pomp.
His character lent itself to that sort of thing (Washington fan-
cied the rather gaudy title of "His High Highness, the President
of the United States"). But there was no clear idea of who
would come after Washington. "The first man put at the helm
will be a good one. Nobody knows what sort will come afterwards," said Benjamin Franklin. The afterwards was therefore
left to providence and to the individual characters of Presidents
to work out.

Providence and presidential character worked fast. George
Washington, the first President, was also the first President to
discover that Article II couldn't be interpreted literally. The
presidency had little positive volition of its own, and that made
it unworkable. By 1793 Washington was in hot water with
the anti-Federalists, partisans of the French Revolution, and a
good many members of Congress as a result of his neutrality
proclamation. With that proclamation he established the principle of volition in the presidency and became the first in a long
string of Chief Executives to pick fights with the Senate over
who had the right to conduct foreign affairs.

The public reaction to all this proved that the Philadelphia
convention had been right when it dealt in timid vagueness with
presidential power. There was a fearful howl of protest. "Louis

XIV in the meridian of his splendor and his power never dared heap such insults on his subjects," wrote one critic of President Washington. "Treacherous in private friendship and a hypocrite in public life!" bawled Tom Paine. The New York *Journal* accused the President of stealing money from the Treasury; another critic referred to him as "the stepfather of his country." All this nonsense was nothing more than a signal that Washington had invented presidential volition and had exercised it. He had started the inevitable process whereby the presidency began to define itself beyond the literal description in Article II.

Most political scientists have graded American Presidents in terms of how much power they snatched away from Congress. The Schlesinger polls of presidential scholars, historians, journalists, and so on operated on this principle. Conducted in 1948 and 1962, both polls ranked Washington, Jefferson, Lincoln, Wilson, and Franklin Roosevelt as great Presidents. Jackson made great in 1948 and was dropped to near-great in 1962. All these men—with the possible exception of Wilson—gathered power to the office they occupied. Wilson seems a dubious choice for greatness in view of his struggles with Congress.

Trying to grade Presidents by the barometers of power is a pretty futile business anyway. There is no evidence that the American people ever adored a President simply because he was powerful. The heaving and bargaining for Process power in an inhouse preoccupation of politicians, journalists, and other President watchers who form a community mostly limited to Washington, newspaper offices, state capitals, universities, and think tanks. It is relatively meaningless to the general public, which judges a President by how much his acts agree with the prevailing popular opinion, by how good he makes people feel or by the things he gives them. Dwight Eisenhower, in abdicating Process power to the Wisconsin demogogue Joseph R. McCarthy, might be judged a weak President, at least in that period. But the public adored him. Besides, a President may have gathered all the conventional symbols of Washington power and still be helpless. Grover Cleveland was such a President (he was ranked as near-great in one of the Schlesinger polls). Cleveland knew that the robber barons of big business were stealing the country blind, buying Congressmen like streetwalkers, and strutting in contempt of the law and popular opinion. "We discover," he said in his fourth State of the Union message (1888), "that the fortunes realized by our manufacturers are no longer solely the reward of sturdy industry and enlightened foresight, but that they result from the discriminating favor of the government and are largely built from undue exactions from the masses of our people . . .," which was saying the least. Knowing all that, Cleveland was still unable to do anything about it. He was a helpless prisoner of his own laissez-faire instincts, which told him that the freer enterprise is the better the nation will be and that the best government is the least government. The force that hamstrung Grover Cleveland and denied the use of presidential power was his own mind.

To General Washington's principle of volition in the presidency one has to add the individual characters of men who have occupied the office, their capacity to create visions and pursue them vigorously. This was the factor that further shaped the insipid clerkship of Article II into the dynamic office that the presidency has become in the late twentieth century. Theodore Roosevelt decided that he wouldn't just limit himself to doing those things that the Constitution said he could do; he would do everything it didn't specifically *prohibit* him from doing. This view, known as the stewardship theory, was first espoused by Alexander Hamilton, a political pragmatist if there ever was one. Energetic, dynamic, and harassed Presidents like Lincoln and Franklin Roosevelt never bothered to work out any profound theories about their office. They just acted, extending the presidency to its limits. It may disturb those who claim to be constitutional purists, but the history of the presidency since Washington indicates that a healthy lack of absolute scruple about Article II is an asset in the holder of the office. Conversely, great constitutional lawyers have tended to make uncertain, dithery Presidents of the United States. They include Madison, Buchanan, Benjamin Harrison, and Taft. In other capacities— Madison as the social, political, and legal thinker, Taft as the

Chief Justice of the Supreme Court—they were splendid. As Presidents they worried too much about the Constitution. As George Washington proved, the document simply can't be interpreted too literally.

The President is supposed to be three different men simultaneously. First, he is chief of state, a monarchical and inspirational role that is supposedly as aloof from the writhings of daily politics as, say, the British monarch is isolated from the unpleasant political realities of Lords and Commons. Second, the President is head of government, his own Prime Minister, which means that he must engage in the hard, Byzantine Process; he must use his powers to help and hurt; he must be a loyal ally and a ruthless enemy in order to demonstrate and thus exert the power that enables him to move men, money, and ideas from one place to another. Finally, the President is head of his own political party, which means that he must be involved in the lowest order of politics—the slush funding and patronage, the nasty purges, the wooing of party blockheads and petty hierarchs who control large number of votes or claim that they do; he must mediate in state party quarrels, toady to rich donors who give the party money (sometimes making them ambassadors), and promise things he can't deliver. Clearly, there is a monstrous incompatibility here. It glows out of the famous photograph of Calvin Coolidge wearing an Indian headdress and a facial expression that suggests that a particularly gamey horse fly has just popped into his mouth. That is a picture of a man trying to hold onto his monarchical dignity while plodding through the banal damn foolery of campaigning.

The west wing of the White House is the hinge upon which the American universe swings. In that compact, three-story warren the President and his closest advisers and assistants spend their working days, which run fourteen hours or more and often number seven in one week. Yet for all the power it symbolizes, the west wing's narrow corridors, with their cream-colored walls, white trim, and soft lights, exude the cool hush of inac-

tion. The main part of the White House, designed by an Irish-
man named Hoban (and criticized by Jefferson, whose design
came in second in the competition, as "big enough for two em-
perors, one Pope, and the Grand Lama"), represents and serves
that part of the presidency that is chief of state. The main floors
lead through museumlike official rooms that are now used for
entertaining and that serve as reminders to thousands of tourists
of the splendors and solemnities of the American past. Above
the state chambers of the main White House, the living quarters
of the First Family compose the nation's grandest railroad flat.
The westernmost, half-oval windows of the living quarters look
down upon the compact west wing, which is connected to the
main building by a series of corridors and press rooms.

The west wing serves that part of the presidency that is head
of government, and there is a certain symbolism in the fact that
this complex is smaller and less splendid than the rest of the
White House. It is an architectural reminder of two of the three
men within one man, the head of state above controversy and the
the lesser, political creature who is fair game for our temporal
gripes and adorations.

On this dark, complaining morning four men leave a rear
door beneath the circular balcony facing south from the main
section of the White House and walk along the outside route
toward the west wing. The President, slender and a shade under
six feet, has set the style by coming out without a coat. Walking beside him, his twenty-nine-year-old son, Peter, reflects the
Chief Executive's patrician, delicate facial features; he has semi-
long hair and a thick but neatly trimmed mustache, and he works
as an assistant White House press secretary. Paul Brasher, the
White House chief of staff, is slightly overweight. He walks
slightly behind the President and his son; Brasher's hands are
shoved into his trouser pockets and his shoulders are slightly
hunched against the cold of the day. Louis Howard, the assistant to the President for congressional relations, is the tallest
of the four men. Howard served eight years in the House
from a tricky urban district in St. Louis. He is a black-haired,
angularly shaped man with a cadaverous face and eyes that

stare oddly out from behind thick glasses. Howard's appearance is deceptive; he looks like a rural causist but is actually one of the shrewdest, most diplomatic men in the President's inner circle. It is 7:30 A.M.; the temperature hovers just above freezing, and the weather forecasters are positive in their prophecies of snow starting about noon.

Walking swiftly, the four men cut through a new path among the fruit trees at one side of the rose garden and go up the narrow strip of lawn toward a columned porch and the glass doors of the Oval Office. Coming out without a coat is an unstudied part of this particular President's style. He and many of the people around him come from upper New York State. They tend to exude the winter-bred hardiness of the northern United States.

They mount the wide steps onto the porch. A White House policeman, summoned so hastily by a call from someone in the main building that he is coatless, holds open the glass doors of the President's office.

"Good morning, Bill," the President says.

"Morning, Mr. President."

The Chief Executive stops just outside the door and takes a deep breath. "It's so cold the air smells fresh."

"Good day for some ice fishing," the guard says.

The President smiles, the famous flash of white teeth and a sort of light coming into the recessed, oddly sad eyes. He puts a hand on the guard's arm. "Maybe next year we can get away for some of that, Bill. Up around the Finger Lakes."

The guard, a large, florid-faced man with thinning hair, nods. "You'd better," he says, "you and Peter both. You spend too much time indoors."

Peter grins. "Come on," he says to his father. "Let's get inside before we turn that office into a refrigerator."

"Okay," the President says. "You'd better beat it back indoors yourself, Bill. It's a cold one today."

The glass doors close behind them as they go into the Oval Office. A new log fire at one end of the room has just reached its flame-spurting full burn. A silver coffee urn and four cups rest on a low table between the two sofas on either side of the fireplace. The President crosses to his desk at the other end of the white-walled room and picks up some papers while Brasher pours coffee. He takes a cup—black, no sugar—across to the President. Peter opens a door and says to someone, "We're in."

Another door opens and a tall man with glasses comes in with a brown leather folder. Without looking up, the President says: "Good morning, Stu."

"Good morning, Mr. President. Most of the leaders are here. Congressman Gaspo's home called and said he'd be a few minutes late."

The President glances at his watch. "Well, we have time. It's only twenty to eight. Do any of them need breakfast?"

"There are coffee and rolls in the Fish Room," Stuart Graham says. He is a retired Navy captain who is in charge of the minute-by-minute running of the President's day. Graham bears— along with seven other men—the title of deputy assistant to the President, a rank vaguely below counselor and assistant and slightly above special assistant. This particular deputy assistant tends to be efficient, anxious, and fussy.

"Anything else this morning?" the President asks, looking up.

"The leadership meeting can run no longer than ninety minutes," Graham says. "Mr. McManus is due in at 9:30."

"Change that to 9:45," the President says. "I want a few minutes with Senator Caldwell when the meeting's over."

Graham squints painfully behind his steel-rimmed glasses. "That will be difficult, sir. You have appointments at ten, 10:30, and eleven."

Brasher, the chief of staff, crosses the room. "Unless it's urgent, Stu, why not get McManus in for lunch at 12:30? If it is urgent, tell him to see me."

"Good idea," the President says. He turns over the last paper on his desk, reads it, and raises his head. "Okay, gentlemen, I'll be going next door in ten minutes. Lou, I think we have the agenda all nailed down; it's rather simple. Have a copy at my place. Paul, are you sitting in this morning?"

Brasher shakes his head. "I've got my own meeting with my people at eight."

"Okay," the President says. "Lou and I will take it. Now everybody out except you, Peter. Stu, I'd like some reading time this afternoon before Professor Kotowski comes in."

Graham jots a note inside his folder. "I'll try."

"And make time for the Secretary of Defense around five."

Graham looks up. "I hadn't heard that he wanted to see you."

"He doesn't. I want to see him. Have Barbara call him."

"Very well," Graham says, writing in his folder. He is miffed, accumulating the first exasperating pressures that will ruin the schedule he has planned and thereby his day. Graham is a worshiper of order, but like everyone else in the new administration he is still learning that the President's day can't be made predictable.

"Any luck on those theater tickets for tomorrow night?" the President asks.

Graham nods. "Yes. Barbara got six—one extra in case your wife decides she'd like to attend. Senator and Mrs. Caldwell have accepted your invitation."

"Can you make it nine?"

Graham twitches. "If you wish, Mr. President."

"I thought it might be nice if you, Mrs. Graham, and your daughter joined us," the President said.

Graham relaxes again and almost smiles as he jots in his folder. "Three more tickets. Thank you, Mr. President. We'd be delighted."

When he, Brasher, and Howard have left, Peter sits down on one of the sofas, stretches out his long legs, and shoves his hands in his trouser pockets. He looks across the room at his father. "Why do you do that?" he asks.

The President puts down his papers, turns, and half sits, half leans against his desk, his hands gripping its rim. "Placate Graham? Oh," he says, looking into the fire, "he's human too."

"Yeah," Peter says quietly, "but you've got to learn that you can't make everybody happy all the time." He smiles. "You have a right to go to the theater with Roy Caldwell without Granny Graham fussing around."

The President doesn't answer for a moment. It is only a few minutes before eight but he feels as if the day is half gone. The temporary restorative of sleep is wearing off and he is resuming yesterday's fatigue. He is fifty-nine years old, looks five years younger, but has now arrived at that time when weariness becomes a habitual condition. He looks at his son. "Did you reach your brother last night?"

Peter shakes his head. "I'm afraid not. I called the state police at Tucson. They said they'd bring him in for a call at 9:30 our time. But when I called the Tucson barracks again they told me he'd refused to come talk to me."

"Well," the President says after a moment, "perhaps he'll calm down after a while."

"I'm not sure it matters much whether he does or not," Peter says, "unless he does something to embarrass us."

"It's not that," the President says. "No family should be choosing sides against itself."

"Come on, Nathaniel," his son says quietly, "we're not choosing sides. Mother isn't really angry. She's just unhappy."

The President nods. "I know, but—why?" He shrugs. "You don't know either. I suppose if it weren't for this—" He looks around the office with its busts of Franklin and Theodore Roosevelt, the Hudson Valley School landscape over the mantelpiece, the photographs, artifacts, and memorabilia that evoke New York State and its politics. "If it weren't for this, I imagine she'd be thinking about a divorce. She's been unhappy for a long time."

"She loves you," Peter says, "really she does."

"Has *she* talked to Richard?"

Peter nods. "Yesterday, I think. That's why I tried to call him."

"I won't embarrass you by asking what she's saying to him."

"I don't know," Peter answers, "but don't brood about it, Dad. Stop feeling guilty about being President."

The President smiles. "Good old Peter," he says. "Your mission in life is really to make everyone feel good, isn't it?"

Peter smiles, takes his hands out of his pockets, and stands up. "My mission in life is to be your assistant press secretary," he replies, "and I'd better get to it or my master, Mr. Bernstein, will have my hide."

They leave the Oval Office, turn left, and walk toward the Cabinet Room. "Do you know," the President says, "that's the first time in a long while you've called me 'Dad'?"

"Big deal." Peter grins as they stop at the Cabinet Room door. "Go fight Congress and stop worrying—Nathaniel." He waves and walks off toward the complex of offices at the end of the hall that houses the press office.

The Cabinet Room, dominated by portraits of the two Roosevelts and Abraham Lincoln, is also cheered by a fire. The curtains are drawn back to admit the gray light that comes through the columned porch from the lowering morning. A dozen men are seated in the leather chairs that line the long table going down the center of the room. They rise as the President enters.

The new administration's party took control of Congress in the election the previous November. The men who are gathered in the room with Louis Howard and the President this morning are the power horses of that Congress' majority leadership—the House Speaker, a tall, melancholy man from Pennsylvania; his Majority Leader; the House Whip, an overweight, sloppy North Carolinian named Mace Applegate; Roy Caldwell, the taciturn, pipe-smoking Senate Majority Leader; and the Senate Whip, the irascible and brilliant Senator James Forrest of California, whose whole nature is driven by a need to ignore the pain and inconvenience of his polio-gnarled body. House and Senate committee chairmen have also been invited this morning—but not all the major ones. Under a new system devised by the President, the regular Thursday morning leadership meetings are attended only by those committee chairmen whose specialities are pertinent to the main topic to be discussed. Louis Howard dislikes the new system because it inevitably means that every week some powerful and often touchy chairman is excluded. But to compensate Brasher and the President have scheduled more weekly meetings with individual chairman as well as a full Monday breakfast meeting with the most politically potent Representatives and Senators from both parties.

As the President goes around the table shaking hands and saying good morning, Senator Forrest is still struggling with his crutch and chair arm in an effort to rise. "Jim," the President says, "you'll be getting a letter from me about what you did on Monday with the public lands bill. I just wanted to mention how grateful we are."

Forrest's smile is a grimace. "If our colleagues in the House would be grateful enough to get *their* goddamn version to the conference, then *I'd* be grateful," he rasps.

There is laughter in the room. The President moves to a seat in the center of the table beside Louis Howard. "Well," he says, "you've got to remember how independent the House is. I was reading somewhere the other evening about somebody in the nineteenth century who used to bring his hounds into the chamber. Who was that?"

Caldwell, the Senate Majority Leader, takes his pipe from his mouth. "John Randolph of Roanoke," he says.

"That was the man," the President says. He turns to Mace Applegate, the House Majority Whip. "What about it, Mace? Can you turn your hounds loose on the public lands bill?"

Applegate shakes his great florid head. He seems in a perpetual state of blush, from the rolls of fat that cushion his neck to his high, shining forehead. "Naw, Mistuh President. We aren't gonna finish with that before Tuesday soonest."

"Well," the President replies, "I'll just leave you to deal with Jim Forrest without my help. You take your own chances."

There is soft laughter again.

The President looks for a moment at the meeting agenda typed on a sheet of paper at his place. He feels better. This is not only his work but his escape. Here he becomes a successful politician and President again; in this milieu he escapes weariness and the haunted feeling that he is an unsuccessful man.

"What we're going to be talking about this morning," he says, raising his head, "is the New Partnership, the matter that Lou and his people have been discussing with you. I just wanted to add my two cents' worth. I wanted to tell you why I think that this and a few other aspects of the same program may be the most important things we can do for the country and the party in this session."

He leans back in his chair, one hand on the paper before him, and looks around the table—at Caldwell puffing on his pipe, at Applegate sitting with his thumbs stuffed into his tight belt, at the gallery of men he has known and worked with for years. But what he has become has slightly removed him from them. Still, he knows them better, he suspects, than they think they know him. Yet there is one man at the end of the table whom none of them are really certain about in those special ways by which veteran politicians reckon one another.

The chairman of the House Ways and Means Committee, seated closest to the door this morning, is neither aloof nor difficult to deal with. He is just somewhat enigmatic. He is a product of the border state politics of Tennessee and cultivates his background with an easy, country-boy manner. Yet he too is slightly removed from his colleagues, not just by virtue of his chairmanship but by the genius with which he operates that chairmanship. He knows the flow and crochets of the House as few others do, what it thinks and feels, what it will buy at any one period, and what it will refuse to accept now but at some other time might. The Chairman—and he is known throughout Washington by that simple title, with heavy stress on *the*—is by virtue of his sensitivity to the House and his profound knowledge of tax, revenue, and tariffs the second most powerful man in the capital. He sits now, hands folded in his lap, pack of mentholated cigarettes on the table before him, listening politely.

"For publicity purposes," the President continues, "we are using this title, the 'New Partnership.' It is based on an idea worked out by Professor Kotowski at Harvard. We've modified it a good deal, considerably as a matter of fact, and we think that while it's a pretty radical idea it's going to work and work well in more ways than one.

"I don't think that any of us are in disagreement over the basic problem in the country today," continues the President.

"We've a majority taxed to the limits and minorities that still need all the programs we've inherited and maybe a few more. What this adds up to is bad conflict. We all know about the tax revolt movement in California, the new activity by the Birchers, and other people refusing to pay their taxes as the antiwar crowd did during the Vietnam business. And I don't think that anybody in this room wants to see any more race riots such as we've had in Los Angeles and Rochester and other places.

"What we need," the President says, looking at the agenda before him, "is to go on doing all those things government has been doing for the poor, the ignorant, and the deprived in this country. I don't think that welfare cheating is a major part of the problem or that eliminating it is a substantial part of the answer. What we need is to go on with most of the programs we inherited—a few need revision and we'll be sending up a few new ones ourselves later on—but we need to do that without raising taxes to pay the increasing costs; we need new sources of revenue for these things. On top of all that we have to demonstrate to people *fast* that we aren't going to raise personal income taxes any more to pay for these social programs. Maybe showing our concern for new, nontax sources of revenue is more important at the moment than anything else."

He pauses. The long, slender fingers pick up a pen lying beside the agenda paper. "Now you all understand the principle behind the New Partnership. Industry can get tax credit, parlayed out over a number of years at fixed rates, for undertaking with its own money any one of the programs as services to local communities or the states—road building, public housing, adult education. Actually, I believe there are 104 different projects to start with. They'll be in the form of standard programs supervised by the federal government but paid for and executed by the private sector."

"One hundred and six," Louis Howard says.

"One hundred and six," the President says. "Now the pilot bills of this program will be our Youth Resources Development Act and a revision of the 1973 Revenue Act. My staff is working on them now."

The room is silent for a moment. The hush is broken only by the fire's small hissings and mutterings and a scratching sound as Senator Caldwell traces large, symmetric whorls on a pad before him.

"Well," says the Speaker, "I don't know." He looks at the ceiling and then down the table at the President. "I just don't know."

The President, who has always privately regarded the Speaker as a pompous ass, is tempted to ask *what* he doesn't know. But he keeps silent.

"Of course, this can't be handled in one bill," the Speaker says tentatively.

"Of course," the President replies.

"You're going to have several sorts of enabling legislation," the Speaker says, "to create the agency for handling the thing, authorizations and appropriations for that, tax bills—"

"As the New Partnership gets going we can request less money for the programs," the President says, "and make sure we publicize the fact of less."

"What reaction are you getting from industry?" Forrest asks.

"More than good," the President says. "We're getting some actual commitments. Ben Saterlee of my staff—most of you gentlemen know Ben—has commitments from half a dozen of the larger corporations already. I haven't got details at the moment, but I can get Ben in here later on if you like. I believe that General Motors has committed itself to a good deal of secondary road building, taking over federal funding in some counties. General Electric—well, their response has been most gratifying." The President nods at Forrest. "We're getting good response, Jim."

"The program hasn't been publicly announced yet," Louis Howard says. "But if the initial response is anything to go by, this ought to be big—with just about everybody."

"An' if it is big," Applegate says, "you're gonna put us right on that li'l old line—dramatic new ideas, pretty glamorous stuff mixin' up the old free enterprise system with Christian virtue. An' if Congress doesn't go along, why then we take the rap."

There is a brief silence again. Then the President nods. "I suppose that's one way of looking at the thing. Still, there's another way too. This is our program, our party's idea, and if we get flak from the other side, they're the ones on the spot."

The President is feeling pleased. The discussion has been going on for forty minutes and already it's turning toward *how* the program should be passed rather than whether it should be tried. "And you'll get my help," he says to Senator Caldwell. "When can you get this on the calendar, Roy?"

"About the middle of April," Caldwell says. "Maybe a bit earlier if we're lucky."

The President looks down the table.

"Oh," the Speaker answers, "I guess we can get to it about then."

"It'll be tougher in the House than the Senate," the President says. He suddenly stops himself. He was about to mention the tour of the West he had planned for July, a time when, he imgines, the tax aspects of the program will be bottled up in the House Ways and Means Committee. Now it strikes him that the Speaker is worried about the chairman of Ways and Means. The Speaker, for all his power and prestige, is a touchily insecure man who intensely dislikes the Chairman. The amateur psychoanalysts of the House think that the Speaker's problem is jealousy mixed with awe of the Chairman's intellectual and persuasive powers. The President realizes that he has nearly allowed himself to be drawn into the logic of the Speaker's complex feelings, risking an appearance of sharing those feelings and thus offending the Chairman, who sits impassively at the far end of the table. "We'll keep in touch on the programing of this thing," the President says. "And I'll be asking you gentlemen for suggestions on what I should do as we move along." He leans forward, the deeply set eyes looking across the faces opposite. "Gentlemen, this whole thing rests on a new logic— not on the old business of shares, who gets what. Think of it as a cost-reducing and conflict-reducing device. Sell it to your people that way."

"That's easy for you to say, Mistuh President," says Mace

Applegate. "But I gotta buncha hound dogs up there on the Hill who got every beady li'l eye *fixed* on shares, on who gits what. An' that, Mistuh President, is how thisyear democratical system of gummint works!"

As laughter overcomes conversation for a moment, Lou Howard leans over and whispers to the President. "Better cut this short and get into the supplementals and the trade bill."

As the meeting resumes, the President switches tactics. The main part is over, with less selling and persuading than he and Howard thought would be necessary when they planned the agenda the previous evening. That means that the President can listen less and act more like a chairman. He swiftly lays out his needs and desires on the two remaining pieces of business and the leaders lapse into receptive listening. They sense that an important psychological divide has been crossed. The President has set the tone and pace of his most important legislative drive for this season, and tacitly his party's congressional leadership has agreed to follow. Or so it seems and is for the moment. The President finishes his discussion of supplemental appropriations and the trade bill, cautions everyone to keep the New Partnership secret until the White House can announce it, and closes the meeting at 10:03.

As he stands up, the President moves instinctively to help Senator Forrest to rise. Behind Forrest's chair Lou Howard lays a hand on the President's forearm. The two men's eyes meet for less than half a second and Howard's eyes say no. The President moves past Forrest, who is struggling with his crutch and chair arm. At the door of the Cabinet Room the Chief Executive shakes hands with Mace Applegate and murmurs a few words to the chairman of the House Appropriations Committee, under whom he served for two terms; he touches Senator Caldwell's arm. "Mind staying a minute?"

Caldwell nods. "Sure."

"Step into my office and I'll be right with you."

Caldwell nods again and goes out into the hall.

Forrest approaches the door with his twisted, body-thrusting limp. He shifts his wrist crutch to shake hands. "Well, you've given us a bitch," he says, grimacing. "It's too damned new, too radical."

"That can make it either a bitch or a real winner," the President answers. "I'm counting on you for this one, Jim. I really am. I need you."

Forrest shrugs a swollen shoulder. "I suppose we'll give the goddamn thing a try. See you." He stumps through the door, wrenching his body from side to side.

The Chairman pauses by the door. He tilts his head up slightly, looking through his thick glasses. He has said nothing during the meeting. "You've certainly given us something to think about, Mr. President."

"Your thoughts about the tax aspects interest me more than any others," the President replies. "Come in and talk to me anytime."

The Chairman turns his head toward the windows. "Looks like we're getting our snow," he says in his soft east Tennessee accent. He looks back at the President and smiles. "I imagine such weather makes you homesick for New York State."

"It does indeed."

"Lovely country up there, lovely," the Chairman replies. "Well, I'll be saying good morning."

"Good morning, Mr. Chairman," the President says.

Walking down the hall with the President to the Oval Office, Louis Howard says, "He's a guy you can't push. Don't try to prod thoughts out of him. He'll tell you what he thinks when he's thought it."

The President nods. "Yes. I made a bit of a blunder there. What about the others? Should I follow up with some calls this afternoon and tomorrow?"

"Maybe one or two tomorrow," Howard says. "Maybe a letter or two. You'll be seeing some of them again at other congressional meetings in the next few days. Don't be too anxious. You've done fine this morning. They're following you."

Senator Caldwell is looking through the French doors of the Oval Office. The rose garden's stretch of lawn flanked by fruit trees is already powdered with new snow. The heavy-set Senator from Ohio turns as the President and Howard come in. He raps his pipe bowl in the palm of his hand and shoves the pipe into his coat pocket. The President crosses to his desk. "Well, Roy, how'd we do?"

"I think you've tentatively sold it," Caldwell says. "But I think it's been sold initially on loyalty to you and the recognition that we've got to do *something* about this damned conflict around the country. We're going to have to persuade some more before we get to the committee-hearing stage."

The President is looking at several messages that have been left on his desk during the ninety-three minutes of the congressional leadership meeting. One from Stuart Graham reads, "Your wife wants to talk to you. Please call her."

The President raises his head and looks at Caldwell. "What sort of persuasion?" he asks.

"Well, what I'm really talking about is more detailed arguments and explanations of the program," Caldwell says. "I'd suggest a couple of briefing sessions pretty soon for the leadership with people from the Council of Economic Advisers, Saterlee, and the domestic affairs people."

The President nods. "Good idea." He presses a button on his desk console. "Barbara, get Paul, will you?"

"Right," says a female voice through the amplifier. "Keith's on his way in."

The hall door opens. A small, wiry man with tousled hair crosses the room toward Caldwell. "Boy," he says, "some of those guys on your team. Jesus."

"What's wrong?" Caldwell asks.

"They're big-mouthing for the press," says Keith Bernstein, the President's press secretary.

"You mean they're spilling the beans about the New Partnership?" the President asks.

Bernstein takes out a pack of cigarettes. "Well, they're not talking about the specific program. But they're going on about an inspiring meeting with you, bold new initiatives to solve the nation's social and economic dilemmas, all that crap. God save me from politicians."

The President moves around behind his desk and sits down. "Inevitable, I suppose," he says. "Keith, give me a cigarette."

Bernstein hands his lit cigarette to the President. The Chief Executive formally quit smoking fourteen years before, but he periodically cadges cigarettes. To his staff it is a sign that times of serious stress are approaching.

"Look," Bernstein says. "I just wanted to know what you'd think about giving *Newsweek* an advance on the New Partnership. They know something's up and say they'd like to do an economics cover story the week you break your new plans."

The President nods. "I suppose—"

The hall door opens and Brasher comes in.

"Paul, what do you think about letting *Newsweek* in on the New Partnership? They want to do a cover story."

"I don't see why not," Brasher answers.

"As long as they don't jump it," the President says.

"Okay," Brasher says. "What's up?"

"Just a sec," Bernstein says. "When do we announce this?"

"Come in after lunch," the President says. "We'll discuss it then. I'm trying to talk to my wife without messing up my whole day."

"Okay," Bernstein says, heading for the door.

"Paul," the President says, turning to Brasher, "Roy thinks we ought to set up some meetings with the council, the domestic people, and Ben to fill in the leadership on the New Partnership arguments and details. Can you take care of that?"

Brasher nods. "Sure." He smiles at Caldwell. "Perhaps Roy and I can work it out right now. Got a minute?"

"Just a minute," Caldwell says. "We go in at noon today and I want to get wrapped up on the public lands bill." He turns back to the President. "You know," he says, "you're going to need all the help possible on this one and that includes the best political advice you can get. I'd have a talk with David Marks one of these days."

"I agree," Brasher says. Marks is a Washington lawyer who for nearly three decades has moved between government and one of the most lucrative practices in the capital.

The President nods. "Set up an appointment for him, Paul."

"One more thing," Senator Caldwell says. "Do me a favor, Mr. President, and tell George Koerner about this whole thing sooner rather than later."

The President nods and writes the name of the Senate Minority Leader on his desk pad. "Perhaps tomorrow when you and he come in at two?"

"I was hoping you'd suggest that," Caldwell says.

The President looks up and smiles. "Then it's done. And we're seeing you and Meg for the theater tomorrow night. Why don't you both drop in for a drink about six?"

"I've got one more thing," Howard says. "When you brief on this, for members of Congress, I mean, I wouldn't lean too heavily on the fact that Kotowski was one of the originators of the idea. I'm sure that a lot of those guys up on the Hill think that Kotowski's a Socialist just because he's at Harvard. What do you think, Roy?"

"Point well taken," Caldwell says. "We'd better get out of here."

After the Senator, Brasher, and Howard leave, the President sits alone for a moment watching the thickened flurries of snow sweep under the porch and spray against the glass of the French doors. The fire has passed its zenith and is now a mound of simmering, glaring coals capped by fitful curls of flame. The President draws on his cigarette and tries to rinse his mind of its preoccupation with the New Partnership legislative program. Within a few minutes he will have to switch to something wholly different. As he sits, however, he is intruded upon by the immediate memory of a white and angry face ringed with auburn hair. His wife was trying to say what was really wrong and couldn't. But her eyes said it all.

"Mr. President," says the amplified female voice from the console on the desk.

The President inhales and blows smoke across the top of his desk. He reminds himself of what his doctor told him a week before while prescribing sleeping pills. "*You* make the pressures," General Hochuli had said. "Don't let the pressures come at you. You're President, you're the ringmaster of this show. *You* make the pressures." If only it were that easy.

The President pushes down his console button. "Yes, Barbara?"

"The First Lady on private line two," says the voice.

The President looks down. The blinking telephone button is angry and insistent.

There isn't much pleasure in being a great king. The most splendid of them howl in misery through the corridors of time, lashing out against the personal torments that made their lives hell while they made their times great. Henry II, that supreme giant of England's gigantic monarchical history, was broken in power and spirit by a plague of sons; Henry VIII of England and Henry II of France both suffered surfeits of women, and the greatness of their genius in history has been obfuscated by their sexual notoriety; Frederick the Great was emotionally crippled by the unpurgeable memory of a bestial father; even that glittering princely perfection, Lorenzo the Magnificent, was terrorized to an early death by the psychotic ravings of Savonarola.

Aside from the personal sufferings that are the dark side of greatness, the king is victimized by furies that are bred of his majesty itself. The first fury is expectation. Great voltages of human hope are focused upon the splendor of the king; the hope is based on the assumption that the ruler is all-powerful and can do whatever he wants to do. Even the mightiest of kings spent their lives in haggling, threatening, being threatened, imploring, and conniving with and against forces that were powerful enough to demand that majesty reckon with them. The second fury is isolation. Because the king is splendid, because so many hope for so much from him, because some are driven to rage by unfulfilled hope, he must remain apart from his people. The world must not see him too often, and thus the king cannot see the world. Others must describe to him as he sits in blind majesty. He perceives reality as the predigested reality of other men. The third fury is finality. The king must make the last and binding decision, and then he must take ultimate praise or blame. But he is not free to decide what and when he wishes. The world dictates when he will make decisions. Prime Ministers swim in the world of mortal politics, which is to say that all they do they do in collaboration with others. The king does not collaborate. In deciding, he acts alone. Only in explaining away the things that he failed to do can the king shift the blame to others. For all that is done by the state or in its name, we praise or damn the king alone. There isn't much pleasure in being a great king.

American Presidents are becoming kings.

Or it might be more accurate to say that the American presidency is becoming a monarchy that imposes the debilities of that political system upon a succession of temporary kings who head it. When one speaks of Presidents becoming kings, one does not mean the amiable but powerless monarchs of modern Europe but rather the great and failed figures of the Age of Kings. American Presidents are not beginning to resemble them because they want to, because they secretly yearn to exchange the harassing problems of governing for absolute rule. The monarchistic traits of the presidency have been imposed upon it by the increasing size and complexity of the United States, by Washington's own obsessions with power, and by the fracturing of the United States into contending blocs of political, social, and economic faction.

In this century the population of the United States will almost quadruple. The sun of the American twentieth century rose on 76 million people and it will go down on 320 million. In the 1960 census it was discovered that of 179 million Americans 125 million lived in cities or close to them and only 54 million lived out in the countryside. In multiplying numbers of people there are multiplying demands and proliferating conditions. In the compressing of such vast numbers into the economic oases of the cities there is immense friction and grievance. What makes the situation impossible is the new American tendancy to aim all demands and grievances at one figure—the President.

Since 1929 the social and political focus of the United

States has narrowed upon him. The new tradition holds that the U.S. government is the only effective activist force left in the nation and that the President is its trigger puller.

The Wall Street crash was more than an economic trauma. It was also the collapse of a certain set of assumptions that had accompanied the industrial growth of the United States after the Civil War. "Modern life is both complex and intense," said Theodore Roosevelt in his inaugural address of 1905, "and the tremendous changes wrought by the extraordinary industrial development of the last half-century are felt in every fiber of our social and political being." What Roosevelt was talking about was a fantastic late nineteenth-century economic growth that, unlike the expansion of 1815–1830, was based as much on machines as on land development, a growth that made far fewer Americans far richer than during the general prosperity of the Madison, Monroe, and Jackson administrations. Government, as the impotent Cleveland grieved, simply conceded power to the greedy spoilsmen of the Gilded Age, and the mass of the people were swept along with the prosperity of the few. The people were not so much kept quiescent by the crumbs that fell from the table of industrial wealth as they were sustained by the dribbling down of an ethic that came to dominate the American mind in the last half of the nineteenth century. Even people as cynical as Jim Fiske, Collis P. Huntington, Armour, Swift, Drew, Gould, and the other robber barons required an ethic. No matter what man is doing, even if he knows that his actions are immoral (or maybe because he knows they are immoral), he needs a philosophy to accompany his endeavors. In the age of the robber barons the operating principle was called "progress," and its reigning philosopher was Herbert Spencer, that lugubrious British prestidigitator who parlayed Darwin's theories of evolution into a justification for unbridled capitalism, because capitalism was ordained as the vehicle of universal and inevitable improvement. Spencer's *Man Against the State* became the ethical bible of conservative economics. It gave a nice tone of philosophical inevitability to what big business was going to do anyway; it linked those activities directly with God Almighty and thus helped to euchre the unrewarded majority of the population into going along with the system. Like the version of Christianity preached to rural Mexicans early in this century, the capitalism preached to the American masses a hundred years ago was rooted in the concept that things may be miserable now but if you behave yourself and believe in the system you'll get yours later on.

And that was the assumption that crashed along with the stock market in 1929. The psychological shock was so deep that its effects didn't surface for some time. What had been demonstrably true to a few nonradical thinkers before 1929—that capitalism, while a perfectly reasonable economic system, wasn't impervious to its own disasters—became everyone's half-conscious realization after 1929. The belief in capitalism as a system of social advancement remained. But it was no longer regarded as the main source of help when things were bad. Suddenly government— which had heretofore been a companion piece to capitalism ("The business of America is business," said Calvin Coolidge) and occasionally, under Theodore Roosevelt and Woodrow Wilson, the regulator of capitalism—became the principal source of help. Government replaced Wall Street as the activist force in American life.

It is interesting to speculate on what would have happened to the public focus if Franklin Delano Roosevelt hadn't been elected President in 1932. He was the pioneer social activist of the American presidency, though not by design. In his first campaign for the presidency Roosevelt sounded at times as conservative and Constitution-bound as William Howard Taft. Addressing the Commonwealth Club in San Francisco on September 23, 1932, Roosevelt solemnly declared that "the Government should assume the function of economic regulation only as a last resort, only when private initiative, inspired by high responsibility, with such assistance and balance as Government can give, has finally failed." Once he was elected the dire condition of the nation lashed Roosevelt into action. FDR's genius was not as an ideologue. It was his very lack of ideological commitment that enabled him to launch upon the vast innovations of

the New Deal. The enormous energy of his presidency combined with the crash of 1929 bequeathed a new and ultimately
intolerable burden upon Presidents to come. The American theory
of action had narrowed the public's focus from the multiple leaders of the capitalist system to one man alone operating the mysterious devices of government. "The buck," said Harry Truman,
"stops here."

The second fury of kings is isolation.

It is bred of the first one, which is expectation. If the people
seek one source for the blame and the cure of their condition,
then they focus on the one part of the government elected by all
of them—the Executive, headed by the President. "There is," observes Sir Denis Brogan, "a vacancy which the President can
make but which no one but he can fill." From the concept of
responsibility for the nation, which strong Presidents have given
the presidency, there derives the immense solitude of the office.
The President may argue with Congress about what ought to be
done and about how to do it; he may be subject to the restraints
and denials of the courts. But as far as the people are concerned
the President is ultimately responsible. It is the first Process principle raised to the level of a national assumption. The people assume that the President has awesome power; they assume therefore that he can do whatever he wants to do and thus they expect him to do everything and blame him when he doesn't.

Along with a lot of other unpleasant things, the President's
isolation imposes upon him a monarchical blindness. George
Reedy, who served as Lyndon Johnson's press secretary says
that "a President does not have available to him methods of
gauging the intensity of the opposition—something any politician
must have to be successful." In order to overcome his inability
to get an accurate fix on the Congress, the bureaucracy, and
the nation, a President needs guide dogs. His staff is supposed
to fill this role by being his eyes and ears in the Process. But
White House staffs suffer from a built-in anachronism: unless
they are composed of men of unusual character, the staffs tend
to become groups of servants vying interminably for their mas-

ters' attention and favor. Neither objectivity nor courage is enhanced in the master-servant relationship.

Obviously, Presidents have always had staffs and helpers. But until Congress voted Buchanan a secretary, a messenger, and a steward in 1857, presidential staffs were recruited either from the Chief Executive's family (and paid by him out of his own pocket) or from other departments of government that went on paying them. The modern proliferation of White House staffs coincided with the explosion of public expectations of the presidency—in 1933.

When FDR came down from New York to be inaugurated in 1933 he brought with him a gaggle of economists and university professors who formed his first "brain trust." Equally divided into liberals and conservatives, the first brain trust withered away and was replaced by a brilliant, disorderly herd of activists who thought while running. Led by the shrewd, ambitious Harry Hopkins, the herd included Thomas "Tommy the Cork" Corcoran, who dealt with politicians, darted in and out of the bureaucracy, told jokes, wrote speeches, and sometimes threatened people; William O. Douglas, who was later appointed to the Supreme Court; Robert Jackson, who worked with Douglas on the economic and mechanical problems of the New Deal; Ben Cohen and Isador Rubin, legal geniuses who drafted bills; scholarly Stanley High, who also wrote speeches; and Steve Early, who handled press relations. Hundreds of lawyers, visionaries, cranks, and causists operated through and beyond Roosevelt's brilliant, contentious Cabinets, tumbling all over one another, duplicating functions, and pulsating enough energy to light Vladivostok on a dark morning. Through it all whirled the most dynamic First Lady in presidential history, advising the President, prowling the country to hear what people were saying, acting as the special White House advocate of women, blacks, and Army privates who didn't like their officers. Eleanor Roosevelt was a brilliant and sometimes difficult woman who was the undeserving target of a lot of malice and smutty humor. She was indispensable to her husband because she helped to keep him informed about the country. Roosevelt's system of running the

White House was one of creative chaos. He liked it that way. He was a compulsive manipulator of people, a great talker, and a greater listener who did his best work in an atmosphere of federal din.

In 1939 the Reorganization Act further increased the number of people working directly for the President. The act was theoretically designed to give the Chief Executive better ways of managing the nation. In addition to enlarging the President's immediate staff to include six new assistants, the act ultimately added on the Council of Economic Advisers, the Bureau of the Budget, the Office of Defense Mobilization, the President's Advisory Committee on Government Reorganization, and a lot of other useful machinery to the Executive Office of the President. Though all this did make it easier for President Roosevelt to run the country, it also resulted in a vast number of new bodies for him to manipulate. The act took all sorts of functions that had been scattered around the federal jungle (or that hadn't existed at all) and whooshed them into the orbit of the President, thereby creating even more chaos. Roosevelt, wrote his loyal Secretary of War, "is the poorest administrator I have ever worked under. . . ."

Thus the first of two theories on how to run the White House, help the President, and mitigate his blindness: get a lot of bright people in, light fires under them, play them off against each other (as Roosevelt and Lyndon Johnson did), delegate work and authority on a who-happens-to-be-around-at-the-moment basis, and hope that from the tumult will emerge ideas that are the supportive genius of a particular administration.

The second thoeory of how to run the White House presupposes that the United States is an economic system that must be administered and that must not be profaned with too much tinkering and grafting. This is the Republican vision of America; Republicans are the modern heirs to the eighteenth-century concept that some things are or ought to be because God and/ or nature has ordained them (self-evident truths, the Founding Fathers called them). In the spirit of that vision the two Republican Presidents of the middle and late twentieth century organized the White House as management offices composed of disciplined specialists with a few generalists sown among them. President Eisenhower vested enormous authority in Sherman Adams, who received the title of assistant to the President and parlayed it into great power before his fall in the Goldfine scandal. Adams made decisions that in other administrations would have been made by the President himself. Once when two quarreling Cabinet members turned up to have their dispute settled by Eisenhower, Adams took over the matter himself with the admonition: "We must not bother the President with this. He is trying to keep the world from war." If that sounds rather pompous, it was a reflection of the power realities of the Eisenhower White House and of the fact that the realities existed because the President wasn't terribly interested in the day-to-day running of the government. All lines of authority flowing to and from the President ran through Adams, who guarded his master's portals with icy authority. He became known in Washington as the "Abominable No Man," but he ran a White House that, whatever else it might have been, was a well-oiled and fixed-duty mechanism.

That sort of organization reached its peak with the first Nixon administration, which came to power in January 1969. If a high degree of efficiency and superb follow-through are maximum presidential virtues, then Richard Nixon is the most virtuous man ever to sit in the White House. He modified the top assistant role so that his chief of staff, Harry Robins Haldeman, wielded great administrative authority but not as much decision-making power as Adams.

The Nixon White House staff is rigidly divided into areas of specialization—international affairs, economic affairs, political affairs, domestic affairs, administration. Haldeman and his dedicated assistant, Jon Huntsman, preside over the flow of work that comes into the White House in the form of problems, letters, crises, demands, telephone calls, messages from Congress, political signals, and forecasts of trouble. At the Haldeman-Huntsman level the work is parceled out to the appropriate area of the White House or beyond to the federal bureaucracy. Each assignment requires expert study, recommendations for action, and a deadline. The completed assignments then flow back to Haldeman and Huntsman, who decide what the President will become involved in and what will be decided elsewhere. Once in the President's office, the studies and recommendations are read and there is discussion with the pertinent specialists. Then a decision is made. The President is kept abreast of the world by a forty- to fifty-page news summary prepared by staff specialists and put in his hands by eight every morning. Nixon's day is carefully parceled into periods for appointments with outsiders, periods for solitary work and thought, and periods for those favored or necessary aides who have, in White House jargon, "direct access." For every meeting with an outsider, the President's staff gives him a one-page brief that includes essential data on the visitor, talking points, what the visitor wants, and what the President might say to him. Appointments secretaries screen applicants for a bit of the presidential time; an aide named Alexander Butterfield hovers in a small, curtained office directly beyond the President's to supervise the coming and going of people, paper, and politics.

There are virtues and defects in both ways of running the White House. The creative chaos method is less effective in follow-through. A President's word is not law, nor are his wishes necessarily demands. He is denied one of the few virtues of a monarchy—the power to get rid of people who don't or won't do what he wants. "In the first year you're in office you assume you have power," said one of President Nixon's top aides. "Then, in the second year, you find out how little you actually have. You discover that it doesn't get down, it doesn't reach out into the whole government." This rueful discovery was also made by John F. Kennedy, who at his inaugural parade asked an aide to find out if something couldn't be done to recruit more blacks into the Coast Guard Academy, whose white ranks were marching past him. Nearly three years later, at the time of President Kennedy's death, the answer still hadn't come back up through the system.

The management theory of the presidency is less effective in generating ideas. The system is so controlled, with so many stopping points and so much categorized order, that it tends to deliver up recommendations and ideas that bear a monotonous similarity to one another. The same sorts of minds tend to process all problems; viewpoints and ideas that are contrary to the accustomed way of thinking tend to be smogged out. Opinions that do not concur with the official thinking of the Executive Mansion are turned away.

Whatever the virtues or faults of the two ways of organizing the White House, they reflect nothing more than the struggle of Presidents to cope with their isolation, which is the second fury of kings. Marooned, at the mercy of other men's tainted vision, Presidents have become noble, blind figures like Oedipus at Colonus, wailing as the Theban king wailed,

> And when you look into my ruined eyes
> Do not look with scorn.
> I am a dedicated man, a holy man,
> And come with graces in my hands,
> Graces for this people . . .

All of which is another way of saying that the road to presidential hell is paved with good intentions whose practicality the Chief Executive has no sure way of judging.

The third fury of kings is finality.

Whatever else the presidency is—and there are a great many theories about that—it is a place where one man must say yes or no. That's bad enough for any sane man of sensitive feelings when faced with mutually exclusive choices. It has always been difficult for Presidents. For some, decision making tended to be an oppressive process. Andrew Jackson, who was brought to power by the first wave of American populism and who was a man of rather complicated feelings, got into a protracted brawl over the Second Bank of the United States, whose extension he vetoed. It was a volatile and tricky decision. The proponents of the Bank and the American fiscal system did not take the decision quietly; battles, problems, and a messy spurt of Treasury deposits followed. "The Bank," Jackson roared at Martin Van Buren, "is trying to kill me. But I will kill *it!*" It was tough on Old Hickory but bearable in light of the sorts of things his successors after 1836 had to decide. The worst calamities that could have befallen Jackson as a result of his decision and the subsequent fight over the Bank were financial disorder in a nation young and resilient enough to bear it and political difficulties that might have prevented him from installing Van Buren as his successor. Abraham Lincoln risked losing a nation. John F. Kennedy in the Cuban missile crisis risked ending the world. In the upgraded stakes that ride on modern presidential decisions, the point about the full monarchical fury of finality is grimly demonstrated.

Decision making in the presidency does not only involve selecting an option; it also demands that the man who makes the decision enforce it. Not only are some of the matters a President must decide dangerous, but the means at his disposal to back up his decisions are positively lethal. They include, along with doomsday weapons, a huge civilian and military force to deploy with sometimes inflammatory results (Kennedy sending U.S. marshals into Alabama to enforce integration; Lyndon B. Johnson escalating the U.S. troop commitment in Vietnam); vast amounts of money that can be misspent (the C-5A transport boondoggle); and the very power of a huge government that, because it is operated by mortal men, is seriously imperfect. The opportunity for a President to make a bad mistake crouches just ahead of him every moment of his years in office. Yet the one thing a President cannot do is refuse to decide, refuse to take a course of action. Events march upon him, imperatives shriek for solution; most great problems incorporate within their perplexities the potential for disasters worse than a bad choice by a President. So the President faces a series of closed doors, ponders, and then opens one of them. He has then embarked upon a course. "He cannot count on turning back," says Theodore Sorensen, "yet he cannot see his way ahead. He knows that if he is to act, some eggs must be broken to make the omelet, as the old saying goes. But he also knows that an omelet cannot lay any more eggs." In describing the limitations upon presidential choices themselves, Sorensen adds: "He is free to choose only within the limits of permissibility, within the limits of available resources, within the limits of available time, within the limits of previous commitments, and within the limits of available information."

This is not to assert that world-shattering decisions are the common or even occasional lot of all Presidents. But they are certainly one of the occupational hazards of the job. They lurk as constant potentials. The commoner misery of decision making is imposed by the first fury—expectation. No man likes to displease others; no politican in his right mind likes to offend large numbers of people. Yet implicit in many routine presidential decisions is the displeasure of a great many Americans. The long-overdue drive for civil rights that characterized congressional politics of the middle and late 1960s and the Supreme Court decisions of the middle 1950s and early 1970s created a situation that forced Presidents of the period to spend a great deal of time displeasing the white South.

The difficulty of even ordinary presidential decision making is compounded by the second fury, isolation. The President can never be sure whether facts are being presented to him in such a way as to prod him toward a particular decision, whether he has enough facts, or whether those advising him even know what they are talking about. Harry S. Truman was presented with an overwhelming case against trying to supply Berlin by airlift after Stalin blockaded the city in the winter of 1947. Political experts assured Mr. Truman that an airlift would only exacerbate the situation; military officers told him that the cargo planes would be at the mercy of Soviet fighters; other experts proved with statistics that it was impossible to sustain a city the size of Berlin by air for any length of time; and meteorologists assured the President from the depths of their expertise that if the airlift were tried, the fogs and winter storms would reduce flight conditions to such a point that Berlin and its lifeline corridors would be littered with wrecked aircraft. Mr. Truman listened to all this advice and then, motivated by some extraordinary confidence and perspective, decided to go ahead with the Berlin airlift. It was a complete success. And that success was due to the uncanny decision-making powers of a great President.

Harry Truman always claimed that decision making never bothered him any more than the names people called him. "When the thing was over with, I'd sleep like a baby," he told this reporter once along with probably 10,000 other reporters. He was proud of the fact that his strong nature permitted him to escape the presidential haunts. It also permitted him to make some of the most hair-raising decisions of American history, from the dropping of the first atomic bomb to the Berlin airlift to the decision to run again in 1948 in the face of what more brooding men would have concluded was an impossible political situation and the decision to throw American and UN troops into Korea to stop a Soviet-contrived invasion that, if successful, would have changed the course of modern history.

Partly because he presided over a more socially unified nation than his successors and partly because of his own talent for moral leadership, Harry Truman kept the first fury of expectation at bay. The disaffection of the Henry Wallace left and the Dixiecrat right in the election of 1948 wasn't serious enough to defeat him—a symptom of the relative harmony of the Truman era. Much has been made of the supposedly "immoral" politics of Mr. Truman's administration, of the deep freeze and 5 percenter scandals, the crooked foolishness of Harry Vaughn, the grubby episodes of cheating and advantage taking by men to whom the President was more loyal than he should have been. But that sort of thing isn't political immorality. It's just petty corruption. Immorality is the misuse of the public instincts for shallow, selfish, or unworthy ends. It is a McCarthy capering about the country with great snorts of self-professed patriotism in the interests of blackening an honorable foe, a Henry Wallace redefining virtue as his own particular political crochets, a Polk cashing in on the westward enthusiasm of his age for his own self-glory. Immorality is also using great office or great political prestige to appeal to the public frailties of fear, greed, and ignorance in order to achieve shallow, selfish, or unworthy ends; it is the encrusted racism passed on for generations in the social South, the class hatreds and regional hatreds of populism in the West, the use of Franklin Roosevelt's presidency to attack Senator George of Georgia with proclamations that he stood in the path of American destiny when in fact the Senator simply opposed Roosevelt's immediate plans for the next session of the Congress.

Harry Truman's capacity for moral leadership—that is, his use of the presidency to demonstrate what he thought was right and useful—was manifest in the recurrently obvious fact that he put the presidency and his version of the national interest above his own political safety. He became unpopular because of his own undeclared war, Korea, and profoundly unpopular with the firing of General MacArthur. He even risked the opprobrium of history by deciding to drop the atomic bomb on Japan. He never indulged in much self-congratulation over his own political morality, but his definition of leadership as displayed by his conduct of the presidency was evident; Truman got an idea of what he thought was the highest good at the time and then tried to lead his people toward it. This *creation* of consensus around an idea contrasts sorrowfully with a later era in which Lyndon Johnson kept groping around for an already existent consensus. Truman, like both Roosevelts, Lincoln, and Jackson, believed that the presidency was a place where objectives and morality were defined in the public view.

One does not dwell at such length on Harry Truman because in his definition of the vague powers of Article II he was the most splendid, best, or "greatest" President of modern times. One uses him rather to illustrate if not to explain some of the human qualities most useful to the presidency. The unique chemistry of Mr. Truman's nature was understandable only to God Almighty but whatever the mixture, it was a good one for Presidents to have: operable but not distracting intellectual capacities, that mental lucidity which makes the essence of a situation obvious, a capacity for decisiveness and enough flexibility to be persuaded, great emotional stability, mixed capacities for contempt and respect, a smoothly functioning digestive tract, and a comforting wife. One also dwells on Mr. Truman to contrast the time in which he was President with the times that followed him. The primary crises that threatened American society during the Truman era were external, and if anything they had the effect of further uniting the American people. After him, after the long, lucky, lazy Eisenhower interregnum, the things that threatened American society came from within, thus splitting that society apart. The two Presidents who inherited that particular maelstrom—Johnson and Nixon—stand in doleful contrast to Harry Truman and his brisk, confident leadership. He didn't have their problems and they didn't have his qualities as President.

He was the last one who wasn't king.

Love.

The search for it, the insatiable appeal for it are the leitmotifs of this President's life and nature. Everything that he is and does can probably be traced back to the search for love, Ben Saterlee thinks as he walks along the narrow, curving corridor toward the Oval Office. The quest for love is neither blatant, neurotic, nor especially visible to the casual observer. It is obvious only to those who know the President intimately, the close friends and aides whose sensory apparatus pick up the unstated facts of his unhappy marriage and the persistent, subtle compulsion of his personality to try to make itself lovable—the worrying about other people's problems as if they were his own, the cultivation of character designed to please, the hatred of saying no to anyone. What's more, Saterlee tells himself, none of this really can be very neurotic because it all works. Those close to the President do love him.

He began thinking about the President and love for no particular reason as he left the Executive Office Building across a private street from the west wing of the White House, made his way, squinting, through the sheets of fine snow whirling across the gloomy Washington afternoon. He had entered a basement door of the White House, passed a white-shirted guard who recognized him on sight, took the elevator to the first floor, crossed the west lobby, and is now heading for the President's office.

Saterlee is one of half a dozen men on the White House staff who don't need to go through channels to get to the President. He is a special counsel and as such has direct access. Everybody knows that when Saterlee goes to the Oval Office it is because the President has summoned him. He talks to the Chief Executive by telephone three to ten times a day and sees him at least once a day, often more.

He opens a door down the hall from the Oval Office. Four secretaries are crowded into a space that is far too small for them. By the same alchemy that creates harmony in a room full of furniture chosen by one person's taste, the four secretaries all seem to be natural parts of the aura cast by the man sitting two offices away. Barbara Claudus, the President's principal secretary, is in her forties, slender, her strawberry-blonde hair going slightly, attractively gray. She is a woman of healthy, clear complexion and blue eyes; this afternoon she wears a cardigan and a tweed skirt. A gold St. Christopher medal twirls and gleams from her wrist as she waves at Saterlee. Two of the other girls are blonde, straight-haired, and equally healthy-looking. The fourth is tall and dark-haired. Her name is Mary Anne Dexter and she spends her White House days withdrawn into a shy dignity.

"Ben," Barbara says, "can you wait a minute? Paul wants to see you."

"Sure," Saterlee says. He looks over at the two blonde secretaries. "You ladies behaving yourselves?"

"Oh God," says the shorter of the two with exaggerated boredom, "we never have a chance to misbehave. Sixteen hours a day and for two weeks it's been seven days a week . . ."

The other blonde punches hard on a typewriter key and pulls a finished letter from the machine. "When I'm President I'm going to run the country in four days and give everybody the other three off."

The office door opens and Brasher comes in. "Hi, Ben. Ladies."

"Paul." Saterlee nods.

Brasher looks up at the windows. The snow has stopped.

Washington is muffled in white. "What a day," Brasher says. He turns back to Saterlee. "I just wanted to tell you that Governor Wharton of Rhode Island was in about an hour ago. Apparently the Atomic Energy Commission licensed a nuclear electric plant at Jamestown. That's an island at the head of Narragansett Bay."

Saterlee nods. "I know the place."

"A group of Jamestown people brought suit," Brasher says. He sits on the edge of a desk, his hands gripping it on either side of his legs. "The claim is that the AEC didn't do proper studies of the effects of water contamination and so forth. They've been turned down in the lower courts and a decision is going to be handed down in the Fourth Court of Appeals next week. If it goes against them as Wharton thinks it will, they're going to petition the Supreme Court to hear them. He wants to know if we can do anything before it gets that far."

"Like what?"

Brasher shrugs. "I don't know. But I'm going to buck this one over to you."

"Okay." Saterlee says. "I'll see what can be done."

"We'd better check with Jake too," Brasher says. "I take it that one reason Wharton came to see us is that he's going after McCall's Senate seat next time and wants to end-run the illustrious gentleman from Rhode Island."

"Okay," Saterlee says.

The console on Barbara's desk buzzes. She turns from her typewriter and pushes down a button. "Yes, Mr. President?"

"Is Ben Saterlee there yet?" says the mechanically distorted voice.

"Yes, sir."

"Paul wanted to see him on the Rhode Island matter."

"They've just finished talking about it," Barbara answers.

"All right. Tell Ben anytime."

"Yes, Mr. President." She straightens up and turns around in her swivel chair. "Ben, go on in and be a pet, get Keith out of there, will you?"

Paul slips off the edge of the desk. "I'll see you shortly," he says. He smiles at Barbara. Brasher's smile is an expression that makes everyone who sees it feel good.

"What's Keith talking to him about?" Saterlee asks.

"He's agitating for another press conference," Barbara sighs. "We haven't had one in six weeks, you know."

"Five," Saterlee says.

"Six," she replies, smiling at him. "February 2."

"The walking encyclopedia," Brasher says. "What day of the week was Christ born, Barbara?"

"Oh Christmas," She laughs. "Go and get Keith out of there, Ben."

Saterlee goes through a small, elegantly furnished room with a large colonial highboy and a console of blinking telephone buttons. This is Stuart Graham's office. It lacks a desk. Saterlee knocks on the far door.

"Come in," says a muffled voice.

The President and Keith Bernstein, his press secretary, are sitting opposite each other on the sofas before the Oval Office's fireplace. Papers and a book litter the cushions on either side of the President; he is coatless, an informality he signaled to his staff an hour after his inauguration when he returned to the White House, took off his morning coat, and met with Brasher, Saterlee, and half a dozen others before going out to the parade.

The President looks tall but really isn't. He is, as a matter of fact, just a shade under six feet. The impression of height is cast by the proportions of his body—narrow shoulders, flat stomach, and long legs. The President is a man naturally constructed for grace and style. His face bears the imprint of the generations of New York merchants and New England aristocrats from whom he is descended. It is a long face; the eyes are deeply set and look upon the world with a faintly mournful expression that his sudden, radiant smile contradicts. His nose is slightly too large and tends, like his teeth, to protrude slightly. "His trouble," wrote a weekly news magazine during the President's last year as a Senator from New York, "is that he looks too perfect. More elegant than Kennedy, with as much natural bearing as his distant cousin, Franklin Roosevelt, his physical manner makes him implausible. People like flaws in their politicians, they relate the man to the electorate he serves. The Senator has flaws to spare but they are all intellectual and emotional, hidden behind his overpowering manner and style."

This afternoon the President wears the slacks of a gray suit whose jacket is draped carefully over the back of a chair beside William Howard Taft's desk, highly polished ankle boots, a shirt of thin blue stripes, a black tie and wide suspenders of flaming red. There is a piece of paper lying in his lap. As Saterlee opens the door, the President takes off his reading glasses. He is looking grave. Bernstein appears anxious, perched on the edge of the sofa. He runs one hand through his tousled hair as Saterlee sits down beside him. "I've just been telling Keith that we'll schedule the next press conference in September, about six months from now," the President says. "What do you think, Ben?"

Saterlee, who knows the man better than anyone on the White House staff except Brasher, immediately knows that a tease is on. "Too soon, Mr. President," he says. "I don't see why we have to have one until at least the first of the year."

"First of the year!" Bernstein says loudly. "For Christ's sake, Ben! Those guys out there'd eat me alive!"

Saterlee shrugs. "That's the way I see it, Keith. We've got more important things to do."

"Besides," the President adds, "we haven't got anything to say."

"Nothing to say! My God, with the New Partnership going up, those bastards in the Senate working themselves up to cut Air Force appropriations—"

The President suddenly laughs, softly, without a suggestion of triumph. "Okay, Keith, we'll have a press conference in a couple of weeks." He smiles at his press secretary. "We're just trying to keep you anxious."

Bernstein looks at Saterlee, who is also grinning. "You guys ought to be ruled off the track," he says, beginning to smile himself. "Jesus, if you knew the pressure—"

"We do know," the President says. "And I also know that

there isn't anyone else in the White House who could handle it as well as you. When do you think we ought to do it?"

"What about March 30?" Bernstein says.

The President nods. "Good. We'll announce the New Partnership program that day. Would you like me to hold it in the morning so that the network news shows will have plenty of time to pull good cuts and get commentary ready for the evening?"

"Great," Bernstein says.

Love, Saterlee tells himself, is being what others want him to be. Bernstein, whom Saterlee doesn't like, is a former network bureau chief. He is obsessed with television news, especially the Cronkite show on CBS. The President is now playing to that obsession, using Bernstein's broadcasting terms, like "pulling cuts."

"Okay, then," the President says. He smiles a terminal smile at the press secretary. "Get Barbara to put it in the book for 10:30 on March 30. If the date's full—well, I'll leave it to you to work out something with Stu and Paul."

Bernstein rises. "Anything else this afternoon?"

The President shakes his head. "I don't think so, Keith."

After Bernstein leaves, the President says, "Keith's all right."

Saterlee doesn't answer, unsure of whether this is a concession to his dislike of the press secretary or a minute persuasion —that Bernstein is useful for what he does.

The President picks up the paper on his lap and reads it. "Ohh-kay," he says slowly, putting it on the cushion beside him. He looks up at Saterlee. "Want some coffee?"

"I wouldn't mind."

The President gets up, crosses the room to his desk, and pushes down the console button. "Coffee for two, Barbara."

"Right away."

"Better make it for three," the President says. "Ask Paul to come in, will you?"

"Right. McManus is here."

"Send him in." The President turns back to Saterlee. "This should only take a few minutes, whatever it is. We've got this damned thing in Peru. It's been going on since morning."

"Want me to leave?" Saterlee asks.

"No, of course not."

McManus comes in through the hall door. He nods at Saterlee. "Sorry to interrupt. But I thought you'd better know what's going on." He crosses the room and hands a folder to the President.

The President opens it. Silence hangs in the room as if awaiting his authority. He raises his head and looks at McManus. "When did this begin?"

"At about an hour ago, at four o'clock," McManus says. His small, professorial face looks anxious behind its gleaming spectacles. "We've just had another radio message from the embassy. The street fighting's getting bad in central Lima and several thousand people are gathering around the embassy."

"Are the authorities doing anything?" the President asks.

"So far, no," McManus says. "There's a good deal of confusion about the loyalty of the troops in Lima. The police seem to be handling the demonstrations and street fighting at the moment."

Sitting on a sofa at the other end of the room, Saterlee listens for a few minutes and then lets his mind drift. Despite himself, he is a little annoyed that Brasher, the chief of staff, is coming in to join his discussion with the President.

In the formal hierarchy of the White House Brasher outranks Saterlee and all the other aides. But in the proximity game Saterlee is acknowledged to be very close and very secure. He knows how the President thinks and the sort of action he is likely to take. He has known and advised the President for twelve years and was a key man in the transition between the outgoing administration and the new one. His official assignment in the organization of specialists is to deal with the legal and academic communities. In addition, he is called in frequently to give an amateur's assessment of the advice offered the President by the other specialists who surround the Chief Executive in shoals of commitment and expertise. Saterlee is a solver of especially delicate problems dealing with other people's power. Above all, he is one of the staff's top political strategists who awes and slightly frightens the party professionals swarming around the perimeters of the White House.

Saterlee, beneath his New England reserve, is a man whose

inner confidence lags behind the responsibilities given him. His personality is arranged consciously never to show his own uncertainties. At times he can be curt and abrasive, at other times he is outgoing. He is solicitously careful of the feelings of underlings, tends to be short with equals. Originally from Camden, New Jersey, he has lived in Boston and Cambridge since his years as an undergraduate at Harvard. His complex and deeply buried feelings are so attached to Massachusetts for all sorts of security and identity reasons that he has come to epitomize the essential Bostonian—but not always to other Bostonians. A prominent State Street banker once referred to Saterlee as "a damned New Jersey swamp mosquito trying to be something he isn't." The Secretary of the Interior, a Bostonian and former Rhodes scholar, has applied a British House of Commons insult to Saterlee by calling him "a desiccated calculating machine." In a sense the label fits—but only in a sense. Benjamin Saterlee is brilliant, efficient, and cold. But he desperately wishes to be a warmer, more outgoing man and has never quite figured out what it is that stands as a barrier between his emotions and his external self. The press, with its penchant for attaching old labels to the new administration's figures, has already begun to refer to the special counsel as the President's hatchet man—even though Saterlee has yet to chop anyone. Saterlee knows all this and it hurts. He genuinely likes Brasher—more, he suspects, than Brasher likes him—yet it doesn't lessen his pain any to know that Brasher is considered the most popular man in the White House.

"I don't want to do anything about destroyers at this stage," the President says. "I do think it commits us to a belligerent position and possibly to future action." He pauses and reads again while McManus watches him. The President closes the folder. "The Secretary of Defense is coming in at 5:30 on some budget figures. I guess we'd better have Mullins and you in with him. I think we'd better all have a deeper look at this thing and at what we can do."

"All right," McManus says. "5:30."

The President turns to his desk console and pushes the button. "Barbara, ask the Secretary of State if he can come in at 5:30 with the Secretary of Defense and McManus, will you?"

"Yes, sir."

McManus leaves and the President comes back to the sofa. "That's all we needed," he says. "If they burn down the embassy or kill some code clerk I'll have every yahoo on Capitol Hill crawling all over me."

"Which may be one reason for making some gesture now," Saterlee says.

The President shakes his head. "I'd rather have a little mud thrown at me here than get into something I can't back off from. We'll have to wait and see." He picks up some papers from the sofa. "I wanted to go over a few things before Paul comes in. I thought we might send a letter to what's-his-name, the chairman of the Bank of America, congratulating them on lowering interest rates ahead of other banks."

"It went out this morning," Saterlee says.

The President smiles. "You still manage to stay ahead of me, don't you, Ben? What about the trip to Ohio next week? If both Anderson and Carlotta are going to try for that Senate seat next year, don't we really have to see both of them?"

Saterlee nods. "I talked to both of them on Monday and I think Joe's talked to Anderson again. Carlotta's no problem. He'll come to the dinner in Cleveland even if Anderson's there too. But Anderson says he won't come if Carlotta does."

"I don't like that situation in the party out there," the President says. "It shouldn't be my job to bang heads together and make people love each other. That's what we have state and national party chairmen for. Can we get Carlotta not to come to the dinner if Anderson decides to show up?"

"Yes," Saterlee says. "He told me he can arrange to be somewhere else that evening—even on short notice if Anderson decides at the last minute to come. Carlotta's a nice fellow. Anderson isn't."

The President puts on his glasses and looks at a paper in his lap. "I just don't want to be double-crossed by Anderson." He reads, the lenses of his glasses making his eyes look large and liquid. "I like Joe Carlotta. I'd like to help him win the primary if I could."

"Yes," Saterlee says, "but Tom Anderson would be a better Senator for us."

The President takes another paper from the pile beside him and scans it. The wind rattles the French doors. "Nobody ever said that politics was pleasant," he mutters.

"No."

A large gust of wind swirls up the snow-muffled rose garden and rattles the French doors again. The flames flatten momentarily upon the logs burning in the fireplace. "Look at this," the Presidents says, waving the paper in his hand. "Do you remember five or six weeks ago when those teaching nuns were in there?"

Saterlee nods.

The President looks at him over the top of his glasses. "I asked somebody to find out if there was any way we could give a little more help to parochial school libraries without legislation. Remember?"

"Yes."

"Well?" The President pauses. "What happened?"

"You never heard anything?"

"No, and it's ridiculous that it should take this long to get an answer to a simple question."

"If I recall," Saterlee says, "Paul turned it over to the Justice Department, the Office of Education, and the Budget Bureau— the last to see if we had any funds left."

The President shakes his head and returns to studying the paper on his lap. "That was your first mistake, letting all those people have a crack at it. They're probably still arguing over who gets to tell me the answer."

"It was Paul who handled the thing, not me," says Saterlee, immediately despising himself.

The President reads in silence. The Oval Office stays alive with the sound of crackling and hissing from the fireplace. "Ridiculous, for God's sake," the President murmurs.

"I'll get on it."

"Yes," the President says, raising his head. "I wish you would. I also wish you'd look into that system the Nixon people had for retrieving assignments handed out to the departments and agencies. Can you call someone?"

"I know Jon Huntsman," Saterlee says. "He worked for Haldeman during the Nixon administration. I'll call him."

The President returns to his papers and reads for a few minutes. There is a muted knock on the door. "Come in," the President says without looking up.

Brasher enters from the hall door, comes around the end of the sofa, and sits down beside Saterlee. "Ben," he murmurs.

"Hello again."

Brasher is tall, slightly overweight, and forty-seven years old. He is a useful specimen in the theory that men's faces reflect their characters. The chief of staff's face is slightly plump; the eyes slightly recessed but luminous, with an attractive capacity for looking into other eyes and sending a signal of kindness. His smile reinforces the impression of kindness; it is never sudden, never full, but breaks across Brasher's face in shy hesitation. His dark brown hair is combed over his forehead. He is a soft-spoken, relaxed man who is a devout Episcopalian. Paul Brasher has some standing as a lay theologian; he has written and published articles and papers supporting the progressive wing of his church. A lawyer in Schenectady, he managed the President's last two Senate campaigns and his election to the White House. He runs the White House staff without ever becoming tense or irritable; he never appears pressed for time. *The New York Times* magazine ran an article on him in early February entitled "The Quiet General Who Commands the White House." The article tried— and failed—to penetrate the chief of staff's private life. It managed only to repeat what was already known, that Brasher is a widower with two daughters and that he has remained devoted to the memory of his wife, who died in an automobile accident ten years ago. Brasher has been close to the President for many years and is said by some people to be slightly afraid of his master. Others contend that Paul Brasher is the man to call— and fast—when presidential rages erupt. The rages are a dark, defeating side of the quest for love.

The President finishes the last paper, takes off his glasses, and looks up. "Paul."

"Mr. President."

"I told Keith we'd have a press conference on the thirtieth to announce the New Partnership."

Brasher nods. "That sounds about right."

"I wanted to have a word with you and Ben before Professor Kotowski comes in," the President says. "Why am *I* seeing him?"

"I think Ben ought to be the one to explain that," Brasher says. "It's his baby."

"Is Kotowski here?" Saterlee asks.

"Waiting outside," Brasher replies. "He was a bit late because of the storm."

"The basic reason we thought you ought to see him," Saterlee says to the President, "is that Kotowski has a rather good-sized following and we may be disappointing him. He writes; he's becoming a pop economic liberal, a sort of latter-day Galbraith. Bob Manning gets him to do pieces for the *Atlantic,* things like that. Since we're taking one of his ideas and using it for something else, we risk being attacked. I thought the explanation had better come from you. We don't need to alienate Kotowski and his friends at this point."

"All right," the President says. His irritation is cooling. "How do I handle him?"

"Kotowski's young," Saterlee says, "about forty, around in there. He's very bright, and like a lot of bright people he tends to be a bit evangelical. Thinks he's in possession of original truth when he comes up with an idea. When he first approached me during the campaign last September, his basic idea was for a new system of tax credits for industry that could be used as an inflation control device by the Executive. He knows that that would have required difficult legislation. I've been softening him up in telephone conversations over the last few weeks. I've told him that Congress isn't ready yet. But I haven't told him we're taking only a piece of his plan and using it as the basis for the New Partnership. I'm not sure how he'll react to that—unless you persuade him we have to do it."

The President has been reading a paper in his lap as Saterlee talks. Without looking up, he says, "What are the dangers to us?"

"Oh, they come mostly from Kotowski's ego," Saterlee says. "He is bright, he does have a following among important people, mostly liberals—the radicals think of him as a slick salesman for capitalism. I think that Jack sees himself as becoming an important outside adviser to us. I think he dreams of being the economic *éminence grise* of the administration. He might get sore at what we've done with his ideas and attack us. We don't need liberals getting sore at us at this point."

"So you said before," the President says, raising his head. He takes off his reading glasses. "All right, Paul, get him in." He nods at Ben Saterlee. "You stay."

Brasher goes out into the hall. The President puts on his jacket. He looks out of the window as he buttons it and brushes the lapels.

He pushes the console button on his desk. "Barbara, get me General Sterling's memorandum on manpower needs for the second quarter, will you? I'd like to have it when the Secretary of Defense comes in for that 5:30 meeting."

"Right. McManus just called."

"Have him ring on the private line," the President says.

The hall door opens. Brasher enters behind a short man with black hair and heavy black eyebrows. He wears a dark suit, white shirt, and striped tie. He comes around the end of the sofa, grinning a teeth-baring smile. "Hi, Ben," he says softly.

A telephone rings on the President's desk. He picks it up. His back is turned to the three men in the room. "Yes," he says. "Yes. Is it only in Lima?"

"Hi, Jack," Saterlee whispers, his hand hurting a little from Kotowski's strong grip. "How was the trip down?"

"American Airlines got lost in the goddamn storm," Kotowski hisses, grinning. "We were forty-five minutes late."

Brasher touches Saterlee's arm. "I'll leave Professor Kotowski with you."

Saterlee nods. "See you later."

The President is still on the telephone. He is listening, speaking briefly, monosyllabically.

"How's Betty?" Kotwoski whispers.

"Missing Cambridge," Saterlee answers softly. "Margaret?"

"Great," Kotowski says in loud softness. "We've been in England for two weeks. Ditchley conference. Great time. Saw a lot of your old buddies."

The President finishes his telephone conversation, hangs up, and turns back toward the sofas.

"Mr. President," Saterlee says, "this is Professor Kotowski."

The President crosses the room, relaxed and unhurried. He holds out his hand. "Well," he says softly, the smile coming suddenly and radiantly, "this *is* a pleasure, Professor. We owe you a great deal around here."

"Mr. President." Kotowski's own teeth-clenching smile seems to be paralyzed across his face.

"Come over here and sit down," the President says. "Ben, have you found out if Professor Kotowski needs some coffee?"

"No thanks, Mr. President. I've had a late lunch."

Sitting down, the President turns to look out the French doors at the rose garden. "I'm afraid we brought you down on a bad afternoon." He turns back to Kotowski. "We're grateful to you for taking the time to come. I take it that you and Ben are old friends."

Kotowski nods. "We taught together at Harvard for a while and used to play a little tennis. I've been in love with Betty for years."

The President laughs. "So's every man in his right senses. She's a lovely person." The laugh abruptly fades. "Well, Professor, the reason we asked you to come down was to get your advice on a program we're going to be announcing on March 30. It's based on your concept of more vigorous use of tax credits." He pauses. Kotowski fumbles in his jacket pocket. "Go ahead and smoke," the President says. "I use the word 'based,' Professor, because every administration, as you know better than I do, has to adapt ideas to suit the immediate needs it faces as it assumes responsibility for the nation."

Love and subtle patriotism, Saterlee thinks as he listens. *He's roping Jack into the national crisis, smothering him with it.*

"Of course," Kotowski answers.

"The political challenge facing this administration," the President continues, "the thing that this administration is going to be all about if we're successful, is defusing the problem of needs in confrontation with the resentment of the taxed while continuing to meet the needs."

He's rehearsing his press conference announcement, Saterlee thinks, as the President slips from a conversational into a slightly oratorical speaking style.

"I don't need to tell you that this country is in a pretty ugly mood," the President says. "We have a working class that's been taxed, as we used to say, to the hilt. Have you ever heard of Harvey Leland?"

Kotowski, who has been listening in rapt, adulatory attention, leaning forward, cigarette smoldering in one hand, shakes his head.

"Well, you're going to. He's a very articulate and skillful man from southern California who's putting together a movemen based on the rawest, damnedest, most romantically nonsensical view of free enterprise you've ever heard. Leland deals in those sweeping oversimplifications we're all familiar with— abolish the income tax, increase corporate taxes, no welfare without work, no government help to anyone who's been in jail—all that sort of nonsense. It may sound silly to you and me but it's appealing because people are overtaxed, and because people don't understand the complications we face here in this office. I don't worry about Leland," the President adds. "I just worry about what he represents.

"So what we have to come up with is a way of going on with the social programs we've inherited while not raising taxes to meet the rising costs." The President pauses, plucks at the crease on his right trouser leg for a moment, and then raises his head. "In the next eighteen months, I'll be sending several programs to the Hill. The first is one we're announcing on the thirtieth. I think it's one of the best. And you gave us the idea for it. To put it simply, we're going to create a schedule of social programs that industry can finance with federal supervision and earn tax credits over periods ranging from two to seven years."

Kotowski is silent for a moment. His eyes, which have been looking at the President, shift to the fire. He purses his lips.

"When you say 'industry,' I take it you mean private business in general."

The President nods. "There are even educational programs that, say, advertising agencies could participate in."

Kotowski thinks again for a moment. He leans back on the sofa. "And the benefit to business is that the tax credits would be fixed while inflation decreases the value of the tax dollar over the payoff period."

"Among other things, yes," the President answers. "It also permits immediate deferment of tax in difficult periods. Some tax."

Kotowski raises his cigarette, draws on it, exhales, and leans forward. He crushes the cigarette in an ashtray on the low table between the sofas. "It's an interesting idea," he says slowly. "I can see why you need it politically—"

"We need something that Congress might be willing to approve to attack the immediate problem."

Kotowski nods. "Mmm. That's what worries me, the immediate problem approach." He looks at the President. "I don't think you're going to get much more than symbolism out of this."

"Symbolism is a big part of governing," the President says.

"Yes, but inflation is going to decrease your tax revenues—"

"And business is going to decrease our costs by taking over some of these programs. We hope that expansion will cut the revenue decrease."

"What I was hoping," Kotowski says, "was that this administration would be willing to take a new—I guess I'm really thinking of a revolutionary—view of tax credits, shelters, and profit taxes. It's all in that paper I sent to Ben in late September—"

"Which I read," the President says.

Liar, Saterlee says agreeably to himself.

"And found to be absolutely brilliant. But you were thinking of basic economic management, the long-term fight against inflation." The President shakes his head. "Frankly, Professor, our vision when we took over this place was fixed on a greater imperative—the social question. We found a more urgent need for your ideas in relation to that."

"Yes, but—"

"Of course, we agree on economic management, and there's a good chance that we'll be having a long, serious look at your basic concept once we get this other thing defused." The President leans forward. "I wonder, Professor, if you know how much this job of mine involves just responding to things? Initiating has become a luxury to the modern presidency."

"Of course," Kotowski says.

"I need to respond and fast," the President continues. "I knew when I came in here on the first day that this confrontation between the overly taxed and the people who need help was the first thing I had to respond to. And, thank God, we had some good ideas around in that paper of yours."

Kotowski leans back and smiles. "Well, I'm glad that I was able to be of some help—"

"And I'm glad you're with us," the President says, smiling, "because I'm about to get to the main reason we asked you to come down here."

Saterlee frowns slightly.

"In it's ultimate form," says the President, "this new relationship with industry will be administered by some form of government corporation. That government corporation will have to be guided by an advisory board of prominent economists, businessmen, labor people, and minority spokesmen." He pauses, looking at Kotowski for a moment. "I'd like you to be a chairman of that board."

Kotowski flushes slightly. "Golly. I'm terribly flattered, sir. Actually, this is a pretty tough year. I'm writing a book and—"

"I'm thinking of something part time," the President says. "Frankly—and you mustn't regard this as cynical, Professor—we need the endorsement and support of prominent people who have national respect. This is our way of getting that support, our way of making it obvious that wise men like yourself are with us. And the program will need continuing supervision, watchdogging, and advising if this thing is to work. How about it?"

Kotowski grins. "When I run for President, will you write my speeches?"

The President laughs and stands. "It's a deal. I'm going to put Ben in charge of you and the board. I'd like you both to come up with a list of prospective members by March 20 so we can choose them, get their agreement, and announce them on March 30 at the same time we announce the New Partnership."

Kotowski is on his feet also. "That's the name of the program?"

The President nods slightly. "That's it."

"Fine," Kotowski says.

"We'll be seeing a good deal of each other in the next three and a half years," the President says. "I wonder if I might call you Jack?"

"I'd be honored," Kotowski says, reddening again.

The President walks him to the office door. "Look in on Paul Brasher, my assistant, before you leave. If the storm gets worse the airlines may stop flying. Paul can arrange a hotel room or make your return reservations for Boston."

At the door Kotowski holds out his hand. "I think it'll work, Mr. President. Good-by."

When Kotowski has gone, Saterlee turns to the President, who has gone back to his desk and is looking at a paper. "I don't recall any talk of an advisory board for the New Partnership," he says.

"There's obviously going to be one, isn't there?" the President replies. He looks at Saterlee. "How did it go? Is he all right?"

"Your slave for life, or at least for the next six months until he comes up with another world-saving idea that you don't use."

"We'll worry about that in six months," the President says. "Maybe we'll appoint him to another board."

"McManus waiting. Urgent," says Barbara Claudus' voice on the intercom.

Saterlee returns to his office, thinking less of the complexities of the search for love than of love's usefulness in presidential politics. Jerry McManus comes and goes from the President's office and returns again at 5:30 to meet there with the Secretary

of State and the Secretary of Defense. On Capitol Hill the public
lands bill runs into a fretful, factional snarl in the Senate.

The time is seven o'clock.

The CBS evening news leads with the Peruvian situation.
"The outcome is still uncertain," Walter Cronkite is saying. "And
so is the fate of the American embassy in Lima. United Press
International reports that four buildings belonging to American
companies in the Peruvian capital have been bombed or set on
fire. On Capitol Hill today there were demands that the President take any action necessary to protect American lives and
property. Senator Jeffrey Hastings of New Hampshire called
upon the President to directly intervene with troops if necessary
to prevent General Chavez from coming to power. That, said
Senator Hastings, would be a mortal blow to this hemisphere."

There was a certain poignant charm in the poster waved before Richard Nixon in Ohio during the 1968 presidential campaign. "Bring Us Together" is a plaintive slogan, an emotive abstraction that was undoubtedly genuinely meant by the child
who carried it and a good many other people besides. But
"Bring Us Together" is also the ultimately unreasonable expectation of the people as they regard their leader. It admits that the
people are unable to find common cause among themselves; it demands that the President do for them what they cannot or will
not do for themselves. This is stretching the possibilities of moral
leadership beyond its capacities. To be led in a moral way, the
people themselves must exercise the minimal political morality
of conceding that, whatever their disagreements with one another, they are bound together by common national interests.

Contemporary American politics is really the politics of guilt
—extravagantly wallowing in it or cynically denying that it need
exist at all. As the American nation faces its present problems
of environmental spoilage, racism, and an industrial ethos that
has become so self-contemplating that it dehumanizes society,
liberals heap guilt upon the country for having allowed these
things to happen and conservatives deny the existence of guilt

on the premise that America is somehow inherently good and therefore blameless. If guilt is not a completely adequate response for a great nation to make to its serious problems, it is still in one way or another the permeating social and political theme of the United States. The trial of Lieutenant Calley in the spring and summer of 1971 marked a turning point in the nation's conscience as masses of people rejected guilt by angrily rejecting the conclusions that a military court had reached. The heavy climate of guilt induced by modern American politics is the source of the ultimately unreasonable demand that the people make upon the President. When they say "Bring Us Together" they are also asking that the leader, the king figure, exorcise the national sense of guilt by taking it upon himself.

The king figure is, in a complicated and deeply rooted way, the father figure. The king is at the same time the repository of the nation's guilt and its protector against guilt. As the author of his people's acts and endeavors, the king assumes responsibility for failure, defeat, and even—in the shadowed world of legend—the harsh visitations of fate upon his people. In the several versions of the Grail legend the wasteland is desolated, and its benign ruler, the Fisher King, sickens and sometimes dies; he is the symbol of the afflictions visited upon his people and the sufferer of their agonies.

The king is thus the barrier against evil as well as the repository of guilt. These roles have been ascribed to the leader throughout human history, and it is not far-fetched to assume that contemporary Americans, under the duress of their own sense of guilt and surrounding evil, are in some way not fully appreciated by themselves, asking their Presidents to absorb guilt and ward off evil as they cry "Bring Us Together," as they take an increasingly monarchistic view of their Presidents.

It is axiomatic that the President cannot absorb guilt, cannot ward off evil of the sort that haunts the American nation, because he isn't really a king. He is assaulted by ultimately unreasonable expectation, is victimized by the anger of his disappointed petitioners, and thus fails.

In the editions of the Washington *Post* of October 3, 1971, there is a highly intelligent discourse on and defense of President Nixon's style in office written by one of his aides, William Safire. It is Mr. Safire's thesis that style—"the way goals are approached—becomes part of the substance, the means part of the ends." In the late twentieth century this is a doleful truth. The elevation of style to a supreme position in the practice of the presidency implies, in a rather chilling way, that the volition that George Washington brought to that office is now threatened with serious crippling.

Washington introduced strong volition into the presidency because the imperatives of governing demanded immediate response, because he, like the greatest of his successors, did see the office as one of moral as well as social and political leadership. Presidents have always had to struggle to keep their freedom of action, the volition that Washington bequeathed them. Most of the time they have struggled against opposing forces within the system of government, forces that were put there as barriers to unlimited presidential power, just as the President has come to be a barrier himself against unlimited congressional power. Thus the normal struggle of the President to act and keep his freedom of action is healthy.

As in the period 1836–1860 contemporary Presidents are struggling against something that lies beyond the planned obstructions of a great democratic system; then and now they struggle against the people themselves, against the public rivalries, jealousies, and bitchiness that make it impossible to govern well. A modern President is so harassed by the contradictory pressures upon himself that he must resort to style to get things done. He must subordinate or disguise his roles as head of state and head of government and engage in the crawly piffle of electoral politics in order to accomplish anything. The public divisions and the public rivalries poison that graceful, if implicit, agreement between the governed and their governors—the former's agreement to concede the moral authority of the latter and the latter's agreement to recognize the capacity of the former to embrace high purpose when it is presented to them. Neither side of this agreement works perfectly at the best of times; it is rather

an assumptive atmosphere within which the process of democratic government takes place. This is what has broken down,
and with it the President's full capacity to govern. That capacity
has been corrupted by the lack of a public sense of commonality
and by the unreasonable expectations visited upon the President,
including the ultimately unreasonable one that he take guilt un-
to himself. Unable to meet the demands, unable to find a majority to whom to appeal, the President loses his choice of action.
He is forced instead, to choose among public blocs and to move
in terms of which bloc he can least afford to offend.

To some degree this has always been true of the relationship
between the President and the public. But premonarchical Presidents could always find one force in the nation to counteract
another they were prepared to offend, as Jackson fell back on his
huge popular support in his struggle against Nicholas Biddle and
the Eastern financial establishment. Alternately the times and
the public's vision of government as a mechanism of several equal
parts were such that a President could take action that offended
a majority and still have sufficient time to demonstrate the wisdom of his decisions. Recognizing this was the genius that gave
Mr. Lincoln the strength to lead the nation into a civil war.

None of this means that government and the presidency as
we have known them since 1932 are doomed by our national
divisions and follies. Rather it means that the presidency is losing much of the volition that its great practitioners struggled for
so long to win. What it might mean is that we are turning back
to the nineteenth-century vision of government as a combination
of collaborative forces. That depends in large part on the capacity
of Congress to reform and reinvigorate itself so that it becomes
once again a forum for ideas and leadership. Another possibility
is that the addled passions of the late twentieth century might
abate, a new sense of consensus might overtake the Americans
again—out of sheer exhaustion, if nothing else—and Presidents
might be permitted to resume the task of administering a nation
that has once again decided to let itself be governed.

The causes of a declining confidence in the presidency, of the
divisions in the nation, and of the politics and policies that helped

to create those divisions go deep and are at least as susceptible to the analysis of a psychologist as that of a writer. But in the end the people of this country must concede something themselves, must themselves give something to politics and government even as they demand that their Presidents bring them together. The concession of moral authority and the recognition of a potential for high purpose must begin to flow again between President and public before Americans are brought back together. The image of the President as king must die. And in the death of kings reasonable life resumes.

3: Foreign Affairs

I believe that it must be the policy of the United States to support peoples who are resisting attempted subjugation by armed minorities or by outside pressures. I believe that we must assist free peoples to work out their own destinies in their own way.

Harry S. Truman, 1947

We deal with governments as they are. Our relations depend not on their internal structures or social systems, but on actions which affect us.

Richard M. Nixon, 1971

Foreign relations are the highest expression of a nation's egocentricity. They are a group activity conducted with one's own interests uppermost in mind, a polity as vain as Pascal's crack about France's dealings with Spain: "Truth is on this side of the Pyrenees, error on the other side." The ancient Chinese were not being uniquely immodest when they named their country *Chung kuo,* meaning either the "middle kingdom" or the "center of the universe." Every nation, privately or in the open vanity of great power, looks upon the rest of the world as a vast whorl of threats and opportunities with itself at the hub.

Because the conduct of foreign relations is such an egocentric pursuit, it can propel nations to the summit of greatness or it can plunge them into profound and expensive neuroses. From the protracted siege of Troy prompted by the kidnaping of Helen to John Foster Dulles' mighty frettings about the evils of neutrality, the conduct of foreign relations is a history of obsession as well as of grandeur.

By "foreign relations" one means all that a nation does abroad in its intercourse with other nations. This can include everything from dropping an atom bomb to haggling over import quotas; it is the business of making multiple alliances as political as a Bedoin sheik's marriages, giving or receiving aid of countless kinds, creating or participating in military blocs, fighting wars in smelly jungles, or issuing visas to old ladies in Beirut who want to visit their nieces in Nashville. Foreign relations also include sending camera-armed satellites into elliptical orbits around the world 150 miles up for the purpose of photographing other peoples' missile sites and parking lots, making educated guesses about the intentions of friends and enemies, or exchanging Egyptian cotton for Virginia tobacco.

In the final anaylsis, perceiving those things that threaten one in the world, identifying one's opportunities, and acting on the perception and the identification are all that foreign relations really amount to. If they are conducted well, the perception of threat and the identification of opportunity are exercised in equal proportion. Where countries get themselves into trouble is focusing too much on one of those foreign relations functions at the expense of the other.

The business of foreign relations is as old as the idea of government itself. That paragon of good government, the Chinese emperor Yao, was receiving emissaries from neighboring tribes as early as 2353 B.C. The ancient Indian laws of Manu decreed that an ambassador should be a cultivated man "versed in all —sciences, who understands hints, expressions of the face and gestures, who is honest, skillful, and of noble family." Centuries before the birth of Christ the Egyptians were making treaties that would be familiar to modern diplomatists. Rameses II drew up an agreement with the Hittites in 1280 B.C. that provided for, among other things, a defense alliance and the resettlement of political refugees. The rules and protocols of diplomacy were so well established in ancient Greece that Thebes decared war on Thessaly because some Theban ambassadors had been arrested. In the Middle Ages the Italians refined the rules of diplomacy and became its masters. In 1268 the doge and assembly of Venice ruled that ambassadors could not take their wives abroad but that they had to provide themselves with Venetian cooks. Wives talked too much, so the reasoning went, but a loyal cook was protection against the common threat of poisoning. So proficient did the Italians become in the arts of diplomacy that they were hired as ambassadors by non-Italian rulers like Czar Ivan III. One enterprising Italian diplomat named Antonio Volpe hired himself out to Venice, the Holy See, the Russians, and the Golden Horde—all at the same time.

American diplomatic history can be roughly divided into four periods. Before and during the Revolution, the United States maintained international friendships by necessity. After it gained its independence, America opted out of European politics and focused on international trade. There was no American foreign policy worth talking about for eight decades of the nineteenth century. Finally, the United States began a morality-ridden emergence as a world power, reluctantly at first, overzealously later.

Isolationism, an enduring theme in American diplomatic history, was a natural consequence of the Revolution. In seeking to separate themselves from Britain, the American colonies also sought separation from the power politics of late-eighteenth-century Europe. While Benjamin Franklin, Arthur Lee, and Silas Deane were in France buying munitions and coordinating French and American desires to make life miserable for the British, John Adams stayed at home to argue against any permanent alliance with France. He feared that such an alliance would drag the United States back into European wars and politics. In his first administration George Washington wrote to a friend that "the great rule of conduct for us in regard to foreign nations is, in extending our commercial relations, to have with them as little *political* connexion as possible. . . ." In his second administration Washington was suddenly faced with a complex European crisis that aroused American passions. France declared war on Britain and Spain and then the French Revolution resulted in the beheading of Louis XVI, a stupid but amiable king whose ministers and admirals had been instrumental in the success of the American Revolution. Despite aroused public opinion, Washington issued the celebrated neutrality proclamation of April 22, 1793, which said in part that the United States would stick firmly to a course that was "friendly and impartial toward the belligerent powers." The War of 1812, into which the country floundered largely because of James Madison's ineptitude as President, restored and confirmed the American penchant for political neutrality and isolation. Isolation became established policy with the doctrine enunciated by President Monroe in his annual message of December 2, 1823, henceforth the European powers should neither seek colonies nor spread their political systems on either the northern or southern American continents; the United States would not disturb existent colonies —there were quite a few of them in Latin America but many of those were undergoing bloody wars of liberation—nor would the United States involve itself in European wars. If John Adams was the first prominent American political isolationist, his son John Quincy converted isolationism into policy. It was largely at his urging that the Monroe Doctrine was promulgated.

In his book *The New American Commonwealth* the British journalist Louis Heren observed that:

> . . . for about eighty years, from the declaration of the Monroe Doctrine to the war with Spain, no need was seen for an active foreign policy. Some Americans believe that the very nature of foreign policy, of what it consists and how it is formed, was largely forgotten in those eight decades, and a few Europeans would agree with them.

The United States, during the eight decades, was having a tumultuous adolescence and young adulthood. Its foreign relations problems—including the annexation of Texas in 1845 and the pro-Southern sentiments of Britain under Palmerston and Russell during the Civil War—were largely extensions of domestic affairs.

Isolationist as far as Europe was concerned, the Monroe Doctrine was also the first expression of a curious quality that has dominated American thinking about the rest of the world ever since; it is a sense of moral instruction to other nations about how they should live and behave. That unsolicited righteousness has alternately baffled, enraged, and gratefully pleased this country's allies throughout our history with them. Undoubtedly America's moral severity in world affairs arises from our deep conviction that upon our part of this continent history's most humane and just system of government came into being—partly through divine intervention. America's experience with its own history has been an evangelical one. Given the American people's implicit view of themselves as a species of latter-day Israelites, singled out and especially cherished by God, it is probably natural that Americans should look upon their work in the world as God's—or at least Jefferson's.

Because the United States has been so derided for its moral righteousness—especially by Americans—American diplomatists and diplomatic historians have tended to deny that the righteousness exists at all. But it does. In the evolution of that strong moral sense, in its institutionalization within the foreign policy–national security machinery created in Washington after World War II, and in its slow fade, coincident with the slow American awakening to the imperfections of the American system, one can trace the beginnings of a new maturity in this country's vision of the world. In the rise of that new maturity, it is acutely embarrassing to remember our past pomposities, like the declaration of Secretary of State Richard Olney, in 1895: "The United States is practically sovereign upon this continent, and its fiat is law upon those subjects to which it confines its interposition."

Yet the American moral sense about foreign relations hasn't been all bad. After isolationism it is the second great theme in the diplomatic history of this century, a voice crying warnings or beseeching American compassion for the sufferings and dilemmas of other people. The moral compulsion struggled to shake America out of its isolationist sleep. And it triumphed in that struggle. In 1939 Congress passed the Neutrality Act, which was symbolic of the country's intense desire to ignore the rest of the world. Eight years later, four of those years spent in the experience of World War II, Congress voted $5.3 billion for the

Marshall Plan—a total reversal of attitude in a very brief time. The first appropriations for the Marshall Plan marked the beginnings of a moral commitment to others expressed in cash terms that by 1961 reached the astounding sum of $80 billion.

Like all systems of morality, the one that formed the basis of modern American foreign policy had its own visions of good and evil. Two world wars and the failure of the League of Nations persuaded American statesmen and diplomats that the supreme international problem was chaos. From that deduction American foreign policy makers came to believe that order—not peace —was the highest international good. The ideal international order would be, of course, that which great and small powers created by mutual agreement among themselves. A lesser but still acceptable sort of order would be that which would result from the stalemate of great power competition. After World War II the world experienced both.

The ideal concept of order, as the Americans saw things in 1945, was the United Nations charter. Created by great power consultations at Dumbarton Oaks in the autumn of 1944 and ratified by fifty nations at San Francisco in April 1945, the charter seemed to politicians and intellectuals alike the best and perhaps the last hope for voluntary world order. That was a brief but beautiful time of optimism. If so-called practical men questioned whether any instrument of words could draw the disparate nations of the world together, Robert M. Hutchins former Chancellor of the University of Chicago, reminded everybody that before 1787, it had seemed impossible to bring the quarreling American states together. "But they did come together," he wrote, "and with the exception of one period, they stayed together under the Constitution." In the United Nations charter the American moral compulsion found the expression of its highest idealism.

The second postwar system of order was one that Americans acknowledged even though they didn't like it much. That second system of order was the east-west division of Europe, accidentally brought into being at Tehran in 1943 and ratified at the bitter, controversial Yalta conference fifteen months later.

America's reluctant acceptance of that order in Europe showed that in 1945 the moral compulsion was mixed with sufficient practicality to recognize facts of international life that nobody could do anything about. Upon the two systems of order—the United Nations charter and the facts of life in Europe—the United States predicated its hopes for a tidy if not completely just postwar world.

It was misplaced optimism. A year after the founding conference of the United Nations, the Soviet Union was on an aggressive rampage in the Balkans and the eastern Mediterranean, threatening Turkey and Iran and triggering the cruel civil war in Greece. Berlin was blockaded and Czechoslovakia was taken over. A year later in Asia, the Chinese civil war climaxed in the crash of Chiang Kai-shek and the triumph of Mao's Communists. A year after that, Soviet-sponsored, North Korean troops swarmed into South Korea.

The United States didn't wait for the dismal events to explode in moral outrage. Having perceived the highest good—international order—it now perceived the maximum evil that was trying to destroy the good. The evil was first identified as the Union of Soviet Socialist Republics. Later it was generalized as communism. To combat that evil, America cranked itself up for the greatest and most expensive moral crusade in history. In 1947, as he appealed to Congress for assistance to Greece and Turkey, President Truman laid down the basis of the moral crusade. The business of American foreign policy, he said, should be the creation of "conditions in which we and other nations will be able to work out a way of life free of coercion. . . . I believe it must be the policy of the United States to support freed peoples who are resisting attempted subjugation by armed minorities or by outside pressures." That implied an immense task. But so pervasive was the American moral outrage over Stalin's cynical breaking of the agreements reached at Yalta and San Francisco that Congress went along with the President.

The course set by Mr. Truman and the 80th Congress consumed the foreign policy energies, finances, and will of the United States for the next twenty-five years. It resulted in the spread of American military power or presence to more than forty countries. It brought about a crucial reorganization of the American government departments responsible for foreign policy and national security. In time the new machinery became so immense, intricate, and overlapping in function that no one could completely master it, not even the Presidents it was supposed to serve. Above all, the high moral outrage of 1947 and definitions of good and evil were locked into the new foreign policy–national security system in Washington, thus perpetuating the American logic of 1947 through subsequent periods of history in which the conditions of the world underwent great change.

The machinery created by the 80th Congress to carry out America's moral mission in the world had its origins in the National Security Act of 1947. That historic piece of legislation was inspired by the realization that the global security that the United States now proposed to guarantee for itself and its client states depended upon more than just money and brute military power. It would require long-range policy planning, keeping track of virtually every nation and area of the world, sophisticated technology, and intimate, all-embracing snooping into the secrets of friends and enemies alike. The new mission would also require the unification of the armed forces and their participation in the shaping of the policies they would have to carry out. Finally, the new moral crusade would impose upon Presidents decisions of such magnitude, delicacy, and awesome implications that the Chief Executives would need constant expert and political assistance in identifying their courses of action, if not in making the final choices.

To all these ends, the National Security Act of 1947 laid down the basic structure of the huge, restless, and cluttered foreign policy–national security system that still exists in Washington. The act created the National Security Council, which sits at the penultimate level in that system; it gave birth to the Central Intelligence Agency and unified the armed forces in a new Department of Defense presided over by a civilian Secretary. As an ultimate consequence of the National Security Act of 1947, the State Department's traditional role as the American foreign ministry in charge of formulating as well as carrying out foreign policy changed, perhaps forever. An elaborate system of gathering and distilling information for presidential decision making and of identifying long-range threats and interests was built into the multidepartmental fusions of the new apparatus. Over the years foreign policy–national security committees proliferated in the fertile bureaucratic soil of Washington; they bear bewildering and eccentric titles, such as SIG, IG, IRG, WSAG, Undersecretaries' Committee, Forty Committee, Senior Review Group, Verification Panel, and Vietnam Special Studies Group. As technology grew more sophisticated and impressed itself upon the processes of diplomacy and security, the original machinery was supplemented by an Arms Control and Disarmament Agency. Because of bureaucratic inertia—which decrees that nothing that exists in Washington can ever be allowed to wither away—the U.S. government ended up with five separate agencies charged with gathering intelligence: the CIA, the Defense Intelligence Agency, the intelligence arm of the Atomic Energy Commission, the FBI, and the State Department's Bureau of Intelligence and Research. In addition, the Defense Department's National Security Agency, operating from a mysterious complex at Fort Meade, Maryland, employs 100,000 people in the world's most exotic code-making and -breaking operation in the world. As Europe recovered from World War II and Japan emerged as a powerful international trade and finance force, the machinery was further supplemented by the Council on International Economic Policy. Foreign policy and national security became such all-consuming occupations in Washington during and after the cold war years that four dozen separate departments and agencies of government got into the act. Thirty-five of them are represented in American embassies scattered around the world, including such obvious ones as the State and Treasury departments and less obvious ones like the Federal Aviation Administration and the Tennessee Valley Authority. In the twenty-five years following the passage of the National Security Act, the number of countries in the world grew to 145 and the United States maintained diplomatic relations with 118 of them while keeping a passionately interested eye on the rest. From the Yalta conference onward American Presidents attended eight meetings with their Communist opponents at what could loosely be described as the summit, and America joined eight regional collective treaties committing it to the physical defense of forty-two different countries.

If America's long and exhaustive history of moral commitment and the mechanism to pursue it did not result in perfect world order, it did save several countries from being submerged beneath some Soviet or other Communist hegemony. If over the decades disorders kept breaking out, a great power stability was achieved and it endured.

But the United States paid heavily for its moral compulsion. The early anticommunism that had prompted the sensible benevolence of the Marshall Plan turned into rancid hysteria in domestic politics. Feeding upon public fear and ignorance, the anti-Communist impulse became a cheap device for the House Un-American Activities Committee, Senator Joseph R. McCarthy and other institutions and men gifted in the cynical arts of self-promotion and oversimplification. They managed to convert the decency of the American moral compulsion into a stewpot of hatred and division unequaled in this country since the Civil War. Later the self-generating momentum of Washington's huge foreign policy–national security apparatus created an economic Frankenstein. And finally, because the moral definitions of 1947 were perpetuated in the institutions of government designed to give them force, the United States committed itself to the tragedy of Vietnam—even though the Communist monolith had long since disintegrated and the relevance of Southeast Asian conflicts to America's real interests in the world was remote.

The United States discovered that it had spent the better part of a generation expending its principal energies on defending itself. Until Richard Nixon became President it seemed that the country had lost its capacity for creative initiatives in pursuit of opportunities. That President, so utterly untalented in domestic affairs, was the man who began to restore the balance of American foreign relations between defensiveness and the pursuit of positive interest. Even though Mr. Nixon made significant reforms in the foreign policy–national security machinery, its flaws still showed.

America had reached the point where the machinery of government was too cumbersome to handle crises adequately. And since the foreign policy–national security apparatus was originally created to deal with a massive and permanent sense of crisis, its basic value had come at last under serious questioning.

He thought of James Joyce, of *Dubliners*, of something somebody said some smoky night or upon some intense noon—that the final paragraph of *Dubliners* is the most beautiful single passage in English literature. That was one of those assertions so outrageously arbitrary that it sticks in the mind. He was reminded of it as he swung slowly in his swivel chair and looked down from his office window upon the White House grounds, upon the west wing and part of the main building. *Yes, the newspapers were right; snow was general all over Ireland. It was falling on every part of the dark central plain.*

He turned back to his desk, amused at himself. It had been a day of quotations. That morning the March issue of *The Washingtonian* had appeared with its piece on—yes, God help them, they *had* used the term—the whiz kids of the national security adviser's staff. The article had begun with him: "Robin Harkness, senior NSC staff member for Latin America, is twenty-eight years old, has a master's degree in government from Georgetown and a Ph.D. in international affairs from Fletcher, and sends his laundry home to Cambridge, Massachusetts, every week. . . ." The page led with photographs of Robin and others on Jerry McManus' staff. He was being shown with his brown hair brushed carefully across his forehead, his round, kid face grinning cherubically, his eyes squeezed tight. Mentioning that Robin liked to illustrate his points in conversation with literary quotations in English, French, and Spanish, the piece concluded with something of Wordsworth's that he had used to express how much he liked doing what he did: "Bliss it was in that dawn to be alive, but to be young was very heaven."

He slouched a little in his chair. Across the desk his secretary was waiting. "Letter to Mr. Damon Thornton," Robin said slowly. He picked up the paper on his desk. "His title is on here, his address, International Cable and Radio Corporation, all that. Dear Mr. Thornton colon thank you for sending me your company's views of the current situation in Venezuela. We will—you can be sure that they will be read with great interest here yours sincerely and sign it McManus." He was tempted to add that the company's self-styled "white paper" on Venezuelan politics was a mishmash of right-wing politics and misinformation, but he didn't. He wouldn't. And while he was reminding himself that he wouldn't, the first call came from the Situation Room over in the White House basement. The Foreign Broadcast Information Service was filing the text of an unusual reception from Radio Iquitos in northeastern Peru. Regular programing had been interrupted at four in the afternoon. After a twelve-minute silence the radio had begun to broadcast appeals to people from the surrounding countryside to come to Iquitos for "our day of salvation—which begins now!" For the next hour the appeals had been interspersed with a recording of a nineteenth-century military march and a voice crying "Land, bread, and democracy!" The second hour had begun with an address by a nameless speaker in the Quechua Indian dialect. The Foreign Broadcast Information Service had no translator who knew that particular dialect. It was waiting for the radio to resume in Spanish.

Robin asked to be informed when the Spanish broadcast resumed. He hung up the telephone, dictated another letter and then a memorandum to his assistant.

His secretary flipped her book shut. "When do you want all that?"

"No rush," Robin said. "Get me Sig Benchley over at State and pull yesterday's copy of the CIA bulletin, please."

The girl left.

Robin was alone in his big, white-walled office. Silence sang against the high ceiling and upon the windows darkening with the fade of a winter day. He clasped his hands together, closed his eyes, and bowed his head. He counted very slowly to twenty-five. Then he opened his eyes and telephoned McManus' office across the street in the White House. The national security adviser to the President was in conference with officials from the Treasury and Commerce departments. Robin insisted on talking to him. When McManus came to the phone, Robin told him what had happened and what he thought it might mean. McManus asked to be kept informed.

Robin hung up and called his brother's former roommate, who was at the CIA. The Operations Center of the intelligence agency was already focusing on the odd broadcasts from Radio Iquitos. The deputy director for current intelligence had ordered the CIA's Peruvian desk to work through the evening. Already someone at the agency was in trouble. The CIA's station chief in Lima had reported two days before that political lieutenants of General Elias de Balaguer Chavez Sumbay had been moving between Lima and Iquitos in the northeast and that the vast interior province of Loreto was alive with rumors that Chavez himself was back in Peru after eighteen months of exile in North Korea, Moscow, and Cuba. But those reports had not been included in either the President's daily briefing or the CIA bulletin. The compilers of both daily papers hadn't considered the Chavez rumors important enough.

By 4:20 in the afternoon the storm that had been dumping snow on Washington since late morning was almost over. At 4:55 the Situation Room at the White House called Robin to say that there were mobs in the streets of Lima and that several fires had been started at the airport and in the downtown area. The State Department had been talking to Joseph Terrill, American ambassador in Lima. Terrill and the Brazilian ambassador had gone to see President Juan Delcorte Mores about measures to protect foreigners. Radio Iquitos was sounding more strident.

To be an expert in something is to acquire new instincts. The relevant departments and bureaus of the U.S. government had begun their specialized reactions to what was now conceded to be a full-blown crisis in Peru. The four crisis control centers—the White House Situation Room, the operations centers at State and the CIA, and the Pentagon's National Military Command Center —were chattering back and forth, listening to the Peruvian radio stations and reading the flow of cables coming in from Lima and other Latin American capitals. There had been a quick meeting in the office of the Joint Chiefs of Staff in the Pentagon; a list of mobile forces—American and non-American alike—available for an operation to rescue foreigners had been compiled. At the Central Intelligence Agency the Peruvian desk and the biography section had begun to compile assessments of the politics and personalities involved in the events. Using its embassies abroad and talking to the embassies of Latin American governments in Washington, the State Department had already embarked upon a campaign to prevent the Peruvian crisis from becoming an international matter. That wasn't easy. Ecuador, Bolivia, and Colombia were already postulating that the return of General Chavez to Peru would signal a Cuban-backed Chilean invasion. They were demanding a meeting of the Organization of American States. The State Department had reached the tentative conclusion that that would be the worst thing that could happen. Sigmund Benchley, the Deputy Assistant Secretary of State for Inter-American Affairs, had tried to get the Peruvian ambassador to come to the State Department. The ambassador refused. He was, he said, giving a cocktail party.

Robin spent an hour and a half on the telephone, rounding up assessments and talking to Benchley and the task force that had been assembled in the Operations Center of the State Department. At 5:45 he was called across the street to McManus' office. Pale blue drapes had been drawn across the office windows. McManus was standing behind his desk talking on the telephone to the Situation Room. Robin sat down and looked at the eighteenth-century prints hung in sets of four upon the walls.

McManus hung up the telephone. "Those damn mobs are getting bigger," he said. "They're burning American buildings. Joe Terrill just made it back to the embassy." He raised his head and looked at Robin. The lights of the office swam in blobs upon his rimless glasses. He ran his hand over his bald head. "The President's upset," he said. "He thinks this one caught us off guard. Did it?"

"The agency's been filing reports that Chavez might be coming back," Robin said.

"Did you read them?" McManus asked, tight and angry. Robin nodded.

"Then why didn't you tell me about them?"

"I didn't want to bother you until we got something more solid than rumors," Robin answered.

"And the goddamn agency didn't say anything in either this morning's briefing or the bulletin," McManus snapped. He put his hands on his hips and looked down at the desk. "Goddamn it," he muttered. "Everybody's screwed up on this thing." He picked up a copy of *The Washingtonian* and slapped it on the desk in front of Robin. "You'd better spend more time on your intelligence cables and less time giving interviews. Okay?"

"Okay," Robin said.

"Goddamn it," McManus repeated.

All this had happened since Robin looked out of his window at the White House and remembered *Dubliners*. Now, back in his office, he is finishing his fifth telephone call to the State Department's Operations Center while watching a television set that his secretary has rolled into the middle of the room. Lots of things are still wrong, but the system has at last gathered itself together and is working. An interdepartmental group is about to meet at the State Department to consider the immediate problems and to make recommendations for dealing with them. McManus, who was supposed to leave for Brussels in the morning with the Secretary of the Treasury, has canceled his trip. He has tentatively called a late evening or early morning meeting of the Washington Special Action Group of senior officials to go over options recommended by the lower-level IG group. Things are getting worse in Peru. The Iquitos garrison of the Peruvian army has joined the Chavez revolt. The mobs in Lima have completely surrounded the American embassy. It is 7:30.

Robin hangs up the telephone and puts on his overcoat. He switches off the TV set and picks up an envelope he has stuffed with the papers that have been coming in for the past few hours. He goes out into the reception room. Like his office, it is large and high-ceilinged. "Are you going home the usual way?" he asks his secretary.

"I can if you want me to," she says.

Robin takes his key ring out of his pocket and hands it to her. "Would you mind going to my place and feeding my cat? I might not get home tonight."

"Sure." She smiles. "I'll leave the keys in my mailbox." She is a Virginian named Betty Smither who is three years older than Robin and feels motherly toward him.

He doesn't know how to handle that. Suddenly embarrassed, he waves awkwardly with his right hand. "Well, thanks for feeding my cat."

"Okay," Betty says. "You'd better go. The car is waiting."

Riding through the dark winter streets of Washington, he flips on the back seat light in the limousine and reads the material that Betty pulled for him from the files. There are also two CIA position-and-biography papers. They fill in details around the rush of memory that hit Robin when the crisis began hours earlier. General Chavez is one of a new breed of Latin American revolutionaries who have realized that military careers can be avenues to political power for leftists as well as right-wingers. Chavez is fifty-two, a career officer in the Peruvian army. He did a stint at the Command and General Staff School at Fort Leavenworth in 1951. A native of northeastern Loreto province, he is half Indian and apparently has great magnetism; his appeal is directed toward Peru's large Indian population, impoverished white farmers, and unskilled urban working people.

Eighteen months ago Chavez attempted a coup against the deeply conservative military junta that has controlled the Peruvian government for years. It was an especially gruesome failure. After Chavez fled abroad, the junta launched a punitive assault on his followers in Lima, Iquitos, and the back country. Villages along the Amazon and Tigre rivers were burned; 71 military officers were publicly tried and executed. The brutality lasted for two months, despite efforts by the United States and other hemispheric governments to stop it. The State Department's Bureau of Intelligence and Research estimated that upward of 32,000 people died or were displaced in the purge. The terror had seared Peru and provided heavy propaganda for the left-wing governments of Cuba and Chile. The United States was blamed because it backed the junta and because tanks bought from the

Americans had cannonaded poor neighborhoods in Lima while American-built jets of the Peruvian air force machine-gunned villages and, according to Radio Havana, even dumped napalm on some of them. Washington had agonized in its impotence as newspapers and television spread news and pictures of the Peruvian blood bath to the world. Now Chavez was back and it was all starting over again.

The limousine swings up the curved drive to the C Street entrance of the State Department. Robin gets out and closes the door. The driver leans over and rolls down the front window. "Want me to wait, sir?"

"No," Robin says. "Thank you."

One security guard stands at the barrier beyond the glass doors. Robin gives his name and shows his White House pass.

He crosses the large, empty lobby hung with the flags of nations. He stops at the bank of elevators and pushes a button. Through the huge glass front of the hall he can see the pattern of stars in the cold night sky. That reminds him of a telescope he got for his thirteenth birthday. He still has it. Almost everything he ever got as a child is stored in two trunks and a packing case in his mother's attic in Cambridge—books, games, chemistry and electricity sets, his collection of toy cars, and even a stuffed rabbit with one ear gone. As he waits for the elevator he wonders, as he often has before, about his reluctance to surrender the artifacts of his childhood and thus release that childhood itself to receding time and dwindling memory.

The elevator shaft buzzes in warning. The doors slide open and Robin rides up to the sixth floor. He walks down a long white-walled corridor to its junction with another corridor. Above a large door there is a black sign whose white letters read "Assistant Secretary for Inter-American Affairs." A plaque beside the door says "Joseph Carpenter II—Assistant Secretary. Sigmund L. Benchley—Deputy Assistant Secretary."

Inside the suite three girls and a man from the consular section are taking telephone calls from the friends and families of Americans living in Peru. "No, m'am," one girl is saying, "there are no reports of anyone being injured or killed."

"We're doing everything we can," the man is saying quietly

into another telephone. "Now if you'd like to give me your telephone number . . ."

A receptionist takes Robin to a conference room at the end
of a narrow hall leading to the rear of the Inter-American Affairs
Bureau. The room's beige walls are dominated by a large top-
ographical map of Central and South America. Its bulges and
contours shine in the diffused overhead light.

Robin already knows many of the men in the room. They
represent various sections of the Pentagon and the State Department—a uniformed colonel named Tarbell from the office
of the Joint Chiefs of Staff; a small, intense man who is the
Defense Department's Assistant Secretary for International Security Affairs. His name is Ridley Peck. He is an abrasive presence in any meeting he attends. There are Latin American specialists from the Defense Intelligence Agency, the CIA, and the
State Department's Bureau of Intelligence and Research. Paul
Vascall, State's Country Director for Peru, is already seated at
the conference table. The CIA's director of current intelligence
takes his place at the foot of the table. He is a tall, pleasant man
named Dickinson who went to school with Robin's father. There
is a senior press spokesman from State and a black man in a
handsomely cut suit who represents the Agency for International
Development.

The time is 7:55. Robin shakes hands with Sig Benchley, the
Deputy Assistant Secretary for Inter-American Affairs. Benchley is a large, bulky man with gray hair and sad eyes. He is a
career ambassador whose avocational passions in life are painting watercolors of ducks and the new Harvard Club of Washington, which he helped to found. "Is there anybody here who
doesn't know Robin Harkness of the NSC?" Benchley asks when
they are all seated. "Ridley?"

Peck, a small man with wispy hair and watery eyes, nods.
"We've met."

"Captain Jameson?"

Robin leans across the table to shake hands with the Navy
representative, who is in a blue civilian suit.

Benchley twists his body to look at a young man with red hair who is sitting on his right. "Peter? You know Robin Harkness?"

The young man stands and leans across the table to shake hands. "Peter MacRae," he says. "I work for the Legal Advisor in this place."

Benchley picks up a piece of paper from among several set at his place at the head of the table. He looks around. "Now you all know what sort of problems we're going to have at this end—God knows, they aren't half the problems the embassy's got in Lima. But we have ours too. Joe Carpenter—who, I presume, everyone knows is Assistant Secretary and my boss—is in Miami, where he made a speech today. He's trying to get back. I don't know what sort of shape the airports are in after this snow, but we're trying to bring him into Andrews." He turns to his paper again. The heavy flesh of his face sags forward and he looks down. "We also haven't got much time. Things are going to move fast if they're going to move at all." He searches among the papers before him. "Now this—no, here it is—this came in from the Op Center here just before we started." He takes his reading glasses from the breast pocket of his gray suit, puts them on, and tilts his head back slightly. "As of seven o'clock there were somewhere between 5,000 and 6,000 people in the streets around the embassy. And I'm sorry to say that one of the Marine guards was shot as he was putting up wire screens over the windows. The embassy has been taking quite a few rocks and a couple of Molotov cocktails. No fires have started yet." Benchley looks over the top of his glasses. "Any comments?"

"Any move to put the military into the streets of Lima?" asks Colonel Tarbell from the office of the Joint Chiefs.

"Not yet," Benchley answers. "There's some mystery there. As you know, Joe Terrill, our ambassador, and the Brazilian ambassador went to see General Delcorte a few hours ago. Joe has been talking to Delcorte on and off by telephone since. The line between the embassy and the President's office is still working. But Delcorte seems reluctant to try to control the crowds."

Dickinson, the CIA's director of current intelligence, leans forward at the other end of the table. "That's possibly because there's been trouble among the members of the junta," he says.

"Those of you who have seen the paper our Peruvian desk put together this afternoon will find a description of that on"—he leafs through a document on the table before him—"page seven. The other five generals haven't been pleased with the way Delcorte is running things. They're especially upset over the fact that Chavez got as far as he did in the business eighteen months ago. I imagine that Delcorte isn't sure about the Lima garrison —whether the other generals will try to use it to get rid of him in the middle of this thing, or even whether it's loyal to the government at all. Our embassy's been trying to talk to the garrison, but no luck so far."

"The Lima garrison's all right," says a uniformed captain from the Defense Intelligence Agency. "At least it's loyal to the government. Whether it'll stick with Delcorte or the other generals—" He shrugs.

Dickinson nods. "In the rest of the country it's still a question of not knowing which military units are loyal and which will go over to Chavez and his people."

"Let's not get ahead of ourselves," Benchley says. "I think that first of all we have to lay out the overall problem. Immediately, of course, we're worried about the embassy and Americans in Lima." He turns to the representative of the Agency for International Development. "Dick, I don't know what, if anything, we can do for your people out in the country."

The black head nods.

"Our friends over at the Pentagon have given me a list of what's available for a rescue operation if we need to mount one," Benchley says. He picks up another piece of paper. "Robin, this list of available forces and carriers should go back to McManus with whatever recommendations we make."

"Okay," Robin says. "I presume that list includes armed forces other than American. McManus, at least at this point, is dead set against sending in any American troops, CINCLANT or anything else. American carriers, yes, but someone else's troops."

"All right," Benchley says. "That, then, is what we'll have to live with." He takes off his glasses and looks down the table.

"Beyond the immediate problem of the embassy and the possible need to rescue foreigners, we have to consider the longer-range possibility that Chavez is actually going to pull this thing off or that he's going to flop again and we'll have a repetition of what happened last time. What we do now on the immediate things will have some bearing on our options later on. Now the President wants some options tonight, and among them he wants a way of making it absolutely clear to Delcorte and the other generals that the United States will not tolerate another blood bath if Chavez fails. Any suggestions on what we can do now to prepare the ground for that will be gratefully received by everybody."

"What's the situation in Iquitos?" Robin asks.

Dickinson leans forward again at the other end of the table. "We've established that Chavez himself *is* in the country," he says. "He came in from Havana on a British Martin aircraft that landed on a strip near Arica in Colombia on the Peruvian border. That's about 150 miles from Iquitos. We think he came into Arica a few days ago and made it by car to Iquitos."

"He's apparently in complete charge in Iquitos," Benchley says. "That isn't our problem at the moment. Our problem is to try to do something for the embassy, plan a relief operation if its necessary—"

"We have only *one* problem," interrupts Ridley Peck of the Pentagon's International Security Office. "We've got a Communist coming to power and a mob surrounding an American embassy and there's only one possible response—that's to go in there with enough fire power to rescue our own people and to put Delcorte's backbone and guts in proper shape." Peck's face is red and indignant. He is glaring at Benchley.

"I think that's a bit premature," Benchley says.

"*Premature!*" Peck shrills. "Of all the—"

Colonel Tarbell from the Joint Chiefs' office turns his head. "Ridley," he says, "shut your trap." He turns back to Benchley. "Go ahead, Sig."

"I might remind everyone," Benchley says, "that the United States has to go on dealing with the rest of Latin America after this thing is over. As we see it here at State, that means no messy showdown meetings of the OAS—there's a Secretary General over there who is extremely anxious to reduce U.S. influence in the organization. It also means that in *no way* should the United States appear to be backing the Peruvian junta in this thing, especially if there's a possibility of another blood bath. If we did that, I can list half a dozen Latin governments whose friendship we need who would drop us like the proverbial hot potato. And the Cubans and Chileans would be delighted to step in as we were thrown out. I don't think I have to remind you of what our own domestic liberals and antiwar people would do if we moved to help Delcorte and the junta. We'd have demonstrations in the streets that would make the old anti-Vietnam things look like revival meetings." He looks down the table at the Deputy Assistant Secretary of State for Public Affairs. "Bob, the longer we can keep the press from finding out that a Marine's been shot, the better shape we're going to be in. They're doing enough yelling up on the Hill as it is."

The department's chief press officer nods.

"Are any other embassies under siege?" Robin asks.

"Yes," Benchley says. "When we last talked to Lima they said that the Brazilians and the Chileans, who are in the same neighborhood, are also surrounded."

"Then it's a rescue-foreigners deal first," Colonel Tarbell says. "I suppose if anyone goes in there tonight it has to be the Brazilians. They have an air base"—he looks up at the topographic map on the wall—"oh, I'd guess six, seven hundred miles to the east. I just hope to God they have paratroopers on that base."

"Could we get them to do it?" Robin asks. "I mean, without invoking any treaty or anything like that?"

The colonel nods. He has a narrow, ruddy face and gray eyes. "Sure," he says. "But *asking* the Brazilians is a political decision."

Robin nods as he writes on a pad. "Okay," he says. "But the Brazilians only, yes? Certainly no approach to the Chileans. Things are bad enough between them and Peru."

"Chile is moving troops already," says Dickinson of the CIA.

"Up in Tarapaca province. It's probably just precautionary."

"Then it's either getting the Brazilians to go in or getting Delcorte to use the Lima garrison to clear that mob away from the embassy," Robin says. "Is that it? How do we get Delcorte to move?"

No one speaks for a moment.

Peter MacRae, the lawyer from the Legal Consul's office in the State Department, raises his pencil. "This may take too long," he says, "but it might work. First, we'd have to get a list of the officers commanding the Lima garrison—"

"We already have it," says the captain from Defense Intelligence.

"Good," MacRae says. "Then we'd have to see if we have anybody who knows any of them."

"That's not too hard," the captain answers. "We've got a computer over across the river that can come up with the names of every one of our people who's ever served in Peru as an attaché, a trainer or you name it."

"Good," MacRae says again. "Presumably your computer has the name of every Peruvian officer who's been up here for training or whatever."

The captain nods. "We've got that too."

"Why not get both lists," MacRae says, "and see if we haven't got someone here in Washington who could call through to the Lima barracks to test the atmosphere? If it's solid for Delcorte, we can have Ambassador Terrill call him and tell him what we know."

The Defense Intelligence captain, Colonel Tarbell, Ridley Peck, and Robin leave the conference room. Robin goes back through the narrow corridor to the main part of the suite. It is 8:30. The three girls and the man from the consular section of the State Department are still on the telephones, talking quietly, reassuring, soothing. Lights blinking on the phone consoles are blobs of anxiety from the heartland, people waiting to talk to the State Department about a relative, child, or lover threatened tonight by alien violence far, far away.

Robin goes into Sig Benchley's office and closes the door. He calls McManus. "There seem to be two options already," he says. "One is to get the Brazilians to send paratroopers into Lima. Their embassy's surrounded too. I have the feeling that State doesn't like that idea much. They want to keep the crisis Peruvian. The second option is to do our own check of the Lima garrison and, if it's sticking with Delcorte, tell him so and pressure him into moving that mob away."

Across the cold, quiet city, McManus is silent for a moment in his White House office. "I'd like Delcorte to handle this himself," he says slowly. "We don't really want to drag in other people unless we have to. But I hate to think of how that Lima garrison would handle it—"

"Do you want someone here to contact the Brazilians?" Robin asks. "Colonel Tarbell says they have an air base near the Peruvian border."

"That's a long way from Lina," McManus says. "But so is everyplace else. Things are getting worse around the embassy. There are 10,000 people out there now and they're feeling ugly as hell. I suppose you know that a Marine corporal's been shot?"

"Yes," Robin says.

"He died half an hour ago," McManus answers. "I don't want that leaking out for a while."

"Sig's already passed the word," Robin says.

Again the telephone circuit stretching through the cold darkness is silent. Finally McManus says, "There isn't time. We haven't got any time. Try checking the Lima garrison and I'll talk to Rio."

"If Delcorte turns those troops loose it could be very messy," Robin says.

"Go ahead and call the garrison," McManus says slowly. "If the people who call can tell them—well, I don't know how you tell Latin soldiers to go easy with a mob." He pauses again. "Go ahead. I'll take the responsibility."

"Okay," Robin says.

"By the way," McManus says.

"Yes?"

"I'm sorry I popped off at you," McManus says. "It's a nice

piece in *The Washingtonian*. I'm going to send your mother and father a copy with a note."

"Oh," Robin answers. He can't think of anything else to say.

The form of democratic government practiced in the United States is almost totally unsuited to the conduct of modern foreign relations. In theory, American democracy presupposes great openness in the doing of the public business. It apportions the power to do that business between an elected President and an elected Congress. The conduct of foreign relations, on the other hand, requires a high degree of secrecy; the matters requiring decision are so complicated and technical that they must be left largely in the hands of unelected experts. "Almost all the defects inherent in democratic institutions are brought to light in the conduct of foreign affairs," wrote Alexis de Tocqueville after his visit to America in the second quarter of the nineteenth century. Among the defects of democracy in foreign relations listed by Count de Tocqueville was democracy's inability to "combine its measures with secrecy." The author of *Democracy in America* also concluded that our form of government lacks patience.

Almost 140 years after de Tocqueville identified the problem, a Harvard professor named Henry Kissinger wrote: "Some of the key decisions [in foreign relations] are kept to a very small circle while the bureaucracy continues working away in ignorance of the fact that decisions are being made." Kissinger, who later moved to the center of the American foreign relations apparatus where he became the focus of a great many arguments about secrecy, wrote:

> One of the reasons for keeping the decisions to small groups is that when bureaucracies become so unwieldy and when their internal morale becomes a serious problem, an unpopular decision may be fought by brutal means, such as leaks to the press or congressional committees. Thus, the only way that secrecy can be kept is to

> exclude from the making of the decision all those who
> are theoretically charged with carrying it out.

The original constitutional design for the conduct of American foreign relations appointed the President commander in chief of the armed forces and permitted him to make treaties (providing two-thirds of the Senate agreed) and to appoint ambassadors with the advice and consent of the Senate. Congress was authorized to provide the funds for the "common defense and general welfare of the United States." It was also charged with regulating commerce with foreign nations and punishing pirates. Congress had the exclusive rights to declare war, raise and support armies, and maintain the Navy.

Obviously, the American concept of foreign relations in the late eighteenth century was a narrow and limited one. It involved only the crudest sort of national defense, and it regarded relations between nations as mostly a commercial proposition. In the 160 years between the writing of the Constitution and the passage of the National Security Act of 1947, the basic American vision of itself in the world was completely reversed. The postwar passion for world order elevated political alliances to a position of supremacy and relegated trade almost to an afterthought.

To the men of 1787 the world of 1947 would have seemed an alien planet. It had shriveled in size as a result of man's capacity to move across it at mind-bending speeds. The multinational nature of political ideas and alliances linked Asia to Europe and both to the Western Hemisphere by interinvolvements that had overcome the geography separating the three great northern land masses of the world. All this rendered the Constitution's concept of foreign relations almost obsolete.

The impossibility of sticking to that constitutional formula for the conduct of foreign relations had been recognized for a long time. Presidents had used executive agreements to make deals with other nations without approval by the Senate. Joint resolutions had been passed by the Senate as substitutions for controversial treaty approvals. These and other devices were used to circumvent the limits of the Constitution in the conduct of foreign relations—not because of the sinister motives so beloved of those who hold conspiracy theories about government but because they were necessary. With the passage of the National Security Act of 1947, the Congress at last formally, if tacitly, acknowledged the impossibility of conducting foreign relations in an open and democratic manner.

The act reorganized the bodies of government in which foreign policy was formulated; it arranged them in a crude tier that, over the next quarter of a century, was improved and refined until one body—the National Security Council—emerged as the commanding and coordinating device for the narrowing, shaping, and polishing of the data and projections needed by Presidents in the final decision making of American foreign relations. In order to understand how that system works, one must examine its three opinion-offering bodies—the National Security Council itself, the State Department, and the Defense Department. Although representatives of many, if not all, of the intelligence services sit on the boards, committees, and study groups in the foreign policy–national security apparatus, they do not offer opinions. Their role, theoretically anyway, is to provide information. Thus intelligence exists as an input but not digestive factor in the elaborate decision-making process.

The National Security Council has become the highest tier in the Washington foreign relations bureaucracy. A layered structure within the more elaborately layered structure of the whole system, the NSC exists just below the President and exerts more influence upon him and upon the bodies below itself than any other piece of the machinery.

Originally created as a committee of senior Cabinet and department officers to help the President identify and sort out options for decisions (or in the case of President Eisenhower, to actually help make the decisions), the National Security Council has had an interesting evolution. In its original form it had a small staff to prepare agendas and other papers for council meetings. Over the years the importance of that staff's director grew while the role of the council itself diminished.

President Truman was wary of the National Security Council, fearing that it would turn into a sort of British-style Cabinet. Sometimes Mr. Truman boycotted council meetings. But President Eisenhower, a man dedicated to staff work as the first principle of government, summoned the National Security Council to regular Thursday morning meetings. The growth of the staff and the diminishing importance of the actual council began under President Kennedy and his brilliant adviser McGeorge Bundy. The same trend continued through the Johnson presidency and into the Nixon years. As Henry Kissinger rose to a disputed but unshakable position as national security adviser to the President and chief shaper of American foreign policy, actual council meetings became fewer and fewer—thirty-seven in 1969, twenty-one in 1970, and only thirteen in 1971. The brain of the National Security Council had outgrown the statutory body. The NSC, operated brilliantly by Kissinger, became the personification of the "very small circle" he had described in his view of the modern foreign relations decision-making technique.

The function of the NSC today is to handle short-range crises, to formulate studies for long-range policy problems and decisions, to coordinate the flow of fact, opinion, and doubt that goes into those functions, and to be in constant touch with the President, advising, listening, and supplying data as he makes decisions.

To perform these tasks, Dr. Kissinger has a staff of specialists in everything from Asian politics to the vast intricacies of disarmament. These analysts, processors of data, and thinkers are housed in and around the White House. Kissinger himself occupies an office on the ground floor, just a few doors away from the President's Oval Office. He has immediate and constant access to Mr. Nixon (one of the few senior Nixon aides to enjoy that disorderly privilege within the highly orderly Nixon White House system). In the basement the White House Situation Room (which is really a suite of rooms) is fitted out with teletype news tickers and devices for receiving duplicates of the thousands of cables that pour in and out of Washington from departments to embassies and agents abroad. In the brown-walled Situa-

tion Room there is a digital clock and a secure-and-open telephone system with direct connection to the operations centers of
the State Department and the CIA and to the National Military
Command Center in the Pentagon. The Situation Room is also
the President's contact point with the hot line (actually a dual
Soviet-American teletype system), which connects him to the
Kremlin. Around the Situation Room complex there are small
offices occupied by senior and junior NSC staff members. The
number of Kissinger's assistant specialists has grown so large
that some of them have to be housed in the handsome, baroque
old Executive Office Building.

On tiers below Kissinger and his staff there is a committee
system that draws top- and middle-rank officials from other departments and agencies into the study and decision-formulating
process. The Washington Special Action Group (WSAG) is the
top crisis committee, bringing from State, the Pentagon, and
the CIA senior executives and specialists to monitor and advise
on events that are disturbing the world's peace or its order as
defined by the United States. Permanent interdepartmental groups
—known by the gruntlike nickname "IGs"—make specialized
studies of areas of the world or particular political-military problems and forward their suggestions and conclusions to the Senior
Review Group, which like WSAG is chaired by Dr. Kissinger.
He is also chairman of the Forty Committee, composed of senior
officials from all five intelligence services, which passes on proposed covert operations. The National Security Council bureaucracy has sprouted other committees for every sort of function
and study from reviewing defense programs to pondering the
complex problems of disarmament negotiations. The committee
system has two roles as it serves the four major functions of the
NSC—to ascertain that all the specialized concerns of the government's departments and bureaus are taken into consideration
in the process of presidential decision making on foreign relations, and to process the stupifying flow of information that
gushes toward the National Security Council. Government is a
perpetually famished monster prowling time and the corridors
of Washington in search of views, details, facts, and sugges-

tions. The nightmare of this city is that some decision will be made without considering every last morsel of information and ramification. The National Security Council is the highest expression of that hunger and fear. In its first three years of operation its staff produced 138 study memoranda from data gathered, processed, and masticated by the bureaucracy. Some of the studies were so long, detailed, and annotated that nobody had time to read them.

If the NSC system has focused all the elements of decision making in one place, that organizational virtue has become an intellectual fault. The NSC staff has become a personal staff for the President, tending to shape its recommendations to his preconceptions. It is a system that lacks abrasive challenges to premises and conclusions. Because no man can know everything, the usefulness of the NSC tends to be limited by the blind spots of its directors (Kissinger's is international economics). Finally, as one of the system's Washington critics observed: "The NSC system tends to create, in its bureaucratic mind, a vision of an ordered world. It becomes glued to that vision, assuming that there are rational, programmatic solutions to everything." All these frailties were summed up in the NSC's handling of the 1971 war between India and Pakistan. Minutes of WSAG meetings in early December of that year were obtained by Washington columnist Jack Anderson. They showed Henry Kissinger relaying the President's demand for a "tilt" of American foreign policy against India; they demonstrated that WSAG, and by inference the whole NSC system, was supposed to give substance to the President's prejudices and rages rather than advise him on the most appropriate American action. It was a bad lapse in Mr. Nixon's otherwise skillful handling of American foreign relations. It was also a demonstration of the subjective role into which the NSC can be forced.

Inevitably, the National Security Council staff's new preeminence in the shaping of American foreign policy has created jealousy and morose feelings of neglect among those who previously shared that position. The principal victim of this malaise is the State Department. Yet its loss of position has not been sud-

den. Power has been flowing away from State in an erratic drain-
out since Roosevelt's second administration.

The State Department and its Secretary are two different en-
tities. The department is based on the foreign service, traditionally the most elegant branch of the civil service. The career diplomats of the foreign service are just what their name implies—
men and women who have invested their lives in the making
and carrying out of American foreign policy. Secretaries of State
are usually political appointees, as are most Undersecretaries.
The process by which foreign policy is made is less important to
them than it is to the career officers of the foreign service. Because Secretaries of State are the creatures of administrations,
they are far more attuned to the particular political styles of administrations.

Cordell Hull, who served as Secretary of State in Roosevelt's first three administrations, was a solid, reliable, undemanding man. He had been a Senator from Tennessee. President
Roosevelt appointed him to the State Department partly to placate the Senate. Mr. Roosevelt had acute memories of Woodrow
Wilson's battles with that body over the Versailles Treaty. Besides, Roosevelt wanted to be his own Secretary of State, especially after 1936, and Hull's personality suited that arrangement.
He had little vanity of position or prerogative. If State's career
officers resented the way Roosevelt dealt under and around the
Secretary, relying on his brilliant subordinates, Hull didn't seem
to mind at all. During Truman's second administration and the
Eisenhower years, policy-formulating power flowed back to State
because two strong Secretaries—Acheson and Dulles—served
Presidents who needed them and were willing to admit it (Walter
Lippmann once remarked that John Foster Dulles was Eisenhower's nanny). John F. Kennedy was the first President to
openly acknowledge his dislike of the State Department—he once
called it a bowl of jelly—so policy-formulating power flowed back
to the White House and the NSC staff, where it has stayed more
or less ever since. Secretary of State Rusk, along with Defense
Secretary McNamara and Walt W. Rostow, President Johnson's
national security adviser, formed the "very small circle" that

made decisions about Vietnam. But that didn't mean that the State Department came back into its own. It meant that Mr. Rusk had joined the opposition at the White House.

The years during and after Acheson's leadership were not kind to the State Department. McCarthy's destructive rampages shattered it and resulted in a purge of China experts that State and the country badly needed (in that, the Senator from Wisconsin performed a valuable service for the Chinese Communists). In 1961 a Senate subcommittee headed by Senator Henry Jackson of the state of Washington made a study of the foreign policy–national security apparatus and concluded, logically, that it was overstaffed. The State Department had entered World War II with eight hundred employees. By the end of the 1960s it had about 12,000—a modest number by the standards of other government departments (State is the second smallest) but still too large in view of the assignments that remain in State's hands after the rise of the National Security Council system. In recent years the State Department has begun to reduce its staff. State still conducts most of this country's daily business with other nations through our foreign embassies. Technically it still oversees the foreign aid program through the Agency for International Development, and it is in at least partial charge of disarmament negotiations through the Arms Control and Disarmament Agency—though final policy in those critical bargainings is squeezed out of exhaustive staff work by the NSC and its committees. The State Department is, theoretically, in charge of America's propaganda efforts through the U.S. Information Agency. State still formulates policy in those areas that the National Security Council staff has neither the time nor the inclination for—the Middle East being the most prominent example at this writing. Yet State was muscled out of decision making on Vietnam, the last, bloody, Wagnerian expression of that moral indignation that fired American global purpose after World War II.

State was never fully attuned to that indignation, even though its Secretaries—Acheson, Dulles, and Rusk—were. Because it is heir to a saner diplomatic tradition which holds that intercourse between nations involves more than a devotion to political and military struggle, the State Department has been in the classic role of an intellectual among activists. It sees the world as the sum of an infinite number of arrangements, interests, relationships, and conflicts. The activist mechanism created by the National Security Act of 1947 institutionalized the moral passion that saw American fortunes in terms of an unending struggle against communism. In the difference between the two viewpoints the State Department is odd man out.

Whereas State has suffered because of its inability to fully accept the post-1947 moral indignation, the Pentagon has had enormous problems because of its literal and total acceptance of that passion. Yet the Pentagon is hardly at fault. It has been toiling at an impossible assignment in the last quarter of a century—staying ahead of the other superpowers in the nuclear chess game while, after 1960, keeping U.S. conventional forces in perpetual readiness to fight brushfire wars.

In the last quarter of a century the world's war-making potential has gone through four stages. First there was a nuclear monopoly by the United States in Britain—a period of safety if not stability. Then the Soviet Union got doomsday weapons. That second period of modern war-making potential was fearfully dangerous and intellectually stimulating. As war theoreticians on both the Soviet and American sides delved deeply into analyses of the destructive power their nations possessed, they conceived of ever more esoteric means of increasing their own attack potential while counteracting the enemy's potential. The practical result was an immense growth of fantastically expensive and dangerous weapons and antiweapons systems built to attack or defend in nuclear war situations fought out on paper with the aid of computers. In the midst of that growth of technology and theory, the third period began, as France and the People's Republic of China developed the basic weapons, if not the global delivery systems, created by the United States and the Soviet Union. Since the new nuclear powers had not studied and probed to the depths of nuclear theology reached by Soviet and American war theoreticians, this third period was also perilous. It is the theory that governs the use of nuclear weapons rather than the weapons themselves that is dangerous. Because of their own supremacy, the Americans and the Soviets, by stalemating each other, created an unadmitted Pax Soviet-Americana. This was first demonstrated in the Cuban missile crisis. As President Kennedy and Premier Khrushchev played out the options open to them during those two crucial weeks in 1962, there were nuclear theorists at each man's elbow warning of the results of each move considered. The Cuban missile crisis, or some variation of it, had been played out in theory a number of times on Soviet and American computers. The 1962 crisis was a practical demonstration of the limits of maneuver in the steps leading to nuclear war. The rules, which the theoreticians had known for a long time, were impressed upon the political leaders in Moscow and Washington. They became the guidelines of the Pax Soviet-Americana.

That didn't mean that all war stopped. It meant only that nuclear war was impossible. The fourth period then began. War became simply a matter of organized violence outside the nuclear ground rules laid down by the United States and the Soviet Union. Conventional war suddenly had a new lease on life because the Americans and the Russians had agreed between themselves not to let conventional wars in the Middle East, Asia, and Africa escalate into nuclear war. Nor did the Pax Soviet-Americana mean that the immense weapons and antiweapons costs were over for the United States or the Soviet Union. The nuclear stalemate was not static. To maintain it, both sides had to go on developing murder and protection devices to stay equal with each other. The expense became so enormous that the two sides began a series of cautious explorations into ways of limiting the arms race before it destroyed both nations without a single missile being fired. Test ban treaties were signed; new possibilities in biological and chemical warfare were blocked from exploration by international agreement. The long series of strategic arms limitation talks (SALT) began in Vienna and Helsinki.

In all this the Defense Department played many crucial roles, from strategy planning to research and development of nuclear weapons and antiweapons systems. That was burden enough for

any department of government or any armed forces establishment. Yet the decades of nuclear involvement were only half
of the Defense Department's impossible assignment. The definitions of evil created under America's original moral outrage
widened to include the whole lexicon of political movements
aside from communism—Nasser's increasingly conservative pan-
Arabism was at one end of the scale of evils as seen by Washington; the muddle of warmed-over ideologies sloshing around in the
Dominican Republic in the middle and late 1960s was at the
other. If one spends enough time defining evil and piling circumstance upon that definition, one can eventually persuade oneself
that, under the right conditions, somebody like gentle, vaguely
confused Juan Bosch is a threat to Western civilization. After the
end of World War II, under the simulus of such rectitude, the
United States sent its military or paramilitary forces into a foreign country on the average of once every eighteen months. In
an address to the American Society of Newspaper Editors on
May 8, 1966, Secretary of Defense Robert McNamara said that
between 1958 and the time of his speech there had been 149
serious internal insurgencies around the world. The United States
by then had gotten itself into the counterrevolution business
full time. The amplification of its original moral outrage led
eventually to the tragedy of Vietnam. The original moral indignation took on decidedly immoral aspects, and the political and economic dilemmas thus created in Washington became more crushing and debilitating than the outraged perception of communism
that triggered the whole cycle of events and consequences in the
first place. Thus does high idealism become a crippling obsession unless periodically reconsidered and refined.

The American ideal, expressed first in the Constitution and
reasserted periodically throughout this country's history, is to
keep the military under civilian control. In simpler periods that
meant taking care that the military did not do things that were
not planned or sanctioned by civilian political leaders. In the
years since 1947 it has come to mean something entirely different; what has gotten out of control is the incredible budgeting
and spending needed by the military to carry out its two assign-

ments. The cost of those assignments has varied over the years
—but it has been a variation in something immense. After
World War II defense spending hit a low of $11.4 billon, or
about 4.5 percent of the gross national product. At the height of
the Vietnam war the military budget went a little over $81 bil-
lion and then slumped back into the upper seventies as President
Nixon began to crank down the Southeast Asian misadventure.

These immense amounts of money create two different sorts of
problems for the United States: they reduce the resources available to solve pressing domestic problems, and they are a narcotic
to American industry. In spending the military budget, the Pentagon awards defense contracts to more than 22,000 contractors
and thousands more subcontractors. More than 4 million people
in the American work force are dependent for their jobs on defense contracts. The system of allocating these contracts is so
complicated and the lure of guaranteed profits (no matter how
much the costs of research, development, and manufacture get
out of control) is so great that firms underbid for military work.
They know that once they have started on a project, cost over-
runs will be tolerated by the Defense Department because it needs
the weapons, devices, or systems being manufactured. The inefficiency and waste in defense contracting became so critical by
1970 that David Packard, then Undersecretary of Defense and
a former executive of a defense contract firm, told the Armed
Forces Management Association: "Frankly, gentlemen, in defense procurement, we have a real mess on our hands."

That mess is the new challenge to civilian control of the military. Within that mess billons are wasted; industry and labor
alike become dependent upon defense spending to maintain the
American economy's momentum, and practices that would normally result in a company going out of business through its own
inefficiency become standard. All that is obviously bad for the
United States, bad for its economy, and disgracefully wasteful of
its resources. All that also is a direct result of the moral outrage
of the United States after World War II.

Regaining civilian control of the American military appears at
this writing to be almost impossible. It is a problem compounded

by the country's legitimate needs for national defense, by the difficulty that civilians have in assessing those needs, by the residue of anticommunism, and by the immense complexity of the Defense Department itself (for one thing, it is the largest money-spending organization in history). The danger posed to the United States is not some fanciful military takeover; the threat is that the military, by simply trying to carry out its two impossible assignments, will spend us into some oblivion of involuntarily screwed-up priorities.

Cutting back on defense spending involves some basic political decisions at home, some highly risky assessments of the world's future, and some leaps of intuition that few people are even equipped to try. Domestic pressure is building for an all-volunteer army. That may be socially desirable. But it could be ruinously expensive. At present, personnel costs take up a little more than half of the defense budget. If one creates the perks and pay scales that an all-volunteer army would require, the cost could go up over 60 percent. That would probably mean a bigger defense budget. The costs of fighting the conventional wars of the postnuclear period are immense. They could be pared down only by making sweeping strategic decisions—that the United States will absolutely never fight a land war in Asia again and/or that it will reduce its ground forces in Europe by 50 percent. If, by some future caprice of events, Burma was attacked by Thailand or the Soviets suddenly began a ground invasion of France and the United States wanted to help in one or both situations without resorting to nuclear war, the budget decisions of preceding years might be bitterly regretted. To cut back on nuclear weapons, to limit production of missile or antimissile systems, would involve problems that could not be fully grasped until the process of disarmament negotiations was considerably further advanced. Yet it is in the limitation of nuclear weaponry that the best hope of trimming the military budget lies; a point comes in the arms race at which sheer overkill compensates for ever-fancier technology. Wherever cuts are made, however the defense budget is trimmed, it is now obvious that military spending must be pared down. The United States simply can't go on living with the industrial addiction and economic momentum that the cost of defense in an age of moral obsession has created.

The hope, ultimately, lies in the present dismantling of that obsession.

The time is 9:20.

Andrews Air Force Base outside of Washington has only one operable runway. The Air Force jet bringing Assistant Secretary of State Joseph Carpenter II back from Miami is stacked over northern Virginia.

Robin Harkness, Sig Benchley, and Colonel Tarbell are in the Operations Center on the seventh floor of the State Department. It is a curiously undramatic suite. It resembles the newsroom of a radio station more than the sinister nerve center of a great power as portrayed in *Doctor Strangelove*. The decor is bright yellow and two shades of blue. One wall is lined with banks of teletype machines in glass-topped boxes. There is a conference room for task forces put together for crises such as this. Glasss-walled offices line another side of the room; one is for the lieutenant colonels who work here as the Pentagon's security liaisons with the State Department (there are foreign service officers assigned to the National Military Command Center across the river). In another office an editor writes the classified, twice-daily intelligence reports for the Secretary of State and other top department officials.

A raised dais dominates the brightly lit main room of the Operations Center. The deputy director of operations in charge tonight is a wiry, gray-haired foreign service officer in shirt sleeves. He sits on the left side of the dais with two telephones and a large, multibuttoned console before him. On the right side of the dais, the associate director of operations, a brown-haired girl with her own console, is talking on the telephone in Spanish. On the main floor below the dais are desks for two operations assistants. They are empty. Everyone except the deputy and associate directors stands below a loudspeaker. A woman translator with heavy blonde hair leans against the wall, head lowered, notebook and pencil ready. The loudspeaker crackles with the sounds of vast distance, with thin mutters of other telephone conversations being conducted far, far away.

The speaker is plugged into a channel that monitors the phone lines of the National Military Command Center at the Pentagon. In the last hour the computers of the Defense Intelligence Agency have come up with the names of two American army officers presently on duty in Washington who have served in Peru and who know two of the officers in the Lima barracks of the Peruvian army. The two Americans—a major and a light colonel—have been summoned to the Pentagon. The situation has been explained to them. Now, from the National Military Command Center, a call is going through to the Lima barracks. It will be monitored in the White House, in the Operations Center of the Central Intelligence Agency, and here.

There is a series of loud clicks in the loudspeaker. A voice speaks distantly in Spanish. A louder Washington voice replies in Spanish. The distant voice answers. There is a pause. The translator raises her head. "They are going to get Colonel Carlos—I didn't get the rest of the name—"

Suddenly the voice from Lima is loud and strong. The voice in the Pentagon identifies itself. There are cries of recognition and laughter. Then the conversation begins, rapidly, fluently. "Very well," the translator says, "and—Margaret? Margaret is well too. She has begun—she has begun to take skiing instruction, can you imagine?" The conversation in Spanish suddenly turns serious.

"Absolutely," the translator says as she listens. "There is no question about it."

"You are certain, even about the soldiers?" Robin hears an American officer say in Spanish.

"Yes, Peter, I am absolutely certain," the translator says, her words lagging only a second behind the Spanish-speaking voices coming through the amplifier. "For one thing, these troops are carefully chosen for Lima duty. Each man is—screened." The Peruvian officer laughs. "Nobody is forgetting what happened eighteen months ago. We wanted to keep Chavez' bastards as far away from the capital as possible, and that is what we have done. We're ready. All we're waiting for is the call."

"Is Luis there?" another American voice asks in Spanish.

The translator bows her head again as she listens. "Yes," she says, "just a minute. Right here." There is a pause. The wall speaker hums for a few seconds.

Suddenly a voice in English cuts across the hum. "This is NMCC," it says. "The officer being summoned is General Luis Ortega Diaz, deputy commander of the 2nd Armored Division stationed in Li—"

"Hello?" says a voice beneath the Pentagon announcement. The message ceases abruptly. "Hello? Peter?"

"Richard Kincaid, Luis," says a Pentagon voice.

"Richard!" General Ortega shouts in English. "Hey, man, this is very nice!"

"Kind of a bad night down there," Colonel Kincaid answers. "How's Dorothea?"

"Oh, she is *fine!* Listen, you should see her. You know, I wrote to you that she went on a trip with Juan to Paris?"

"Yes?"

"I wrote that she was going to get fat over there?"

"Yes?"

"Listen, Richard," Ortega says. "She lost thirty-one pounds!" He laughs. "What about that?"

"Great," Colonel Kincaid says. "Listen, Anne is sending something for the grandchild—"

"Oh, fine. Listen, Richard, we are having some fun down here tonight. Is that what you called about, yes?"

"That's it," Colonel Kincaid says. "We've been in touch with our embassy this evening, Luis."

"Yes," Ortega's voice is suddenly serious. "Yet, those sons of bitches are surrounding your people. I wish Delcorte would give us the word. The Brazilians too, they're having a bad time. And the Chileans. Screw the Chileans. All we need is the word from Delcorte, Richard, and we'll have everything nice and peaceful again—all over Lima."

"They've killed one of our Marine guards," Kincaid says.

"The bastards. Listen, all we need is the word—God, what a mess we have here."

"You know what I'm calling about?" Kincaid asks.

"Oh sure," Ortega answers. "I was listening when Peter talked to Carlos. We're ready, Richard, and the troops are reliable. Carlos told you the men are hand-picked. Alongside that, we've got all other units pulled back from Lima, more than a day's drive. Listen, Richard, you know what we've got here?"

"No."

"A division. One big, tough division. All the equipment. All we need is for Delcorte to give the word. You know, it's getting very bad out there. Those people up around the embassies aren't just going to stand in the street all night. They want to do something. So we had better do something before they do something."

"What's the problem, then, Luis?"

The deep voice in Lima makes a sound of contempt. "You'd find out if you were the woman who washes the underwear that Delcorte is wearing tonight."

There is a soft ripple of laughter in the Operations Center.

"Is Delcorte afraid of the other generals?" Kincaid asks. "Is he afraid they'll use your troops to get rid of him tonight?"

General Ortega is silent for a moment. "Richard," he says finally, "believe me, that is no problem, that thing you mention, not tonight. Tonight the problem is that bastard Chavez and all his hooligans who are tearing Lima to pieces. We want to move, Richard. Without Lima, nobody has anything. Tonight the problem is to get control of Lima."

"Okay, Luis," the American says. "Thanks for the information. Give my love to Dorothea."

"Yes, okay, Richard. *Embracos* to Anne. Okay?"

"Okay. Good night, Luis."

The line clicks and the speaker starts humming.

Robin turns to Benchley. "He sounded as if he meant it—that Chavez is the only problem. I think we'd better relay that to the ambassador."

"McManus takes responsibility?" Benchley asks. His heavy face is gray with weariness.

"Yes," Robin says.

Benchley looks at him a moment longer and then crosses the room to the associate director. "Have you got a line to the embassy?" he asks.

She nods. "We're holding a commercial circuit open. The shortwave's no good. There are storms in the Pacific tonight."

"Let's have it," Benchley says. "The ambassador."

The brown-haired girl punches a button on her console and picks up a telephone. "Hello, Mike? Got the ambassador there?" She listens a moment and then hands the telephone to Benchley.

"Hello, Joe," the Deputy Assistant Secretary says, holding the phone to his right ear. His head is slightly bowed. His free hand is in his jacket pocket.

"Who's that?" says the voice of the American ambassador to Peru through the loudspeaker.

"Sig Benchley."

"How're things up there, Sig?" says the ambassador.

"We've had a couple of people talking to the Lima barracks," Benchley says, "to a general named Ortega. He says that the Lima garrison's loyal to Delcorte."

"If he says it I believe it," the ambassador says. "Luis Ortega's a hard man, but he's pretty steady and reliable too."

"More importantly," says Benchley, "how're things where you are?"

"Hard to say," the ambassador answers. "I don't know if you can hear the noise. It's pretty loud. But nothing much has happened in the last half-hour. We took some rocks and Molotov cocktails again. They set one of the garages on fire, but it's across from the main buildings. Since then there's been a lot of speeches and shouting and waving banners, but not much else."

"Any shooting?" Benchley asks.

"They've shot out all the upper windows of this building, and you know about the Marine guard."

"Yes," Benchley says. "Are you talking to Delcorte?"

"All the time," the ambassador answers. "I think he's focused mostly on what's happening up in the northeast around Iquitos rather than on the situation here in Lima. But he ought to be thinking about Lima. There are bad fires and the streets are out of control."

"Can you tell him what Ortega told us?" Benchley asks.

"I can," replies the ambassador. "But Delcorte's a little miffed with the Americans tonight. The Brazilians have been talking tough to him. They're threatening to come in with paratroopers unless their embassy's relieved. Delcorte thinks Washington put them up to it."

Benchley looks at Robin.

"McManus talked to the Brazilian foreign minister," Robin says.

"He's right," Benchley says into the telephone. "But don't tell him so. Just tell him that the President is very angry about the embassy and the Marine guard. Tell him the President of the United States wants action."

"Okay," the ambassador answers.

"What are the Lima police doing?" Benchley asks.

"They're marvelous," the ambassador says. "Two officers came through that crowd in a jeep. They could have gotten themselves killed. They're down in front of the embassy now arguing with the guy who seems to be leading this thing. My agency man says his name is Joronez. He's one of Chavez' operators."

"Tell Delcorte that the United States is just as worried as Brazil," Benchley says. "You can say that the President is personally following the situation and that we expect our embassy to be relieved immediately."

"Right," says the ambassador. "I'll get back to you later."

Benchley hands the telephone back to the brown-haired girl. "McManus has obviously been in to see the President," he says to Robin. "They've obviously decided to do the Brazilian thing. I wish McManus had let the Secretary give his opinion before he decided to do that."

Robin doesn't answer.

Benchley turns and looks down the bright blue and yellow room. Members of the task force are returning to their glass-fronted conference room. Colonel Tarbell and the duty colonel from the Pentagon are at the bank of teletype machines reading

something. An operations assistant—a heavy young man in a loose
shirt with crisp, curly hair—is talking on the telephone at one of
the desks in the middle of the room. The deputy director of
operations is also on the telephone, talking in a low, urgent voice
to the embassy in Lima. Benchley shrugs. "Well," he says to
nobody in particular, "maybe they've got Delcorte in enough of a
squeeze so that he'll move. I wish the Brazilians hadn't—" He
shrugs again.

Another operations assistant comes into the main room with a
strip of copy from the Foreign Broadcast Information Service
wire. He brings it over to Benchley and Robin. "Radio Iquitos,"
he says. "They're back broadcasting in Spanish." He hands the
copy to Robin. "Look at the fourth paragraph." They claim
the garrison at Trujillo has gone over to Chavez. That's the 24th
Infantry Division."

"Where's Trujillo?" Robin asks.

He goes with Benchley and the operations assistant to a table
in the center of the room. A *National Geographic* atlas lies open
at a detailed map of Peru. The lieutenant colonel from Pentagon
liaison comes to the table and looks over Benchley's shoulder.
The operations assistant points to a coastal city north of Lima.
"Up there," he says.

"Can we check that claim about the 24th Division?" Robin
asks.

The lieutenant colonel goes into his office and picks up a telephone. In the conference room the CIA man on the task force
makes a telephone call to his office across the river at Langley.

It is 10:45 P.M.

At the bank of teletype machines Colonel Tarbell swears softly. He straightens up, still reading the copy that is chattering out
under the glass. "Sig," he says, "come take a look." Tarbell's
face is flushed and angry.

Robin and Benchley cross to the teletype bank. A United
Press International machine is moving a bulletin slugged "WASH-
INGTON."

> . . . Senator Jeffrey Hastings of New Hampshire said
> tonight that he has learned from "highly placed sources"

that a Marine guard at the American embassy in Lima, Peru, was killed by the mob that has had the embassy under siege since late this afternoon.

Senator Hastings called upon the President to take "immediate and decisive action" to relieve the embassy.

"The murder of an American serviceman is an absolutely intolerable insult to this country," Hastings said in a telephone interview with UPI. "It is obvious that a major Communist revolution is under way in Peru," he said. "The Cubans are definitely involved."

Senator Hastings added that the present Peruvian government seems to be unable to control the situation in Lima.

"Only immediate and decisive action by this country can prevent another Communist takeover in Latin America. . . ."

Colonel Tarbell looks at Benchley. "The only person who Hastings could have gotten that from is Ridley Peck," he says. "That little son of a bitch."

"With friends like Ridley we don't need enemies like Chavez," Benchley says. "Come on, we have a lot more to do downstairs."

The interdepartmental group reassembles in the conference room on the sixth floor. Ridley Peck does not come back to the meeting. At 11:35 the Operations Center calls to say that troops from the Lima garrison are rolling through the streets of the Peruvian capital. Trucks, weapons carriers, tanks, and water cannon are under the direct command of General Ortega. At midnight the American embassy reports that the mob that has been surrounding it has been dispersed. The cable says that heavy street fighting is taking place; the Peruvian army is using live ammunition. At the same hour the Central Intelligence Agency reports to the IG conference that Radio Trujillo is saying that troops of the 24th Division are arresting their officers and declaring their support for General Chavez. The Defense Intelligence Agency says that another division in the northern part of the country is leaning toward Chavez. Shortly after midnight President Salvatore Allende Gossens of Chile puts his armed forces on full alert. Radio Lima says that Chavez is being backed by Chile and Cuba and that a Chilean invasion of Peru is imminent. Radio Iquitos, now broadcasting in Spanish only, says that Ortega's troops have killed over 5,000 people in Lima; it calls upon the United States and Brazil to "leash their dogs of the Delcorte military clique to prevent another butchery of the Peruvian people." At 12:30 the Army attaché at the American embassy in Lima reports that six Peruvian air force jets, probably F-104s, have taken off from Jorge Chavez International Airport northwest of Lima and are heading up the coast toward Trujillo.

The State Department's Assistant Secretary for International Organization Affairs calls Benchley to report that Cuba and the People's Republic of China have called a meeting of the UN Security Council for three o'clock this afternoon. The subject will be Peru. The U.S. mission to the United Nations is worried that an operative resolution will be passed calling upon the United States and Brazil to take no military action in a matter that is strictly Peruvian and strictly internal. That could cripple any operation to rescue foreigners. The U.S. mission is recommending that the Organization of American States be summoned later in the morning to go counteract whatever happens at the United Nations. Benchley goes upstairs to see the Secretary of State. He returns and tells the IG conference that the Secretary is still opposed to any internationalization of the crisis. But the group can recommend an OAS meeting to the President with a State Department dissent.

At 2:10 A.M. Robin leaves the State Department. He stands under the porte-cochère at the C Street entrance, breathing in the fresh cold air. Beyond the delicate black lacework of tree branches sheathed in ice, the Lincoln Memorial gleams in late starlight. Suddenly Robin realizes how stale and fatigued he is. His adrenalin is running too high to permit sleep, but his brain is numb after hours of listening, querying, absorbing information, and discussing. He rides back to the White House in the limousine. In the silver light Washington has lost all its color. It is a cold, empty city, its shapes and forms reduced to black and shades of gray trimmed by snow lying in precise lines along roofs, window ledges, and cornices.

He enters the White House by the basement door on West Executive Avenue and goes directly upstairs to McManus' office. The national security adviser looks fresh and impeccable in his three-piece suit despite the long hours he has been working. He takes off his glasses and polishes them with a white handkerchief, which he then tucks back into his pocket. He puts his glasses on and looks at Robin. "At least Delcorte's finally moved," he says. He sits down. "All right. Let's hear what you've got. Want some coffee?"

"It keeps me awake," Robin says. "Could I have a glass of milk and something to eat?"

McManus presses a button on his desk. A secretary's distended voice says, "Yes, sir?"

"Have the mess send up a glass of milk and some sort of sandwich for Mr. Harkness," McManus says, holding down a button. "I'll have some tea, and get whatever you want for yorself."

"Yes, sir."

Robin takes off his coat, lays it over an arm of the sofa, and seats himself before the desk. He takes three sheets of paper from an envelope. "Before I begin," he says, "I think I should tell you that State's a little rumpled because you called the Brazilian foreign minister. Benchley says that the Brazilians are acting tougher than they ordinarily would because they think they have American backing."

McManus nods. "I imagine that's true."

Robin looks at the first piece of paper lying on his lap. His intellect is struggling to achieve clarity through the burden of his fatigue. Somewhere beyond his focus a clock is ticking in the large, blue-walled office. "There are three possibilities," he says. "The first is that Chavez will win; the second is that Delcorte and the junta will win. The third possibility—and it looks most likely at this point—is for a protracted conflict. In all of them, the United States should appear to take no unilateral action of a military or political kind."

Suddenly the tide of his fatigue recedes. His mind begins to work and he changes abruptly from a tired young man to what he was trained to be—a detached analyst working within a cage of limitations imposed by national interests, threats to American political and economic positions, the internal politics of the Washington foreign relations apparatus, and the larger limits imposed by national politics. Tonight, in this crisis, the military and the intelligence community are neutral—which means that they will side with whatever the national security adviser recommends. The State Department is at odds; it will dissent, doubt, and worry. Now, verbally, Robin gives McManus the immediate options as the interdepartmental group saw them.

"If Chavez wins," he says, "the United States should suspend diplomatic relations with Peru, withdraw its military and police training programs, and suspend but not dismantle its economic aid programs until the new government's policies and nature become clear and until the influence of Cuba, Chile, or other states hostile to the United States has been discerned. The resumption of aid programs and full diplomatic relations should be used as a lever to get the new Chavez government to compensate American firms for the damage to their properties in Lima. The Chavez government—if it comes to power—should be pressured into paying an indemnity to the family of the dead Marine, or at least into conducting an inquiry into his death and punishing those responsible. At the first indication of a Chavez victory, a diplomatic delegation composed of representatives from the United States, Brazil, Colombia, Ecuador, and Chile should meet with Chavez or his responsible lieutenants to arrange for the safety and/or evacuation of all foreigners who wish to leave Peru."

"Have we a complete rundown of aid programs and trade arrangements?" McManus asks.

Robin nods. "It's being compiled at State. You'll have it later in the morning."

"Okay. Go on."

Robin drops his first page on the floor beside his chair. "The second possibility—that Delcorte and the junta will win—presents problems that are in some ways more difficult," he continues. "The immediate problem posed by a victory for the junta is a repetition of what happened in April 1974: court-martials, quick civil trials, public executions, and reprisal raids in the cities and in northeastern Loreto province."

McManus is leaning forward. His elbows are on the desk and his hands are clasped before his face. His chin rests on them. He is looking intently at Robin through the light-smeared rimless glasses. "Yes," he says.

The clock in the office ticks loudly and steadily.

Robin looks at his notes. "The United States cannot afford to be associated in any way with another blood bath. It is reshaping its whole Latin American policy, and the thrust of Latin American politics is changing. More young, university-educated intellectuals are moving to positions of power. The old rigidities of military dictatorships are relaxing. American policy now seeks to identify left-wing states such as Cuba and Chile as aberrations, not as prophecies of the political future. American policy could be seriously damaged if it were linked in any way with repressing violence in Peru."

"Therefore," he tells McManus, "if it appears that President Delcorte and the junta are going to win, the American ambassador in Lima should be instructed to tell Delcorte in the most forceful terms possible of Washington's concern over another blood bath. This expression of concern should be backed by a letter from the President, with threats to suspend all military aid and training programs and economic aid. To reinforce the warning the Peace Corps programs in Peru should be suspended but the personnel should be left in the country. If there is a blood bath, all American military and police training programs should be stopped immediately, and if it continues diplomatic relations should be suspended. The problem of a Delcorte victory is compounded by the conflicts within the junta. If Delcorte falls, the United States is in an even more difficult position. It has a great deal of information about the other members of the junta, but U.S. diplomats don't know any of them very well."

There is a knock on the door.

McManus raises his head. "Come in."

The door opens. A blonde secretary enters with a tray. She

puts it on the side of the desk. "There's one milk, one turkey sandwich, and one tea," she says. "Anything else?"

Robin looks up. "No, thank you."

"Somebody from the Situation Room's waiting," the secretary says.

McManus nods. "Send him in."

A short, solid man enters as the secretary leaves. He hands McManus several teletype tear sheets. "It's spreading," he says. "The top one is Radio Lima. They're still talking about a Chilean invasion. The other stuff is Radio Iquitos. It repeats the claim about the 24th Division at Trujillo joining Chavez." He goes around the desk, looks over McManus' shoulder, and points to the copy. "There's the paragraph about a solidarity message from the 24th Division."

"The CIA station chief in Lima says that the 5th Division, which is down in the Madre de Dios, may join too," says the watch officer.

McManus nods again as he reads. "What's going on at the embassy?"

"The State Op Center talked to them about ten minutes ago," says the watch officer. "The army's cleared the area. There's a lot of shooting going on and a good many people are being killed. But the embassy says it's out of danger—at least for the moment. A Colonel Cambray from the President's office has gotten through by car. He presented President Delcorte's apologies for the attacks on the embassy and regrets over the death of Corporal Biggs."

"That the Marine they killed?"

"Yes sir."

"All right," McManus says. "Thanks. Keep me informed. I'll be sleeping here tonight."

"Yes, sir." The watch officer leaves. For a moment the large office is silent except for the steady ticking of the clock. That sound enlarges the silence.

McManus swings his chair sideways and takes off his glasses. "It looks like a full-scale civil war," he says.

"Yes, it does," Robin says.

McManus pushes down a lever on his telephone control box. "Mary, get the chief of current intelligence over at the agency."

"Yes, sir."

McManus looks back at Robin. "You were about to go into the third possibility, civil war."

Robin drops his second sheet of paper on the floor beside his chair. "That might involve a rescue operation fast," he says. "Most Americans and other foreigners are in and around Lima. Our Peace Corps people are mostly in the back country. Unless they got themselves to Lima there wouldn't be much we could do for them. But if Lima is threatened, if the airports are bombed or closed, we'd have to—"

The buzzer on McManus' desk interrupts him. McManus leans forward and pushes down the lever. "Yes?"

"The chief of current intelligence, Mr. Shepherd, is on 2027, sir," the secretary's voice says.

"Okay," McManus answers. He picks up his telephone. Mr. Shepherd? Jerry McManus here." He takes a deep breath. "It looks as if this Peruvian thing is getting messy and complicated and we may want to go to the OAS in the morning. Yes, exactly. The President would like everything your bio people can pull together on Chavez' Cuban and Chilean connections—or his connections with any other unfriendlies. What?" He listens for a moment, looking at Robin. "Yes. Yes, that's fine. By eight this morning. Another thing, Mr. Shepherd. We'd like your people to put together anything they have on General Delcorte and the other generals in the present Peruvian arrangement." He listens and nods slightly. "Yes, deep bio. Even the dirty stuff if there is any. All right. Thanks." He hangs up.

The desk amplifier hums. "The President is on 2028," says the voice of the secretary.

McManus picks up his telephone again and punches a button. "Yes, sir?" He pauses and listens. "Yes, that's the way it looks. Chavez seems to be picking up some—" He pauses, takes a silver pencil from his desk, and toys with it. "I didn't want to wake you at this point—oh, I'm sorry to hear that." He smiles. "Well, there's a difference between my staying up all night and you doing it.

This is all I have to worry about. Yes, sir. It broke up about forty-five minute ago. Mr. Harkness of my staff is here now filling me in on what the group recommended. Yes, sure. We can skip WSAG and SRG meetings. What Mr. Harkness has is—yes, all right. Right away." He hangs up. "I have to go upstairs," he says to Robin. "Better give me all your notes."

Robin picks up the two sheets from the floor. "They aren't typed," he says.

"That's okay," McManus says. "Let me have them." He rises. "Why don't you catch some sleep? You can use the sofa in here."

At the mention of sleep Robin's fatigue crashes back upon him. His head is throbbing, his eyes burn, and he wishes he could take a shower. "Thanks," he says. "I will."

McManus leaves. Robin switches off the overhead light, leaving only the desk lamp burning. He takes off his shoes, loosens his tie, and lies down. For a few minutes he is too full of thought to sleep. Then the thoughts begin to break up and he becomes drowsy. He begins to slip. The march of images begins to cross his conscious mind. His consciousness burns low, surrendering to a detached mixture of things remembered, things seen, toys in a trunk, a dark-haired army officer standing on a burning plain in the morning, his cat, jets screaming silently across a cloudy sky, someone speaking reproachfully, the words, in piecemeal, obliterating the ticking of the clock in the shadowy office. He drifts from the office—he is walking through a marsh; his shoes and trousers are soaked and that makes him feel guilty. He is trying to say something to someone who is present but beyond his immediate vision. Something imperative needs to be said. He is standing in a bare room of an old house and again it is morning. He walks through a narrow cave with dark green velvet walls that fold together in the darkness immediately ahead. He goes deeper into the abstract chambers of his mind where God and all the men who ever lived talk to him. Exaltation hums at the junction where he meets the dreamer who dreams his dreams. The answer to the secret of the cosmos is whispered to him by an eternal wisdom that is unrememberable, and then once again he is walking across a great ballroom floor and the officer from the burning plain reaches out and clasps his shoulder. He feels himself being shaken. He turns and says something in Spanish. The general replies in English, speaking with the voice of a girl. That is too improbable, even for dreams, and so Robin awakes.

He opens his eyes, stunned with sleep. Like frightened creatures the images of his dreams scatter and flee back into the slowly closing doors of his deeper mind. He lies motionless for a moment, becoming aware that he is lying on the sofa in McManus' office, that the room is filled with sunlight, and that a red-haired girl in a print dress is shaking his shoulder. "Mr. Harkness," she says, "it's seven o'clock."

He sits up, feeling stale and unwashed. "Golly," he mumbled, rubbing his eyes, "I'm sorry."

"It's all right," she answers. "Mr. McManus said to let you sleep until seven. He's been asleep himself down in the Situation Room."

Robin swings his legs off the sofa. He puts his hands over his face, trying to force the last sleep from his mind. He looks up. "Can I have a cup of coffee, please?"

"I'll get you one," she says. She hands him some papers. "I was told that you might want to look at these when you woke up."

He takes the papers. "Thank you. Cream, no sugar in the coffee."

He puts the paper on the sofa beside him and stands up. He stuffs his shirt back into his trousers and tightens his tie. He sits down again. As he puts on his shoes he wonders why McManus let him sleep so long. His mind suddenly fills with his last realizations about the Peruvian crisis. He looks around the office. It is full of sunlight.

Robin picks up the papers from the sofa. The first one has been torn from an Associated Press teletype machine.

LIMA, March 23 (AP) . . . An attempted coup d'état by former Peruvian General Elias de Balaguer Chavez Sumbay collapsed today after a violent crackdown by the government of President Juan Delcorte Mores.

The effort to crush the Chavez revolt apparently split

the military junta, which has ruled Peru for years. Radio Lima announced this morning that President Delcorte had resigned during the night.

A new, provisional "government of national order" was proclaimed. No leaders were named.

The first sign of the Chavez revolt's failure came just before dawn when the radio station at Iquitos in northeastern Peru, the Chavez stronghold, resumed normal government programing.

Radio Iquitos had been broadcasting revolutionary messages since late Thursday.

Peruvian army units started rolling through the streets of Lima shortly after midnight, routing demonstrators who had come by the thousands in support of Chavez. Machine gun and rifle fire was heard in the capital through the night.

F-104 jets of the Peruvian air force attacked an army camp near Iquitos at four o'clock this morning, government sources said. Troops stationed there had joined the Chavez revolt. An unidentified eyewitness said that the army camp was burning and added that "many bodies are on the parade ground and on the road leading away from the main gate."

There were unconfirmed reports that Chavez himself had been killed trying to cross the border into Colombia.

Using trucks, army teams were picking up bodies in main squares and in the streets around the diplomatic quarter of this capital city. There was no official estimate of the death toll, but it appeared that hundreds had perished in the Peruvian capital.

The sunlight streams into the Oval Office, laying its paths of bright illumination across a bust of Theodore Roosevelt and a framed photograph of an old house in Seneca, New York. The President lifts his head after reading the Associated Press dispatch. "Who authorized American encouragement to those troops in Lima?" he asks, his voice barely controlled.

"I did," McManus answers.

"And who do we talk to to"—he gestures with the piece of wire copy—"to stop this damned carnage?"

"We don't know who's in charge now," McManus answers.

The President turns to the director of the Central Intelligence Agency, who is standing in the middle of the room beside McManus. "How bad is it?" the President asks.

"Bad," answers the director. "They're moving on the army camp at Trujillo. They've begun to bomb it."

"With aircraft we sold them."

The director nods.

The President turns and looks through the French doors at the snow-smothered rose garden. "Is Chavez dead?" he asks.

"Yes," the director answers.

"Did the Colombians, or whoever killed him, find out about his escape route to the air strip from us?"

"Possibly," the director says. "We don't know yet who else knew about the air strip."

"Where else are they—" The President stops and shakes his head.

"A couple of villages are burning in northeastern Loreto province," McManus says.

For a moment no one speaks in the Oval Office. The crackling of the fire is the only sound.

"Christ," the President says softly. He crumples the Associated Press dispatch. "Can't we do something?" he asks, turning to McManus.

McManus shakes his head. "I'm afraid not, sir, not until we know who's running things in Lima."

The President's face is taut and pale with fatigue. "Then what good are we?" he asks.

Of all the splendid or corrupt men who governed and ruled imperial Rome, only one emerges to us through time and the brittle memories of glory as lovable. Marcus Aurelius Antoninus, who died on the Hungarian marshes in the year 180 A.D., spent his last months trying vainly to prop up a doomed empire and organizing his feeling and experience into a book of meditations. In that sublime volume, Marcus relates men and nations within the framework of moral principle and then, as a true Stoic, offers them up to the inalterable rules of the universe. He wrote the logic of his own demise as well as that of Rome when he said: "Nothing happens to anybody which he is not fitted by nature to bear." Dying, Marcus was no longer able to bear the guilt for Rome's past, which he had taken upon himself. Dying, Rome was no longer fit to bear the burden of a world it had tried to order. In one way or another, nature knows best.

There is a mysterious revelation composed of a number of signs and portents that is presented to nations when they overburden themselves with irrelevant pursuits. This revelation is seen in myriad crude or subtle events. The nation's official logic begins to crumble; voices murmur in drawing rooms or howl in the streets the message that the state is paying so much attention to vast abstractions that it has forgotten its own children. Demagogues arise, crying scorn in oversimplified terms upon the complex problems of government.

All that was happening in the late 1960s to the United States. A vast paradox was revealed; America was in serious disorder. Grown old and changing, it was too rich and too poor; it was pursuing its enemies around the world while neglecting its decaying society at home. Disordered, it could no longer strive to build order in the world. What was needed was a conversion of that energy churned out of its righteous (and originally justified) moral outrage at Stalin's tampering with the postwar world. Now the United States needed to be outraged at the incompleteness of itself.

Intelligent nations pay attention to the revelation thus presented to them. But the processes of their wisdom aren't precise or clear; change comes in confused and contradictory ways. In the case of the United States in the late twentieth century, a man who was first catapulted into national prominence by the messy, domestic anticommunism of the late 1940s became the President who began the business of dismantling America's moral obsession with international communism. Perhaps the conventional wisdom about Richard Nixon is right—only a politician who had thoroughly established himself as a master of the rituals and in-

cantations of professional anticommunism could have decided
to start withdrawing troops in Vietnam. Perhaps only a man
who had won his first election by inferring that a liberal California Democrat named Jerry Voorhis was really a sinister Red
could have persuaded this country that Chou En-lai was more important as the Premier of the most populous nation on earth than
as a member of the Chinese Communist party.

The means by which Mr. Nixon did these things is less important than their final significance. Operating on some vision un-
articulated in public, the President began to correct the imbalance
in American foreign relations that had ultimately gotten this
country into serious difficulties. For the better part of a quarter of
a century the United States had focused on defending itself and
its client states against communism. It had neglected to pursue its
positive opportunities in the world or—worse—had persuaded itself that that opportunity was largely a business of thwarting rival
powers. Mr. Nixon saw positive opportunities in beginning dialogue with China, in advancing relations with the Soviet Union,
in repairing the dreadful damage done to America's international
economic position. This, plus the withdrawl from Vietnam and
the enunciation of a doctrine that warned former client states
that they would have to fight their own Vietnams in the future,
started the process of rectification in American foreign relations
and ended the era of moral obsession

The sum of these new departures and the healthy result of
them will be Mr. Nixon's monument to history. What he did was
not easy because the original 1947 moral obsession had created
its own logic as well as its own definitions of good and evil. The
logic held that patriotism and anticommunism were indivisible—
that the God who had especially blessed Americans meant them
to scourge his Marxist enemies in the latter day; that America,
being perfect in itself, could rightly order the world and that he
who doubted American perfection was an ally of the enemies of
order. Such reasoning had waned slowly since the fading of Mc-
Carthy, but Mr. Nixon put it to a final, decent rest as he switched
off the moral obsession about the world.

It is unjust now to say that the original moral obsession was foolish, because it was not. It was the sum of a great benevolence at its point of origin; it was the loudest cry of warning and charity to awaken America from its isolationist coma. Only later did the moral obsession lead to sorrow and foolishness. It did so because the original 1947 righteousness, like all righteousness, was inflexible. The rest of the world moved beyond it and changed. In the tumult of the late 1960s America received a message that it, not time, was out of joint. In the presidency of Mr. Nixon it began to act upon that wisdom.

Marcus would have understood. Nature had not fitted America to go on with a moral crusade that, if incomplete, had still done its best work. The time of obsession was over.

4: The House of Representatives

Your representative owes you, not his industry only, but his judgement; and he betrays instead of serving you if he sacrifices it to your opinion. . . .

Edmund Burke, speech to
the Electors of Bristol

. . . the first duty of a Congressman is to the area he represents. . . .

Clem Miller, "Letters of a Congressman"

Senators, in their chamber, get to sit at desks.

Members of the House of Representatives just have chairs.

In practical terms this reflects nothing more than the fact that you can equip the workroom of a hundred people with desks but you can't do the same for a chamber that is supposed to accommodate 435. In symbolic terms, however, the question of those who get desks and those who don't sums up the difference between Senators and Representatives as parts of the legislative whole, as the beaus and drabs of the great Washington dance, as figures on two different landscapes of political art.

The symbolism implies that a Senator comes to his deliberations burdened with books and papers and therefore great thoughts. He is thus a microcosm of the body that contains him, a precious archduke who, because he is the very symbol of his rank's splendor, is to be cherished and accommodated by those who provide a setting for his labors. By the same symbolic inference, a member of the House is of no greater individual importance than is one beige leather chair of his chamber over all the other beige chairs. The implication here is that a House member is a professional fraction, someone who personifies nothing more than 1/535 of the legislative chowder until and if he endures many seasons in Congress. Unless time hoists him to legislative eminence, we are asked to believe, he will play out his days and years in the House's deskless chamber, committee rooms, and halls, whose decor resembles the third act of *Aida,* as nothing more than a spear carrier in democracy's play within a play. The Process lifts its leg on Representatives and dares them to stick around long enough to trade their innocence for power.

At least that's what the interior decorations of the Capitol imply. And there's some truth in it, but, as always, symbolism exaggerates and oversimplifies. In its attitude and conciliatory little practices, Washington tries to pretend that there is no difference in the importance and value of Senators and Representatives. Both, technically speaking, are called Congressmen. Except for the Speaker of the House, the President pro tempore of the Senate, and the Majority Leaders and Minority Leaders of both chambers, all members of Congress receive the same pay ($42,500 a year, plus a dazzling array of perks that includes free mailing privileges, allowances for travel, telephones, and stationery, and a gym to play in).

Yet in function, symbolism, and atmosphere—and as works of political art—the two chambers and therefore the people who occupy them are profoundly different. The Senate is often called splendid, and sometimes it is. The upper chamber is a caucus of delegates to the national consensus, whereas the House is supposed to represent the people. Senators serve the longest terms of any elected American officials (six years); they share with the President—and often fight him for—the awesome power to make foreign policy. In the devices of political ascent the Senate has become the trampoline that bounces men into the White House —three of the five Presidents who governed between 1945 and 1972 first emerged to national notoriety or importance from the Senate (Richard Nixon also served there but first made national headlines while serving in the House).

There is no single adjective that completely describes the House. There are several ways of looking at it, all of them leading the observer to valid conclusions, but none of the conclusions are conclusive. The House is a proving ground upon which the problem of reflective representation in a late-twentieth-century industrial democracy is faced and sometimes accomplished in unexpected ways. It is a management mechanism with a unique system of producing laws (or changing or blocking them); it is an institution cursed with schizophrenia as representation and management pull it in opposite directions; it is an arena in which power goes to the survivors and from which that crochety clout vies with power elsewhere in the Process. The House is all these things but never just one of them. It is a graveyard of good intentions and also their birthplace. As a means, a continuum of style, it is a closed world with its own mores and values, which can never be fully grasped by outsiders. Like the marital beds of the great, the House is often speculated upon but known in all its truth and reality only to its occupants and God.

At its beginnings in the eighteenth century, the House of Representatives was called by George Mason "the grand depository of the democratic principles of the government." Such a description implies a gathering of souls as disparate as the United States itself. That disparity is one of the few characteristics to have endured over two centuries. In any season the House will contain four or five authentic heroes, a few geniuses, a few unreconstructed sons of bitches, clusters of left- and right-wing evangelists, a few apolitical opportunists who will believe in anything or nothing depending upon the price offered, and a large body of able, useful members whose relative anonymity obscures the fact of their exhausting labors and their desire to do good. Originally the House was supposed to be the throat and amplifier of the people's voice in government affairs. From its beginnings it was popularly elected—something not achieved for the Senate until 1913. Time, however, is the enemy of original ideals, and in the nineteenth century the House became a different machine from the one originally envisioned. Its essential parts were no longer its members but its rules and procedures. Its fuel was not so much the popular will as the power to enact legislation for which speakers, committee chairmen, and occasional rebels contended. Then and now its other uniqueness, aside from structure, was the important but uninspiring fact that the House originates all revenue bills in Congress. This in turn makes the House Ways and Means Committee the most powerful one in Congress and its chairman—if he is as skilled and determined as Wilbur Mills —the most powerful single member of Congress. If it is the right of the Executive to tax, it is the chairman's right to say how much, providing he can get his colleagues to go along with him.

"Congress in session is Congress on public exhibition," wrote Woodrow Wilson in 1885, "whilst Congress in its committee rooms is Congress at work." This is still the bitter, necessary, complicating truth, the reason that the pure ideal of popular representation has been sacrificed to the torrent of complex technical demands gushing upon the House. To ask the membership as a whole to debate, hear testimony, and rewrite on every measure that comes before the Congress would be equivalent to asking any group of 435 fallible human beings to bring their collective wisdom to bear on matters as diverse as feeding starving Asians, revising Public Law 480, reassessing the submitted military budget in all its bewilderment and trickery, and judging upon the feasibility of a program to explore the industrial uses of seagull droppings. You can't do it. You need to break the 435 into groups of specialists who hopefully become experts; you need to create more time by parceling out the demands to sectors of the legislature that will work simultaneously on them. You need, in short, a committee system, and the committee system needs a subcommittee system, and the committees and subcommittees need chairmen. The whole thing becomes enormously unwieldly and absolutely necessary.

The chairmen begin at the bottom of their party's hierarchy on a particular committee and inch their way upward. It is a rather macabre business. You move when somebody ahead of you in the Republican or Democratic pecking order of, say, the Agriculture Committee dies, is defeated, or retires. If enough people are dispensed with before nature or the electorate nail you, then you get to be chairman, which means that everybody beneath you—that is, everybody in your party on the committee —develops a vulturelike interest in your demise.

But before you expire in one way or another, you have a hell of a time as chairman. Your views become the subject of absorbed scrutiny by anyone in any way connected with the work of the Agriculture Committee. Because you have spent so much time on the committee working your way up, because you have dealt in exhaustive detail with so many agri-issues for so many years, heard so many hours, days, and months of testimony, rewritten so many bills, and consulted with so many experts, it is assumed that you are an expert yourself. You suddenly wield enormous power of the classic Process sort—everybody believes that you can help or hurt, which means that you can. As chairman, your personality is studied for its pliabilities, crank points, and vulnerabilities. You become the autocrat of a large committee staff, the guiding baron of the other committee members. You become the darling of lobbyists, the archbishop of agribusiness, the overseer of the Secretary and Department of Agriculture (you and your opposite number in the Senate have a great deal more to do with shaping agricultural policy than the President, who is busy with saving the world and solving weightier social problems). In the grand anatomy of the American legislative body, you are a key link in the lower colon through which everything that emerges must first pass.

The possibilities for corruption of the common sort used to be enormous. Nowadays Congress has developed a fussiness about even minor perks like free airplane rides and call girls snuck into motels in Nashville during inspection tours. You may still decide that, after a particular session ends, the future of American farming absolutely requires that you go to Paris, Nice, and Copenhagen to compare their grocery prices with those in Waukegan, Biloxi, and Medford. But that isn't corruption. Corruption in Congress is something that most people have no desire to do. Most members have no wish to snitch free airplane rides or visit with call girls, but some do have a passion for travel.

The deeper and subtler sort of corruption available to committee chairman is far more sinister. It lies in the fact of their supposed expertise. Because that supposition grants them psychosomatic power over almost everyone else, a committee chairman, if he is really corrupt, can manage to inflict his own opinions on public law to a frightening degree. If his views are reasonable and really do arise from a deep knowledge of his subject, the law is relatively safe. But if his views are nutty, stupid, or derived from sheer prejudice, everybody is in trouble. The effect of such committee chairmen's opinions is usually negative. A ruthless chairman can manipulate hearings, staff, and fellow members to eliminate things he doesn't like from bills. During the 92nd Congress Representative William H. Natcher of Kentucky, chairman of an appropriations subcommittee, made an unenviable reputation for himself in Washington, D.C., by stubbornly blocking funds for a much needed subway in the capital until certain highways were built. Nobody ever accused Representative Natcher of anything but a passion for highways, but he caused a vast amount of trouble by combining that quirk with his chairman's power to obstruct. In such a case the public good is clearly abdicated to the views of one willful man who has the means of exerting his will because of the committee system.

The potential for corruption in the committee chairmanships doesn't mean that all or even a majority of the House's committee and subcommittee chairmen are prejudiced, vain, or stupid. Most of them are guided by their expertise, flavored by some unusual personality traits and views that are for the most part reasonable. But it does disturb one's sleep somewhat to realize that thirteen people—the chairmen of the House Appropriations Committee's subcommittees—pretty much have the basic say on how much money the government can spend and what it can spend it for. The congressional capacity for caprice is also rather unsettling. The late Congressman Michael Kirwin of Ohio developed the whimsical notion that what Washington, D.C., really needed most was an aquarium. Senator Wayne Morse of Oregon, who was a member of the Senate District Committee, blocked the project. In retaliation Kirwin cut off all public works funds for the state of Oregon until Morse caved in.

Yet for all these defects and the openings they create for mischief and dottiness, there is no other plausible way for the House to operate. The sheer volume of work requires expertise, and the committee system is the only way to get it. In the 91st Congress 29,040 bills were introduced, and 695 of them were actually voted into law. The range of matters dealt with would buckle the intellect of a Diderot. All of which underscores the truth of Woodrow Wilson's contention that "Congress in its committee rooms is Congress at work."

Wilson was also right about Congress in session being Congress on public exhibition. The exhibition is sometimes unedifying. On any typical afternoon or early evening when Congress is in session the House resembles a Balkan auction more than a child's vision of a great deliberative body.

The House members meet in a huge, sloped chamber in the south wing of the U.S. Capitol. The chamber, lit from its upper walls and ceiling, often is shrouded in half-light. Like the French National Assembly, the U.S. House of Representatives has no windows in its chamber. The ironic humor of that condition, so appealing to the people of Paris, is lost on the earnest burghers of Washington. Around the tops of the House walls are plaques depicting great lawmakers of history—Edward I, Alphonso X, Lycurgus, Colbert, Pothier. On the floor below their contemporary heirs sit in the beige leather chairs placed in curved rows around the chamber, some listening to the debates, some reading, some gossiping with their friends or writing letters. Others wander in the aisles, waving, staring, entering, or exiting, while still other Congressmen hang over the brass rails at the back and sides of the chamber, smoking, chatting with aides, or listening to the amplified voices of the debaters.

The action is centered in front of the Speaker's dais—known as the well of the House. There the Congressman allotted five minutes for his speech stands at a lectern equipped with a microphone. Set among the seats in the main sections of the chamber are two long tables, also equipped with microphones. Above the soft din of chatter, laughter, rustling papers, and the occasional belch, debaters address each other from the well, the tables, or other points in the chamber, using ornate terms like "the gentleman from Utah" and "the gentlewoman from New York." More often than not, they conduct complimentary colloquies in support of each other's views, with each speaker pretending to be pleasantly amazed at the sagacity, perception, and wit of his ally. While the speeches issue forth or the dialogue crackles, shorthand reporters wander about taking it all down for posterity. On the top of the Speaker's dais the reigning majority member presides, or if the House has dissolved itself and is meeting as the Committee of the Whole on the State of the Union (a device to streamline the rules), a chairman appointed by the Speaker oversees the proceedings. House parliamentarians sit below the presiding personage or hover at his elbow to guide him through the labyrinth of rules, traditions, and precedents (20,000 of the last are on record, and if the House ever runs out of them it turns to the precedents of its parent, the House of Commons in London).

Above the chamber floor the press and broadcast reporters take notes in their reserved galleries, and the public watches—for the most part uncomprehendingly, since those on tours of the Capitol are whisked in and out of the galleries at intervals of a few minutes. A House debate, encountered after its start and left before its finish, might as well be conducted in Lithuanian for all the clarity it offers.

Periodically the presiding officer responds to the debate in a jargon of his own, usually with some phrase like "withoutobjectionsoordered." And sometimes he bangs his gavel at the hum and din and bawls "The House will be in order!" but the House rarely is. In the cruel truth of the play within a play, 80 percent of floor debate is pointless; it is Woodrow Wilson's Congress on public exhibition. The real business is done elsewhere.

And for most of the history of the House it has been. In 1809 the Federalist Representative Josiah Quincy of Massachusetts lamented that the House "acts and reasons and votes and performs all the operations of an animated being, and yet, judging from my own perceptions, I cannot refrain from concluding that all great political questions are settled somewhere else than on this floor."

The statistics on the conduct of House business in 1809 are sparse, but what happens on the floor of the House today in the full stare of public notice rarely influences the final outcome of the body's deliberations. The vast majority of the legislation that reaches the floor is noncontroversial. It is the dross and necessity of government and neither evokes argument nor prods many sensitive ideological glands among the members. The leadership tries to keep tight control over the relatively small amount of legislation that *is* controversial. If the chairman of the committee that processes the bill has done his work well (including the critical work of figuring how much of the measure the House will accept), if the Rules Committee has forwarded the bill to the floor with the right formula for debate, if the measure's floor manager is persuasive, if the party leaders have led well, if the Whips have done their arithmetic properly (a good Whip can usually predict the fate of most bills within half a dozen votes), and if the Speaker's timing has been right, not much of what is said or done on the floor alters the programmed outcome.

But there is a small portion of the small number of controversial bills on which floor debate and chamber politicking can alter the outcome. Such debates are aimed at influencing public opinion. On days when one of these comes to the floor, attendance usually trebles. Members are attracted by the imperatives of their own prejudices for or against the bill or amendment and by the lure of the unpredictable. Majority Leaders, Minority Leaders, and Whips prowl the floor; passionate oratory erupts from the well, and sudden jousts break out between parliamentary judo artists. Bewildering phrases like "Strike the last word" and "Move the previous question" strew the record as masters of the rules slam one another with nuance and surprise. If the controversial matter is of sufficient national symbolism or importance, the press and radio-TV galleries above the Speaker's dais are filled with reporters lured by the gusts of contention that awaken the House like gas pains bringing the invigoration of agony to a sluggish body. A sense of exhilaration churns the chamber because suddenly every member is, for a little while, equal and in direct touch with the legislative process. The despair born of the fact that most things are programmed and arranged by the lords and barons of the House behind its Byzantine scenes vanishes. Suddenly the play within a play is a real drama of winner take all, and everyone is excited except the lords and barons, who de-

test the unexpected as a Puritan hates sin and for the same reason
—it is disorderly.

None of this is meant to suggest that the House of Representatatives is completely in the power of its seniors and leaders who
lure or herd the rest of the members like cattle. Nor is it meant
to imply that the House is totally undemocratic. The House simply isn't democratic in the way it claims to be. In the final analysis each of its members does have one vote; he controls 1/435
of every outcome. Thus at the barest minimum he must be reckoned with in the calculations of the elders and leaders who decide what will and won't go through the machinery. If a member so completely identifies himself as a predictable, visceral liberal or knee-jerk conservative, he is puzzled over and reckoned
very little and it is his own damned fool fault. The mass democracy function of the House—what there is of it—is thus partly
manifest in the calculations of its overlords. They maintain their
power in the House by correctly sensing its moods, its preoccupations, and the limits of its tolerance. The leaders are not in
the business of espousing issues or promising the successful outcome of legislative debates and then losing. Nor can they exercise
completely dictatorial power and block *all* legislation that doesn't
suit their ideological fancy—which in most cases of House leadership runs from cautious to deeply conservative. The life and political death of Joseph G. "Uncle Joe" Cannon teaches the lesson
of restraint to all House leaders who have followed him.

The most accurate statement that this reactionary tyrant ever
made about himself was: "I am one of the great army of mediocrity which constitutes the majority." Cannon, who served as a dictatorial Speaker from 1903 until 1910 and as a humilitated
and chastened one for another year, was a blinkered conservative of the most stringent sort. A contemporary described him
as "probably the most unimaginative man in public life." Cannon
thought that his congressional district, centered around Danville,
Illinois, epitomized the nation, and he regarded all reformers
as dangerous demagogues. "Everything is all right out west
around Danville," he once bawled. "The country doesn't need any
legislation." He was that profound. Cannon's chief characteristic

—aside from a certain gent's room charm manifest in telling dirty stories—was his obsessive insistence on imposing his own preposterous views on everything that came before the House. He considered America a howling success and loathed anybody who tried to change anything. Eventually he became too much even for the House of Representatives, where eccentricity was a way of life. A revolt led by George Norris and other Progressives stripped Cannon of much of his power in 1910. Among other things this meant that Cannon, through the diligent application of arrogance and stupidity, deprived future Speakers of powers they might have considered handy. His chief value in history was to instruct his successors in the leadership that one can go just so far in trying to impose one's own views upon the House. Go too far and the House and the nation won't stand for it, no matter how powerful you think you are.

The lesson remains. No leader can make the House accept things that the majority finds objectionable. So if one assumes that the majority in the House does in some way reflect the national majority, then the will of the majority sometimes rules in its own peculiar way. If the backstage head counting, persuading, bargaining, and committee work are more important than floor debates, the members are still being coaxed and considered— even if it is in private. As one English observer of this complicated American process once said: "It's all just a matter of location."

Yet by the commoner definitions of democracy, the House isn't very democratic. This is not because its nineteenth- and twentieth-century leaders were necessarily evil or totalitarian men. Rather the present clogged condition of the House results from the fact that its assigned role in the Process has become a staggering management problem ever since the 51st Congress (1889–1891), when the number of bills submitted in one session went over the 19,000 mark. Even if most House bills are doomed by the mere fact of sending them to committees— crossing "a parliamentary bridge of sighs to dim dungeons of silence whence [they] will never return," as Woodrow Wilson put it—the basic problem of having to comb through such a mountain of notion, thought, and fancy to extract the gold of legislative possibility is overwhelming. Add to that burden the task of organizing 435 human beings who, because they are politicians, are cursed with ego problems and the dimension of the management problem is obvious.

Liberals and libertarians are constantly shocked—but corporation presidents, generals, and kindergarten teachers are not—by the harsh reality that good ends require the unpleasant means of restrictive machinery and rigid rules. There is plenty of room for arguing that the present House machinery and rules aren't the right ones, but there can't be much debate over the need to control and order the place.

In their pure forms, total management and democracy are natural enemies. They erode each other as ideals; any combination of them results in a reduction of both. Since management must exercise its function—which is to get business done—in a forum dominated by at least the idea of democracy, what tends to emerge from the committee system, the politicking, and the interminable reconciling of views is that which is least offensive to the greatest number of Representatives. That means in turn that the House leadership tends to compromise on the lowest common denominator of the ideas, programs, and innovations that go through the machinery.

If the U.S. House of Representatives no longer is the grand depository of the government's democratic principles, it is still the grand heart of American politics. There are, as a matter of fact, three different political systems in simultaneous operation while the House is in session. First, there is the raw simplicity of national politics, which dictates that the party that elects the most members to the House gets to run it. "The best system," said the greatest and wittiest Speaker, Thomas Brackett Reed of Maine, "is to have one party govern and the other party watch." That's about the way it still works as far as organization is concerned. The winning party gets the speakership and the committee chairmanships. In the external view, the leaders of the majority party are the victorious masters of the House. Seen internally, the party affiliations of the leaders blur before the fact that old Republicans and old Democrats have been there a long time, have together waited out the weary seasons and years until the old boys plodding ahead of them vanish, leaving vacant the baronies and the parochial satisfactions of House leadership. In this century the waiting has been long indeed. Sam Rayburn came to the House as a freshman in 1913 and finally made it as Speaker in 1940. In the 92nd Congress the average member had served eleven years; the turnover at election time is only 15 or 20 percent. A man crawls slowly in an institution so undisturbed by time and attrition. As he crawls he comforts himself with the comradeship of his fellow creepers and with a determination that slowly turns into an obsession about the House itself; it, and not the results it produces, becomes the fixation of its elderly survivors. Party differences fade before the mutuality of years and fixation. Like old polo ponies turned into pasture, veteran Republicans and Democrats will shoulder and kick at one another because the rituals and procedures of the House demand it. But party is unimportant to their real relationships. Thus, aside from its role as a means to organize the House, *party* as such is the least exciting sort of politics practiced there.

Ideology is the second political division of the House. With the exception of the left- and right-wing nuts who dwell on the periphery of the membership, most Congressmen think of themselves—at least privately—as moderately liberal or conservative in one form or another. If they aren't moderate in their liberalism or conservatism when they arrive in Congress, they become so because the first lesson learned in the House is the lesson about the limits it places on world-saving and nation-reforming. In plotting his course through the House, a member draws a complicated mental graph composed of his own political instincts, the interests, instincts, and crochets of his constituents, the turgid systems of the House itself, and the memory that history will have of what he does there. Composing the graph is a gradual and very painful process. Unless the member has an extremely safe district (the fortunate possessor of one such district says he could rape his grandmother on the main street of the biggest town at high noon and still be reelected; there aren't many like that), the drawing of the graph involves the member's own confrontation with the basic problem of representation—whether, in Burke's words, he should be guided solely by his own judgment or whether he should adopt Clem Miller's view (which was also Madison's, Mill's, Thomas Paine's, and the Abbe Sièye's) that a Representative's first duty is to mirror his constituents. In 1967 Democratic Congressman Lee H. Hamilton of Indiana became so bothered by the basic problem that he polled his district on it. Of the 7,474 people who answered his questionnaire, 69 percent thought he should "vote according to the majority wishes of the district as he interprets those wishes" and 31 percent thought he should vote according to his own judgment and conscience.

Within the House of Representatives ideology is the key driving force—indeed, it is what the House most clearly mirrors in representing the American people. Representatives are relatively free to follow the dictates of their own ideology and expertise because the average constituent has a short memory. Districts usually forget the positions that a Congressman takes until they are reminded at election time. Only special-interest groups follow House members' votes closely—full-time, committed liberals and conservatives, farmers on agricultural matters, Jews on military aid to Israel, and so on. Members of the House dispute the theory that their constituents don't pay much attention, but most of them will admit that constituent pressure is sporadic and selective.

In purely practical terms, it is almost impossible for a conscientious Representative to function in the House as a simple mirror of his constituents. He is present in Washington, close to and devoting all his time to matters upon which other men, including his constituents, form part-time opinions. Occupationally the House is not now and never has been a reflection of the nation as a whole. "Ours," said some wit somewhere, "is a government of lawyers, not men." In the nineteenth as well as the twentieth century the dominant precongressional profession of House members was the law—by a huge percentage. Business backgrounds formed and still form the second largest category.

Beyond these two occupations no other profession, following, or job has accounted for more than 6 percent of the pre-House careers of all members of any Congress since the 60th, which ended in 1909. The clear implication is that the average Representative is better equipped by training and by his place amid great issues to form judgments on those issues than most of the people who vote for him. They live far away from Washington and spend most of their time thinking about things other than politics and government. If this makes Congress a sort of closet aristocracy of politics, it can't be helped. If it leads a Congressman to opinions and judgments that differ from those of his constituents, that can't be helped either. But the fact of his proximity to government, his knowledge of it, and his expertise in some aspects of it can occasionally put the Congressman in one hell of a bind between his own judgment and that of his less tutored constituents.

Whichever way the House member finally chooses to be motivated—either by his own ideology and judgment or by the views of those who elect him—after a while his voting and debating fall into a pattern, and a knowledge of that pattern helps the House leadership to calculate the outcome of votes. A man's position along the ideological spectrum is a better guide to the way he'll vote than his party affiliation. Any tally of how the House divides on gut-churning issues such as Vietnam withdrawals, foreign aid, and civil rights will show members splitting along ideological rather than party lines. Liberal Republicans and Democrats vote together. Conservative clout in the House derives from the well-known coalition of more orthodox Republicans and Southern Democrats.

The third sort of politics practiced in the House of Representatives is the one least known to outsiders. Yet it is critical to the problem of modernizing the U.S. Congress so that it will be more reflective of and responsive to a nation that has evolved into a whole new social entity from the time it—and Congress—began. This third type of politics is the struggle to reform the House itself, to break it out of the worst aspects of its dodder-glorifying seniority system, to revive its party caucuses so that

individual members' voices will be louder and clearer, and to
slash through the Sargasso of rules and procedures. On one side
of this third political struggle are the power-encrusted committee
chairmen, the older members who are dogging them, the party
leaders—and tradition. Aligned against them are the snorty young
rebels fired by the general reform spirit coursing through the
country.

But in its essentials the House remains what it has been for
decades. The seniority system—originally introduced as one of
the liberal reforms to break Joe Cannon—remains. And committee chairmen can abort federal programs they dislike by keeping them from the floor, so that the rest of the House can't vote
on them.

In the final analysis, the House of Representatives is cursed
by a schizophrenic pull between its two incompatible functions—
representing the people in the corridors of their federal government and still remaining efficient enough to pass the legislation
that the nation needs. Under the intense stress of the opposite
pulls of management and representation, representation is losing. Whatever else it is or does, the House of Representatives
does not represent the American people in anything like the full
dimension of their being. Maybe it can't. Perhaps, even, it
shouldn't. But it doesn't.

If one can find the charity to overlook the willfulness of some
of the House's chairmen, their tendency to boil legislation down
to its lowest common denominator, and the sniggery privilege enjoyed by favored members who pass special bills for favored
constituents behind the respectable façade of committees like
Ways and Means—if one can overlook these and a swarm of other
functional absurdities and inefficiencies—the House does tolerably
well at its management function. But as the problems of the
United States grow and compound themselves, as new programs
gush forth from successive administrations, and as national finances become increasingly complex, the management function
of the House is strained to its limits. And that means that the
real work of the House—which is conducted far from its floor
or open committee hearings—becomes even more inaccessible to

the people. That in turn means that the representational function of the House diminishes.

Democracy is an eighteenth-century ideal, a nineteenth-century pursuit, and a twentieth-century problem. Kings once regarded it as evil because it threatened their sovereignty. Modern governments like Mussolini's and the one that junked the constitution of Thailand in November 1971 regard democracy as bad because it is inefficient. Perhaps the dichotomy between management and representation is irreconcilable, but an imperative for the rest of this century is the need to search for ways to restore the representational function of the House of Representatives— or perhaps to find new ways in which that function can be exercised. Government is becoming remote from the people. They are frightened and angry. More now than in the late eighteenth century, the Americans need a grand depository of the democratic principles of their government.

North Carolina is the porch of a frame house on a rainy Saturday afternoon in the early autumn of 1923. A red-haired boy sits on the porch steps just out of the rain watching rivulets of water gush from the O-mouth of a drainpipe across the uneven grass and wash mud from the path so that the white and gray stones are laid bare and clean like the bones of a rotted animal. Great oak and elm trees along the street sway in the wind that brought the thunderstorm, their leaves glistening. The tarred street is clean. The white posts of the porch have been washed clean of dust by the rain. The boy sits and watches, transfixed by more than just the free, hurtling path of the water. He is playing a game of looking-straight-ahead-and-not-seeing-anything-else. It is a game he plays walking home on dark nights or when he is going past that house on Aspen Avenue where they've got that Doberman pinscher dog that would just as leave tear you to pieces as look at you. Looking-straight-ahead-and-not-seeing-anything-else usually works because if you don't let yourself get scared of a thing it won't hurt you. But this dark afternoon it isn't working, maybe because the boy can't quite figure out what he's scared of. Behind him, in the shadowy recesses of the house, his mother and father are going at it again. He's heard it lots of times before. Sometimes it starts the minute his father gets home from the garage where he works down at Turner and Grace streets; sometimes it's late at night after the boy has gone to bed. You can't say they're both going at it because his father is a smoothy-man, that's what Aunt Elle calls him, a smoothy-man. "Always tryin' to smooth over," she says, shaking her head and making a cluck. "Always tryin' t' make everything smooth. He's a smoothy-man." It's the boy's mother who's going at it. Sometimes she's just mad; sometimes it's different and he can tell the difference in her voice, like now. He's only seven but he knows what the difference is, or almost. "It's when old John Barleycorn's got her it's the worst," Aunt Elle says. The boy knows that John Barleycorn isn't a man or the devil or anything like that. It's when the stink fills the kitchen and the little passageway leading into the front hall, the same bitter stink that's on her mouth when she comes to kiss him and blubber over him after she's been going at it. Sometimes she even wakes him up in the middle of the night, her hair all pulled loose from the bun on the back of her head, tears half dried in the cracks on either side of her eyes, hugging him, breathing the bitter stink and sobbing, "Oh God, Macey, I didn't *mean* what I said . . ." That's going to come later, he knows, and it's going to scare him for reasons he can't figure out. Right now she's going at it in the kitchen, her voice cut loose and screeching, his father's voice trying to soothe, trying to make her tone down and the boy is out on the porch watching water gush across the path and trying his hardest to play looking-straight-ahead-and-not-seeing-anything-else.

"The boy," he hears his father say softly, almost whining. "Please Marie, honey, please don't let Mace hear what you're sayin'—"

"Fuck the boy!" she screams. "Fuck him! Fuck you!"

North Carolina.

Mace Applegate, U.S. Representative for the Second District of North Carolina and Majority Whip of the House, fifty-seven years old, 248 pounds heavy, his florid bullet head tufted with wisps of red hair, concludes with a tightening in his gut that it's not going right.

The evidence has been coming in through a myriad of those little nuances and portents that are the diagnostic devices of people who make other people the materials of their work. Nobody has yet told Mace that the bill which symbolizes the new administration's whole program and promise is going to have a hard, maybe fatal time in the House. Rather his feeling is being translated into a distinct impression through events and signs telegraphed out of the House to its majority leadership: several meetings of the Southern caucus, to which Mace, as an administration man suspected of having caught the liberal virus in late years, was not invited; the wintery, distant attitude of Maynard Crockett, chairman of the Rules Committee, which this very afternoon is meeting to decide the procedures for floor debate on the bill; the jitteriness of half a dozen middle-road members who feel demands for party loyalty closing in on them; the especially harried air worn by Lou Howard, chief of congressional liaison for the White House; the faint impression of smugness hovering around Congressman George Stetson of the state of Washington, one of the more fiery members of the black caucus. Stetson, to Mace Applegate's eternal exasperation, is a new boy still hooked on the political airs that got him elected, and he loves to see orthodox liberals and conservatives brawling with one another. That and a dozen other signs, some of them highly specific, add up to the Majority Whip's conclusion that there are all sorts of trouble ahead and maybe even a bruising, humiliating defeat.

He sits now in the second row of the House chamber beside one of his two chief assistants, Congressman John Stermas of Colorado. It is a hot, hushed Monday afternoon in early June. The chamber is three-quarters empty. The members of the Tuesday-to-Thursday club aren't back from their long weekend, and the business before the House is routine and dull. The press gallery is nearly empty. In the public galleries the doorkeepers are sitting inside, their glazed, bored eyes fixed on the floor below. In the well of the House GP "Professor" Dunston of Kansas is using up five minutes with his annual speech on how farm price supports are undermining the morals of the nation, of Kansas, and of his district. This view would outrage Representative Dunston's farm constituents if they paid any attention to it, but they don't. Nobody pays much attention to Prof Dunston. "Every legislature," Mace Applegate once said, "has got to have a right-wing nut. Prof Dunston's ours. Now I like that boy. Can't see much sense in him. But I *like* him."

Liking Dunston and listening to him are two different things. This afternoon Mace isn't listening. The matter under discussion is a continuing appropriation for the Agriculture Department. It will pass despite Prof Dunston's quixotic fulminations against it. The Agriculture Department will get its money. That's no problem. That stuff never is.

"Spent most of Sunday readin' testimony," Mace says to Stermas as they stare into the well. "All that horse crap they've been hearin' over at Public Works and Education and Labor. It's a blue-eyed wonder how many folks feel threatened by this thing. Like we was gonna turn the churches into whorehouses."

"Like who?" Stermas asks.

Mace takes a dead cigar from the side pocket of his blue coat and twiddles it between his thumb and forefinger. He is stting with his arm hooked over the back of his seat, his six-foot, two-inch frame sloped down in the chair, legs spread to bear the burden of his gut. His chin is lowered into its supporting jowls. "Hell," he grunts, "you name it. They got federal employees unions comin' in hollerin' about forest rangers' jobs, local governments claimin' we're gonna violate their constitutional right to educate, an' a bunch of folks from Michigan yellin' about drugs. You name it."

"Drugs?" Stermas says. "What've drugs got to do with it?"

Mace turns his head to look at his deputy. "Thisyear bill's gonna put underprivileged kids into work-study camps 'round the country, right?"

"Right."

"An' when you say underprivileged," the Whip continues, "what're you sayin'?"

Stermas shrugs. He is a tall, russet-haired man in his middle forties. "Poor," he murmurs, "ghetto children—"

"*Niggers*," Mace says, jabbing Stermas' chest with the fingers that are holding the cigar. "That's what underprivileged means. An' when you got one of them fancy suburbs in Michigan with a closed-down Army camp right north of it an' you hear that the President's got a new program to put underprivileged kids in camps where they're gonna get schoolin' an' work on the 'viron- ment an become the future leaders of the goddamn universe, you know what that means. It means that a whole lot of teen- aged coons are gonna be runnin' all over the neighborhood smokin' dope, crappin' on your lawn, and rapin' your daughter. Jesus." He sticks the dead cigar in his mouth and turns back to contemplate the well. "Jesus," he repeats in a mumbled grunt. "We better watch out or we're gonna strangle on all the goddamn Christian charity in the goddamn country."

Stermas is silent for a moment. He sits slumped down in his chair, his elbows on the arms and his hands folded before his face. Mace is on one of his grumps. They never last long, but he's impossible to talk to when he is besieged by one of these sudden onslaughts of pessimism.

Stermas, a former Rhodes scholar who is respected in the House as an intellectual who doesn't disdain practical politics, has served for two terms as Majority Floor Whip—or deputy —to Mace Applegate. He has a deep affection for and under- standing of the beefy North Carolinian despite the fact that the two men have totally opposite natures, move in totally different spheres of Washington life, and came to politics along routes as disparate as scholarly idealism and the hard realities of the South's rural courthouse system. John Stermas has long since perceived that Mace Applegate is a complicated man, a creature of sensitive impulses and humane instincts entwined around the devices, guises, and personality traits of a coarse, cigar-chomp- ing pol. Mace is the master of the House's written and unwrit- ten rules and a postive genius at exercising its parochial bon- homie. But those who bother to study him come to realize that all this blather has nothing to do with the personal political pro- motion of Mace Applegate. He is, Stermas concluded long ago, an almost selfless man with a disguised passion for causes. The Majority Whip has fought prolonged battles for legislation dealing with federal aid to education—an anomaly since his own lack of education is as evident as a belch at a chamber music concert. When some of his fellow Southerners drop those phrases that are an invitation to join in racial denunciations or grievance over the march of civil rights, Mace cracks jokes, repeats his famous dictum that "Seg's as dead as Jeff Davis," or walks away. Mace is an astute sensor of national moods and of those issues that are likely to turn into debates about morality. In the late 1960s he announced his opposition to the war in Vietnam, sweated out a close reelection, and then became comfortable again as the country and his own constituents caught up with him.

Now, Stermas deduces, Mace is heading into another of his bouts of inarticulate but passionate caring about an issue. The Majority Whip's latest cause is House Resolution 1418, a bill to establish a Youth Resources Development Agency. Beneath the innocuous-sounding title lies the first venture of the President's New Partnership policy. The bill would let private industry fund social welfare projects. If it passes in the House and gets through the Senate, it would create a new independent agency that would supervise 220 camps for underprivileged children across the country. The camps would be year round. In them children from thirteen to eighteen would receive schooling; in addition, they would work on environmental projects like clearing and maintaining waterways, helping the National Park Service on grazing lands and in national parks, and the like. HR 1418's four parts have been through the preparatory process in the Public Works and Education and Labor committees. Now the bill is heading through the Rules Committee to the House floor. All that remains after Rules has established the sort of floor debate the bill will have is for the Speaker to schedule the debate itself.

"We gotta move faster," Mace says suddenly.

Stermas turns his head. "Why faster?"

" 'Fore folks in this place get too worked up," Mace answers.

"What does the Speaker say?"

Mace takes his cigar from his mouth and looks down at it. "Aw, he wants to let the House talk its way through the thing. You know how he is."

Stermas nods. *Scared of his own shadow, scared somebody's going to get mad at him,* he says to himself. *That's how the Speaker is.* Which leaves Mace dangling in a vacuum of unexercised power. By a consensus that is seldom voiced in the majority party, Mace Applegate is the strongest if lowest-ranking member of the triumvirate of leadership. Between him and the Speaker is the unpredictable figure of Randolph Hatfield of Ohio, the Majority Leader. Once an ebullient, confident man, Hatfield has been stunned by personal tragedy and has now turned inward. Eighteen months before, his second son died from an overdose of drugs. On some days he is moody and withdrawn; on others his mind seems present and the ghost of his old charm and command is back. It is said that he is drinking heavily. His colleagues in the House are sympathetic, but the recognition of power is a ruthless thing and for day-to-day leadership the majority now looks to Mace Applegate.

". . . The principles of moral independence, " Prof Dunston is shrilling in the well, "the principles of taking the good with the bad, of betting your *own fortunes* on the American free enterprise system, *that's* what I'm asking this House to remember! *That's* what I'm standing here—"

The Speaker cuts him off. The time for debate is over.

Clanging bells echo through the chamber, the corridors, and the office building across Independence Avenue. The burble and murmur of the chamber rise in volume. Doors swing open and members begin coming in for the voice vote. A page hurries down the aisle and stops at the row where Mace and Stermas are sitting. "Mr. Crockett's coming to the floor, Mr. Applegate."

Mace looks up. The globular face with its flushed, shining cheeks, eyes buried in strands of flesh, and large, moist mouth suddenly breaks into a smile. "Okay, Jackie. Thanks, boy."

The page nods and starts away.

"Hey there!"

The boy turns and looks back. Mace twists himself around in his seat. His face reddens. "How y' all comin' on history now?"

"Better, Mr. Applegate."

"Better be better," Mace says, pretending to be severe. "I

ain't too busy to get myself over to the McCormack School to check, y' know."

The boy grins. "Yes, *sir,* Mr. Applegate."

Mace turns back in his seat and chuckles. "Nice kid. Bob Gates brought him in."

"And he was flunking history in the page school?"

Mace grins his wide sloppy grin. "Pretty near as. Poor little feller thought the Missouri Compromise had somethin' t' do with old Harry Truman."

"And you straightened him out," Stermas says.

"Yeah," Mace chuckles. "I straightened him out. Had him on the lookout all afternoon for old Crockett." He raises his head and looks across to one of the side sections. "And speakin' of the devil . . ."

A tall, gray-haired man who is chairman of the Rules Committee is coming down an aisle among the members who are trying to decide where to sit. Mace dislikes Maynard Crockett, not for his region, which is Mississippi, or for his politics, which are as Mace says " 'long about to the right of ole George the Fourth," but because of his demeanor. As he comes down the aisle toward a section usually occupied by Congressmen from Mississippi and Alabama, Crockett exudes the chilly aura of a middle-aged virgin at a dirty movie. Mace sighs. "Might's well get it over with. Looky at him sittin' down. S'prised he didn't wipe the seat with his hanky first."

Stermas laughs. "Good luck."

Mace gets to his feet with a tired heave and yanks his suit jacket down around the equator of his girth and butt. "Can't say I feel lucky," he says, dropping his dead cigar in his pocket. "Old Granny Crockett looks like he et somethin' bad for lunch."

"Whip's meeting right after the vote?" Stermas asks.

Mace nods. "Right after. You be there." He goes down the aisle and starts across the well amid the crowd of wandering chatting members. As he crosses the well Mace Applegate is an ambulatory bulb that lights up in recognition of everyone it passes. "George." "Tom, you keep on makin' speeches like yesterday and we're gonna have to *elect* you to somethin'." To a

Congressman who has just turned eighty-two, he says, "Well now, there's young Billy Benson. Harya, Billy? That's *good*." He grasps hands, touches arms, and gives a broad wink to a young member of the opposition who is in bad odor with his own leadership. Mace pauses to put his arm around a freshman from Maine who came to him with a grievance a week before. "Don't go writin' the folks about it yet, Pete, but I think we're gonna find you that seat on Merchant Marine and Fisheries." To the surprised blurt of gratitude the Whip responds with a squeeze and a joke.

Watching from his seat, Stermas reflects that all this would be corny and offensive if done by someone with a different chemistry. What makes it plausible, what makes Mace almost universally liked in the House, is his capacity to really mean everything he says and does. He is that rare man who is so free of the coils of self that he can be genuinely interested in everyone else. Mace is the House's quickest sympathy tender, its most productive doer of favors for the troubled and the helpless. He is a fat, glad-handing politician who is as genuinely glad as he is fat. When he calls in his IOUs of affection and gratitude, those who return them by supporting or voting for things as Mace has asked them usually consider that they have made a satisfactory bargain.

The chamber is as full as it is going to get for the voice vote on the Agriculture Department's continuing appropriation by the time Mace has worked his way across the well up the aisle to where Crockett is sitting. He squeezes himself past two members who are occupying aisle seats. Cracking a joke about being too fat, he settles himself beside the chairman of Rules. Mace takes out a handkerchief and wipes his forehead. "Like gettin' through a hog pen in the mornin', Maynard."

Crockett smiles his thin, unmeant smile. "And saying good morning to every hog."

Mace chuckles and stuffs his handkerchief back into his hip pocket. "Yeah, well, every hog in thisyear pen's got a vote too."

Crockett turns his head slowly and looks at Mace. "Does the name George Orwell mean anything to you?"

"English writer, wasn't he?"

The slender, impeccable Missisippian nods. "He wrote something about some animals being more equal than other animals. It was intended as satire but it comes out the truth, a hard truth, Mace."

"Yeah," Mace says, leaning back in his seat. "That's the main reason I came over to give you the pleasure of my company—you bein' one of those 'specially equal animals." He turns to look at Crockett. "You folks written a rule for HR 1418 yet?"

"We haven't finished with the bill," Crockett replies, turning his gaze back to the well and the Speaker's dais.

"I know you don't like it worth a damn, Maynard," Mace says, "an' the Speaker, the Leader, and me all know you don't like it, and we all reckon you're gonna make a speech against it and then vote against it."

"That's right," Crockett answers, eyes fixed on the dais.

"Which is what you oughta do feelin' like you do an' comin' from where you do," Mace continues. "But what you do up there in Rules is somethin' else again." He pauses, sniffs, and squirms slightly. "I s'pose you know how much the President wants that bill?"

"I'm aware of it."

"An' you know that the whole program isn't gonna cost the taxpayers a cent. It's gonna be administered New Partnership style—private industry's gonna pay for the whole thing in return for tax credits."

Crockett turns his head and looks at Mace. "You mean private industry will pay for the program *if* Ways and Means agrees to revise the 1973 Revenue Act. There are two bills involved in this thing, you know. Your HR 1418, which is just enabling legislation, and the bill Ways and Means is holding hearings on."

Mace reddens and puts a hard clamp on his temper. One of Maynard Crockett's least attractive traits is his tendency to give lectures on truths that everyone knows; the intended effect is to make the recipient of the lecture feel like an idiot. "I was aware," Mace says. "I do believe I heard about that. I came over to talk to you 'bout HR 1418."

"Yes?" Crockett says. "What about it?"

The vote is called. Both men shout "Aye!" They pause while Prof Dunston's lone "No!" echoes in the chamber and is followed by a small murmuring sound that could be the sum of comments of derision in multiples. Members get up and begin to leave the chamber. General noise breaks out and the Speaker's gavel cracks twice.

"I came over," Mace says steadily, already anticipating more humiliation, "to ask if you couldn't see a way of sendin' that bill out with a closed rule."

Crockett turns to look at him again. "Is this the President and the Speaker asking me or is it Mace Applegate?"

"Just Mace—but with a pretty good idea of what the President wants and a damn good idea of what thisyear country needs right now, which is welfare services—and let's not you an' me get into a socio-loggical argument over *that,* Maynard—an help for the poor but no more load on th' taxpayers."

"Interesting," Crockett murmurs, turning his gaze back to the floor. "That means you don't think you have enough votes to pass your bill and you want to cut out debate and amendments so you can try to shove it through."

Mace stands. "I just thought I'd ask, Maynard."

Crockett looks up at him and smiles. "Of course, I can't say what the Rules Committee will do—that's up to the committee. But you know better than to ask me to do a thing like that, Mace. I'm going to recommend extended debate and amendments. I might even have an amendment or two myself."

"Horse shit," Applegate says quietly. "It ain't a matter of me knowin' better than anything. It's really a matter of whether you— as a member of thisyear leadership—want to get on the wagon and help with something important. I suppose I was wonderin' if you wanted to do a little leadin' for a change." He sidles himself out into the aisle, leaving Crockett staring down at the well, still wearing his December smile. Mace curses himself for having no talent at giving insults.

Humiliation burns upon him as he leaves the chamber and takes the elevator down to the floor below. He had no real hope of trying to get the Rules Committee to report out HR 1418 with the stringent limits on debate and amendments that would have made its passage easier. But somebody had to ask, and it was certain that the Speaker wouldn't—he is too awed by Crockett —nor would the Majority Leader, distracted as he is by his dark personal torments.

Mace is a great believer in asking as a first political principle. During one of his early runs for the North Carolina state legislature he campaigned hard everywhere except in his own neighborhood. He assumed that the people who had always known him would vote for him. After he lost he ran into one of his neighbors, Mrs. Lukey, who had been a friend of his Aunt Elle for thirty years, and was astonished to hear that she hadn't voted for him. "I woulda, Macey," she said, "but you didn't ask." Ever since losing that election—and he now likes to say that he lost it by the exact number of neighbors he didn't ask—Mace has preached the gospel of asking to young politicians. "If I hear about Mrs. Lukey one more time," Mace's late wife used to say, "I'm going to throw a fit."

Getting off the elevator on the ground floor, he walks around a corner toward his office. The day is still and muggy but the corridors of the House are cool. Tourists mill through them; policemen stand guard while colored waiters from the House restaurant hurry along with trays of food to be delivered to the hidden offices allocated to senior House members.

The walls of the long corridor that leads through the Capitol to its Senate side are faced with dull pink marble. The columns that stand in front of them are of gray stone. Between the columns are statues of men that earlier periods of history regarded as important. Now frozen in various stages of illustrative animation, they are forgotten—James Harlan of Iowa, Zachariah Chandler of Michigan, Blair of Missouri, Aycock of North Carolina, and a purposeful rendering of a General James Shields, whose pedestal lettering proclaims him Warrior, Jurist, and Statesman. Mace lumbers past them, ploughing his way through the slower-paced jetsam of gawkers, guards, and petitioners. He passes under the crystal chandelier and is about to turn down a smaller hall that leads to his office when a colleague stops him. It is a New Jersey Congressman named Jerry Cressap who is given to suits that fit too well, shiny ties, and a little pencil-line mustache. "Mace, I gotta see ya a minute."

The Majority Whip stops, takes Cressap's hand, and looks down at him with a sudden frown of concern. "Why sure, Jerry. What's on y' mind?"

"Mace," the New Jersey Congressman says, trying to retrieve his hand, "I got word a coupla days ago that the labor people were putting a guy into the primary against me." He squints and the pencil-line mustache ripples with his mouth's pout. "Now I'm no flaming liberal, Mace, but I've always gone pretty good for labor and I'm always here when you need me, aren't I?"

Mace gives the hand he clutches an affirmative shake. "Why, you sure 'n' hell *are,* Jerry."

"Well, why do they want to do that to me then?"

"I dunno," Mace answers. "But I'll tell y' what I'm gonna do. I'll find out why. I know some of those labor folks."

"I'd sure appreciate anything you can do, Mace."

"I'll call. Y' hear?"

"Thanks, Mace."

The Whip releases Cressap's hand and goes on down to his office. Two pretty blonde girls from North Carolina are at the reception desks; each desk has a large, blinking telephone console. Mace winks at the girls and goes into a small hallway outside his office. His assistant, a tall young man named Henry Rutherford, is waiting for him. "They're all in there, Mace," he says. "And so's Lou Howard and a guy named Plessy."

Mace nods. "Sam Plessy. Used to work over at Interior. He's congressional lee-aison for HEW. Good boy. Lookyear, Henry, get a hold of what's-his-name over at the AFL-CIO—"

"Don Mengert?"

"Naw." Mace squeezes his eyes shut and shakes his head. "Old —what's-his-name—Gus Freeman. I just run into Jerry Cressap and he's cryin' because the labor folks are puttin' someone in the primary 'gainst him next time. See if you c'n get Gus to come up for breakfast tomorra."

"Okay. Your brother-in-law called."

"Aw fer—what's wrong now?"

"They had to take your sister back to the hospital. She's been drinking again."

"Kee-rist," Mace mutters. "Okay. I'll call him tonight. He want anything?"

"No. Just wanted to tell you."

"Okay. What time is it?"

Rutherford looks at his watch. "Quarter to six. Here's the memo on the meeting." He hands over a paper and Mace goes into the big office. It is a room done in soft colors—pale green walls and rug with one window looking out over the front parking lot of the Capitol. Twenty-five men are sitting or standing around the office, some crowded onto a sofa, some in chairs, one or two of the younger Representatives sitting on the floor. John Stermas and a man named Lloyd Davidson from Minnesota are Mace's immediate deputies. Nineteen of the others are Assistant Whips, each a contact man with one regional group of Congressmen. Lou Howard, the President's chief of congressional liaison, leans against a wall, a briefcase clutched under one arm. His angular body is slightly bent forward and his near-sighted eyes peer out from behind thick steel-rimmed glasses. A younger man leans against the wall beside him.

Mace waves a greeting as general as a benediction. He shakes hands with Howard. "Harya, Lou? We winnin' or losin' today?"

"That's what I came up here to find out," Howard answers. "You know Sam Plessy? Mace Applegate."

Mace smiles and shakes hands. "Why, hell yes, I do. Me 'n' ole Sam did a coupla stunts together when he was over at Interior. Harya, Sam?"

"Fine," Plessy answers in a Boston accent. "And you, Mace?"

"Well, I'm all right. We're gonna need you right soon and right urgent, Sam."

The Whip moves his tall, bulky body behind a desk at the end of the room, sits down, and lays the paper that Rutherford gave him on the blotter before him. He smooths it out with one beefy hand and leans over to read. "All right," he says, scanning down the list of items. "Anybody got any questions 'bout the agenda?"

"I think there's a mistake here," Stermas says, looking at his own copy of the memorandum. "Under 'Conference Reports' you've got 'S 8761—Public Health Service hospitals. Passed Senate May 3. House acts first.' " Stermas raises his head. "I think the Senate's got to pass the conference report before we do."

Mace leans over the memorandum on his desk and peers at it. "I forgot to tell you 'bout that, John. We switched that. We're doin' it first. Henry!"

"Right here," Rutherford says from his position beside the hall door.

"You wanna tell the Speaker's office 'bout the change on S 8761?"

"Okay."

"Any problems, John?"

Stermas shakes his head. "No. We can get rid of it on Thursday."

The Assistant Whip for Georgia and South Carolina raises his hand. "Mace, under 'Appropriations' you've got 'District of Columbia—ready to go.' I think we may get tied up on parts of that. Some of the people in my zone want a debate."

Mace makes a mark on his memorandum. "Okay. I'll let the Speaker know. Anything else? Any complaints today?"

The assistant for Maryland and New Jersey says, "I'm getting some bitching from the New Jersey guys about the list for the interparliamentary conference in Rome. They want to know why none of them ever get to go on these trips."

Mace is sitting with his hands folded on the desk before him, his wide shoulders hunched forward. He purses his lips. "Gotta favor th' guys on Foreign Affairs first."

"Inche is on Foreign Affairs," the assistant says.

Mace nods. "Yeah, an' he's a pain in th' ass. We sent him to that conference in Paris three-four years ago an' I'd hate to tell his old granny the scrapes he got into."

Complaints and queries from several other delegations are brought up. As Mace deals with them one of the blonde secretaries brings in a can of Fresca and a sheaf of oblong blue slips. Mace rips the seal off the cold drink and shuffles through the slips. These are zone lists. There are nineteen of them, each bearing the names of all the majority party members in the regional categories of the House represented by the Assistant Whips. The slips that Mace is studying are the results of a Whip's poll on HR 1418, the bill to establish a Youth Resources Development Agency. Beside each Congressman's name there is a blank space in which the Assistant Whips have written "For," "Against," "Undecided," or "Unanswered." Mace reads quickly. With his wide knowledge of the House he can usually predict how most of the members will vote. Now, adding what he knows of most majority and minority members' proclivities, he scans the "Undecideds" and "Unanswereds" for possible switches and converts. As he reads, he takes the cold cigar butt from his jacket pocket and puts it between his teeth. He looks up. "HR 1418," he says to Howard. "How urgent are you folks downtown feelin' about that bill?"

"Well," Howard says, "you were down at the leaders' meeting on Friday. The President told you he wants a bill by the end of the month."

Mace shifts the cigar from one side of his mouth to the other by a rolling motion of his lips. He shuffles the blue slips in his hands again. "I dunno," he mumbles. "Way I figure it, we're 'bout twenty votes short right now."

"Thirty," says Davidson, the elder of the two deputies. "If you go for twenty votes you'll be trying to win by one or two. Too close."

Mace raises his head. "Listen, Lloyd, if we're gonna win this thing atall, it's gonna be by one-two votes. Lou, what's so special 'bout the end of the month?"

"The President's going on a speaking tour of the West in July," Howard answers. "He needs to talk about this. He wants to be able to say that his campaign promise to increase public services without any more burden to the taxpayers was real."

Mace drops the slips on the desk. "I dunno," he says thoughtfully. "Ole Crockett's bringin' the bill out on a bad rule, lots of debate and amendments. The Speaker wants to let the boys talk themselves out on it. I've been readin' testimony they got over at Public Works 'n' Education 'n' Labor. Everybody's gettin' their bowels in an uproar about nigger kids runnin' loose around the country an'—"

"Mace," says the Assistant Whip for Alabama. "You can't stampede folks. You've just gotta—"

Mace takes the cigar out of his mouth. "Aw, come on, Tom. Let's not you 'n' me get to bashin' our asses over seg. I just done that with old Granny Crockett." He picks up the slips again. "Lessee what we got here. Henry, you put Bill Sturdevant down as undecided."

The Assistant Whip for Hawaii, Oklahoma, and the Dakotas nods. "I called him personally after my girl put him down that way. Bill's interested in the reuse of old federal properties like Army camps. He might go with us on this one if he thinks it won't hurt him."

"Hell," Mace answers, "it isn't gonna hurt him any. He won last time with seventy-three point four. That district of his is mostly farmers and ranchers, 'cept for the two big towns. There isn't any race stuff out there worth spittin' at. You want to talk to him some more, Henry, or you want one of Lou's fellers to go 'round and see him?"

"Let me try first," the Assistant Whip says.

Mace nods. "An' old Pete Tucker?"

"Unanswered," says the assistant, "but you can put him down as against."

"Thought so," Mace says, marking on the slip. "Just 'cause he's in his against mood. Sumbitch. Okay. Larry, you got a couple of promisin' fellas down here as undecided."

The Assistant Whip for Massachusetts, Maine, Connecticut, and Rhode Island is leaning against the wall beside Howard and Plessy. "Bob Marsh is possible," he says. "I think it'd take some heavy persuading, though."

"What's Marsh's problem?"

"I don't know if he really has one," the Assistant Whip says, "but he thinks he does. He's just gotten divorced and he's got a lot of Catholics in that district. You know how he's been all this session, Mace—kind of scared of anything controversial."

Mace nods. "I s'pose it'd help if he could say the President asked him."

"A lot, I think."

Mace looks at Howard, who nods. "The President will call Bob Marsh—but you can't have too many of those, Mace. He's only got time to deal with six or eight guys. He doesn't like to do any more than that on one bill."

Applegate turns back to the New England assistant. "Ole Tom Finelli's got a real problem," he says. "Two mills closed up there last winter and there's a lotta unemployed ethnics and a lotta unemployed blacks an' an old Army camp down away from Providence. Maybe it'd look like Tom was votin' for his blacks and not his ethnics." He pauses and writes. "Maybe we'll get the leader or the Speaker to talk to him."

The meeting goes on for forty minutes more, all of it devoted to the search for converts to HR 1418. Howard doles out promises of presidential help; names are shifted back and forth from the "Undecided" column to possible "Fors" and "Against." Mace makes notes to pair those irretrievably against the bill with possible supporters who may be traveling abroad or around the country on House business. The pairs can't be finalized because the Speaker hasn't scheduled the bill for floor debate yet and won't for another week. Persuasion teams are made up from the Assistant Whips and Deputy Whips, Howard and Plessy's congressional liaison staffs, senior members of the House who are for the bill and who will be able to influence younger, undecided members. Knowing that big city Congressmen are more likely to be for the measure than suburban or rural Representatives, Mace makes a note to have the Speaker schedule the bill for a Tuesday, Wednesday, or Thursday so that the urban Congressmen will be present. Study groups and informal luncheons are planned; Mace or one of his deputies will attend the meetings to persuade. For the fact-oriented and more scholarly members, teams of experts will come to the Hill with charts, figures, and explanations. They will be assigned from the Department of Health, Education, and Welfare and from Ben Saterlee's staff at the White House. A coalition of lobbyists will be put together to work for the bill. All this would normally be done by the Majority Leader, but Hatfield is lost in his preoccupations. So Mace Applegate has taken over the planning. With his knowledge of members' districts, Mace begins to compile lists of hometown bankers, mayors, community leaders, lawyers, and old friends of various Congressmen who can be called on to exert pressure for the bill. Even Hollywood actors and Wall Street superstars who can be counted on to support the measure are listed as people to call members vulnerable to their particular charismas and persuasions.

But when the calculating and assigning are finished, the measure still appears to be nine-to-twelve votes short of passage. As the day of debate draws nearer, the computing, figuring, and head counting will be done over and over. But as it stands now, Mace knows that his gloomy hunch of the past few days has been justified. If the vote were tonight, the President would take a beating on the pilot bill of his whole program. And precedents once defeated in the House are hard to resurrect.

The meeting breaks up. Outside, the parking lot in front of the Capitol's majestic sprawl has begun to empty. Street lamps switch on in the gray, cool dusk. Lou Howard stays behind. He has moved to the sofa and has put his old briefcase on the cushions beside him. "Where are we going to get them, Mace?"

The bulky Whip lights his cigar, shakes out the match, and drops it in an ashtray. "Where we gonna get what?"

"The votes."

Mace puffs out a cloud of smoke, takes the cigar from his mouth, and examines its glowing end. "Thisyear's a pretty conservative Congress, Lou—lookin' at it from the socio-loggical pointa view."

"Obviously."

"So we gotta get a new view."

"What new view do you think you can put on this thing?" Howard asks.

Mace puts his cigar back in his mouth. "How 'bout patriotism?" He grins. "That's always kinda nice, isn't it? I mean, it works."

"Sure," Howard says, "but—"

"S'pose," Mace interrupts, "that you got the President to tell the Secretary of Defense to tell th' Army generals that thisyear bill's the greatest thing since the invention of mule crap for cabbages because it's gonna reactivate a lotta them old Army camps and take th' expense off th' Army's back an' they can keep the money to build rockets to bomb the Russians with?"

Howard raises one eyebrow. "That's not a bad idea. It isn't really accurate, though. We weren't planning on using all that many old Army camps—"

"Well, plan on usin' more."

"And I'm not sure the money saved would be left in the defense budget—"

"You want this goddamn bill?" Mace grunts.

"Sure."

"Then you tell them boys down at th' Budget Bureau to leave the money in the goddamn defense budget. You do that, Lou, and we're gonna have a whole lotta them high-class military-congressional lee-aison types runnin' around up here tellin' the old goats over on Armed Services that thisyear bill's more patriotic than Flag Day." He grins suddenly. "You'd be s'prised how patriotic the soldiers can make somethin' sound if they're gonna get money out of it."

Howard stands and picks up his briefcase. He shoves it under his arm. "Okay, Mace. I'll check it out at the White House. You've probably got something there."

The House has adjourned.

Suddenly the Capitol is almost empty. Across the street in the office buildings some members and their staffs are still at work. But here the tourists, lobbyists, and bored-looking doorkeepers have evaporated into the dusk. Suddenly the thing that fuels Mace Applegate and makes his life possible has stopped. The House is his source; for many of its old boys, it is not only a place of great purpose and endless dealing but a beloved campus on which members rollick together with all the jokes, secrets, and camaraderie of boys anywhere. Mace sits in his empty

office and toys with the idea of calling the chairman of Ways and
Means to see if a hint can be pried from him about the progress
of the other bill the President needs—the revision of the Revenue
Act, which will enable private industry to pay for the New Partnership. But if he did that, Rutherford and the girls would have
to stay another half-hour while their boss gabbed on the telephone. Mace is always anxious about that, fretful that his staff's
loyalty will keep them with him when the day ends and the
depression of suspended purpose creeps upon him. That might
deprive Henry and the girls of something they wanted for themselves on this balmy summer evening.

He picks up the telephone and buzzes Rutherford. "Henry?
Close 'er up. You 'n' Ruth 'n' Maude skedaddle."

"You staying?" Rutherford asks.

"Naw, I'm gonna go eat."

"Don't forget to call your brother-in-law."

"I won't. Now you git."

"Goodnight, Mace."

" 'Night."

He hangs up the telephone and sits for a moment, listening
to the silence sing. Tonight all over Washington there are places
where Mace Applegate would be welcome—in hired hotel suites
where lobbyists are offering bourbon and shrimp on toothpicks
in return for the presence of the important; at Paul Young's,
where junior colleagues or reporters would love to treat a House-
worn wheelhorse to dinner in return for his reminiscences of
how it used to be and what the great shadows of the past were
like when they walked these corridors as living men. There are
also places to which Mace Applegate would never be invited.
He has never been to a Georgetown dinner party or had cocktails in one of the old houses of dignified character in Cleveland Park. The difference between the places in which he is
revered and those to which he would never be asked doesn't
bother him. He isn't in politics to satisfy hungers of that sort.
He is here because being here, performing the House's rituals,
skills, and jousts, *is* his source. Barely knowing that about himself, he doesn't brood much beyond it.

But days end, and in the lapse Mace Applegate is faced

with the rest of life. In the evenings his dead wife's goodness makes him ache with continuing love; the little apartment he shares with another member from North Carolina beckons in barrenness, and he thinks sometimes about his father, who deserved a lot and never got it.

He stands up, drops the blasted remnants of the cigar in an ashtray, pauses beside the door to turn off the lights, and walks out into the empty corridors. He passes the gray columns and the lifeless forms of human statuary, a big man all alone in the hallways of the House of Representatives. Devoid of its people, the building is a grand, illuminated tomb.

"Mr. Mace Applegate."

Mace stops. A tall, slender black man with a beard, Afro, deep-collared shirt, wide tie, and hip-hugger pants has stepped out from the row of columns. It is Stetson, the new black member from the state of Washington who so far has irritated Mace with his posturing. The press calls him militant, but when he speaks, now and on the floor, his voice is soft.

"Well," Mace says, "it's young George Stetson."

They are five feet apart, two tall figures in an empty place. "I hear we got a fuss coming," Stetson says.

Mace chuckles. "More 'n' one, son. You stay here a time an' you'll count your history in fusses. What's on your mind?"

Stetson smiles slightly. Mace suddenly notices that he is handsome; he has never thought of a black man as handsome. "A bill to send nigger kids to the country," Stetson says.

"Kids," Mace answers.

"I said nigger kids," Stetson says.

"You sound like a fella tryin' t' bait somebody," Mace replies. "Fact is, son, you sound like a damn fool."

Stetson raises one eyebrow. "Yes? How's that Mr. Applegate —suh?"

"Forget that nigger stuff," Mace says.

"Have you forgotten it, Mr. Applegate?"

"Lemme ask you somethin'," Mace says. "What d' you s'pose is the difference between a nigger kid and a white kid?"

"I wouldn't know," Stetson replies. "I've never been a white kid."

"Well, I've never been a nigger kid," Mace says. "Now do you want to stand around wastin' a tired fat man's time or do you want to talk about how we're gonna get some votes for this goddamn thing?"

"I hear you're leading the hounds on that bill."

"You hear right."

"I've got some ideas," Stetson says. "Maybe I could help."

"Good," Mace answers. "Ever had dinner with a white man?"

Stetson laughs suddenly, loudly, with a tilt-back of his head and a flash of white teeth.

"I had dinner with a nigger once," Mace says. "It didn't hurt none. I reckon I can do it again. How about Paul Young's?"

"You're on," Stetson says, still chortling.

"Okay, son, then let's get to it."

They walk on together down the empty corridor, beneath the glittering chandelier and past the posing statues. The presence of Stetson means that Mace's confrontation with the rest of life on this particular night has been postponed. He is relieved.

Turning down another hallway, he breathes the air of a new night. Something that had begun to gnaw at him with an old, inexplicable pain has been washed away by someone else's pain perceived as vain strut. They walk toward the steps and the darkness together.

North Carolina.

The U.S. House of Representatives is a classic example of the tendency of American political institutions to begin as one thing and to become something else. The House began as "the most exact transcript of the whole society," as James Wilson put it. It has become, after nearly two centuries, a management mechanism that bears a closer resemblance to a badly organized Chinese tong than to a New England town meeting. It still represents—but not in the manner originally intended and not very successfully.

All great ideas are to one degree or another reflective of the historic and intellectual settings that produced them. The eighteenth-century ideal of representative democracy reflects the

historic experience attendant upon the waning of the Age of
Kings, the growing complexity of mercantile societies, and the
emergence of a philosophy of optimistic rationalism. The representative ideal was rooted in two assumptions. The first, derived
from natural law, holds that mass desires for liberty and justice,
while potentially dangerous, are basically reasonable. The second assumption maintains that the people in their mass are capable of wisdom, that they are so imbued with love of liberty and
justice that they will transcend their own selfishness in great matters—in short, that the people know good law from bad and
will be tireless in paying attention to their own interests. Once
one has made such dazzling optimistic assumptions, it only remains to work out a mechanical system of government based on
them.

The basic formula for the House was representation plus highly specified powers—such as the power to originate all tax and
appropriation legislation. The philosophical role of the House in
the larger federal structure was that of the voice of popular will
in creative conflict with senatorial power, executive exercise and
judicial restraint. The House was to be the insurer of social justice, the embodiment of the people's presumed capacity to safe-
guard their individual and several interests within the greater
good. To achieve all this, the House was to be a reflective representation of the people. This is fairly explicit in Madison's argument that the House should have "an immediate dependence on
and an intimate sympathy with the people. Frequent elections
are unquestionably the only policy by which this dependence and
sympathy can be effectually secured."

The society that the new government set out to order was a
fairly simple one. The American population in 1790 was a little
under 4 million. There were only five Eastern seaboard cities
with more than 8,000 inhabitants, and settlement to the west
reached only a little beyond Nashville. Postrevolutionary America was more a continuum of the last years of British rule—in the
social sense, anyway—than a violent upheaval of new forces. The
tendency was to tinker with nationalism and to grope for a new
culture that would express it. Noah Webster decided that Ameri-

ca should be "as independent in literature as she is in politics."
He designed his *American Spelling-Book* and his first anthology
of American lessons in reading and speaking to that end. Ethan
Allen of Vermont wrote a tract of wretched length and tedium
proposing a new world deism as a Republican substitute for
Christianity. It never caught on. So relatively unchanged was the
social climate once the Revolution and its memories had faded
that many loyalists who had fled abroad in 1775 and 1776
came drifting back. One of them, an enterprising gentleman
named Henry Cruger who had been a member of the British
Parliament during the Revolution, returned and managed to get
himself elected to the state senate of New York. The make-up
of the country, in other words, had not altered radically. It was
perceivable and representable.

To represent does not mean to mirror. The House has never
been a microcosm of the whole nation. The first Congress had
fifty-nine House members. A third of them were lawyers. Their
average wealth was far above the national average. What the first
House did mirror to some degree was the people who elected it
—which didn't mean all the white males in the nation over the
age of twenty-one. The right to vote in national elections was restricted to those who, under the laws of their states, could qualify
to vote for "the most numerous" chamber of the state legislature. Many states had property requirements restricting eligibility
to vote.

The Founding Fathers were not ungifted in prophecy. James
Madison wrote in *The Federalist*:

> At present, some of the states are little more than a
> society of husbandmen. Few of them have made much
> progress in those branches of industry which give a variety
> and complexity to the affairs of a nation. These, however,
> will in all of them be fruits of a more advanced popula-
> tion; and will require, on the part of each state, a fuller
> representation. The foresight of the convention has ac-
> cordingly taken care that the progress of population may
> be accompanied with a proper increase of the representa-
> tive branch of the government.

In the last half of the nineteenth century the United States became too complex a country to be represented easily. By 1890 the population had swollen to nearly 63 million people—and it was a population that differed radically from the one with which the nation embarked upon its independence. Immigration had come in stunning waves. It spewed 800,000 people into the country in 1881, with central and southern Europe providing 50 percent of the new Americans in the last half of the century. On the West Coast Chinese immigrants accounted for 17 percent of the population of San Francisco. A hundred years earlier American society had been rather simply divisible into farmer, mechanic, laboring, and property-owning classes. Until 1860 the statistically average American was still a farmer. After 1900 he was a wage earner. The organized labor movement was on the rise as one of the new American special-interest groups. Roman Catholicism had become a power in a largely Protestant country. Urbanization increased with such rapidity that the population of New York City grew from 1.3 million to 2.05 million in the last thirty years of the nineteenth century, and Chicago exploded from 443,534 inhabitants to 1.7 million in the same period. The United States had become a much more complicated society in its first century, and the only thing that could have accurately represented it would have been a split-level Tower of Babel.

It had also become a country of vast focused wealth. In the extraordinary post-Civil-War expansion of American industry, business outran all reasonable expectations and became the god and central rationale of national life. Interrupted by the panic of 1873 and the crash of 1893, business boomed in the last half of the nineteenth century, with a veritable disgorging of profits from railroads, steel, oil, timber, and land—to list but a few of the more lucrative enterprises. A new ethic howled in the land. Mark Twain fixed his cynical eye on Jay Gould and cracked: "The people had desired money before his day, but *he* taught them to fall down and worship it." The ensuing corruption of Congress by big business led Henry Adams to the conclusion that "the progress of evolution from President Washington to President

Grant was alone evidence enough to upset Darwin." If the species was in reverse evolution according to Adams, so was the original shimmering idealism of the men who had created the House of Representatives.

In addition to becoming corrupt after the Civil War, the House became incredibly complicated. Its rules, customs, and precedents accumulated to such an extent that obstruction and turgidity reached serious proportions. The management function was in jeopardy and the new American megasociety was producing problems and demands faster than Congress could deal with them. The cluttered and constipated condition of the House was so preposterous, said its great Speaker Thomas Brackett Reed, that the problem of trying to pass sufficient legislation was as hopeless as "trying to run Niagara through a quill."

Reed, a Maine Republican who presided over the House from 1889 to 1891 and again from 1895 to 1899, was a spectacular, hilarious, strong, and good man who symbolized the final triumph of the management function over the purest ideals of the representative function. Six feet, three inches tall and weighing close to three hundred pounds, Reed glittered in an era of pompous, venal mediocrity. He is something of a paradox in the history of the House because he was and is vastly admired despite the fact that he was a ruthless autocrat. The difference between Reed and his successor, Joe Cannon, is that unmeasurable quality that can have no definitive place in political science—character. Cannon was the prototype of the American superpatriot who yaps endlessly about national perfection. Reed was a man of enormous guts who had a clear vision of the national good and pursued it. What mitigated the iron control he exerted over the previously chaotic House was his character and his style. Of two long-winded members Reed remarked: "They never open their mouths without subtracting from the sum of human knowledge." It was Reed who turned the Rules Committee into a vehicle for passing the Republican program. He would confer with the majority members of the committee and then summon the Democratic minority and announce: "Gentlemen, we have decided to perpetrate the following outrage." Reed is the man who is credited with the observation that a statesman is a dead politician. Before the convention that rejected him for another of his protégés, the amiable, empty William McKinley, Reed was asked if he thought that the Republicans would nominate him. "They could do worse," he answered, "and they probably will." They did, and American history is poorer for not having had T. B. Reed in the White House.

The beginning of the House's reconversion to an instrument of effective management came on January 29, 1890. On that day the House was to decide which of two West Virginia Democrats had won a particular seat. The Democrats, then in the minority, pulled one of the commoner delaying tactics of the day. They first declared that a quorum wasn't present and then, when the roll was called, refused to answer so that a quorum could not technically be present. One could tie up the House for days with that device. When the stalling began, Speaker Reed took over the counting from the clerk and listed all members in the chamber as present. Pandemonium broke out. A Kentucky Congressman leaped to his feet, bellowing: "I deny your right, Mr. Speaker, to count me as present."

"The Chair is making a statement of fact that the gentleman from Kentucky is present," Reed replied. "Does he deny it?"

The Democrats counterattacked the next day with another delaying tactic—refusing to vote on the routine approval of the previous day's House journal. Cries of "No quorum!" echoed through the chamber and again Reed counted the House and declared a quorum present. Members roared "Tyrant!" and "Czar!" (a nickname that stuck with Reed ever after) and rushed about the chamber waving their arms and shouting insults at the Speaker. Reed dug in. The brawl continued until the next day. Reed once again counted the House, listing all members in the chamber as present. Members tried to hide under their desks (they had desks in those days) and behind screens. Reed ordered the doors locked so that no one could escape. One member, Representative Constantine Buckley Kilgore of Texas, won a sort of immortality in the events of that day. He became so worked up that he tried to kick down one of the chamber doors. It flew open in the face of another member, giving him a bloody nose. Thereafter Kilgore was dubbed "Kicking Buck." He was pointed out as a tourist attraction.

Ultimately the farce ended, Reed won, and his dictates were voted as new House rules. The management function had triumphed. It is still supreme. That doesn't mean that the House has ceased to be a representative body. Because its members are elected, they obviously represent something having to do with the people who elect them.

The House certainly does not represent, in any reflective way, the demographic components of the United States. Blacks form 11 percent of this society, but in the 92nd Congress only twelve of the 435 House members were black. Women account for more than 50 percent of the U.S. population, but there were only twelve women in the House. The majority of members still list law as their primary occupation—which hardly reflects the economic or intellectual level at which a majority of the American people make their living. The House thus does not accurately reflect the United States as a microcosm of the whole society—and it never has.

Nor does it accurately reflect the prevailing national opinions on major social questions. In the autumn of 1970 a group called the American Business Committee on National Priorities polled the districts of ten leading House members on issues like the SST, Vietnam, and the draft. They found that most of the ten members were voting against the prevailing sentiments of their constituents. These ten were powerful Congressmen whose long tenure implied that they had pretty safe seats. There have been dozens of similar studies that demonstrate more or less the same thing.

If it no longer represents America by section or region, if it does not mirror the social composition of the country, reflect its prevailing opinions, delineate the nation's classes, the House still does exercise a representative function, however poorly. By "representative" here one means that the House expresses currents running in the country. The currents are mostly intuitive, and for political purposes they are translated into the left- or right-wing instincts of ideology.

To be more precise, what the House represents is ideology

qualified by expertise and sometimes limited by various sorts of pressure. It sounds complicated but it isn't. Most members of the House tend toward either liberalism or conservatism. Most members also become specialists in some aspect of legislation. Detailed knowledge of a matter usually qualifies one's ideological instincts about it.

The modern Congressman, swimming in a morass of technically complicated issues, putting in on the average a fifty-nine-hour week that includes everything from committee work to answering mail, cannot possibly know everything about everything, so he decides to become a specialist in a few things. Sam Rayburn's famous advice to House freshmen "To get along, go along" has been replaced by the political command "Know something!" An individual Representative, faced with an issue that neither he nor his legislative staff has had time to research, usually checks with a fellow ideologue who is an expert in the field; everything else being equal, the member follows the voting advice of his expert soulmate. A conservative who doesn't know anything about aerospace legislation will usually go along with a conservative who does.

All this leaves us with the question: Whatever happened to the eighteenth-century ideal of a legislative body that would be the voice of the people in the councils of their federal government? The "common interest with the people," which Madison insisted be an intrinsic part of the House, is now expressed through the vague smear that is the spectrum of ideology represented. It is also expressed by the frequent elections that Madison thought necessary. Indeed, in the latter part of the twentieth century the principal lever of American democracy has been the power to remove from office those Congressmen (or Senators or Presidents) whose actions and ideologies don't conform to the majority view of what ought to be done.

If democracy is, in the final analysis, the measure of how much the people actually govern themselves, then the modern reality of American democracy is considerably more modest than the eighteenth-century theory of it. Even its principal device, the power of recall, is vulnerable to the contemporary means of mass persuasion, the hopelessly complex nature of events, and the apathy of a huge, semialienated population. The ability of the people to influence their government becomes increasingly difficult even though the antiwar movement of the late 1960s and early 1970s showed that it can still be done. What really should keep an administration—which is an ideological force—in check is the presence of opposing ideologies in Congress, plus the periodic opportunity for the voters to get rid of leaders whose ideology is displeasing to the majority.

The eighteenth century believed, with Rousseau, that the mass was capable of wisdom. The statistics on voter participation and the various measures of public interest in what goes on in the House of Representatives put some dents in the theory. American democracy today is composed of a relatively inert mass of disinterested and preoccupied people who are courted, manipulated, and persuaded by political minorities committed to ideological points of view. That is the modern American reality, and insofar as the House represents anything that is what it represents. The result is that the various ideologies of the House make perpetual war against one another, with the commitment of the majority as the prize. In that cross-fire the lords and barons of the House continue to work their turgid will on the legislative process, and Congress as a whole becomes less able to check the ideological impulses of the Executive.

And that, in the end, is why Presidents grow stronger and Congress becomes less and less able to check them.

Willis Dern, who is generally credited with having the best intellect among Washington columnists, is eating shrimp salad for lunch. Congressman John Stermas of Colorado, one of Mace Applegate's deputies, has theoretical abstractions. Lou Howard, chief of congressional liaison for the White House, satisfies two different appetites with steak and pessimism.

The three men are lunching together in the plush House restaurant, which at ten minutes to two is almost deserted. Afternoon committee meetings are getting under way. Favored constituents taken to lunch by their Congressmen have resumed their wanderings around the Capitol. Dern, Stermas, and Howard have lingered over coffee to talk about HR 1418. Lou's anxieties have accumulated since Mace Applegate held his first Whip's meeting on the bill two weeks before. The impression then was that the majority didn't have the votes. It still doesn't. Lou and Mace, working with the poorly focused interest and sluggish participation of Randolph Hatfield, the Majority Leader, have assembled a coalition of government and private lobbyists for the bill. The Pentagon has turned loose four captains and three majors from its own congressional liaison staff in return for a White House promise that any money saved by reactivating dormant Army camps would remain in the military budget. Lobbyists from the AFL-CIO have been enlisted after White House consultations and persuasion; other special groups such as the NAACP and even a few industrial operatives are working for the messure. In addition, Mace has a new ally in Representative George Stetson, who is bringing pressures to bear on big city Congressmen from various segments of the black community. The search for votes has tightened and narrowed, but the controversies have grown louder and more heated. The conservative press and commentators have begun to focus on HR 1418 as part of a general attack on the whole New Partnership program. "Some of the tougher black separatists are accusing the administration of planning concentration camps where ghetto children will be brainwashed. Conservative Southerners who had originally disguised their opposition under the old principle that the government that governs least governs best are now being more openly racist. Congressman Crockett, the chairman of the Rules Committee, received a flurry of national publicity for a statement he made during an appearance on *Meet the Press*: "We will never achieve racial harmony in this country by giving the federal government new ways to perpetuate the old habit of making one race pay for the misfortunes and failures of another." In the face of all this the intensified drive by the majority and the leadership still leaves HR 1418 some eight to ten votes short of passage in Mace and Lou's calculations. The Speaker is getting impatient. The session is lagging and he wants to get HR 1418 to the floor, where it can be disposed of in one way or another. And the President is growing edgy and angry.

"You know there's a leadership meeting at five," Stermas says.

Lou nods. "Mace is going to ask for more time."

Stermas sets down his coffee cup. "I wouldn't count on his getting it. The atmosphere's turning ugly. Your President's leaning on the Speaker too much, Lou—and the Speaker's building up a big resentment."

"I know," Lou says. "We've been trying to get him to lay off." He looks at Stermas. "My boy resents too much too. He thinks the Speaker's dragging his feet. He thinks the leadership up here can find the votes if they really want to."

"And then we've got a few fires building up under the Speaker from here," Stermas says. "A lot of chairmen have stuff ready to come to the floor and HR 1418 is sitting in the way."

"Hell," Dern says, "they can just bypass it." He is a tightly built man in his late forties with tousled black hair, a ruddy complexion, and an addiction to a rumpled version of the Princeton style of dress as it was practiced around 1959. Dern's uniform usually consists of gray suits, blue button-down shirts, and striped ties.

"We're caught in a bind," Stermas says. "The President wants the bill passed for his speaking tour. So what we're arguing about is really a rather narrow range of time—whether to get the bill up next week and take our chances or wait another ten days and hope we can find the votes. What I'm afraid of is that the Speaker will get so irritated at the pressure from the White House that he'll push the bill out and let it be defeated just to teach a new President a lesson about who runs the House."

"You aren't serious," Dern says.

"I'm very serious," Stermas answers. "Between us, this is a complicated and rather petulant man."

"I thought the Speaker was supposed to be a scaredy-cat."

"He's not scared of the President," Stermas says. "Just of the House."

"Which brings us back to the main point," Dern says. "This

administration and this congressional leadership haven't found each other yet, so the process of leadership is failing."

"It isn't really a failure of leadership," the tall Colorado Congressman says. "And I'm not saying that just because I'm a very junior member of the leadership. What we've got here is a confusion of focus."

"In a general lack of political focus," Dern says.

Stermas nods. "Well, yes, I suppose. Granted that the Speaker is weak and that Hatfield isn't functioning very well, what the House is really looking for is a definition of its function in a new situation—new administration and all that."

Lou Howard looks up. "Heresy," he says. "Willy's column this morning said that you guys and us guys were simply failures in leadership. Nothing complicated about focus."

Dern laughs. He turns and looks at Howard, tilting his head slightly to look over his glasses. "I didn't say *you* were failing, Lou. I said your President was failing. Isn't he?"

"My President," Lou answers, "is getting angry about this whole snafu up here. He's funny angry, though."

"How?" Willy Dern asks.

"He's sore at Ways and Means for taking so much time over the hearings on amending the Revenue Act."

"He isn't worried about HR 1418?" Stermas asks.

Lou shakes his head. "He's got this idea that the Speaker and Mace can pull it off—if they really want to. Meanwhile, he's sore at the Chairman and at Willy here and the other people who are focusing all the attention on HR 1418. I must say," Howard adds, "I wish you'd hung your thesis of failed leadership on something else."

"Why?" Dern asks.

Lou raises his head and looks across the restaurant. Congressman Jerome M. Cressap of New Jersey is having lunch alone. He is a short, thin man in his sixties. Cressap's dapperness is utterly without style; he is offensively neat. "Because of people like that," Lou says, nodding toward Cressap.

Dern turns to look. "What's he got to do with it?"

"We need him on this bill and we're not sure that we have

him," Howard says. "We ought to. Jerry was all anxious a few weeks ago because the unions were putting up someone against him in the primaries. Mace seems to have fixed it, but Cressap's still jumpy. He may have read your column this morning." Lou looks at Willy. "You did make it fairly plain that you were for the Youth Resources Development Act. If Jerry Cressap can grasp that much of what you wrote, it may make him nervous about the bill. He thinks you're a Commie or something."

Dern and Stermas laugh. The sound of their amusement breaks into the train of Congressman Cressap's thought.

Jerry Cressap's mind as he sits alone eating a bowl of vegetable soup, with a cracker held between two manicured fingers and his thumb, is held prisoner by a series of compulsive images, all of them conjuring up threat. Threat in many subtle forms dominates Jerry's inner life.

Hearing the laughter, Cressap looks up. Lou Howard and John Stermas are two of those Washington figures whom Jerry describes to people in his district as "big men." It is one of his recurring phrases. Whenever someone in New Jersey mentions a name heard on television or printed in the New York *Daily News,* Jerry will answer, "He's a big man in Washington. I know him." Only on rare occasions does his gratification at being able to say that succumb to his private admission that he has never had real intimacy with any of the big guys. Something happens between those people that Jerry Cressap can't quite put his finger on. They are comfortable with one another, but he's not comfortable with them. They're always using words and phrases that refer to private things or to people Jerry doesn't know. One gets the impression that the big men of Washington were all at one another's houses last night and that their wives are all friends. Jerry wishes that his wife, Marion, was the kind of woman who could make friends. But she can't seem to find anyone in Washington to be friendly with, someone who would call her up for no reason in particular. Jerry and Marion live across the river in Arlington, Virginia. Marion is a wonderful housekeeper.

Jerry looks at Willis Dern for a moment. Stermas is beckoning to one of the waiters. They're going to leave. Dern's wife is a beautiful woman with deep eyes who sometimes gets her picture in the "Style" section of the Washington *Post,* where they write about parties and Georgetown goings-on.

Stermas is crossing the restaurant with Lou Howard and Dern behind him. They pause by the table. "Hi, Jerry," Stermas says.

Jerry looks up. "Hi, Johnny." He uses "Johnny" for anybody he knows named John. He uses "Mac" for anybody whose name begins with "Mac" or "Mc."

"You know Lou Howard and Willis Dern, don't you?" Stermas says.

Cressap nods. "Hi ya."

"Hello, Jerry," Lou says.

Dern nods. "Hi."

(Tonight over dinner Jerry will suddenly say to Marion, "I was talking to Willy Dern today.")

"Going over to Ways and Means?" Stermas says. He looks at his watch. "I think the Chairman called us back at three."

Jerry nods. "Yeah. You run along. I'll be over in a few minutes." He pauses, wondering whether to leave it there. But he can't. "I've gotta finish my soup," he says. He immediately feels stupid and irrelevant.

Stermas smiles. "Okay, Jerry. See you over there."

The big men leave.

As he continues eating, Cressap is again overtaken by the compulsive thoughts about how you get from one place in life to another. Jerry sees, for the thousandth time, a huge asphalt parking lot in his New Jersey district. It is rimmed by a big supermarket, a hardware store, an ice cream shop, a dry cleaner, and a drugstore. The sunblasts of a hot August afternoon glint from the bodies and windshields of cars. In the vision Jerry is campaigning again. He is forever approaching people who, he is sure, are going to reject him or be angry at him.

Jerry Cressap is a man whose anxiety to please and whose inability to please arise from his feeling of being an unpleasing person. He is frightened of his white constituents. In his cumulative portrait of them, they always seem to be angry. He thinks of them at the lowest common denominator of their malaise, and he begins all his thoughts about them with the assumption that they resent everything that the federal government does and thus resent him. He hardly knows his black constituents, who live along a rim of ghetto that borders his predominantly suburban district. There are outsiders agitating among his blacks, Jerry is sure of that. The candidate that labor was going to put up against him in the primary was a big-mouthed black man with a college education.

In his campaigning Jerry uses the media to reach the blacks and devotes his personal work to the white majority. He roams the shopping centers, ethnic picnics, high school auditorium meetings, and the Jerry Cressap Appreciation Dinners that he and his brother-in-law arrange. In his imaginary movie he is forever walking across that great, sun-baked parking lot, forever screwing his face into a smile, sticking his hand out, and saying, "Hi! I'm Jerry Cressap, your Congressman." And he is forever afraid. In that same *cinéma nonvérite* he is constantly being assailed by pot-bellied men in shirt sleeves, men with angry red eyes who pound their index fingers against his chest and demand to know when the goddamn government is going to pull the niggers off the public tit.

As he spoons the remaining vegetables out of the bottom of the soup bowl, he turns once more to the contemplation of his last goal. Jerry Cressap once took a night course that instructed him to think in terms of goals. These thoughts too are permeated with anxiety. Jerry has to serve just one more term in the House to be eligible for a pension worth three-quarters of his salary. He needs it. But the malevolent spirit lurking in that hot parking lot threatens him.

The House Ways and Means Committee room in the Longworth Office Building is splendid, austere, and cool. The large chamber is dominated at one end by a high, curved dais that stretches from one side of the room to the other. Behind it the Chairman and his committee are enthroned like judges of a great court. The colonnaded wall behind them is hung with a huge, green drape. Oil portraits of the present chairman and the ranking minority member hang on one side of the rear wall. The committee—its majority members at one side of the curve in order of seniority and its minority members on the other side of the Chairman—stares down at witnesses who sit at a table just before the dais. Behind the dais staff members lounge in chairs against the wall, listening or answering telephones in hushed voices.

When Jerry Cressap arrives, coming in through a rear door and going to place in the third seat from the end on the majority side, only four other members of his party are present aside from the Chairman. Prof Dunston is the lone minority member present on the other side. The audience section is nearly empty. Two reporters sit at one desk talking to each other in low voices.

Congressman John R. MacKenzie of California is the first witness this afternoon. He is a trim, emphatic man with blue eyes who is known for the insistent hardness of his views. He is finishing the reading of a long prepared statement. As Jerry Cressap sits down, Peter Jaffe, the staff chief of the committee, leans over behind him and whispers, "Revision of the 1973 Revenue Act."

Cressap nods. "Yeah."

MacKenzie is hunched over the witness table, holding the last page of his prepared statement. He is dwelling on the familiar welfare-now-pay-later theme that is being used frequently by opponents of the President's New Partnership concept. "When the time comes for these corporations to cash in their tax credits," the California Congressman is saying, "it obviously detracts from federal revenues. Mr. Chairman, if we make the simple assumption that money that the government does not receive is money lost, money that it cannot spend, then we see that his proposal is hardly novel. It is not a new departure to solve the old problem of the federal government's supporting the unfortunate, subsidizing the lazy, and paying premiums to those who breed children out of wedlock. The President, in his campaign, promised a new departure." MacKenzie raises his head. The blue eyes look into the Chairman's face. "This isn't it," he says. He looks down and resumes reading. "This is just a continuation of the same old wasteful, unjust system. All that is new here is a gimmick designed to give the impression that private industry is funding these programs." He looks up again and takes off his reading glasses. His mouth is set in a straight line across his pale face. "I urge this committee to reject the proposed revision of the Revenue Act just as I will urge the House as a whole to reject HR 1418, the enabling legislation for this so-called new program."

The Chairman nods. His face is expressionless. His eyes are blurred behind his own thick glasses. With his unremarkable features, hair combed straight back, gray suit, and plain tie, he appears to be a shapeless man. Nothing that he will say here in questioning witnesses or in commenting on their testimony will hint at his own views on revising the Revenue Act. Only those who have served with him for a long time (or worked for him or studied him) will detect his opinion in the drift of his questions, the scheduling of witnesses, and the flow of evidence before the committee goes into seclusion to write its final bill.

The Chairman looks down at MacKenzie. "The committee is grateful for your appearance, Congressman," he says in a deep voice brushed with a border state accent. "We are also grateful for the obvious time and thought that went into the preparation of your statement." He looks to his right and to his left. "I have no questions. Does the committee have any?"

No one on the majority side makes any sign of wanting to question.

On the minority side Prof Dunston raises a pencil he holds in his right hand.

"Mr. Dunston," the Chairman says. He sits back and folds his hands.

"Am I to take it that you regard the so-called New Partnership as a trick?" he asks MacKenzie. "Something based on a trick?"

MacKenzie lowers his head and thinks for a moment. He looks up again. "I prefer the word 'deception,' " he says. "A trick implies something done—well, deliberately."

DUNSTON: But you think that this tax credit device is a deceptive thing?

MAC KENZIE: I do. It's obvious. Sooner or later the federal government will have to pay for these programs by not receiving money in taxes from the corporations that have paid for the programs.

DUNSTON: Why do you think that this deception has been sent here in the form of these two bills?

MAC KENZIE: Well, sir, it's obvious, isn't it? Federal revenues were over $310 billion last year, federal expenditures were $331 billion. The public's patience with such profligacy is exhausted. A major share of that—now that we're out of Vietnam, the *largest* share—47 percent, goes into what they call "human resources." The public has had enough.

DUNSTON: If we are to look at legislation about to come to the House floor—

MAC KENZIE: HR 1418, the so-called Youth Resources Development Act.

DUNSTON: Yes, that bill. If we are to look at that bill we can only deduce that the President wants to spend more—

MAC KENZIE: And that he's perpetrating the deception that he is spending *less* by postponing payment of it and disguising that payment through these tax credits. The whole thing would be a little more plausible—not much, but a little—if this new payment gimmick were applied to the programs we already have. But it comes to us with demands for new programs . . .

The colloquy of mutual agreement continues. As Jerry Cressap listens, he begins to like the raw, solid logic of what Dunston and MacKenzie are saying. Jerry Cressap has been feeling funny about this whole program, anyway. He hasn't really thought it through, but everything connected with it churns up the images of threat in his mind. George Stetson is for it, and Stetson is a militant. The idea of putting up a whole new program for *them*— Cressap can see the bulky men in shirt sleeves pounding their fingers against his chest and shouting about still more for the niggers. The threats make him want to vote against the program. Now Dunston and MacKenzie are giving him good arguments. He writes the budget figures on a pad. He jots down "human resources" and underlines it.

He makes a note about the expensive old programs and the demand to get them off the public's back first. He feels a mild tingle of excitement. He can get his staff to work out how much the people of his district pay in taxes and then show how much of that goes to pay for "human resources." He can send copies of the speech to the local newspapers, making the point graphically in terms of local income.

And yet.

And yet, ten days before he had had lunch in the Whip's office with Mace Applegate and a man named Gus Freeman from the AFL-CIO. Freeman had explained to Jerry the situation in a few local unions which had led to a threat by one of the unions to put up a primary candidate against him. Urged on by Mace, Freeman had suggested to Jerry what he might do about it— voting right on several bills endorsed by labor, threading strong prounion passages into his weekly newsletter, arranging speeches before labor groups. All this was way beyond Freeman's duty or even discretion. He did it for Mace, and since that luncheon, Mace has twice asked Jerry for his vote on HR 1418.

Jerry hasn't committed himself yet. He hasn't known how. He has thought of pleading threats to his survival—an argument that always evokes sympathy from Mace. But Mace has just done Jerry a large favor in the survival department and Mace knows a good deal about Jerry's district. Cressap can't figure out how he could explain to the Whip these vague feelings of threat. But in the dialogue between Dunston and MacKenzie, now coming to an end, Jerry is finding new arguments based on principle. Mace is profoundly respectful of men's principles. Principle could justify Jerry Cressap in voting against his leadership and his President.

"Once again, Congressman, we are grateful to you," the Chairman is saying.

MacKenzie rises, nodding.

The Chairman lifts a sheet of paper and reads from a paper beneath it. "Our next witness is Mr. John Bevins Kane of Princeton University."

A tall young man with prematurely gray hair gets up from his seat and walks to the witness chair. He carries a briefcase and a bundle of papers under one arm.

The Chairman nods. "Mr. Kane. Good afternoon, sir."

Seated, the young man smiles. "Good afternoon, Mr. Chairman."

Peter Jaffe, the staff aide leaves his chair at the back of the room and whispers something in the Chairman's right ear. The Chairman listens, nods, and then smiles at the witness. "I am guilty of rudeness, sir." He raises the paper and reads beneath it. "I should have said *Professor* Kane. My apologies, sir."

Kane smiles. "I'm not a stickler for titles, Mr. Chairman. Not my own, anyway."

"A good principle," the Chairman says. "But yours, as we know, is a very respected title. I imagine quite a few of the members of this committee have read your two books on taxation and appropriation. I know I found them very instructive."

Cressap leans forward. The Chairman is signaling respect for the witness. Cressap has heard of John Bevins Kane but hasn't read anything by him and doesn't know what his opinions are. But the fact that Kane comes from New Jersey and that the Chairman respects him makes the professor important.

"Thank you, Mr. Chairman," Kane says. "I wonder if I might break precedent and comment on something the previous witness said before I begin reading my statement."

The Chairman is silent for a moment. "I think that would be all right, if the previous witness doesn't object."

MacKenzie, who is standing in the audience section putting papers in his briefcase, raises his head. "No objection," he says.

"I am sure it was inadvertent," Kane says, "but during his responses to Congressman Dunston's questions, Congressman MacKenzie used the phrase 'human resources' and left the impression that this referred only to welfare costs, aid to dependent children, and the like."

"So I believe," the Chairman answers quietly.

" 'Human resources,' " says Professor Kane, "is a generic political term applied to a budgetary category. It was first used, I think, during the last years of the Johnson administration or the first year of the Nixon administration. It refers to a wide range of programs. It is a budgetary category covering all sorts of things from various forms of welfare to federal aid to education, veterans' benefits and services, manpower training, health programs, and so forth. When Congressman MacKenzie speaks of 47 percent of the current budget going for 'human resources'—the figure is actually 47.8 percent—that isn't just for so-called welfare."

The Chairman nods. Watching him, Jerry Cressap thinks that the Chairman is suppressing a slight smile. "Thank you, Professor Kane," the Chairman says. "That is a useful point to make, although it is one that I am sure all the members of this committee are aware of. Perhaps we could hear your statement now."

Jerry Cressap takes his pencil and crosses "human resources" off his note paper. He also crosses off "47 percent."

Kane begins to read. Jerry had expected to be confused and to lose interest. Professors do that to you. But Kane's statement is plain, clear, and brief. It is in support of the tax credit principle and of the 1973 Revenue Act revision.

Since 1963, Kane points out, tax policy has been based on the principle of economic growth. The basic function of taxes is to raise enough money to meet federal expenditures. The corporations being offered tax credits could not claim all the credit in one year. It would have to be taken in percentages over several years. The amounts taken thus would not have a harsh effect on tax revenues all in one year. Indeed, economic growth would naturally increase tax revenues to compensate for the credits being cashed in by corporations. Growth would be faster because the credits would stimulate corporate expansion and reinvestment. Meanwhile, government expenditures would not be going up for new human resources programs because the new programs were paid for by the private sector. Professor Kane cites the program proposed in HR 1418, now pending House action, as an example.

The Chairman questions the witness, expanding on the points made in his brief statement, coaxing from him the details and examples that Kane is obviously prepared to give. After the Chairman finishes, John Stermas takes over the questioning, re-

lating the whole New Partnership program to the social tensions
now boiling in the country.

> KANE:　Social science isn't my field, Congressman, but
> I read the newspapers like everyone else. It is my be-
> lief that we have to do something like this if we are to
> restore the confidence of a majority of taxpayers in
> their government's basic sense of fairness.
> STERMAS:　You are something of an authority on appro-
> priations, or at least the appropriating process, sir. Now
> we aren't really *appropriating* under this new policy—
> KANE:　No, you're keeping federal control over the spend-
> ing of money from the private sector for the public
> good. To me, that's the genius of the thing.
> STERMAS:　Exactly. Let me ask you something. You use
> the phrase 'the public good.' Is there any question in
> your mind that these expenditures would be for the
> total public good?
> KANE:　(smiling)　I can say what you, perhaps, can't,
> Mr. Stermas. I take it that some of the opposition to
> this program is based on racial—well, let's call them ra-
> cial considerations, that this money is going to be spent
> mostly for the benefit of black people.
> STERMAS:　There is opposition along those lines.
> KANE:　My colleague Professor Kotowski of Harvard was,
> as you know, named by the President last Tuesday to
> be chairman of the board of the new federal corporation
> that is going to oversee the whole series of programs.
> STERMAS:　Yes.
> KANE:　I don't think it was an indiscretion on his part
> to discuss with me the kinds of programs the adminis-
> tration already has on the drawing board. Secondary
> road building? That doesn't benefit blacks alone. Day
> care centers? If anything, they will permit welfare
> mothers to work by providing care for children. That
> benefits everybody, not just blacks. Manpower retrain-
> ing? My God, what that alone is going to do for the
> whites of Appalachia. The point is, Mr. Chairman, Con-
> gressman Stermas, when you spend to reduce, not pov-
> erty, but the *dependence* of poverty on federal assist-

ance, you help everyone. And some of these programs are of direct benefit to all the taxpayers but at no cost to them.

Listening intently, the depression of his old confusions growing again, Jerry Cressap crumples up the paper on which he had made notes during the Dunston-MacKenzie dialogue.

Kane is finished. The Chairman thanks him.

Jerry Cressap drops his crumpled paper into a wastebasket near his feet below the dais.

The Chairman calls a ten-minute recess.

Jerry Cressap stands. John Stermas, three seats away, is also standing. He comes down the dais. "What'd you think, Jerry?"

"Of what?"

"John Kane."

"Smart man," Cressap says.

"We were at school together," Stermas says. "Would you like to meet him?"

"No," Cressap says. "I gotta go, anyway. Got some people from the district coming in at four."

"Before you go," Stermas says, "could I ask you about HR 1418? We're going to need all the votes we can get. It's close. We'd like to have you with us."

The sun-baked parking lot flashes a threatening image in Cressap's mind. The heavy, angry faces shout silently. "I haven't made up my mind," Jerry says.

"Look," Stermas says in a low voice, "I don't mean to put on the pressure, but this one's terribly important, Jerry."

"When I make up my mind, I'll let you know," Cressap says. He goes away, knowing how you get from one place in life to another and knowing that he won't be going.

Stermas stays to hear two more witnesses and then he too leaves in order to keep an appointment in Mace Applegate's office.

He walks through the dark hallways of the Longworth Office Building. Revolving doors take him out into the blinding sunlight of a Washington summer afternoon. The heat is so thick that for a moment he can hardly breathe. People walk in clusters down the sidewalks from the Capitol; cars crawl by on Independence Avenue. Stermas walks to the curb, where a Capitol policeman nods. "It's a scorcher, Congressman."

"I don't know how you take it standing out here all afternoon," Stermas says.

"Oh, we get a break every so often," the cop answers. " 'Tisn't too bad. Here, lemme change the light for you." He reaches for a switch in the bowels of an open control box.

"Don't bother, thanks," Stermas says. He stands waiting until the light changes. A taxi stops close to the curb. Its front window is rolled down. An American flag sticker on the rear window bears the slogan "Pro-America." Inside, a radio is disgorging the strident voice of one of the fundamentalist preachers who exhort Washington and the world from little radio stations scattered across the hills of Virginia.

Stermas nods to the policeman, crosses the street, and starts up the sidewalk toward the Capitol—a tall man in a brown suit, hands in his pockets, his head slightly bowed as he traverses the heat of the day.

He had been thinking about John Kane's testimony until his run of memory was snapped by the policeman and the broadcast voice from inside the taxi. Stermas has always been annoyed by the oversimplifications that every politician inevitably encounters in campaigning. But the people who think and speak thus are also part of America. They are the clingers to symbols, the adherents of some unclear dream of nirvana. All philosophies of government that ignore them are as immoral as the politics that appeals to the symbol-clingers' fears. The unattractiveness of the uptight and the angry conceals the pain from which they speak and blurs the justice of their ugly plea for succor and order. There is a point, Stermas tells himself as he mounts the Capitol steps, at which the unattractive plea is frustrated by official appeals to better nature. At that point the strident oversimplifications surrender to rage.

And that is where the United States is now—or nearly. He had read that morning the Washington *Post*'s story of a serious riot in Milwaukee—only it wasn't something that could be simply dismissed with the word "riot." It had begun the evening before with a senseless and—police said—apparently unmotivated attack by whites upon a Roman Catholic ghetto project. Before sufficient numbers of police could be summoned to break it up, hundreds of blacks had poured out to engage the white attackers in hand-to-hand combat. More whites had gathered. Guns were produced. The television news this morning said that the sniping and brick throwing were still going on, that five houses in affluent white suburban neighborhoods had been set on fire during the night, presumably by blacks. The *Post's* front page carried an article that was the first of an investigative series on a similar outbreak in Portland, Oregon, six weeks before. Below the fold of the paper there was a story about yet another huge rally in Anaheim, California, where the mesmeric demagogue Harvey Leland was speaking. Leland has been loud in the land this year, proclaiming a mass movement whose members will refuse to pay all taxes until socialism has been expunged from government and common sense restored, until income taxes have been abolished along with all the "do-good, hoodlum-supporting, bastard-sponsoring" federal programs they paid for. Leland has been proselytizing far beyond his home base in Orange County, California. He has filled stadiums in Chicago, Boston, and Atlanta too. "Let 'em try to arrest 5 million patriots!" was his wind-up cry, and he was right. It couldn't be done.

Stermas has never been a servant of the moment in American politics. During the late 1960s and early 1970s he believed that the ghetto outbursts, the student riots, the burnings, the antiwar marches, and the popularity of flagrantly exploitive figures like Agnew and Wallace were flaring symptoms of deep grievances. The symptoms wouldn't endure for long. They would recede, he thought, and give government a chance to respond to the grievances themselves. Stermas has always believed that the human capacity for embracing vicious politics, for sustaining open hatred, or for sheer outburst was limited.

But the present symptoms are different. They are a warning that government didn't respond well enough after the first wave of violence and hatred. The dimension is also different now—broader, engulfing more people. Now riots are not just conflicts between blacks and authority or students and authority. They are open clashes between the races, face-to-face confrontations instead of the symbolic burning and smashing of property. The Leland movement may not be any more permanent than the appeal of Agnew and Wallace, but it is more direct, touching more explicitly upon the divisive grievances. Leland is a dealer in more than symbols. Unlike Wallace and Agnew, he is not a politician. He aspires to no office as far as anyone can tell. Therefore he can be blunter and he can do more damage than the politician who risks loss of office by offending moderates. Leland is well financed and magnetic. He is proposing that the first mass refusal to pay selected taxes begin on the first day of next year. Thousands of lawsuits will be thrown at employers to make them stop withholding taxes.

This time, Stermas believes, several serious calamities are in the making unless government can make convincing response to the roiling grievances in the country. The symptoms are appearing with increasing and more violent frequency; the tumult is getting louder. Therefore government must make its reassurance soon or the sound of it will be lost in the uproar. This is why the President is touring the West in July. But he needs to have something positive to say, something to calm the rampant fear that the burdens of solacing poverty will bankrupt the wage-earning majority. Yet the minorities, the poor, and the deprived cannot be denied either. What the administration urgently needs now is a victory in Congress for HR 1418 as a start—as dramatic evidence that the New Partnership is actually going to be. The tension leading up to the House debate and vote on the bill is good; it is drawing attention to the policy that the administration is trying to launch, making the facts of that policy clearer. That dramatic tension must be climaxed with a victory exciting enough to make the top spot on Walter Cronkite's nightly news program. It must become a screaming headline in the New York *Daily News* as well as a sedate one in *The New York Times*. The administration needs to be able to cry "Hey! Cool it! Everything's okay now!"

That won't calm rioters immediately. But the reality will seep down to them through the layers of angry people who believe themselves persecuted and euchred by the welfare state. It will also deflower the logic of demagogues like Leland who are fomenting tax revolts in the country.

The trouble is that HR 1418 is all there is at the moment. Aside from securing its passage and getting the revision of the 1973 Revenue Act through Congress, the administration has no other way to positively demonstrate a new beginning, to display a new logic that will, as Kane said, restore the confidence of the people in the basic fairness of their government.

Stermas walks through the main corridor of the Capitol and turns down the little hallway leading to Mace Applegate's office. The crowds are swirling slowly through the building, gazing in awe at the architecture and decor of their Congress. For the first time in his ten years on the Hill, John Stermas wonders how much longer that awe and reverence will last.

One of the pretty blonde receptionists looks up and smiles. "Haryawl, Mistuh Stermas?"

Stermas smiles at her. "C'mon, Maude, don't 'yawl' me."

The girl giggles. "We're s'posed to, Congersman." She rolls her eyes in a caricature of a flirt. "We-all's Suth'n girls."

"Okay," Stermas says. "Where's Mace?"

"Inside with Senator Yeats," the girl says. "Yawl can go right in. He tole me to tell yawl."

"You spilled hominy grits on your blouse at lunch," Stermas says. He walks through the little hall to Mace Applegate's office, leaving the two girls laughing shrilly behind him.

Mace is sitting at his desk, holding a can of Fresca. "Harya, John?" he says. "Y'know Sam Yeats."

Stermas shakes hands with a tall white-haired man. "Hi, Senator."

"Congressman." Yeats is a junior Senator from Georgia.

"I was just tellin' Sam what a pisser we got here," Mace says. "You talk to Jerry Cressap, John?"

Stermas nods. "Just now over at Ways and Means. Still undecided."

Mace leans forward and makes a note on a blue Whip sheet

before him. "Sumbitch," he grunts. He looks up at Stermas. "Bad news from 'nuther quarter. Young Pete Grimes of Maine just switched from 'For' to 'Undecided.' "

"Christ," Stermas says. "What's the matter with Grimes?"

Mace is still writing something. "Beats the hell outta me," he says. "Mebbe you oughta go talk to him."

"I'll try," Stermas says.

Mace finishes writing and drops his pen. "Ole Sam here's gonna be seein' thisyear bill through the Senate. He jus' dropped over t' check on the fine progress we was makin'."

"I'm not sure we'll even get a bill over to you, Senator," Stermas says.

"We can always try to push it through from our side as a Senate bill," Yeats answers.

"It hardly ever works if we've killed it on this side," Stermas says.

Yeats nods. "I know."

"Well," Mace says, I gotta leadership meetin' over at the Speaker's office." He pulls himself to his feet and tugs his jacket down. "John, I wanted you t' come over and fill Sam in on our troubles."

"Glad to," Stermas says. "I like shoulders to cry on."

Mace grins at him. " 'F you fellers want anything, jus' ask Henry or the girls."

"Thanks, Mace," Yeats says.

Mace goes out through his office, winking at Maude and Ruth. He heads down the hallway to the main corridor, thinking about the goddamned contrariness of the human race. The same people who are always hollering about welfare bills are now hollering about a bill to get social policy costs off the government's back.

He walks to the elevator marked "Members Only," rides up to the next floor, and chugs through the Speaker's lobby with its red carpets, portraits of past Speakers, and side rooms draped with newspapers on racks. The area exudes the rich, leisured atmosphere of a Victorian gentlemen's club.

The Speaker's rooms, a corridor's width from the House chamber, are among the most ornate in the Capitol. The ocher walls are painted with elegant trim that flows toward an arched ceiling covered with murals depicting, via the nineteenth-century passion for allegory, democracy's nobler sentiments. Immense chandeliers bathe the outer office in glittering white light. Mace sits down in a leather chair, his heavy body tilted forward, hands resting on his hams, the dead cigar butt between two fingers, a booklet entitled "House Worksheet" in his lap.

At times like this Mace Applegate doesn't know how he does what he does, because for the moment he has forgotten how to do it. He has always sensed the House before trying to analyze how it will go on a particular bill. That initial perception has always given him a feeling of how to direct his analyzing and persuading efforts. Now he is baffled. He can't sense the thing at all. His new ally, Stetson, has even reported peculiar pressures running against HR 1418 in the black caucus. It doesn't make sense.

"The Speaker will see you now, Mr. Applegate."

Mace looks up at a girl who has come from the inner office. "Thanks, Mary. Mr. Hatfield shown up yet?"

"Yes, sir. The Leader's in with the Speaker." She lowers her voice. "They've been talking to the President. Mr. Howard is on his way over."

The Speaker's office is a miniature in elegance of the outer room of the suite. It has its own chandelier. From the walls portraits of earlier, greater Speakers look out in tolerance.

The Speaker, a tall, morose-looking man from Pennsylvania, is on the telephone. He holds his hand out and shakes with Mace. The Whip sits down on a sofa beside Randolph Hatfield, the Majority Leader. Hatfield has put on weight in the year and a half since he gave himself over to brooding about his family tragedy. His body strains at the seersucker suit wrapped around it. He has a square head, curly, moist black hair, eyes cushioned by deep folds. His face looks haggard as he reads some papers in his lap. He looks up. "Hello, Mace." His voice has the deep whispery hush that one associates with old, kegged bourbon.

"Harya, Randy?"

"You smoking that cigar or just carrying it?" Hatfield asks.

Mace chuckles. "I'm always pretendin' I'm about t' smoke it."

Hatfield makes no response, facial or verbal.

The Speaker hangs up the telephone. "Well, Mace," he says jovially, "how are you this hot, miserable day?"

"Hot 'n' miserable," Mace says. "Looky, Mistuh Speaker, Mary tells me Lou Howard is comin' over. Anything you want to tell me 'fore he gets here?"

The Speaker tilts back in his chair, his round face relaxed in a contemplative grin. "Oh, I guess I'd better—" He breaks off, the smile fades as he thinks. He looks back at Mace. "We've just had a conversation with the President. He's angry. He wants action."

"Yes, suh, Mistuh Speaker, I know that. An' he's gettin' action, the best kind we got."

"He wants the revision of the Revenue Act out of Ways and Means and he wants HR 1418 out on the floor and passed." The Speaker's tone is curious, almost pleased, as he describes the President's impatience.

Mace is suddenly alarmed. He knows that the Speaker is churlish and defensive about his power in dealing with Washington and unsure of that power in dealing with the House. Mace knows specifically that the Speaker hates the President's guts— as he hates anyone who outshines him. And now Mace is alarmed. "Mistuh Speaker," he says, "I hope you're gonna hold that bill 'til we're ready for it."

The smile returns and the Speaker tilts back in his chair again. He shakes his head, looking down at the floor. "Why, Mace, I'm surprised at you." He looks up, still smiling. "You know I'm a good party man. I try to accommodate the President."

"Yes, suh, Mistuh Speaker, but—"

Still smiling, the Speaker says, "I've scheduled HR 1418 to come to the floor a week from today, Mace. Next Thursday."

Mace sits silently for a moment, trying to stifle his panic. "Mistuh Speaker," he says slowly, "I wish you wouldn't do that. Goddamn, I wish you wouldn't. Mistuh Speaker, we ain't gonna have the votes by then."

And you know it, you sumbitch, Mace says to Mace.

When Thomas Brackett Reed was elected a freshman member of the 45th Congress in 1876, the Democrats were in control of the House and the clutter of rules, procedures, traditions, and precedents had become such a self-defeating morass that individual Congressmen could indulge themselves in conduct that ranged from the indolent and the arrogant to the bizarre. The House itself, wrote Reed, "led a gelatinous existence, the scorn of all vertebrate animals." The 51st Congress, to which Reed was elected Speaker and in which he won his celebrated showdown with recalcitrant Democrats on the nonsensical rules, probably passed more legislation of historic importance than any Congress since the Civil War. Burdened by the junk of tradition, the House was barely functioning when Reed took charge of it. He was a strong man who cleaned it out, repaired it, and made it work again.

The last strong Speaker was the great Sam Rayburn of Texas, who parlayed his own granite character, his network of alliances in both parties, and his mastery of the rules into a force that made the House work. But the exemplary political characters of Reed and Rayburn illustrate what is wrong with the House: by itself it doesn't work very well; its representative function slumps and its managerial function bogs down.

Reform of the House of Representatives is usually a boring subject for outsiders. The reformers of the present years seem to go on interminably about altering obstruse details of operation —modifying the seniority system, strengthening the Democratic caucus, persuading the Speaker and the leaders to more activist roles, restoring the twenty-one-day rule, changing the system of committee assignments, and so forth. Yet this isn't just tinkering with inhouse trivia. It is an effort to change those procedural parts that, when assembled, create the political whole. If the House of Representatives is a failure, it is a political failure.

In arguing for such a House, James Madison expounded his theory that the body couldn't perform its real function without an "immediate dependence upon and an intimate sympathy with the people." To guarantee that relationship, Madison concluded, "frequent elections are unquestionably the only policy. . . ." That is as good a mechanistic theory of representative democracy as anyone has ever come up with. It presumes that the American people will express something of themselves as they elect men and women to the House. It further presumes that the thing expressed will be reckoned with in the making of law and the process of government.

What is reflected by the membership of the House of Representatives is the sum of reasonable American ideologies. As it emerges in the House, left- or right-wing irrationalism may occasionally find expression there too. But that sum *is* the American median, the point from which the House can safely proceed in the making of laws.

But in its *results* the House doesn't express the American median—even though its membership does. The House's will is suppressed by its procedures. The procedures limit legislation to that which the leadership and the committees think will go through. The chairmen influence what the committees think. The maze of rules, precedents, and traditions leaves too much House power in the institutionalized hands of its leaders and chairmen. Although the shifting voting patterns of the nation are alleviating the situation somewhat, it is not happening fast enough. The accumulated years of the House's great survivors and its accumulated procedures prevent the political median that is the House of Representatives from expressing itself. That is why the reformers, who must always work from within the House, hack away at changing the procedures.

All this still leaves us with the question: Should the median even be expressed any longer? The question is not whether it can; the House's capacity to reflect the spectrum of American ideology insures that it can. But should it be expressed, and if so why?

In practical terms, the ideological median is a reflection of what the American majority will permit the Process to do. Sometimes it is even a reflection of what the majority would like the Process to do. There is no magic in majorities. A vast number of people can be as wrong as a small number. And a system that bases itself on functioning majorities, as the American system does, is ignoring the persistent problem of minorities. But in the final analysis democratic government, even a modified democratic government such as ours, is a bargain between the governed and their governors. The bargain is based on plausibility. If the governed believe that the policies governing them are plausible, government can work. If they cease to believe that government is plausible, the system is in trouble. In recent years Americans have believed less and less in the plausibility of their government. By enacting legislation whose political intent and motive are derived from the American ideological median, the House could assist in the restoration of plausibility.

Madison believed that justice is the end of civil government. In the sense of a mass watching its government operate, "Justice" is a hard word to define. The French theological *penseuse* Simone Weil did better than most when she wrote: "Justice consists in seeing that no harm is done to men. Whenever a man cries inwardly 'Why am I being hurt?' harm is being done to him. He is often mistaken when he tries to define the harm, and why and by whom it is being inflicted upon him. But the cry itself is infallible."

Justice in this sense, then, means to heed that cry, to assuage its pain, and to raise the infinite possibilities of improvement. That is what representative government should do—what the House of Representatives does not do by failing in its representative function. And that is why the reformers pick at House procedures and why they must continue to do so until the political system is restored and great justice may be achieved—for it is *the* end of civil government.

5: The Power Brokers

> . . . show me my faults and make me recognize them.
> . . . This being most necessary for a ruler, since there are
> few or none at all to be found who will do this, commonly
> refraining out of awe or self-interest. . . .
>
> Maria Theresa of Austria to
> her adviser, Count Tarouca

A mythical beast slithers and hisses through the American political imagination. It lurks in the shadows cast by Presidents, muttering Iago-like advice and counsel that invariably result in disaster. It reveres nothing but the bitch goddess of self-profit. Foul and repellent, it manipulates those hoisted to glory by the people and then writhes away, shaking in asthmatic laughter while others suffer the catastrophes it has caused by its whispered counsel. Despite the fact that the mythical beast is nonexistent, Americans need it. Who else can be blamed for bad or unpopular presidential actions? The President and thereby the people who elected him? God forbid. The beast who is the secret adviser is to blame.

The myth of the evil genius lurking in the background behind administrators, governors, and kings has always been with us in one form or another. The American manifestation of the legend was personified by a man named Amos Kendall, one of the key figures in Andrew Jackson's celebrated kitchen cabinet.

Born and brilliantly educated in New England, Kendall moved to Kentucky and became a newspaperman. Jackson met and was impressed with him and eventually brought the editor into his administration as fourth auditor in the Treasury. There, as a good reporter, Kendall dug up evidence of some dazzling swindles perpetrated by his predecessor, which impressed Jackson even more. Kendall moved closer to the President. The public began to know that somebody named Amos Kendall was exerting influence over Jackson, but few people ever saw him because Kendall's health was chronically frightful and he rarely appeared in public. Bent, prematurely white-haired and pale, cursed with a hacking cough, and given to wearing a bandage around his head for migraine, Kendall was a Uriah Heepish sort of man. He was superbly typecast as an evil genius of power to those who did see him. "He is supposed to be the moving spirit of the whole administration," wrote an English visitor, Harriet Martineau, in a flutter, "the thinker, the planner, the doer." "He was the President's thinking machine," wailed Congressman Henry A. Wise a year after Jackson left office. "Ay, and his lying machine! . . . Nothing was well done without the aid of this diabolical genius!" As late as 1840, eighty-one-year-old John Quincy Adams was tottering around obsessed with the idea that the baleful vapor of the adviser had engulfed not only Jackson but Martin Van Buren. "Both," he wheezed, "have been for twelve years the tool of Amos Kendall, the ruling mind of their dominion."

The facts about Kendall are a good deal less exciting than the hair-raising legends. He was a good writer and an articulate speaker, and Andrew Jackson wasn't. Kendall would sit for hours beside the President's bed while Old Hickory smoked stogies and poured out his thoughts, notions, prejudices, and visions, which Kendall would then translate into the orderly prose of presidential speeches and messages. He made himself useful in other literary, clerical, and advisory ways and was rewarded by being appointed Postmaster General. In the last year of his life Jackson tried to get Polk to name Kendall minister to Spain in place of Washington Irving, whose name Jackson couldn't spell. Whatever his intimacy and proximity, it is absurd to think that Amos Kendall could make a political genius like Andrew Jackson surrender power or do things that he didn't want to do. Still, it was useful for people like Congressman Wise to have a minion close to the center of power to shoot at when they wanted to hit a popular former President. So the American legend of sinister-advisers in the White House was born, and presidential aides as varied as Bernard Baruch, Henry Kissinger, William Henry Seward, Averell Harriman, Edward House, Sherman Adams, Elihu Root, Abe Fortas, and Clark Clifford have been hounded or amused by it ever since.

Modern nations are complexes of soluble, insoluble, and disaster-tempting problems and of people who don't like one another much. When bad things happen the tendency is to blame the leader, who has to defend himself while trying to keep hundreds of other bad things from happening. There are few nations with the civilized decency of the British, who, as Sir William Blackstone points out, constitutionally decree that their king can't do anything wrong.

History has never produced the perfect ruler because God or genetics has never produced the man of infinite capabilities. Rulers and governors need other abilities and perspectives to supplement their own. Around each of them in history there swarms a clutter of chamberlains, grand viziers, deputies, ministers, and wizards to share in the burdens of state and sometimes even in the consequences. George Washington had an absolutely admirable personal character, but as he wrote to Henry Knox in the spring of 1789, he lacked that "competency of political skill, abilities, and inclination which are necessary to manage the helm." Without political skill Washington couldn't govern, so he found several people to fill the gap in his own nature. The most durable of them was a tornado of intellectual energy with something slightly less than an admirable character, Alexander Hamilton. Though he was a thoroughly arrogant snob who thought of the American people as a "beast" and the Constitution as a "frail and worthless fabric," Hamilton had a first-class mind, amazing drive, and visions of American industrial greatness; in addition, he was a tough, shrewd political strategist (with the enemies to prove it). He became indispensable to Washington.

Americans, who tend to adopt an oddly ambivalent, love-hate attitude toward their federal government, would probably like to worship their Presidents as kings—once the Presidents are dead. Hence they intuitively dislike the people who gather in the White House to help Chief Executives govern. The commonest complaint is that presidential advisers, counselors, and power brokers aren't elected by anybody, yet they exert great influence. That may be just as well. The greatest of presidential advisers have been so long on intellect, glacial discretion, and intense personal loyalty and so short on charisma that they probably couldn't get themselves elected to anything.

Now and in history, presidential advisers are goading reflections on the imperfection of man and democracy, and that too makes them unpleasant to contemplate. But one fact mitigates the distaste with which great presidential advisers are regarded: government and the American past would be a lot sorrier without them.

Dusk comes. Washington goes slack.

The Senate chamber has been empty since four o'clock. Now the dome lights on the Capitol dim as the Speaker gavels the House into adjournment. The evening traffic thins in the city's center and reclots on the bridges and arteries leading to the suburbs, to the forested rise of Cleveland Park and the slatternly sprawl of northeast Washington. On this cool, soft evening the western sky is streaked in pale blue and flame behind Mr. Lincoln's memorial. Jefferson looks north from his cage of Grecian columns and the night lights come on around the Custis-Lee mansion above Arlington Cemetery.

This is the hour—cocktail hour in Georgetown, children's hour in the suburbs—that enigmatic passage between day and dark when old women die and men depart from the strivings and mutterings of government and become once again failed or fulfilling husbands, good or bad fathers; when they turn away from the groaning of the world on its axis to the somehow more maddening problems of disposal units with forks stuck down them, sons who can't (or won't) pass algebra, and overdue bills from the garage.

Day's ending or no, many of the Process' people are still involved in it. Senatorial aides are plotting strategy or angling for new jobs at the Rotunda or in the bar of the Congressional Hotel on Capitol Hill; typewriters prattle overnight news stories behind the frosted doors of the National Press Building; four Cabinet officers are still at work, one in the long, gallery-shaped office of the Secretary of Defense. On the twelfth floor of an office building just up Connecticut Avenue from the White House a short, middle-aged lawyer in a rumpled suit is mixing an Old Fashioned for his partner. He looks like an aging boy—tiny hands, bright eyes lying on the surface of his face, a youth with the creases of years worn around the eyes' edges and the flares of the pug nose, whose tousled quarter-bushel of hair is laced with gray. As he drops ice cubes into a glass, cigarette dangling French style from the corner of his mouth and eyes squinting against the smoke, he discusses an amendment to a tax bill before the Senate and how the outcome—up or down—will affect two of the firm's clients, a Massachusetts bank and a chemical company in St. Louis. He speaks with the lingering ghost of an Alabama accent, most of it lost through the years in Cambridge, New York, and Washington. It is a voice famous in this city for the causes it has espoused in Washington's inner councils—civil rights and labor (when that counted), public power, and the protection of the accused.

The flow of raspy, precise talk is interrupted by a buzzer. The rumpled lawyer puts down the glass in his hand, crosses the room, and picks up the telephone. "Yes, Mrs. Dunn?"

"It's the White House, Mr. Marks."

The lawyer puts his hand over the mouthpiece and turns back to his partner. "I wonder if you'd excuse me, George?"

The partner nods, rises, whispers "See you tomorrow," and leaves by a side door. Like everyone else intimately connected with David Marks, the partner knows by some imprecise sense what those calls mean. They are summonses for the talents of a somewhat inexplicable man—talents as specific and yet indefinable as those of an artist's for line, color, perspective, and the translation of feeling into form. David Marks is a compilation of distinct abilities—an immense intellect carefully compartmentalized into sections for conception and sections for detail, an abrasive sort of charm, utter discretion, common sense, and an uncanny set of instincts about what will and won't work in Washington. He has parlayed all this into a rarefied, offstage role close to the very center of the Process.

Alone, Marks raises the telephone again. "Put 'em on."

After a few clicks another female voice says, "Mr. Brasher's office."

"This is David Marks."

"Oh, good evening, Mr. Marks. Can you hold on a moment? Mr. Brasher would like a word with you."

"Yeah, okay," Marks says. "I'll hang on."

Within twenty seconds the telephone line is punched back to life again in the White House. "David?"

"Hi, Paul. How's everything?"

The appointments secretary laughs. "Listen, if Ways and Means hangs on to the revision of the 1973 Revenue Act much longer, we'll all be back practicing law in Schenectady. Aside from contemplating that sobering fact, I'm fine. And you?"

"Well," Marks says, "some hot-rock columnist wrote today that the Chairman is about to chew the President up and spit him out in little pieces. Your tax revision problem is going public. Somebody over there is crying on the shoulders of the press."

"Don't I know it," Brasher says. "It's getting a lot of people down."

"They ought to keep it to themselves," Marks retorts. "This isn't a political struggle between the President and the Chairman, but if you keep thinking it is and saying it is, it will be."

"If only we could figure out which direction Ways and Means is going and how long it's going to take them," Brasher says.

"Yeah," Marks says. "I suppose the President's edgy."

"To say the least. I understand you called me this afternoon."

"Um," Marks answers. "On the revision of the Revenue Act, as a matter of fact. You remember he had me in last week and asked me to think about it, gave me some data."

"Yeah, I sure do. We could use a little good advice at this point, if just to relieve the atmosphere. You ready to come in?"

"Anytime."

There is a pause at the other end of the line as if something were being studied. "Ohh-kay," Brasher says slowly. "How about this evening? Going out?"

"Yeah, but that's not important."

Another pause. "How about half an hour from now?"

"Fine," Marks says. "I'll catch up with Dorothy at the Grahams' later. I'm still not sure I should get mixed up in this."

Brasher laughs. "You won't get hurt. Listen, if we get the act amended, it'll be those $50,000-a-year clients of yours who have to earn their tax credits. So nobody can accuse you of self-interest when the press finds out you're helping us with the New Partnership."

"Nobody but those clients," Marks says.

"Yeah, but they'll be so dazzled at all the stories about how you help Presidents that they won't mind that you've heaped a lot of work on them. Besides, you'll be a popular hero. We think we have the country with us on tax revision."

"Shouldn't be surprised," Marks says.

"Want me to send a car for you?"

"No, it's a pleasant evening. I'll walk."

"All right," Brasher says. "Basement door. I'll tell the northwest gate you're coming. And David—thanks. He needs you."

"Don't mention it," Marks says. "We'd hate to lose you to Schenectady. See you in twenty minutes." He hangs up the telephone, takes a light gray tweed coat and a battered hat from the closet, and goes to the outer office, pausing at his secretary's desk. "Will you call my wife? We're dining at Senator Graham's house. You tell her to go on and I'll meet her there."

Mrs. Dunn nods. She is a handsome, brown-haired divorcee who has been David Marks' secretary for eleven years and combines at least one of his qualities—total discretion—with a chronic and sometimes annoying irreverence for what her boss does around the thrones of Washington power. "I'll tell her not to expect you too soon." She grins. "Don't start any wars."

"Good night, Mrs. Dunn."

"Good night, Mr. Marks."

Overcoat tossed over his shoulders and crumpled hat on his head, Marks rides the elevator down to the first floor, wondering if somebody couldn't get Mrs. Dunn to stop that.

Globular gas lamps cast pale light onto the façades of the handsome nineteenth-century town houses lining the west side of Lafayette Park. Marks pauses to look at the Decatur house on the corner of I Street and Jackson Place. Something he read long ago is prompted out of a pocket of his mind, something about Stephen Decatur being a lecherous and intemperate man. He was bull-headed, anyway. The lawyer remembers that much.

He walks slowly down the park side of the street so that he can admire the houses, whose restoration was originally the idea of Mrs. John F. Kennedy. The plan for Lafayette Park was one of the last things considered by the doomed President before his assassination. The houses are redolent of a more parochial and intimate Washington—of the time of Henry Adams (though he lived on the north side of the park), James G. Blaine, Roscoe Conkling, and that half-forgotten but quite lovable President, Rutherford B. Hayes, a victim of the filthiest era in American politics. Hayes was alternately sneered at as "His Fraudulency" because a gaggle of Republican politicians stole his election for him and as "Old Granny" because of his personal rectitude (he wouldn't serve hard liquor at the White House). As he walks, Marks remembers reading—or somebody telling him—that Hayes wrote beautiful letters. He reminds himself to get Mrs. Dunn to find out if a book of them has been published.

A cluster of tired people stands beneath a street lamp waiting for a northbound bus. They barely notice the small, slightly rumpled man strolling by, his coat thrown capelike over his shoulders, the crushed hat worn at a slight tilt, which permits clusters of his thick hair to protrude from beneath the brim. They cannot know that he is depressurizing his mind, and thus preparing it for work, by permitting himself the pleasures of reflecting on Mrs. Kennedy, the bull-headedness of Stephen Decatur, the curious death of Mrs. Henry Adams, who committed suicide by drinking photo developer, and the letters of Rutherford B. Hayes. They cannot know that, as the hour ends and the Process proceeds along its evening course, Washington's most celebrated power broker is going to work.

The primary social difference between the capitals of the United States and Great Britain is that one is obsessed with rank and the other is not. Washington is fascinated by—indeed, orders its life through—the delineation of a person by his rating in the political administration of the moment. London isn't, possibly because Britain has a built-in system of rank. Washingtonians are attuned to who counts most with the President at any particular time. London couldn't care less about who influences the Prime Minister. Washington will invite the most appalling people to dinner if they're important. London populates its dinner tables with the interesting, the brilliant, and the eccentric. In Washington a man wears his authority like a case of elephantiasis. If you don't know he's on the White House staff when you meet him at a cocktail party, he'll usually find a way of telling you. In London a droll, slightly collapsible man who has listened all evening to your theories about Germany will, if pressed about his occupation, murmur, "Oh, I fiddle about at the Foreign Office. I do krauts." That means that he's head of the Northern Department, which deals with Germany.

There are a few basic rules that rank-conscious Washingtonians must follow if they want to understand the game. The first is that not everyone close to a President has influence with him. Almost every President has had his pals, his friends who come in purely for diversion. Theodore Roosevelt's famous "tennis cabinet" was a collection of buddies—some political, some not—who played with the President (to stay in, you couldn't beat him). They included the French ambassador Jusserand, a Secret Service man, and sometimes an Oklahoma cowboy named Abernathy. Inclusion in the tennis cabinet didn't necessarily mean that one could speak to Roosevelt about policy. Calvin Coolidge had a remarkable friend named Frank Stearns, a wealthy Boston department store owner who had an absolute genius for saying nothing. He was once clocked in the company of a large group of friends with whom he stayed for twelve hours without uttering a word. Stearns and Coolidge used to sit together in taciturn silence looking out the window. That was Coolidge's idea of great fun. Once when Stearns did manage to get out a few words in recommendation of a particular man for a federal judgeship, Coolidge told him to mind his own business. Herbert Hoover was addicted to the pleasures of medicine ball tossing and used to have a few friends in before breakfast to toss with. Inevitably they came to be called the "medicine ball cabinet," but none of them had any great influence on the President's actions or decisions.

Presidential advisers obviously must be men of far greater dimension than skills at tennis, medicine ball tossing, and window gazing. Depending upon the service they render to a President, they are chosen either for a particular talent (press relations, economic administration, and so on) or for a whole range of attributes including political sagacity, intelligence, and the ability to judge the effect of a particular act or decision upon a diverse gallery of people affected by it.

In its original form the Constitution makes only a veiled reference to people advising the Presidents. It says that his department heads must report to him in writing. There is no other provision for advisers. When Franklin Roosevelt came to office —at a moment of an immense quantum jump in the problems of the nation and the responsibilities of the President—the law permitted him only four aides above the level of clerk. Previous to that, presidential advisers had come from a variety of sources— from the Cabinet, as in the Washington-Hamilton relationship, from sinecures salted away in other departments of the government, like Amos Kendall's at the Treasury, from Congress, and from outside government altogether. The two fundamental categories of advisers now and in history are those who in one way or another are within government, making their living at it and those who at the time of their advising have no formal connection with government. With political Washington's passion for giving trendy names to spectacular men or events, the greatest of the outsiders have come to be known as power brokers.

Most Presidents have had them—the brilliant, intuitive outsiders who counsel, do errands, act as intermediaries, and sometimes stand in the full glare of a collapsed policy or disastrous action to take the blame. Jefferson got to know, be impressed with, and ultimately rely on the French émigré Pierre Samuel Du Pont de Nemours, a struggling businessman who bolstered Jefferson, advised him, and even undertook a delicate private mission to France to dicker with Tallyrand over the Louisiana Purchase. In return Jefferson gave Du Pont de Nemours' powder factory government business, thereby helping in the establishment of the Du Pont industrial empire. Tyler had a collection of Virginia educators and jurists who advised him as outsiders; Grant, predictably, used soldiers. Wilson formed, with Edward M. House, the most intriguing President-adviser relationship in American history; FDR had his cabal of Columbia University professors. Kennedy and Johnson had Clark Clifford, and almost everybody between Wilson and Truman had Bernard Baruch. Because of the unique position of such detached outsiders as advisors, almost all eighteenth- and nineteenth-century presidents and all modern Democratic Chief Executives have used power brokers.

Some of them object to the name. "It implies a man who's buying and selling," says one, "and there simply isn't any profit in advising Presidents." In that they get no paycheck, he's right. But invariably profitable law practices, high government jobs, and shimmering awe come to power brokers as an indirect result of their service to a President. In the rank-happy milieu of Washington they are durable objects of splendor. In addition to their proximity to the top, power brokers have the glamour of secrecy and mystery. Inevitably they are sought after for more than their value as dinner table adornments. If one is brilliant and discreet enough to advise a President, the logic goes, one is worth a good deal of deference and reward as a counselor to lesser men.

Seen in another light, the title "power broker" is quite apt. Fundamentally, the adviser is helping his President to retain and broaden his personal power in the Process, his capacity to move things from one place to another. The adviser to Presidents carries about him the implicit aura of a President's power; he has authority, which is the belief of others that he can make powerful men do things. Hence, like any other broker, he deals in and with something that belongs to somebody else.

In the twentieth century all great power brokers except Elihu Root have been Democrats. This fact arises from the alchemic mysteries of political personality. Either pressured by or themselves deeply rooted in modern American conservatism, Republican Presidents tend to distrust power and dislike it. The innate pessimism of the conservative presents them with dark visions of power gone berserk. That is why Republican presidential candidates like Richard Nixon talk about stripping power from Washington and returning it, in some way or another, to state and local governments. Fearing power, most Republican Presidents have tended to limit its uses to those methods precisely defined by law. Among many other things that excludes the use of outsiders, of unlicensed brokers, to help Presidents harvest and expand their power. General Eisenhower was advised by his brother Milton, but he relied mostly on the White House staff. Democrats, on the other hand, have an equally intuitive *fascination* with power. Tending to be liberals, Democratic Presidents look upon power as something good, as an essentially benevolent force, something you can't get too much of because you use it to solve problems. They are students of power, have been tutored in its use by their Democratic predecessors, and have no compunction about drawing in outsiders—Democratic outsiders—to advise and help with the deploying of power in the Process.

The greatest power brokers employed by Democratic administrations from Wilson onward have had a good many qualities in common. They have been as discreet as Clark Clifford, who served Kennedy and Johnson, as worldly as Bernard Baruch, who advised Wilson and subsequent Presidents, as rarely intuitive about Washington as Abe Fortas, the Johnson power broker, as passionately devoted to their particular man and his cause as Wilson's adviser Edward House.

The power broker tends to emerge from the gross national

crisis of his time; he is a man who is an expert or becomes an expert on some aspect of that crisis and whose expertise, coming to the attention of a President in one way or another, is sought. Thus Bernard Baruch, who once described himself before a congressional committee as a "speculator," was a Southern Democratic progressive with an enormous knowledge of the ways and men of Wall Street, which meant that he also knew a great deal about American industry and the economy. He had made, lost, and made again fortunes on the stock exchange; he was a scholarly man who could read Greek and Latin. All these abilities attracted him to Woodrow Wilson, who put him to work on the economic and financial aspects of World War I. Baruch's brilliant maneuvering and his talent for bringing hostile forces together in conciliatory meetings staved off what could have been a painful confrontation for Wilson between Southern farmers selling cotton to Germany and Germany's enemy, Britain, which wanted them to stop it. Operating more or less on his own, Baruch combined his vast knowledge of stock and commodity markets with his broad range of friendships in Washington and London and the strange, compelling power of his amiable nature to work out a compromise. Later he turned the same talents against the British, who refused to control the price of jute on the Calcutta market. In a display of the power broker's requisite talent for hard-nosed rough stuff at the right moment, Baruch got the U.S. Treasury to cut off the silver payments that stabilized the Indian economy. The British discovered that they could, after all, control the price of jute. Using sentiment, patriotism, and appeals to conscience, Baruch got the usually choleric H. C. Frick to set a fair price for steel plates considerably below that being asked of the government by the rest of the industry. In all this Baruch's advice and actions produced the results that the President wanted, sometimes before the President even knew he had a problem. Baruch's performance so enchanted Wilson— who called his power broker "Doctor Facts"—that he became an adviser on all sorts of matters that had nothing to do with money, commodities, the economy, or industry. He worked with Wilson at the Versailles conference and tried later to persuade the

President to accept a modification of the treaty's controversial Article X as the price of Senate ratification. From a specialized adviser he had become a general one.

This has been the pattern through which all outside advisers have progressed to the status of power broker. Clark Clifford, who began as an assistant naval attaché to Truman, made himself an expert in the gross national crisis of *his* time, the cold war, and as special counsel to the President he ended up advising Truman on such diverse matters as strategy in the 1948 election and how to handle John L. Lewis, the ferocious and obdurate boss of the United Mine Workers. Clifford was a master of the requisite power broker ability to detach oneself from one's own instincts in order to give cold, objective advice. Along with Oscar Chapman, Clifford was a leader of the liberal forces around President Truman, and presumably he was imbued with the liberal's sensitivity to the rights and reputation of others. In the 1948 election Truman was threatened with the loss of liberal votes by the Progressive party of Henry Wallace. A former Secretary of Agriculture, former Vice President, and a rather messianic man, Wallace was running a third-party movement in the election, apparently to steal Democratic votes, defeat Truman, and thus position himself as the Democratic candidate in 1952. In advising Truman on how to fight off the Wallace ploy, Clifford wrote that efforts should be made to "identify him and isolate him in the public mind with the Communists." It was unattractive advice and it probably made the liberal in Clifford writhe a bit, but it seems to have worked.

Clifford and most other latter-day power brokers have moved in and out of government. Clifford was on the White House staff when he advised Truman, made a fortune as a Washington lawyer during the Eisenhower years, advised Kennedy on the transition between the outgoing Eisenhower administration and the New Frontier, and was outside adviser and then Secretary of Defense for Lyndon Johnson. The alternating government and nongovernment roles seem to enhance each other, especially if the power broker is successful in private life. Government and the business world tend to be frightfully naive about each other, and a man who does well in one tends to be vested with a rather shiny mystique in the other. Two of the greatest power brokers, Baruch and Edward House, refused Cabinet posts because they felt that the jobs would make them too visible and controversial and therefore less useful to Woodrow Wilson. Also both were wealthy men who didn't particularly need to parlay their government reputations into personal fortunes after their government service was over.

There are both obvious and not so obvious reasons for the special value of outside advisers to Presidents. The relationship they have with the Chief Executive and the things they are able to do for and with him differ from the relationships and functions of staff advisers. Obviously the power broker can afford to be more candid, to tell Presidents those unpleasant but necessary things that Chief Executives and other mortals don't like to hear. The power broker can't be fired because he has never been hired. He can just be expelled from the presence of the President or, at worst, maneuvered into a position where he takes the rap for something that misfires. "All Presidents are cannibalistic," says one veteran Washington power broker. "They should be allowed a certain number of advisers to devour for self-protection. The adviser mustn't mind." If the devoured man is a staff adviser he obviously minds a good deal more than the power broker because his career and livelihood are sacrificed. The power broker is able to just shrug and go back to his law practice, having lost nothing but a delicious proximity to importance—and that loss is usually only temporary if his value is proven and his relationship to the President sound.

Being an outsider, the power broker escapes the intense, introverted atmosphere of the White House, in which the world, the nation, and Washington are viewed with a partisan distortion. That atmosphere is in itself part of the problem of presidential dealing in the Process; it can make for touchiness, belligerence, and the unique exasperation of those who are under great and constant pressure. Outsiders with influence—power brokers and leaders of the President's party in Congress—can temper the intensity of the White House. Furthermore, as an outsider, the power broker is known to the rest of political Washington as one, close to but not of the President. Other Process people tend to be more candid with the power broker than they would be with the White House staff member, who carries the full aura of partisanship in the President's cause. The candor that the power broker receives is carried back to the White House in the form of realistic advice.

The power broker may or may not be the sort of man to whom people reveal themselves fully; he may or may not have detailed factual knowledge of every important event taking place in Washington at any given moment. But he is invariably someone of keen intuition about the city, the Process, and the people who hold power. His intuition is partly a gift of nature, partly a result of his long experience in Washington and his participation in the Process. That well-honed ability to instinctively sense what will and won't work in Washington and the nation—to know when trouble is brewing, when the hounds of opposition are being gathered into a pack under the pressure of some issue or debate, when a foe is weakening, when the time of a particular idea or policy has or has not come—that is the essence of what the power broker has to offer a President. Good advisers have kept Presidents from making intemperate, damned fool speeches, from pushing programs that are better shelved for a more auspicious day, from lying and taking impulsive actions that could start wars and lose elections. Cruising through the mottled, Florentine atmosphere of the Process, picking up its downcurrents of anger, obsession, confusion, hope, and desire, the power broker becomes a grid upon which warning lights flash and bells ring when something is about to go wrong.

Political history, like all other history, is compiled from what happened, not from what didn't happen. Those things that power brokers have prevented Presidents from doing are nonevents. Hence the best illustration of the power broker's preventive value is something bad that happened because no persuasive, intuitive man was around to stop it.

The worst wound that President Nixon inflicted upon himself before the 1970 midterm elections was the nomination of G.

Harrold Carswell of Florida as associate justice of the Supreme Court. Having just been rebuffed on the nomination of Clement Haynesworth for the same seat, the President was angry and baffled. He had battled the Senate into an exhausted, ugly mood, had disenchanted Senators of his own party, and had already lost power because in the Haynesworth affair he had publicly shown himself unable to do something he wanted to do. Hostilities were running high; storm signals were up all over the place. Senators, congressional aides, reporters, and other Process participants sensed the mood. Inside the White House the ruling desires were (1) to force the Senate to take whomever the President chose and (2) to use the whole Carswell squabble as a bloody shirt in Mr. Nixon's drive to woo the South. What was badly needed at that point was someone from the Process mainstream, who had the requisite clout and the President's confidence to wrench the perspective around toward reality. The otherwise able Senate Minority Leader, Hugh Scott of Pennsylvania, seems to have tried and failed. The White House forwarded the name of Carswell, an amiable but unqualified man (so unqualified that the Republican voters of Florida later rejected him as a senatorial candidate). In the ensuing debacle Carswell was defeated and the President made a public statement that amounted to the preposterous claim that Carswell had been turned down because the Senate hated the South.

In this Mr. Nixon was operating largely on the advice of John Mitchell, his Attorney General, who was a member of the circle and therefore a victim of its mood, a man almost completely inexperienced in the subtleties and warning signs of the Process. In his inadequacies, Mr. Mitchell was a mirror image of everything a good power broker should be, and the episode is a pretty good illustration of why power brokers are useful people to have around. Mr. Nixon didn't have one.

As advisers on presidential decisions and actions, as consultants on presidential problems, power brokers are usually saved for the big crises. They come into a problem or decision-making struggle at its penultimate moment. Along with their intuition, common sense, and studied detachment—that quality that Abe

Fortas calls "deliberate schizophrenia"—the power brokers' final, unique value is that they share exactly the same perspective as the President.

As a matter moves upward toward the moment of decision by the Chief Executive, all the nerve ends and glands of the relevant government departments and agencies begin to quiver. Special pleaders gather upon the White House, funneling in data to bolster this department's interest in the matter, maneuvering to negate the importance of that agency's information. Politicians, generals, civil servants, and experts vie and quarrel as the President's staff sifts, winnows, chooses, and discards among the facts and arguments presented. A final brief is ultimately packaged and sent to the President. In the process of selecting the information that it thinks pertinent to the President's decision, the staff itself becomes bruised and blurred; bits of discarded arguments, lost causes, and old disputes cling to the Chief Executive's men.

Because he comes in at the penultimate stage, the power broker is unsullied by all the intermediary jockeying; he sees what the President sees, works from the data that the President receives, testing it for implication and possibility and placing it against all his intuitions about the Process. He may participate in weeks of debate (President Johnson used to invite his power brokers to sit in on staff meetings that dealt with the problems they were advising on), but he debates on the highest level. His perspective on the problem is focused from the same angle as that of the chief executive. The staff advisers, the regular White House people, are immersed in the preceding clutter.

How to advise is a matter of contention among power brokers themselves and depends largely on the President they are serving. Abe Fortas, for example, received data on a problem or a decision from President Johnson, took it home, studied it, thought about it, and then returned to lay out a series of options before the President. "I was never a bottom-line man," Fortas commented afterward. He saw the relationship as one of lawyer and client, the lawyer spelling out the various courses that were open and the President-client making the final choice. Averell Harriman has contempt for the option system. He believes that

Richard Neustadt, the political historian, first identified the option approach in a book read by John F. Kennedy between his election and his inauguration. Kennedy thereafter liked his advisers to bring him options. Harriman was more direct and blunt with Roosevelt and Truman. "We used to give the President flat recommendations for action," he says. "The President would say 'What's the best thing to do?' and we'd tell him. He could either take our advice or ignore it."

The President uses his friends for diversion and his advisers for solace and reassurance as well as wisdom. Sometimes that is the most valuable function the adviser can perform in assuaging the terrible pressures of presidential decisions. During or after a period of agonizing decision making, Harry Truman would privately summon Supreme Court Justice Fred Vinson and House Speaker Sam Rayburn. In deference to Vinson's sacrosanct isolation on the Court, the meetings were always secret. Mr. Truman didn't necessarily want their advice on the matter at hand. Vinson and Rayburn were simply two men he admired and for whom he had enormous respect. One supposes that he used them as rudders for his presidency, as touchstones with a sort of higher wisdom that he regarded as almost infallible.

Sometimes too a President will use advisers in a public show of keeping in contact with party elders or other distinguished people. During the duress and sorrows of conducting the Vietnam war, President Johnson made great displays of conferring with Dean Acheson and General Matthew Ridgeway and other heroes of a somewhat less controversial war—Korea. The publicity surrounding such consultations was helpful in borrowing the respectability of men who have outlived their controversies for a President wallowing in the middle of his.

In arguing the value of the power broker, one doesn't argue that he is infallible. Power brokers have been horribly wrong, abetting Roosevelt's disastrous attempts to pack the Supreme Court and purge the conservatives in his party, encouraging Johnson's myopic escalations in Vietnam. Unvisionary advisers egged on Andrew Jackson in his self-defeating destruction of

the Bank of the United States and so tainted William Howard
Taft by their swarming presence that the most corpulent of all
Presidents was once described as "a large body surrounded by
people who know exactly what they want."

Yet the power broker is what he is because of his rare intuitions about Washington and the Process, and he has earned
them by a long record of wins and losses that spans many administrations, many seasons of many controversies in this tough,
remorseless, and subtle city. He offers the absolute loyalty of
the high-risk taker and the detached wisdom of one who contemplates his master from among the rabble in the piazza while
the rest of the advisers stand with the leader on the balcony of
state. Because of his immense discretion, the power broker flees
journalists and eludes history, doing what he does in the closeted
confines of personal friendship; thus the myth of the beast remains, hissing in the shadows of the American political imagination.

In the evenings the white-walled Oval Office of the President
of the United States radiates the afterburn of the day. In the
tranquil hush framed by darkness pressing upon the panes of
French windows, the late visitor thinks he can feel all the day's
expended hope, power, and persuasion quivering like the glow
in well-used muscle.

It is a room that retains its own identity as a place of Presidents. No one President has ever been able to impose his own
personality upon it with the placing of the totems and artifacts
of his own life. This President is from New York State. He has
hung the walls of the Oval Office with portraits of Martin Van
Buren, Grover Cleveland, and Washington Irving, with dry-
point etchings of rural life in Kinderhook and a warm, light-
flooded landscape View of Sing Sing. In two corners there are
bronze busts of Theodore and Franklin Roosevelt. For all that,
for all the books on New York history, the photographs of a
country house in Seneca, and a Revolutionary war musket from
the Hessian Hills, the Oval Office transcends its present occu-

pant to embrace the shades of all the Presidents who have used it—the good, the bad, the simply forgettable—as well as radiating the exertions of this particular day's exercise of power.

The President is standing at one side of his desk reading a paper as David Marks and Paul Brasher are shown in. He doesn't look up and they don't speak as they cross to the two white sofas on either side of the fireplace with a low table between them.

"What about a drink?" Brasher says softly.

"Bourbon Old Fashioned," Marks murmurs, leaning back on the sofa and digging in his jacket pocket for a pack of cigarettes.

Brasher smiles at him. "I should have remembered that by now," he says. He crosses the room to a polished mahogany washstand used by Millard Fillmore and now converted into a small bar.

The President lowers the paper he is reading. Still looking at it lying on his desk, he says, "David, what do you know about a man named Joe Sharret?"

"Not much," Marks answers. "Not offhand. Rich, I'm told, Chicago lawyer, does some teaching at Northwestern Law School." He shrugs. "Securities, taxes, that sort of thing. Didn't he work pretty hard to defeat you?"

The President raises his head, looks at Marks, and nods. "I'm thinking of appointing him to that vacancy coming up on the Securities and Exchange Commission."

"Is he any good?"

"Yes," the President says, taking a deep breath. "All the checkouts we've made up to now indicate that he is. He's clean, he's written a couple of books on the right things. Intelligent and able man, apparently."

"You'd better expect bitching from the party if you appoint somebody from the opposition."

The President's tired face breaks into a small grin. "Oh, well, sure. I do expect that. But appointing Sharret will sit well with the voters and the press for the same reason." He slips the paper into a blue folder and pushes a button on his desk. The far door opens and a tall dark-haired girl crosses to the desk. The President hands her the folder. "Have Lewis come in and see me about these in the morning. Have I some time open?"

"9:15," the secretary says. "Anything else you need this evening?"

The President raises his head again and smiles suddenly, the famous bright and warming grin breaking from the face that looks, at least, as if it had been burned and creased by sun and wind, the most celebrated political face in America. "Nothing else thanks, Molly. You can go home now."

Watching, Marks notices the girl's color rising, hears the minute suppression of a tiny gasp. The magic still works, he thinks, even up close.

"Thank you, Mr. President. Good night, Mr. President."

"Good night, Molly."

She leaves unobtrusive as a low whisper. The door closes behind her without a click.

The President crosses the room, taking a drink from Brasher as he passes. He sits down on the sofa opposite Marks. He takes off his reading glasses and puts them on the polished table surface before him. "Well now, David," he says in a low voice. "What about this mess we've gotten ourselves into?"

Brasher hands Marks an Old Fashioned and sits down at the far end of the sofa. Marks looks down at the amber surface broken by ice cubes. "Oh," he answers, "I wouldn't call it a mess, not yet anyway. How long's the Chairman been sitting on the revision of the 1973 Revenue Act?"

"Six weeks," Brasher says.

The President turns his head and looks at his appointments secretary for a moment. "Yes," he says, "about that." He sips at his drink and sets it down again. "The trouble is that we've focused too much on the Youth Resources Development Act. We haven't attended to our politics with the Chairman, and now he has us over a barrel."

Marks continues to stare at his drink, agreeing by not responding.

The President's forehead and cheeks redden a little. "I keep on being bugged by two things," he says. "First, a piece of legislation that we want and, I suspect, the country wants and needs is going down the drain. Second, it's a serious setback for a new administration to have one of its flagship bills shot down by one Congressman. We send Lou Howard up to the committee—"

"The Chairman eats congressional liaison people for breakfast," Marks says.

"It's bad for us politically," the President answers. "If we lose on this one the rest of the program is in trouble."

Marks lights a cigarette, holds the match until the flame is almost at his fingertips, then shakes it out. "You know," he says quietly, "I think you're more worried about taking a beating than you are about getting the tax law revised." He raises his head and looks into the President's face. "Your people are bitching too much. The press is beginning to smell a power struggle between you and the Chairman. If that sort of crap becomes the common gossip this thing *will be* a power struggle."

"Will?" The President retorts. "It already is."

Marks shakes his head. "No, it isn't, not yet. But you can turn it into one if you and your people think of it that way. That would be a bad mistake. The issue here is the revision of that act not the underlying power struggle."

The President straightens up, lifts his glass, and looks across at Marks, his expression radiating annoyance, the corners of his mouth twisted down and his eyebrows pinched into a tight frown. "Somebody's going to control our program in this Congress," he says, "and I'd just as soon use this occasion to demonstrate that it's going to be me."

"Bad idea," Marks says. "You're getting mad before anybody hits you. You're also getting into a brawl—unnecessarily— that you can't win."

"But—"

"Look," Marks says sharply, "you've served in the House and Senate and you can remember the perspective from there. The Congress worships its own gods and the Chairman is one of them. He has thirty-five years of tax experience behind him and you've been President for four months. If you choose to make this a me-or-him issue, it's going to be him."

"Damn it," the President says. "I'm not saying I won't co-operate with him. I've even thought of having him down here and asking his advice on how to get the bill through."

"Bad idea," Marks repeats. "You may not like his advice, and the worst thing you can do with somebody like the Chairman is to ask for advice and then not take it."

As the President leans back on the sofa, Brasher looks at him. The color on the high forehead and cheeks is deepening. Marks' tone, his interruptions, have nettled. Brasher knows that Marks is steering the President toward the real issues. But, as he listens the President is becoming angry. He is good at stress but doesn't handle fatigue very well. The day has been a wearing and difficult one. "Well, maybe," the President says. "But if it could be explained to him that tax credits will ultimately produce enough revenue—"

"That's a faith statement," Marks says.

The President leans forward. "Now what in hell's that supposed to mean?"

Marks flicks his cigarette over an ashtray. "You believe—or hope—that tax credits will result in enough revenue in the long run by taking some of the social-need load off the federal budget and stimulating expansion. Maybe it will. It's a great concept and it's worth a try. But when you ask the Chairman to act on your own faith that this might eventually happen you're asking too much. You're asking him to sell something to his committee and to the House based on a faith he might not share. That," Marks says, mashing out his cigarette, "means that you're asking him to put his power on the line. He won't do it. He didn't build his reputation by going out on suppositional limbs."

Gently, Brasher pleads silently, *softer, be kind . . .*

"I suppose you're asking *me* to help *him*," the President says.

The rumple-haired lawyer nods. "I suppose I am. I've read your bill and the staff memoranda and I've done a little sniffing around. I think that the real problem is that the Chairman hasn't got enough votes to revise the act as things stand now."

"Then, damn it, he should go out and get them," the President says. "That's what he's supposed to be famous for! He said he was with us on this thing in principle. Now he's got to do his stuff."

Calmly, Marks shakes his head. "Uh-uh. It doesn't work that way. The Chairman is, first of all, a consensus taker. He keeps his mouth shut, does a lot of listening, senses what the committee and House majorities will and won't accept, and then acts accordingly. He hasn't got a consensus for revision yet."

The President starts to say something angry and then checks himself. "Okay," he says in a quieter tone. "If that's the situation—and I'm not agreeing that it is because my congressional liaison people don't tell me anything like that—what do you think we should do about it?"

"Rewrite the bill," Marks answers.

"How?"

Marks looks at a point somewhere above the President's head. "Well," he says, "as I understand it there are two sections to the idea. The big one, the sexy one, is the New Partnership tax credits. Your people have also put in some lesser parts—tax breaks for families without fathers, tax breaks for one-time big earners like prize fighters, writers, and the like—the scattered stuff. That's what I'd drop. I'd rewrite the bill, confining it to the New Partnership. That's big stuff, Mr. President. It's revolutionary enough for this year."

The room is silent for a long, ticking moment. The President sits slumped back on the sofa, his drink cradled between his hands, his eyes on Marks' face. "That," he says slowly, "is the damnedest poorest advice you've ever given me, David."

It is Marks' turn to shrug. "In my opinion it's the only way you'll get the real gut of tax revision passed this year."

Again there is a long silence while the President stares. Brasher's stomach tightens.

"For God's sake," the President mutters, his eyes shifting from Marks' face to the table between them. "Of all the gutless backdowns." He looks at Marks again. "This fight hasn't even begun yet and you're sitting there telling me to compromise." He pauses. "For Christ's sake."

"I'd try to help the Chairman if I were you," Marks answers calmly.

"Help him!" the President says in a low voice. "Goddamn it,

David, I'm President of the United States. He should help me. I'm trying to save this country billions of dollars and get back its confidence in the free enterprise system. He ought to be helping me!"

"I think he's trying to," Marks says. "I think he's trying to keep your bill from being chewed up in the House by Southerners and others sick to death of any more tax breaks or other federal help for blacks. That's what families without fathers and prize fighters means to them. The poor got a break in the 1969 Tax Reform Act. It's enough for a while according to a lot of people in the House and that's what the Chairman's trying to save you from. You're in enough trouble there with the Youth Resources Development Act." He pauses. "And I'm trying to keep you from turning a rather delicate difficulty into a brawl you'll lose."

The President puts his glasses on and stands up. "It was good of you to come," he says tightly. "I understand you're dining with the Grahams this evening. I won't keep you."

Marks rises. "You can always tell yourself that my advice is worth about what you pay for it," he answers calmly. "You asked for my opinion on how to break tax revision out of the House Ways and Means Committee and you've had it. Good evening." He walks swiftly toward the door.

"Oh, you get paid," the President says in the room behind him, his words bursting softly from him. "You get the clients."

In the narrow hallway outside the Oval Office Brasher hands Marks his hat and coat. "I know it was tough," he says, "but you told him what he needed to be told—not to turn this thing into a silly power struggle. He'll think about it when he calms down. You know how he is."

Marks mutters something incomprehensible as he struggles into his coat.

"I'm sorry he gave you a rough time," Brasher says. "He isn't himself this evening."

"Yeah?" Marks says, putting on his crumpled hat. "Who is he?"

In the final analysis the myth of the beast is based on the assumption that the adviser manipulates his master. The adviser's ability to do that depends on the reasons a President needs him. The myth imagines the President to be a weak, befuddled poltroon while the adviser is in smooth, deft control of himself and his master. In the sum of American political history, the myth is rubbish. Obviously Presidents have some sort of need for their men, but the quality of the need varies.

It is when a President needs an adviser because of some character deficiency, some short circuit or failing that manifests itself in halting self-confidence, blurred vision, or moral confusion that the ability to manipulate is present and the myth of the beast has a chance of being fulfilled. In such President-adviser relationships—and there has been only one that is clearly a case of character support as well as intellectual and political assistance—the man elected to the office and the great adviser blend together to literally make one President.

"Power," said Woodrow Wilson, "consists of one's ability to link his will with the purposes of others, to lead by reason and a gift for cooperation." It is an interesting definition because Wilson alone was unable to execute it. He was a man with a very exacting sense of his own position in the order of things. It was a removed position, aloof and distant from the vulgarities of life and politics. Woodrow Wilson was simply incapable of the forced bonhomie, the crass horse trading and sacrifice of a part of a principle for a final result that politics requires. He was a deeply moral, outwardly cold, and at times bitterly unyielding man. His inabilities were more than the intellectual shortcomings of Washington and Jackson. He was a man imprisoned by himself upon the upper reaches of an Edwardian sense of nobility. "Talking to Wilson," said Clemenceau, "is something like talking to Jesus Christ."

There has been a great deal of speculation about Wilson's character, including a book written by William Bullitt and Sigmund Freud on the role of the President's mama in making him incapable of communicating or dealing with all sorts of people and situations. The potty-training school of analysis is probably no more pertinent than any other, and besides the reasons aren't as important as the plain fact that that's the way Woodrow Wilson was. He seems to have been fairly realistic about his own deficiencies. His secretary was a veteran of Jersey City precinct politics, Joc Tumulty. Since the President was withdrawn and remote from most of Process Washington, he brought in his future son-in-law, William Gibbs McAdoo, as confidant and Secretary of the Treasury. McAdoo was ambitious, outgoing, and very well known indeed. Wilson couldn't abide dealing with tobacco-spitting, deal-making Southern Congressmen of his own party so he gave the job to his Postmaster General, a former Texas Congressman named Albert S. Burleson who, though a somewhat pompous cornball, had a bucolic shrewdness and rather liked the smoky, vulgar precincts of the House. To pay off a political debt and to keep the public reminded that God Almighty was alive, well, and working hard in the administration, Wilson employed William Jennings Bryan as Secretary of State. Bryan's blowhard, Bible-thumping antics bore about as much of a resemblance to the subtle nuances and niceties of diplomacy as the Nebraska Platte does to the Indian Ocean. But it didn't matter. Wilson was his own Secretary of State.

In all these appointments the President got men who could do things he couldn't do. He was fulfilling the simplest-need principle.

But Wilson's relationship with the greatest power broker of this century, Edward M. House, arose from needs much more profound. Underneath his glacial exterior, Woodrow Wilson was a man almost desperate in his lack of confidence, his need for love and reassurance. "There surely never lived a man with whom love is a more critical matter than it is with me," he said. The genius of Edward House was to recognize all this, to provide ease and comfort and to become one of the crucial psychological props that permitted Wilson to function under the duress of the presidency. "I nearly always praise first," said House of his technique for dealing with Wilson, especially when he had to disagree, "in order to strengthen the President's confidence in himself. . . ." Wilson's closest friendships were with women. House was once described by a carping observer as being "almost feminine in his solicitousness." On top of all that House's grasp of politics, his capacity for work, and his consummate diplomacy made him the most durable adviser of Woodrow Wilson's presidency. "What I like about House," Wilson once said, "is that he is the most self-effacing man that ever lived."

He was a lot more than that. Born in Texas to considerable wealth, educated in the East and in England, House was a shrewd, stable, intelligent man who was rich enough to do what he wanted with his life. He once described himself as being so full of ambition that "it has never seemed to me worth while to strive to satisfy it." He got into agrarian-progressive Texas politics, backing and advising Governors, but became bored with his native state by 1900 and started looking around for someone on the national scene whom he could back. His ambition apparently was of a clean and rather depersonalized nature. It was a desire to participate in the doing of great and important things, "to put someone else nominally at the head," he wrote, "so that I could do the real work undisturbed." In 1911 friends introduced him to Woodrow Wilson in New York. Wilson, then preparing to become a candidate for President, was lonely, uncertain, and charismatic. House was small, sickly, and rich in confidence and intellectual capacities. He had already published a fantasy of what he wanted in the form of a rather frightful novel entitled *Philip Dru, Administrator*. It is a clumsy tale of a political genius who leads his people to the good life. The most interesting character in the novel is the supersecretive adviser to the super-President Dru. His name is Selwyn and nobody ever sees him.

During the Wilson presidency House was fairly invisible, operating mostly from his apartment in New York, then and later a meeting place for some of the world's most important people. In effect, the characters of House and Wilson fused together to make one President. House was the embodiment of that spirit of cooperation in Wilson's definition of power. He enabled the President to fulfill it.

Tireless and discreet ("He can walk on dead leaves and make

no more noise than a tiger," wrote one admirer), House was the very model of a modern presidential adviser and confidant. With his authority he assembled information for Wilson's decisions, made recommendations of his own, forwarded the opinions of others, and dealt with national politicians. While Wilson was preoccupied with the conduct of World War I, House collected ideas, facts, and views on the forthcoming peace. In October 1918 Wilson made an extraordinary gesture. He sent Edward House, uninstructed, to the Supreme War Council to negotiate with the Prime Ministers of Britain, France, and Italy. "I have not given you any instructions," Wilson said to his power broker, "because I feel that you know what to do." In effect, Wilson was saying, "Insofar as I am President, you are me." In this and in other exercises in trust and dependency no American President has shared so much of his power. Wilson was giving House, as emissary, the power of formulating policy as well as the assignment of executing it. This is delegation of far greater magnitude than that given, say, to Averell Harriman by Roosevelt in dealing with Churchill and Stalin. "We weren't really instructed," Harriman observes of himself and Harry Hopkins, "but we had an acute sense of the administration and its policies." In 1918 House was more than a presidential alter ego; he was part of the ego itself. House was sensible, patriotic, and responsible enough to use his position wisely and without any evident self interest except that overwhelming desire to do important things. A potential for evil riddled the whole House-Wilson relationship. But it was not accomplished; the beast did not manifest itself largely because Edward House was a decent man. The potential evil in the American political experience has not been the exercise of power by unlicensed brokers in it. Great power exists—it is there, it must be wielded by someone. Americans were fortunate when it was wielded better by the combined forces of Wilson and House than it could have been by Wilson alone. The potential evil is that of the unscrupulous man gaining dominance over a President who is cursed with character inadequacies. The supreme opportunity for evil was offered Edward House but he didn't take it. He rendered instead the supreme service of helping a fragile President to stay whole in one of the most arduous periods of American history.

The king is alone; in the theoretics of rule he presides in solitude at a pinnacle and with a rectitude that no mortal man can accomplish within his own character. To rule successfully—or in the case of the President, to govern successfully—he needs perspective; he needs the truth as it is perceived beyond his majesty. For this he needs power brokers, the grand chamberlains of Process politics. They are despised and distrusted as the counselors of great men have always been despised and distrusted—partly because of envy, partly because of fear. They abide in the shadows of the Process, operating in a quasi-private capacity as advisers to their Presidents, stigmatized by hazy public memories of all the ruthless or self-serving outsiders who in one way or another have tried to prey on Chief Executives. The stigma attached by the public to the power broker is amplified by the incurable public need to blame someone or something when a President takes wrong actions or decisions—or actions or decisions that conflict with the opinions of the blamer.

If as a result of their service power brokers get plushy jobs, lucrative law practices, and awe and celebrity in Washington, they probably deserve it. They apply proven judgment to their country's mightiest problems, invest their years of experience and trained intuitions. They may be devoured by cannibalistic Presidents, forced into jobs that they don't want or that result in their eventual downfall and anguish—as when Abe Fortas was armtwisted onto the Supreme Court or when Clark Clifford was sent to the Defense Department. Their motives are complex, including a fascination with power, a desire to live life near greatness, a love of risk taking, a quest for fame.

One Washington school of thought divides power brokers into two groups—those who serve for no ultimate reward and those who, in the judgment of this sometimes bitchy city, cash in on their former proximity to greatness. It is a question of diffuse and multiple moral components, not susceptible to easy answers, and maybe it isn't even a useful measure of a man's value at the time of his service to an American President.

In the end, that value is hard to fix exactly upon the latitudes and longitudes of history and politics. To a considerable degree their value is something that must be gauged by what never happened. Like the authors and negotiators of disarmament treaties who are rarely credited with the awful things that don't happen but who are always blamed for the awful things that do, the power broker is a hero of political nonevents as well as one who has counseled successful decisions. He is the least visible of the great Process game players, and in the popular imagination he is a sinister beast.

The telephone rings at 1:47 A.M. in the large bedroom of a Cleveland Park house. David Marks fumbles for his bedside lamp and switches it on. Speaking softly so as not to awaken his wife, who sleeps beside him in the huge double bed, he says, "David Marks."

"David," says the voice of the President. There is a long pause. "David, I'm sorry."

"Don't worry about it," Marks says quietly.

"Did you have a good evening with Graham?"

"Yes, just fine."

"David—"

"It's all right," Marks says. "I was a little rough on you too. God knows, I should understand why you get mad. That's part of what I'm here for."

"We'll talk about it again. I've been thinking. You may have something there—"

"We'll talk," Marks says soothingly. "Any time, Nathaniel." It is the first time he has used the President's Christian name since the election.

"Good night, David. And thank you very much."

"Good night, Nathaniel." Marks hangs up the telephone.

"Who was that?" his wife asks sleepily.

Marks switches off the light. "Just somebody who needed a kind word. Go back to sleep."

He, however, stays awake for a long time, lying on his back and thinking about ambitions and desires that, when fulfilled, put good and gentle men under such pressure that they rage in the evening and brood sorrowfully at night.

6: The Press

Were it left to me to decide whether we should have government without newspapers, or newspapers without government, I should not hesitate for a moment to prefer the latter.

> Thomas Jefferson
> before he became President

Even the least informed of the people have learnt that nothing in a newspaper is to be believed.

> Thomas Jefferson
> after he became President

"It has been proved to us by experience," wrote Plato, "that if we would have true knowledge of anything we must be quit of the body—the soul in herself must behold things in themselves." In other words, there is no absolute truth this side of paradise. Everything perceived is perceived through man's fallible senses. Everything retold is tainted by the teller's interpretation.

Once one has grasped this familiar metaphysician's dictum a great many things about Washington are easier to understand—why General Sherman exulted in the deaths of three Civil War correspondents, why Spiro T. Agnew flew into a passion at television and the press, why congressional aides and mighty White House advisers alike believe that press manipulation is one of the essential crafts of government. Above all, Plato's point lies at the nexus of that psyche-rattling mixture of anxious love, raw hatred, blubbering resentment, and alternating desires to murder and caress that is the true relationship between the politicians of Washington and the press corps of Washington.

The relationship is like a marriage conceived in an excess of passion and with a minimum of reason. The two personalities involved are too similar ever to be happy together. Like all miserably married couples, the politician and the journalist play to a gallery of witnesses to their misery, each attempting to portray himself as a martyr to the flaws of the other. Yet they are bound together inexorably by the imperatives of the Process. It cannot function without either of them.

By "politician" here one means not only those elected but the officials of government who are their surrogates. And by "press" one means all the journalists of this city—whether they transmit news as wire service copy or as broadcasts, whether they write for daily print or for weekly or monthly magazines.

By their very functions in the Process the politician and the journalist are incompatible. Yet the heart of their love-hate relationship lies in something shared—the great and curious American confusion about words and the things words describe. "There is a deep-seated human tendency to confuse unhappy news with unhappy events," writes George Reedy, former press secretary to Lyndon B. Johnson, "and to assume that if the news can be altered, so can the events. This tendency is particularly accentuated among monarchs. . . . Peter the Great strangled the courier who brought him the tidings of the defeat at Narva. John F. Kennedy (or someone on his staff) canceled the White House subscription to the New York *Herald Tribune*." This peculiar belief that if a thing isn't reported it may not have really existed persists.

In addition, the politician and the journalist have different visions of the truth because each has different uses for the truth. The politician is a soul driven across the world by a compulsive search for approbation. As he searches, he justifies his place in the Process with reminders of past approbation; he is there because a sufficient number of people approved of him to elect him. That continuous need for approbation dictates the politician's definition of truth no matter how vociferously he denies it. The truth is that arrangement of facts which makes him look good.

The best journalists are also driven men because they are creative men. Like all creative people, they are hounded by a compulsive vision of order, by a desire to take a mass of events, utterances, misdemeanors, and triumphs and reduce it to some sort of comprehensible schema. Like the politician, the journalist justifies himself in the Process, but not with an event. He uses a principle: the people's right to know.

When they are locked in their bitterest combat, the politician and the reporter belabor each other with the opposites of their own justifications. In his celebrated denunciation of the TV networks on November 13, 1969, Vice President Agnew snarled at a "tiny, enclosed fraternity of privileged men elected by no one and enjoying a monopoly sanctioned and licensed by government. . . ." The key phrase is, of course, "elected by no one." The press retaliates in this interminable argument by trumpeting the people's right to know. It accuses government of secrecy and trickery. It throws the First Amendment like a thunderbolt. It publishes the Pentagon Papers.

The politician is the proposer of the means by which men, money, and ideas shall be moved from one place to another. The journalist, starting with that fact, performs four functions. He is the simple purveyor of the news that the politician has proposed something. He is the analyst of the matter proposed. He is the diviner of the politician's motives in making the proposal. He is the prophet who attempts to forecast the results of the proposal. And therein lies a cauldron of mixed feelings because the politician adores the journalist in only one of those four roles—as the purveyor of the news. He distrusts the journalist in his roles as analyst, diviner, and prophet because in them the journalist is likely to arrive at different truths from those held by the politician.

The journalist's feelings about the politician are just as ambivalent. The politician is the basic source of the information from which the journalist fashions his visions of order. But the journalist realizes that the information that the politician gives him is likely to be trimmed and pruned to make the politician look good and his opponents look bad. This means, in the final analysis, that each is a distrusting supplicant of the other.

But along with everything that divides them, there is much that unites them. Beyond their bifurcating obsessions and the incompatibilities of their roles, the politician and the journalist are joined together by the essential linkages of the Process itself. They share its concept of reality—that those things that may happen or those that are happening a great distance away or those that are happening in the abstract are just as real as the events that touch one's own life. The politician and the journalist are companions in witness to a continuity that will endure as history. They are ranked in Washington by exactly the same measurement of importance—how much power the rest of the Process players think they have.

In order to do his job the contemporary Washington correspondent needs to be well educated (and his life continues as an endless process of self-education, including an onerous amount of homework). He better serves his masters and himself if he has good manners. He must have a lot of physical stamina—a White House correspondent is expected to give up his evenings, weekends, and family in order to travel with the President. He cannot operate without a good deal of skilled energy, and he must have a gift for human association because his success depends to some degree upon knowing people and persuading them through long association to trust him. Honor can't be faked. In return for all these qualities or a reasonable combination of some of them, the Washington correspondent is usually fairly well paid and has the mysterious gratification of being close to important events and the men and women who make them. "I was the guy to whom Robert Kennedy first admitted that he was a candidate for Vice President in 1964," one of Washington's better correspondents remarked. "That was gratifying. It still is. I don't know why but it was a reward of some kind to be kept in the memory."

There is no precise or predictable hierarchy in Washington journalism. A lot depends on who controls the White House. Reporters who share an administration's general ideology are usually more favored than those who don't. Importance doesn't always depend upon the power of the news organization one represents, though some correspondents do rate highly because of the organizations they work for. If there is any hierarchy at all, successful columnists and commentators for the three major broadcasting networks are close to the top of it. They are opinion journalists, and politicians have a special awe of printed or broadcast opinion. They think that an opinion offered is an opinion widely accepted. Hence the better-known columnists and commentators are the knights of Washington journalism. Special background briefings are held for them, and they rank just below Cabinet members (or on a par with Senators and ambassadors) as dinner guests—a reward more important to those who don't receive it than to those who do. (Washington journalism is still chortling over the correspondent who, upon being made chief of his bureau, wrote a form letter to all the embassies in town asking to be put on their invitation lists. "P.S.," he added, "there is a Mrs. Jones.")

Celebrated specialists also rank fairly high in the vague hierarchy. State Department correspondents are regarded as instruments of diplomacy. Those journalists who work for weekly publications and who resort to the signed essay as their analytical device are widely admired if they do their job well. Outsiders who come frequently to Washington can also be important in the city's press hierarchy. Good interviewers are prized in Washington.

But the majority of the more than 3,000 journalists who cover Washington for organizations as mighty as *The New York Times* or for specialized journals devoted to everything from nuclear physics to hog breeding sift down to varying degrees of celebrity and anonymity largely dictated by a combination of who they are, what they do, and which organization they represent. Specialization can mean obscurity as well as celebrity. There is one lady who appears every year at the background briefing that precedes the presentation of the budget. Every year she asks one question about the amount of money allocated for education. Then she vanishes into the tumult of the Process and remains, invisible to her colleagues, until the next briefing the following year. If anything close to absolute truth is achievable, it probably exists in either the sum or the distillation of the billions of words that gush out of Washington every year from the great and the creeping of its press corps.

The Washington obsession with Plato's impossibility is a product of the American Revolution. Before it there was no great tradition of press freedom in the American colonies. The first newspaper published in America was shut down after its first edition. Ben Franklin's brother James was the editor of the *New England Courant,* which was closed in 1722 for printing a story of a government expedition to chase coastal pirates. The paper reopened after a year and was promptly closed down again for poking fun at the Massachusetts General Court. In 1735 John Peter Zenger, a printer who published the *New-York Weekly Journal,* was hauled into court for permitting his newspaper to be used as a vehicle for attacks on William Cosby, a lascivious and greedy boob whom King George II had appointed Governor of New York. The Zenger case became the catalyst for a brilliant and vicious political brawl among the politicians, intellectuals, and lawyers of the day.

During the American Revolution the press wasn't much freer. Newspapers were told by quasi-official groups like the Newport, Rhode Island, Committee of Inspection that they were free to print "liberal sentiments" but not "wrong sentiments respecting the measures now carrying on for the recovery and establishment of our rights. . . ." Those papers that printed "wrong" sentiments were closed down or their editors were beaten up by mobs of self-appointed patriots.

Thereafter the first American administrations paid great obeisance to the principle of the truth and the openness that supposedly derived from it. Jefferson uttered his euphoric remark about preferring newspapers without governments to governments without newspapers. Alexander Hamilton, always more interested in the operation of government than the ideals it operated for, didn't share Jefferson's enthusiasm for the newspapers. "What is the liberty of the press?" he asked in *Federalist* 84. "Who can give it any definition which would not leave the utmost latitude for evasion?"

Nobody, of course, could or can. The press of the early years of American independence was a mixture of horror and virtue. Newspapers are frequently owned by politicians, who used them to praise themselves and to flay the opposition. Out of a particularly ugly feud between the Federalist *Gazette of the United States* and the Republican *National Gazette* grew the notorious Alien and Sedition Acts of 1789. This nasty parcel of legislation was a Federalist attempt to throttle Republican newspapers and to deport some of their editors and reporters who hadn't yet become American citizens. The acts were also the first example of what has become a well-known practice of some Washington administrations—to use simplistic logic in portraying their own political interests and the national interest as indivisible and then, wrapping themselves in the flag, to take out after their critics with the bludgeon of righteousness and the dagger of national security.

The Alien and Sedition Acts were subsequently allowed to die and the American press went rollicking off into the nineteenth century, alternately brawling with government and making obsequious love to it. Andrew Jackson was a great manipulator of the press in his battles with Congress. He favored cooperative newspapers with government printing contracts. Lincoln was the first real media genius, keeping up a steady flow of news to all papers and frequently writing and publishing articles about his own views.

When the Civil War broke out, Lincoln warned correspondents covering the front that they could be tried for espionage if their stories aided the enemy. General William Tecumseh Sherman nearly shot one reporter before Lincoln intervened. Sherman hated the press and blamed all his troubles on the leaks printed in newspapers. When he heard that three reporters had been killed by artillery fire he whooped: "Good! Now we shall have news from hell before breakfast!" The press retaliated by writing stories that Sherman was insane.

The government cracked down on newspapers during the Civil War, seizing the Chicago *Times,* indicting the editor of the Ohio *Statesman,* and suppressing the Philadelphia *Evening Journal* and the *Christian Observer.* The newspapers fought back by attacking Lincoln. He was, according to one article, "a half-witted usurper." Another newspaper weighed in with the observation that the President was "mole-eyed."

After the war was over, President Andrew Johnson became

the first Chief Executive to hold a news conference. Theodore Roosevelt loved press relations. He considered the White House "a bully pulpit." Woodrow Wilson made the presidential press conference a regular event.

The Washington press corps grew at a pace comparable to the growth of government. At first Congress excluded reporters from its sessions. After some skirmishing the House admitted them in 1790, and the Senate went public in 1792. But in 1813 there were only four men covering the Congress. By 1868 the number had grown to fifty-eight. Today Congress is still the most heavily covered branch of government. There are 1,300 members of the House press gallery. Although the White House has issued around 2,000 passes, its Correspondents' Association has only eight hundred members. The State Department Correspondents' Association has four hundred members.

The public attitude toward the love-hate relationship of politicians and journalists is ambivalent. Mobs have wrecked newspaper offices throughout American history—including one spectacular episode in Baltimore in which a newspaper office was burned because the paper had called President Madison a traitor. The American public clings to its facile and unjust conceit that most politicians are crooked, or at the very least interested only in their self-improvement. But the same public will raise unshirted hell with the press for confirming the notion in specific cases. One of the most fascinating of all contemporary opinion polls was taken by the American Broadcasting Company after Vice President Agnew's celebrated blast at television. Of those polled, 88 percent knew about the attack and 51 percent agreed with Agnew that television was biased, but only 25 percent felt that the news media had been unfair to the Nixon administration. Agnew had vented his rage on what he called "instant analysis" by news commentators after presidential speeches. But 67 percent of those polled wanted commentators to go on with such analysis—which isn't instant.

In other words, the public is just as confused about the truth as are politicians and journalists. Perhaps Mr. Agnew's chief contribution to the whole subject is his novel definition of truth. He is reported to have told representatives of the Radio and

Television News Directors' Association on December 18, 1969, that news coverage should be based on whatever the majority wanted to hear.

Most politicians recognize that truth, though never absolute, is not something that can be defined by popularity ratings. The question that bedevils the politician in his dispute with the press is the exact measurement of the journalist's power to influence people and events.

The press has certainly had a sporadic influence on events. At the turn of the century muckrakers goaded Congress into passing the Seventeenth Amendment, which provided for the direct election of Senators; in the same era the flamboyant and vain William Randolph Hearst created the public hysteria that caused the Spanish-American War; crusading reporters led by Mark Sullivan of *Collier's* magazine helped cut Speaker Joe Cannon down to size. Using a combination of chicanery and blasting comment, a group of correspondents teamed up with a handful of myopic Senators to thwart Woodrow Wilson's efforts to obtain ratification of the Versailles Treaty. The filthy Teapot Dome scandal, which besmirched the Harding administration in history, was first uncovered by reporters from the Denver *Post* and the Albuquerque *Morning Journal.* Television made and then broke Senator Joseph R. McCarthy of Wisconsin. The censure of Senator Thomas Dodd of Connecticut and the fall of Representative Adam Clayton Powell of New York began with newspaper stories. And so on.

Yet its power of revelation is not the principal means by which the press influences events. Persistence is journalism's main weapon. It appears daily or weekly (or hourly in the case of radio news programs). For the politician this persistence can be sheer hell because part of the art of politics is the art of timing. There are times when a man wishes to recede from the news; there are other times when he wishes a particular campaign to be waged *sotto voce* in order to make its later loudness all the more dramatic. With a persistent press, doing these things is difficult. The press is always there, always looking over the political shoulder, always talking.

The press also has memory. It remembers, for instance, that a

President who pleaded for reticence from critics of his war policy was, as a Senator, a savage critic of another President fighting another war. The memory of the press is sometimes ruthless and irrelevant. It hounds the politician who has changed his mind with stories about his past utterances—as if consistency was an especially great virtue.

Yet for all its maddening traits and its spasms of unfairness, the press remains an essential ingredient of government. And the politician infinitely prefers a world with the press to a world without one. This is not a judgment of vanity so much as a necessity to the endless perception of government by the people, which is one of democracy's fundamental principles. Without the press, the governed would be blind in one of the eyes that sees their Governors.

It breaks upon Washington at 3:27 on a Thursday afternoon in June. A telephone call from the congressional correspondent of the Columbia Broadcasting System to his bureau chief is the device by which a flung rock of sudden controversy shatters the predictable cadences of the capital. It has to do with Randolph Hatfield, Majority Leader of the U.S. House of Representatives. "He claims," says the correspondent, "that the President wants him to lead a revolt against the Speaker in the next Congress."

In his office at the two-story CBS building on M Street the bureau chief looks out of the window while holding the telephone. "What kind of revolt?" he asks.

"Hatfield says that the President has offered three times to back him if he'll run for Speaker next time."

A large CBS mobile unit is blocking the near lanes of the street as its crew maneuvers the van back into the garage. "When did Hatfield tell you this?" the bureau chief asks.

"About ten minutes ago."

"Was he sober?"

"Near as I could tell."

"Okay," the bureau chief says quietly. "Find out if Randy or the Speaker will hold still for an interview and call me back in fifteen minutes."

At the same moment the first story conference of the afternoon is going on in a glass-walled office on the fifth floor of the Washington *Post* building on Fifteenth Street. Assistant managing editors and their staffs are discussing the play positions of stories in the next day's editions of the paper. The managing editor presides over the meeting and makes the final decisions. At 3:31 the assistant managing editor for national affairs is summoned for an urgent telephone call. He walks down the length of the crowded, cluttered newsroom and picks up a telephone on his desk. He talks to the *Post* reporter who covers the House of Representatives, asks a few questions, and then returns to the meeting. "We'd better not make any final decisions about tomorrow," he says.

"What's up?" asks the managing editor, a slender, gray-haired man in his middle forties.

"Randy Hatfield's telling people that the President is putting him up to shafting the Speaker—wants him to take on the Speaker at the start of the next Congress. Randy says he's forced to tell all because of the constitutional implications or his great patriotism or something."

"Oh Jesus," says the managing editor softly. "Okay." He slides open a glass panel that separates him from his secretary sitting outside the little office. "Judith," he says, "track down Dan Stock and call over to the Supreme Court. If Jack is there tell him to get down here because we may need him."

"Okay," the girl says.

"And tell the editor we're going to have to see him right after we've finished here."

"Okay," the girl says again.

The story conference continues.

Also at 3:31 this afternoon Willy Dern is leaving the west wing of the White House and is walking up the drive toward the northwest gate. It had rained heavily in Washington around noon. A few dead leaves are still glued by moisture to the black asphalt. The air smells damp. Brilliant sunlight gleams on the roof of the baroque Executive Office Building. Willy doesn't know yet about the new break on Capitol Hill, but it doesn't matter. Columnists' methods of dealing with sudden events are different from those of hard news writers for the wire services, newspapers, and broadcasting networks. The columnist tries to focus on the meaning of the new development in the larger context of events.

All week long that larger context has been dominated by the administration's first showdown with Congress. On Monday *The New York Times* and the Washington *Post* led their front pages with articles on the struggle to round up votes for the Youth Resources Development Act. Every day since the papers have carried running stories, profiles of the principal protagonists, and analyses of the New Partnership concept. The *Wall Street Journal* published a poll of business views on the program (mostly favorable). Wednesday's newspapers headlined a departure the President made from the prepared text of a speech he delivered to some civil service award winners the previous afternoon. "Those who deny the legitimate grievance of American taxpayers," he had said, "and the legitimate needs of our unfulfilled friends and neighbors deny the greatest possibilities of our form of government. Those who delay the amelioration of those grievances and the fulfillment of those needs—for whatever reason—should be the subject of some very serious doubt on the part of their colleagues in government and their fellow citizens." It was regarded as an intemperate presidential outburst and it was clearly aimed at the Speaker. The network news shows have led with the White House–Congress struggle since Monday evening. *Time* and *Newsweek* both ran cover stories on "Taxpayers in Revolt," the former with a color photograph of a riot after one of Harvey Leland's rallies, the latter with a stark drawing of an angry, shouting man holding a crumpled income tax form in his fist. Since Tuesday reporters have been trying to get the Speaker to reply to the President's blast. But the Speaker has just smiled.

At the CBS building on M Street the bureau chief has talked to the executive producer of the Cronkite show in New York. Hatfield's revelations, exploding into an already overheated Washington controversy, will lead the CBS evening news. The Speaker has refused to be interviewed on film; so for the moment has Hatfield. The network will limit its coverage this evening to "stand-uppers" by its congressional and White House correspondents—straight pieces without film inserts, narrated by the two men.

At this hour CBS doesn't know how much Hatfield has talked —whether it has sole proprietorship over the story. The Washington bureau's problem is to find out as much as possible without spreading what it knows. The bureau chief has already fended off a request by radio news to have the congressional correspondent do a one-minute piece for the 5 P.M. broadcast. The story is being saved for the Cronkite show. The Sunday talk program *Face the Nation* is trying to find someone to appear and discuss the feud between the President and the Speaker.

At the moment the congressional correspondent is in the Speaker's office discussing that feud—but for background only. The Speaker leans back in his chair, slowly raises a polished shoe, and rests it on the edge of a drawer. "The President's anxious, of course," he says comfortably. "He believes that this new program of his—what does he call it?"

You know damn well what he calls it, the correspondent thinks. He is sitting on a leather chair, body hunched forward, notebook held in one hand.

"The New Partnership—the President apparently believes that this is the answer to the country's problems." The round face assumes an expression of doubt. The eyebrows move up. He shrugs. "Now I'm not going to argue with that. I just don't know. But that isn't the point. Naturally the President is anxious. But the House has its duty too." The doubting expression fades, replaced by a smile. The Speaker's eyelids lower, half-shuttering the eyes. "The House's duty is to have a thorough look at all these things Presidents want in such a hurry. I've seen it happen before. I've been in this place a long time. I've seen my share of Presidents."

"Do you think the New Partnership is what the country needs at the moment?" the correspondent asks.

"Oh," the Speaker answers quietly, "I wouldn't know about that. But, as I say, that's not the issue at the moment."

"Let me put it a specific way," the correspondent says, leaning back in his chair. "Have you and the President had a disagreement—specifically—over the New Partnership or the Youth Resources Development Act?"

"I'm a good party man," the Speaker says, smiling again. "We've done all we can for him on this bill. You know that. You've been here every day watching this thing. You've watched me and Randy working for it."

I've watched Mace working while Randy looked at the wall and you sat on your ass, the correspondent thinks.

"The Youth Resources Development Act is a difficult bill. I can't make my chairmen rush. I can't lay down the law to Rules. You know how things work up here."

"Were you angry when the President blasted you on Tuesday?"

The Speaker looks surprised. He takes his foot off the drawer and moves his tall body forward, resting his elbows on the desk. "Blasted me? I didn't hear any blast that applied to me."

"Did you suggest that Randy talk about these threats the President is alleged to have made?"

The Speaker laughs suddenly, briefly and mirthlessly. "Oh, I wouldn't call them threats. Like all new Presidents this one is— oh, what shall I call him? A bit of an evangelist?"

"Did you suggest that Randy Hatfield talk about this?"

The Speaker shrugs. "Randy Hatfield can do whatever he likes. He's an elected member of Congress. He's his own man."

"Do you believe that the President did offer to back Randy against you?" the correspondent asks.

The Speaker smiles again. "I'd like to help the President if I could," he says. "I'd like to help him to work better with the Congress. That's why I'm not going on your television tonight. I don't want to blow this thing all out of proportion."

Going through the Speaker's lobby on his way to the radio-TV gallery, the correspondent sends a note to Congressman Hatfield on the floor. Hatfield comes off, smiling, his heavy face flushed, hands shoved into the pockets of his seersucker jacket. "Randy," the correspondent says, "you've started a real stink."

Hatfield puts one hand on the taller man's shoulder. "I didn't

tell you all that to make a stink," he says. "I just think we've got
to keep the record straight."

"I wish you'd agree to go on camera tonight."

Hatfield gives the correspondent's shoulder a shake. "Not
tonight, friend. Tomorrow."

"Is that a promise?"

Hatfield smiles again. He is calm and looks happy for the first
time in months. "That's a definite promise. Want to set a time?"

"If I can get tape facilities, how about ten tomorrow morning?"

"Ten it is," Hatfield says, taking a little diary from his breast
pocket. He jots a note. "Ten o'clock at CBS."

At the Washington *Post* a second meeting in the managing
editor's office is breaking up. In the two hours since the editors
first heard what Hatfield has been saying, the paper's House reporter has assembled a good deal more: Hatfield has repeated
that the President made the offer to back him against the Speaker
at least three times, that he can name other people who were
present—but won't at the moment. The *Post*'s House man has
also seen the Speaker, who is still putting on his tolerance-and-
forgiveness act. The reporter thinks that the Speaker has gotten
Hatfield to make the accusations—and so do the editors downtown. But it is unprovable, a hunch that arises from rather intimate knowledge of the personalities involved. Therefore it is
unprintable.

The Washington *Post* has decided that the story is important
for several reasons—because it reveals the bitterness that has been
growing between the President and the Speaker during the battle
for the Youth Resources Development Act, because it is a continuation of the week-long story about that struggle, and because it raises some important political and possibly constitutional
issues. The *Post* has learned from Hatfield that CBS is also on
to the story. Hence the newspaper can afford to be open in its
pursuit of details. At the meeting just ended, the editors decided
to "task force" the Hatfield story. Tomorrow's paper will have
double leads written by the House and White House reporters.
Daniel Stock, the paper's political correspondent, has been as-

signed to write an analytical piece on the President-Speaker dispute. Jack Sterling, the Supreme Court reporter, has been called off a series he has been writing to do 750 words on the constitutional implications of presidential interference in congressional leadership elections. The time is 5:35.

Willy Dern has returned to his office in the basement of his house in Georgetown. His secretary gives him several telephone messages. His wife has left a note saying that she is across the street having tea with a friend. The air conditioner has gone on the fritz. The office is muggy and close.

One of the telephone messages is from John Stermas. Willy calls him at the Cannon Office Building of the House. Quickly Stermas tells him what has happened.

"It's ridiculous," Willy says. "It doesn't work—the combination of Hatfield, the President, and the Speaker."

"That was my initial impression," Stermas says. "If the President wanted to knock off the Speaker, he wouldn't pick Randy Hatfield as the man to do it."

"Exactly," Willy says. "And he wouldn't use this device—I mean, the President wouldn't put Hatfield up to this a year and a half before the next election for Speaker."

"Unless he meant it as a threat."

Willy shrugs out of his jacket, switching the telephone to his left hand as he pulls his right arm out of the sleeve. "But he still wouldn't use Randy Hatfield," Willy says.

"No," Stermas answers, "he wouldn't."

Willy sits down at his desk and takes a pencil. "I can see the President putting somebody like you up to this—"

"No," Stermas repeats. "I couldn't get elected Speaker any more than Randy Hatfield could. Look, Willy, my main reason for calling aside from making sure you knew about this is to ask you for God's sake to keep Jerry Cressap in mind when you're writing about it."

"What's Jerry Cressap got to do with it?"

"I've just been over talking to Mace," Stermas says. "He's wild. This is the last thing we needed at this point. There are guys we've got listed as 'Undecided' on HR 1418 who could come down on the 'Against' side because of this. House loyalty to the House, resentment against a President trying to mess up the Speaker—no matter how much such guys may dislike the Speaker themselves. You know, that sort of thing. If you blast the Speaker and Randy—"

"Do you think the Speaker's behind this?" Willy asks.

Stermas pauses. "I don't know," he says slowly. "He owes the President one. He is a vindictive bastard and he's pretty Byzantine too. Randy might have picked up something—God knows what the President actually did say to him—Mace is trying to find out right now—and the Speaker might have suggested to Randy that he go talk to the press. Oh, hell, I don't know. My main point is that if you and guys like you come out on the President's side, you're going to turn off people like Jerry Cressap."

"Look," Willy says, "I've got to make some telephone calls. What're you doing this evening?"

"Wait a minute," Stermas says. There is a moment of silence. "Nothing."

Willy flips over a page on his desk calendar. "Neither are we, unless Sally's made some last-minute— Look, why not come over and we'll have dinner and talk about it?"

"Okay," Stermas says. "I'll bring a bottle of wine. About eight?"

"Fine," Willy says. "But forget the wine. We have that."

He hangs up and tells his secretary she can go home. Then he sits thinking for a moment in the warm, moist hush.

Willy knew the President well during his years in the Senate and watched him closely, if sporadically, during his campaign the previous autumn. He knows that the President blows under the combined stresses of fatigue and impatience and is likely to say reckless things that will be regretted later. But Willy also knows that the President is neither mean, stupid, nor capable of protracted malevolence. What seems most likely is that he lost his temper over the delay in passing his two bills and said some foolish things that Hatfield somehow heard or found out about. What puzzles Willy is Hatfield's claim that the President urged him three times to challenge the Speaker at the beginning of the next Congress.

Hatfield himself is a tragedy. Willy feels sorry for him and suspects that Hatfield is being used by somebody else, probably the Speaker. The Speaker in turn is vindictive. He had some vague hopes of getting his party's nomination for President the previous summer and would now begrudge the presidency to anyone who won it. To Willy, the Speaker is best analyzed as a limited man who has been elevated by the Process. He is in a semipermanent state of anxiety about himself in the House and is touchy in his dealings with power outside it.

It is 6:05. Willy Dern now comes to his first conclusion about the piece he will write for Sunday; he cannot afford to get into the merits of the Hatfield-Speaker-President imbroglio. On the coming Sunday Willy's column will exert some influence in Washington itself; people will turn to it to find out what Willy considers to be the real issue. Now, as it was before Hatfield started all this, the issue is HR 1418 and the differing visions of it at the White House and on Capitol Hill.

He makes a few notes and then calls the White House. He asks to speak to the assistant press secretary, who is the President's younger son, Peter. Like most reporters who cover or who have fairly constant dealings with the White House, Willy thinks that Peter is calmer, more candid, and less combative than his boss, Keith Bernstein.

Peter comes on the phone. "Hey, Willy," he says quietly.

"Hi," Willy answers. "I'll bet you know what I'm calling about."

"I wouldn't have a couple of hours ago, but I do now," Peter says. "Keith's just had a go-round with the *Post* and CBS."

"What're you saying?" Willy asks.

"Well," Peter says. He pauses. "I guess we're saying that we don't quite know what Hatfield's talking about but we're looking into it. If the guys who've been in with Keith are feeling nice that's the way they'll put it."

"Keith blown up?"

"Well," Peter answers, "let's say he isn't at his coolest right now." He pauses again. "It doesn't look good at this moment, does it?"

"Not to people outside of Washington, it doesn't," Willy answers. "To anybody who knows Randy Hatfield it probably sounds a little crazy. Look, I'd like to talk to Paul tonight or maybe Lou Howard."

"We'll see," Peter says. "Call me later in the evening. I'm afraid I can't help much at the moment. Paul's in with the President and the rest of us are trying to figure out what it's all about."

"I'm not too interested in the brawl itself," Willy says. "But one thing is odd—Hatfield says the President did this three times."

"That's what he's going to have to prove," Peter says. "We've had Barbara going over the appointments schedule and one of her girls checking the telephone log. We want to find out if Randy and the President have even talked three times—you know, under the circumstances in which this thing could have been said."

"Interesting," Willy says.

"I've got to go," Peter says. "I'd appreciate it if you didn't tell Keith I've been talking to you."

"Oh, sure," Willy says. "When can I call you?"

"Right after the Cronkite show at 7:30," Peter answers. "I imagine we can get Paul to talk to you sometime tonight."

Willy hangs up. He calls Mace Applegate and talks for ten minutes. Then he telephones a legislative specialist at the Brookings Institute on Massachusetts Avenue. They discuss the late-committee stages of the Youth Resources Development Act, Willy probing for those times when the Speaker could have intervened to hasten the bill through the House machinery and for ways in which the Speaker could have used his office and prestige to get more votes for the bill. It is now 6:29.

"Direct from our newsroom in New York," says a network announcer, "the CBS evening news with Walter Cronkite. . . ." The program is not shown in Washington until seven. A Baltimore television station carries it at 6:30. Baltimore is within television reception distance of Washington, and on nights of major news breaks the CBS news is seen by hundreds of people in the capital at the earlier hour.

"Good evening," says Walter Cronkite. "There was a new development tonight in the White House drive to pass two bills that are key to the President's New Partnership program. In Washington this afternoon, House Majority Leader Randolph Hatfield said that the President had threatened the Speaker of the House unless passage of the bills was speeded up. The two are, of course, the administration's Youth Resources Development Act and a revision of the 1973 Revenue Act, which would provide the authority for private industry to finance social welfare programs. Our correspondent on Capitol Hill has the story."

Standing in a darkened control room in the CBS building on M Street, sleeves rolled up, thumbs hooked into his vest pockets, the bureau chief watches as technicians in New York switch to videotape. The congressional correspondent had finished recording his stand-upper twenty-five minutes earlier and it had been fed up to New York.

"The details are still somewhat obscure," says the recorded correspondent, "but if Congressman Hatfield is correct, the fight over the administration's two bills has turned decidedly personal. Hatfield claims that the President wants him to run for Speaker when the next Congress convenes. If true, this would amount to open warfare between the President and the present Speaker, a signal that the President's impatience over the slow pace of his program in the House has led him to try a purge of his party's congressional leadership. Such attempted purges by the White House are not uncommon. Franklin Roosevelt campaigned against Georgia's Senator Walter George in 1936, Richard Nixon worked directly to defeat Senator Charles Goodell of New York in 1970. In this one Congressman Hatfield—clearly siding with the Speaker —says he was forced to reveal the President's threats because of what he calls the grave constitutional issues they raise . . ."

In the little glass-walled office off the main newsroom of the Washington *Post* the managing editor and Dan Stock, the paper's political correspondent, watch the snowy picture on the television screen. The managing editor sits with one leg stretched across a corner of his desk. He twirls his glasses slowly by one stem. Stock sits on a small sofa, his notebook open on his lap.

The CBS congressional correspondent cues to his colleague who covers the White House.

"Administration officials appeared surprised when they first heard about Hatfield's charges this afternoon," says the White House correspondent. "The initial reaction at the White House was astonishment—but no outright denials. At the moment it seems questionable that whatever has happened between the Speaker and the President is part of a concerted White House drive to undercut the Speaker's authority. If there is a campaign on, it is probably a presidential appeal to members of Congress for action on the two crucial bills. It is no secret that the President and his top aides are dismayed by the slow pace of action on the Youth Resources Development Act and the revision of the 1973 Revenue Act. It is also known that the President has held several strategy sessions without the Speaker being present. But sources here say that the consultant from the House was Majority Whip Mace Applegate of North Carolina, not Mr. Hatfield . . ."

In an office on the third floor of the Rayburn Office Building on Capitol Hill the shades are drawn against the lingering sunshine. In the dusk of the white-walled room a square of cold light glows dully. At the other end of the office a solitary man sits at a desk watching. He is physically motionless, arms resting on the sides of his chair, tired, puffy face slightly lowered with the eyes fixed on the screen. But the brain inside the head is alive and churning, groping for absolutes among a cacophony of regrets and doubts.

Even Randolph Hatfield himself isn't quite sure what triggered his decision to go to the Speaker two days before. It all began when he woke up at 4:30 in the morning and couldn't get back to sleep. He had lain on his back looking at the ceiling, rethinking it all for the thousandth time. He had tried to find, in his exhausted reason and used-up vocabulary, some new argument that would force from Dorothy the forgiving words that she didn't know he needed. Scores of times before Benny's death she had reproached him for not spending enough time with his sons. But she had never said it after Benny died. Yet the prior reproaches had had their full impact on Randy only after the boy was gone.

At seven o'clock he had gotten up, put on his dressing gown, and gone down the hall to her room. She was sitting up in bed with the morning paper in her lap. Her hair was tousled and her face was chalk pale and taut with weariness and grief. She was wearing a blue silk bed jacket with a coffee stain on it. "Dot," Randy had said, sitting on the edge of her bed, "I've been thinking about this thing, about Benny, and it occurs to me—"

She had lowered the newspaper. Her eyes were dry. "Oh Randolph," she had said, "for God's sake, let's not start all over again."

"You mean you don't want to talk to me about it?"

She nodded, slowly, deliberately, three times. "That's exactly what I mean. Too many words. Too much asking ourselves why."

"You don't want to talk to me?"

"That too!" she had said, her voice rising. "I have nothing more for you. Just go away and *give me some peace!*"

Coming downtown in his car forty-five minutes later he had thought about his two lives—one as a private human being trying to make it with other human beings, the other as a public figure, as a journeyman of Washington power, as an instrument of history. If a man failed totally at one of his lives he could compensate by being great in the other. He had resolved to do better in the House, to snap out of the doldrums, to crank up new resolve, not thinking out every word that he said. He had gone to the Speaker that morning. He had told him about the President.

Walter Cronkite makes a final point on the lead story and the television picture switches to a commercial for denture adhesive. The telephone rings. Without taking his eyes from the screen, Hatfield picks it up. "Hello?"

"Randy? It's Willy Dern."

"Hel-*lo,* Willy," Hatfield says. "Been watching Cronkite?"

"I just saw the lead on the Baltimore station."

"What can I do for you, Willy? As if I didn't know." Hatfield rumbles in a small chuckle.

"I'd like to hear about it," Willy says.

"Why, we've got a fight on our hands," Hatfield says. "We're back in 1940 with Roosevelt purging—"

"1936," Willy interrupts.

Hatfield reaches for a little box on his desk that switches off the television sound. "Right, of course, it was 1936," he says. "That's where we are now, me and the Speaker. Those folks downtown are trying to gang up on us, but—well, you know that won't work, Willy."

"There's one funny part of it," Willy says.

"Yes? What's funny, friend?"

"If I have the story right, you say that the President has suggested three times that you run against the Speaker at the beginning of the next session. You also say that you can give the names of other people who heard him say this to you. Can you tell me when the three times were and who the witnesses are?"

Hatfield shakes his head as if Willy were standing before him. "I'm not willing to go into details yet."

"It'd help if you could verify the three times, Randy."

"That sounds like you don't believe me," Hatfield answers.

"I think a lot of people are going to want details of those three separate occasions," Dern says. "Most of us can believe that the President blew his lid, that he might have said something like this once in a temper tantrum, but—"

"I can't even confirm that there were three times," Hatfield says. "Maybe there were, maybe there weren't."

"You mean—"

"Not now, Willy," Hatfield says. "Not now." He leans forward and hangs up the telephone. He sits looking at the silent, blurry screen. Walter Cronkite is talking but there are no words. Hatfield ponders the number three for a moment. Then he decides that he just can't think about that now. He thinks instead about Dot, about the President, and about his own new closeness to the Speaker. He is back on the team again. He and the Speaker are in a real fight together against a morose and overbearing White House. It makes a man feel alive to be in a fight.

Hatfield gets up, crosses the office, and mixes himself a drink. He goes back to his desk and sits down. He will watch the seven o'clock rerun of the Cronkite show on Washington television. He drinks, tasting the smoky, soothing bouqet through the ice's chill. He won't think about three. Randy Hatfield leans back in his chair, able to think better now about Benny, able to fix and hold on the thought that Dot's talk all those years before Benny died was just female talk. Her accusation that he didn't spend enough time with the boys was just a woman's judgment and not necessarily rational. He thinks of all the times . . .

Governments are like operas. In order to exist they need audiences. They need to send out impulses and receive impulses in return. The public judges the quality and reality of government from a combination of the impulses it receives. Government charts its course toward public need and through public desire and mood from the impulses it gets back. This sending and receiving of impulses is the essential, if subjective, dialogue of democracy.

The public receives two sorts of impulses from Washington. The first and most potent type comes in the form of the practical effects of Washington's policies on people's lives—farmers feeling the effect of price support policy, housewives sensing government through its capacity or lack of capacity to deal with inflation, Southern blacks voting or not voting in terms of Justice Department energies expended, industry gauging Washington in terms of countless regulations covering everything from export licensing to pollution control. These are action impulses, the results of policy at its final destination.

The second set of impulses coming out of Washington is generated by the press (and once again by "press" one means all the devices of journalistic communication). Reporting from Washington, the press sends out declarative impulses—news about what government says it intends to do, about the controversies attendant upon shaping and starting policy on its course.

Receiving the action and declarative impulses, the public compares them and from the comparison forms its opinions about government. The results can be beneficial or devastating depending upon how the public thinks the two sorts of impulses compare. When the President claims that he has taken action to calm social disturbance, the public judges him to be truthful and virtuous if there have been fewer riots lately. When an unemployed aircraft worker whose jobless benefits are about to run out hears that people in Washington are claiming that the economy is improving, he deduces that the government is full of goddamn fools or liars or both.

Since 1932 Washington has become acutely aware of the potential promise and perils of public relations as a craft. It has erected a mighty information apparatus that, in 1971, included 6,144 people who were *acknowledged* to be working on information policy, information manufacturing, and information dispensing. (Some observers believe that if all the information specialists squirreled away in the bureaucracy by one device or another were counted, the number would be closer to 10,000.) The annual public relations price tag for government was officially put at $165 million for the same year. (Again, if hidden budget items or budget items indirectly applied were taken into account, observers say that the information bill might have been closer to $400 million.) The Defense Department's public relations staff ran to several thousand people. Health, Education, and Welfare was the second largest organization, employing 737 people. The Department of Agriculture listed eighty information specialists, the Department of Transportation 236, and so on —all figures for 1971.

Not all these people—indeed, not even a majority of them— deal directly with the press or engage in that political flack that is the vague public concept of government public relations. Maintaining a flow of pure nonpolitical information to the public is an essential function of government. Without it, nobody would hear governement's warnings about dangerous or deficient drugs, epidemics, bad weather, and spoiled food. The economy couldn't operate without government information on unemployment, the cost of living, industrial output, and other fiscal and economic data. The civil defense program—such as it is—is based largely on information. America talks to the world about itself through the

U.S. Information Agency. All this and much more is the legitimate and indispensable function of Washington's information industry.

At the upper levels of that industry dwell its princes and archbishops, who do deal with the press (or who command the troops in charge of press relations). These exalted figures are charged with the highly political task of trying to shape or influence the declarative impulses that the press sends from Washington to the public. The most exalted information officers bear commensurate titles, such as Assistant Secretary of Defense for Public Affairs, Deputy Assistant Secretary of State for Press Relations, and special assistant to the Secretary of the Treasury.

Information policy is indivisible from policy itself. In Washington's most successful public relations operations (in recent years government has come to prefer the vaguer, more respectable term "public affairs") top information officials sit in on policy planning sessions and have access to the data and judgments from which policy is shaped. This means that the information officer who is really clued in on policy becomes an expert source for reporters. In most cases, the most expert of the information officers seem to be the least defensive. The best of them—President Eisenhower's press secretary, James Hagerty, and Mr. Johnson's men, George Reedy and Bill Moyers—regard themselves as liaisons between the press and the politicians, trying to accommodate the needs of both.

Since World War II two vital developments have complicated the relationship between the politicians and the press of this city, sometimes exacerbating the relationship. Both changes have made the jobs of politicians and journalists more demanding and difficult.

The first change was the explosion in the size, complexity, and domain of government. The War and Navy Departments were consolidated into one superagency; three new departments were added in the postwar years—Housing and Urban Development, Transportation, and Health, Education, and Welfare. The budget spurted from $94 billion in 1961 to $202 billion in 1971—all symbols of a dazzling growth in government's size and in its areas of endeavor. Joseph Kraft, one of Washington's leading columnists, called this "a Copernican revolution in the field of public affairs." Suddenly government was dealing in every corner of the world and in such esoterica as space satellites, telecommunications policy, voyages to the moon, economic problems so complex that even the most brilliant experts could understand only parts of them, urban transport, weapons technology that boggled the mind, rarefied social dilemmas, and so on. "To apply common sense to what is visible on the surface," concluded Kraft, "is to be almost always wrong."

Obviously, such a change in the circumstances and tasks of government meant that everybody—press, politicians, and public alike—was flying dimmed if not downright blind. Because events and issues were so difficult to understand, journalists became more and more dependent upon government information officers or experts to provide data and explain it. That irritated the press and made it more wary of politicians and their official surrogates. In translating the complex information about policy in the postwar world, journalists had to generalize and simplify in order to make it comprehensible to the general reader and listener. That irritated the politicians and their surrogates, who felt that they were not being adequately portrayed.

The second change since World War II was the advent of television and its growth as a reigning information medium. Close to 80 percent of the American public regards television as its primary source of news. Since television is both a vehicle for the reporting journalist and an electronic witness to actual events, its arrival created new abrasions between politicians and journalists. It also added a new and not completely understood dimension to the declarative impulses coming out of Washington. Suddenly the natural drama of politics and its practitioners underwent a metamorphosis in which the political leader and his surrogates became the superstars of a showbiz whose dimensions dwarfed the most lurid daydreams of the late Cecil B. DeMille. Not even the wildest partisans of John Connolly, Treasury Secretary and prime don of the first Nixon administration, claimed that he was a great economist or a prescient fiscal expert. Half of Mr.

Connolly's genius was invested in a capacity for superb political management. The other half was manifest in his talents as a great public performer who could take the creakiest policy script and turn it into a smasheroo of political histrionics.

In addition to making the jobs of politicians and journalists more difficult and exacerbating their relationships, the Copernican revolution in public affairs has injected new rituals and practices into the interdependency of the two groups. The most celebrated and controversial ritual is the background briefing, or "backgrounder."

Basically, the backgrounder is nothing more than a device to standardize the dispensing of a large amount of information to a large number of journalists on complicated or delicate matters; it is an audience for journalists given by officials. The spokesman may be as exalted a personage as the President of the United States or a Cabinet member, an expert, or an information officer. The difference between the backgrounder and the open press conference lies in the rules under which the information dispensed may be used.

At a press conference the spokesman is identified and everything he says is publicly quoted. Many press conferences by Presidents are televised so that the public hears what the Chief Executive says at the same time that the journalists hear it. (This is the main reason for televising press conferences. They have become speeches with journalists acting as straight men.) At its loosest level the backgrounder is conducted under the rule that everything said at the briefing may be quoted and that the spokesman may be identified as an administration official, a White House source, or some other title that underscores his authority. If the session is on "deep background," no direct quotes may be used and no attribution to any spokesman may be given. If the briefing is off the record, the information itself may not be used; there are no quotes and no attribution. Off-the-record briefings are rare. Their usual purpose is to prepare reporters for some coming event.

Backgrounders vary in the number of correspondents invited, in their settings or forums, and in the hours at which they are held. They can be as relatively intimate as former Secretary of State Rusk's Friday afternoon chats with favored reporters covering his department or as large as the East Room briefings at the White House before President Nixon's televised speeches. In the latter, reporters are summoned a few hours before the President speaks. They are given copies of his address to read. Then the presidential aide most involved in the subject of the President's talk offers analysis and answers questions. These sessions are especially helpful to broadcast commentators who have to go on the air immediately after the presidential speech. This useful practice by the Nixon White House means that Vice President Agnew's accusations of "instant analysis" of Mr. Nixon's speeches are pure sham.

Periodically the Washington journalistic community picks a fight with itself over the morality of backgrounders. These controversies reflect the press' feelings about vulnerability because of the dependency of reporters upon officials for information. They also bespeak some of the absurdities practiced by government under the backgrounder rules. Once during the Johnson administration three prominent officials held a not-for-attribution backgrounder for the writing press and then repeated most of what they said for television film crews.

But for the good correspondent backgrounders aren't the only source of information. He also has private talks with officials; he reads, gathers fact through dogged legwork, and even uses his social life in the pursuit of information. Few if any great news breaks have been blurted in the presence of journalists by a drunken Cabinet officer just before he slid, belching, beneath a Georgetown dinner table. But in the intermingling of reporters, officials, and politicians in the mainstream of Washington social life there are useful opportunities for all sides to meet, gain insights about one another, and engage in that exchange of opinions from which a synthesis of reasonable understanding is achieved.

Along with their external role of sending out declarative impulses to the public, the journalists of Washington also play a vital role within the Process. News is written as generalizations by outside observers with inside information. Because they are paid by somebody other than the U.S. government and because their survival in Washington does not depend upon the political fortunes of an administration or a Congress, journalists in this city are still outsiders of a sort. The combined output of the press results in an overview of Washington politics that relates the various parts of the Process to one another. That overview is the device by which the President sees the Congress and the Congress sees the President not as separate, contending clusters of ego but as elements in the larger Process scenario. "If the press did not report Congress, Congress could hardly function," wrote the late Representative Clem Miller. "If the sound of congressional voices carried no farther than the bare walls of the chambers, Congress would disband." In this way, the press is a sort of maddening mortar that holds the Process together.

What mitigates the declarative impulses that the press sends out to the public and the role the press plays within the Process itself is television. The medium doesn't convey ideas very well, especially not complicated ones. But it does convey aspects of personality in some enigmatic, ruthless way.

Television has enormous appeal to politicians because in it they see a chance to bypass journalists and throw their own declarative impulses directly at the public. Unfortunately for some politicians, that is sometimes exactly what happens. They display themselves in the full dimension of a reality they don't intend. Their carefully manufactured prose becomes a mishmash to their listeners. Their real personality burns through to the viewers from behind the contrivances of their natures. What remains after one of President Nixon's televised speeches is the memory of how perspiration sometimes forms on his upper lip. It isn't his fault. Mr. Nixon makes very good speeches on television but they are subservient to himself.

Yet this hasn't deterred the few Presidents who have governed in the television era. They all reach eagerly for the tube, presuming it to be a simple communications device. The National Broadcasting Company did an interesting tabulation of three eighteen-month periods in the administrations of John F. Kennedy, Lyndon B. Johnson, and Richard M. Nixon. During these periods Kennedy took to the box forty-seven times, Johnson went on forty times, and Nixon used television twenty-eight times. The difference between Mr. Nixon and his predecessors lay in the times he chose to appear. Fifteen of them were in what is called prime evening time—when the folks in videoland are immersing themselves in their love for Lucy, in the clean-shirted dauntlessness of a fictional FBI, or old movies. For all that, Mr. Nixon was sensitive to mass tastes. On May 8, 1967, he delayed a press conference for one hour so that the televising of it would not interfere with a basketball game on ABC between the Los Angeles Lakers and the New York Knicks.

What eludes most politicians is the fact that television is not the simple medium they think it is. Most of them have never grasped the first lesson the television commentator learns—that he is not speaking to 50 million people out there. He is speaking to two people sitting in a living room. The average politician tends to exhort on television when he should be conversing. Mr. Nixon's best performances were his talks with network correspondents. They were intimate and low-keyed.

Television has exacerbated the love-hate relationship between politicians and the press, intensifying the hatreds and converting the love into a lust for television's attention. During the first years of the Nixon administration considerable savagery was turned upon the press and television. There were the carefully orchestrated attacks of Mr. Agnew, the sicking of FBI agents on Daniel Schorr of CBS, the series of subpoenas slapped on reporters demanding their notes and film for grand jury investigations, the brawl over the publication of the Pentagon Papers.

To some degree all this was occasioned by the administration's fascination with television, its desire to get more televised attention for itself and more favorable coverage by television news departments. For that reason the Vice President made television his primary target and the Pentagon flew into a passion over a CBS documentary on its public relations practices. Aside from demonstrating the politician's abiding belief that television could be his salvation if he could only wrest it from the hands of those dreadful journalists and executives who control it, there was a startling logic behind the belligerent nonsense. What the Nixon people wanted—what any administration wants —was a good press, a press that wrote nice things about it. The Nixon people seem to have thought that the way to obtain that was by yelling and threatening.

Press power in the Process is almost but not quite like other Process power—it is based on the belief that the power holder can help or hurt. To a small degree the press does have the power to help and hurt; it sends out those declarative impulses that are half of the ultimate public perception of government. But the press' power to help or hurt must be carefully defined.

There are three sorts of bad impressions that the press can create. The first is instantaneous: something derogatory is written about a politician and for a brief time those reading or hearing the report think badly of its subject. But the impression fades quickly. The press raised hell about the Kennedy administration's use of FBI agents to try to pry sources of information from reporters. But it was raised only once as an issue and the Kennedy administration did not suffer a long-term reputation for being anti-civil libertarian.

The second bad impression created by the press is cumulative: a barrage of unfavorable stories is written about a politician or an administration over a protracted period of time; those who read or hear the reports form a vague but lasting impression that the politician or administration is bad. The classic unjust example of this is the enduring bad impression of President Andrew Johnson. Because a malevolent Senate impeached but did not convict him and because reporters wrote so often that he was a drunk (he wasn't), he suffered a permanent, cumulative bad reputation. It was created by shoddy politics and crummy journalism.

The third is institutional: highly specific press criticisms of a politician's performance in one area create a lasting bad impression of the politician among people particularly interested in the area under criticism. President Nixon prides himself on his expertise in foreign policy. The Anderson Papers' revelations of his handling of the India-Pakistan War in late 1971 dented his claim of expertise.

Politicians can survive the instantaneous bad impression because it doesn't last long. They can endure the institutional bad
impression because the receivers of the impression don't form a
majority. It is the cumulative bad impression that politicians
fear most.

All of this has to do with the basic problem of keeping people informed about their government, the problem of sending
out reasonable and accurate declarative impulses, which is the
press' real external role in the Process. In the aftermath of the
Copernican revolution in government and public affairs that problem is becoming a dilemma.

At 10:30 in the evening a black limousine leaves the White
House motor pool. The streets of downtown Washington are
brilliantly lit and almost deserted. The limousine goes down
Pennsylvania Avenue to Seventeenth Street, turns right, crosses
K, and turns right again into L Street, the night lights glinting
and swimming on its polished black body. It goes two blocks
east on L and draws up in front of the Washington *Post* building on Fifteenth Street. The driver gets out and goes inside. At the
reception desk he buys six copies of the first edition of Friday's
paper and returns to the White House.

A guard takes the newspapers from the driver at the basement
entrance on West Executive Avenue. He gives them to another
guard who goes up to the next floor by elevator. With the papers
under his arm he walks down to a door next to the Oval Office,
opens it, and gives the newspapers to Barbara Claudus, the
President's principal private secretary. Barbara pushes down the
button on her intercom. "The newspapers are here, Mr. President."

"All right," says the mechanized voice through the box.
"Bring 'em in."

She opens the door. Six men are scattered around the Oval
Office. Through the windows and French doors the lights of the
Washington Monument and Pennsylvania Avenue gleam and
sparkle in the hot darkness.

The President is behind his desk. His chair is pushed back. He is in his shirt sleeves; it is his usual striped shirt with a plain maroon knit tie. He wears seersucker trousers and highly polished black shoes. He is leaning forward, elbows on his legs, hands clasped. His patrician face is etched with the marks of that growing and permanent weariness—deepening lines at either corner of his mouth, dark-hued circlets of flesh curving below his eyes. He turns to look at Barbara as she enters. "Pass them out, will you?"

"Yes, sir." She lays one newspaper on the President's desk. She takes one to Keith Bernstein, the President's press secretary, who is standing by the French doors. Barbara hands a newspaper to Peter, who is sitting on one of the fireplace sofas next to Paul Brasher. Peter's tie is unknotted, his shirt collar open. Paul smiles, his eyes nearly closing, as he takes a newspaper. "Thanks," he murmurs. He flips it open and scans the front page as Barbara gives copies of *The Washington Post* to Mace Applegate and Lou Howard, who are sitting on the opposite sofa.

Brasher notices to his relief that the headline is not smeared across the top of the front page. It is compressed into a space above two columns on the right-hand side: "Presidential Threat to Speaker Alleged." Beneath it in smaller type there is another head: "Hatfield Cites Three Offers of Backing in 95th Congress Leadership Race." Below the headlines are two news columns written by the House and White House reporters for the paper. Paul glances down both columns and then opens the paper to page seven for the bleed-over.

"It could be worse," he says.

Lou lowers his newspaper. "Saved by the number three."

"Why three?" Bernstein asks.

"Both reporters keep coming up with the fact that Randy claims the President did this three times," Lou says. "They also lean on Randy's statement that he can name witnesses to each time but won't."

"It is worse," the President says from behind his desk. "Look at the editorial page."

Newspapers rustle in the Oval Office. Below the Herblock cartoon—which is devoted to another subject—there is a main article by Jack Sterling, the *Post*'s Supreme Court reporter, on the possible constitutional implications of presidential interference in a congressional leadership election.

"Jesus," Bernstein murmurs, "that's rough."

"You bet it is," the President answers, still looking down at the newspaper. "The bastards are impeaching me before they've heard all the evidence on whether I committed a crime." He finishes reading and then closes the newspaper. He lays it on his desk and looks up. "Mace," he says, "what're the chances that Randy Hatfield will drink himself to death before the next time I see him?"

"Ain't much," Applegate says, lowering his own newspaper into a crumpled heap on his lap.

"Any of you gentlemen like some coffee or something to eat from the kitchen?" Barbara asks.

The President nods. "Have them fix some sandwiches and coffee. And call Ben Saterlee."

"Yes, sir," Barbara says. "I think Ben's still in his office." She leaves.

"Like I was sayin'," Mace resumes, "thisyear mess is gonna make leadership meetin's right lively for a while. I think you oughta see Randy alone before the next one—and let folks know you've seen him."

The President nods. "I suppose so. Lou, do you think you ought to try Randy again?"

Howard shakes his head. "I've tried his office and his house. Dorothy says she hasn't seen him all evening and she's worried."

"She ought to be," Bernstein says. "The son of a bitch."

"If he's in his office he's prob'ly drunker 'n' a Baptist owl," Mace says. "You want me to go over there, Mistuh President?"

The President shakes his head. "No thanks, Mace. You're in enough trouble already with CBS coming out and saying I've been talking to you separately about the bills. And you're risking more problems by just being here this evening. It's still us against the House."

Paul Brasher folds his newspaper and puts it on the coffee

table between the two sofas. "Well," he says quietly, "it isn't going to be us against the House for long." He smiles at the President. "We've got our story straight and it's a pretty good one—"

"Ben's here," says Barbara's amplified voice from the speaker on the President's desk.

The President leans forward and pushes down a switch. "Send him in."

The door opens. Ben Saterlee comes in. He is wearing a rumpled olive-drab suit. His eyes behind the glasses appear tired. "Still at it?" he says.

The President nods. "Paul was just recapitulating where we are now."

"Okay," Saterlee says. He takes the chair that is beside the President's desk, turns it to face the room, and sits down.

"We've done a check of the visitors' schedule and the telephone calls," Paul says to Ben. "Randy's only been in here with the leadership or with delegations. Never alone. The last time was last Saturday, when he brought in a steel manufacturer from Cincinnati for a courtesy call."

"What about telephone calls?" Saterlee asks.

"We've only made one to him—that was on March 18 and it had to do with a postal bill. We've been dealing mostly with Mace and the Speaker."

"Anybody'd believe that," Saterlee says. "Randy's been pretty much out of action all session."

"If we're guilty of anything," Brasher says, "it's ignoring him too much."

"When he was in here last Saturday," the President says, "we began talking about the Revenue Act and the youth bill and I said that the Speaker wasn't really leading forcefully enough. Then—I really did this, you know, to make Randy look good in front of an important constituent—I said 'Randy would make a great Speaker' or something like that. I remember saying 'Maybe I'd better get with all of those Congressmen who want Randy to run for Speaker next time.' I think I also said that the country could use a great Speaker. That was it."

'What'd Randy say?" Saterlee asks.

The President shrugs. "Oh, he laughed or made some wise-crack. I remember that the man with him laughed too. I suppose I let my feelings about the Speaker show a little bit, but—"

"The only other thing we can think of," Paul says, "was when two British MPs were in here last month. One of them was named Sherborne and the other was—well, Barbara has those names too. They are both Tories and were on some sort of State Department tour for members of Commons. The President talked to them about the different roles of the Speaker here and in the House of Commons. The President said something about difficulties with the Speaker and Sherborne asked if he had any real influence in disposing of a Speaker. The President said no."

"Did you mention Hatfield?" Saterlee asks the President.

"Good God no," the President says. "When I did it that once it was just a way of flattering Randy in front of an important constituent."

"He must be crazy," Saterlee says.

"He's a very disturbed man," Howard says.

"Why don't we just tell the truth," Saterlee says. "Just say that you were trying to make Randy look good?"

The President shakes his head. "No, because the two members of Parliament are still in the picture. They probably dined around Washington or reported their conversation in here to their embassy and, in the natural course of things, repeated what I said. That's probably where Randy gets another proof of my anti-constitutional plottings." He doesn't smile.

"Then what do we do?" Saterlee asks.

"Call Randy Hatfield a liar and a nut," Bernstein says angrily.

"No," Peter says. "Excuse me, Keith, but we can't afford that."

"He's right," the President says. "We'd just end up creating sympathy for him. Mace, what's this going to cost us in the House?"

Applegate pushes his large mouth into a contemplative pout. "Depends," he says slowly. "We gotta lot of old boys who're on the fence on that bill right now—not all of 'em because they don't like the bill. Me 'n' John figger we need nine-twelve votes. May-be thisyear thing'll make some of them fellers drop down on the 'no' side." He takes a deep breath. "House's a funny thing, Mistuh President. The boys'll fight like hounds 'n' polecats among theirselves, but if they think somebody outside's pickin' on the House," he looks directly at the President, "why, then, they'll crawl all over that feller."

"And I'm the feller picking on the House," the President says with a small smile.

"That's 'bout the way it's gonna look—at least first off," Mace replies.

"Have you heard of the Speaker telephoning any members to persuade them to vote for our bill?"

"Nawsuh."

"We have a timing problem," Brasher says. "We have to get our side of the story out fast and clearly before Randy's version sets."

Bernstein sits down on the sofa beside Peter. "Then we have to orchestrate what we have. Look," he says to Saterlee, "a lot of the guys have been pressuring me to see you. You've become the mystery man behind the White House scenes and all that crap." He turns to Paul. "How about staging a backgrounder with Ben tomorrow morning for a dozen of the top guys?"

The room is silent. The President, once again leaning forward, elbows resting on his knees, looks inquiringly at Brasher.

After a moment Paul nods. "Yes. Good." He turns to the President. "Ben could lay out what *we* think is the basis for Randy's accusations—the meeting with you last Saturday and the discussion with the two MPs."

The President nods.

"Forget the goddamn MPs," Keith says.

"No," Paul says, turning back to him. "It's better that we mention them than have the American press corps in London dig them up and spring them—even though what the President said to them hurts our case."

"Ben doesn't have to repeat the bit about us wishing we had another Speaker," Bernstein replies.

"Okay," Brasher says. "He'll just repeat the discussion about the roles of the two Speakers and—"

"And that's all," Bernstein says.

"One thing," the President says, straightening up. "I don't want anyone in any way impugning Randy's mental state. If we suggest that we're in trouble."

"Right," says Saterlee. "I won't."

"*Nobody* will," the President says. "Is that clear? I think Randy sounds about half bats and the rest of you may think it. But we don't say it—not even in private conversation. Right?"

"Right," Brasher says. "What about television tomorrow?"

Peter has been leaning back on the sofa. Suddenly he straightens up. "Hey," he says softly, "who was the guy Randy had in here with him last Saturday?"

The President leans across his desk and presses the switch on his intercom. "Barbara, what was the name of that man Congressman Hatfield had in here last Saturday?"

"Hold on a sec," Barbara says. In a moment she answers. "His name was Frederick Porter. He's—wait a minute. He's president of Ohio Sheet and Tube."

The President looks at Paul.

"Let's try," Brasher says.

The silence hangs with the President's indecision. He presses the switch down again. "See if the switchboard can get him for Paul, Barbara."

"Right."

The President leans back in his chair again. "We have to do more than this," he says. "We can't just waste our energies defending ourselves against poor old Randy. How're we going to turn this thing around so that it's an argument for our bills?"

"Anything on the Speaker?" Bernstein says.

"No," the President answers. He is tilted back in his chair looking at the ceiling.

"Any value in you going on television?" Lou asks.

"No," the President answers, still gazing at the ceiling. "It'd appear defensive. We need offense."

The silence embraces a full minute. Mace sits with his hands clasped between his knees looking at the landscape above the fireplace. Lou takes out his pipe.

"We haven't talked to anybody about the weapons caches," Ben Saterlee says.

The President lowers his gaze. "What about weapons?"

"Two FBI reports," Ben answers. "One on caches of weapons found in St. Louis, Providence, and Anaheim. They're like the ones black revolutionaries have, only bigger. They were stock-piled by Leland's secret paramilitary bunch."

"I didn't know about that," the President says.

"The reports just came in this morning," Ben answers. "The other one is on the paramilitary group."

"How big is it?"

"Three or four thousand people," Saterlee says.

The President nods. "All right. Have Justice leak the reports where they'll do the most good."

"Great," Bernstein says. "That'll make great Sunday stories. It'll show how urgent this program is."

"Will somebody start wondering why we haven't made arrests?" The President asks.

"The paras haven't done anything yet," Ben says. "Except for storing weapons."

Mace turns to the President. "I got 'nother idear," he says. "Whyn't you fellers get the chairman of Ways 'n' Means t' go on the television for yawl? He'd prob'ly say something good."

"No, Mace," the President says. "He's got us too far over a barrel already and he knows it. He's sitting on that Revenue Act revision and God, I wish I knew why."

"It's his way of doing things," Lou says. "I really don't think he's deliberately—"

"That's nonsense, Lou, and you know it," the President says. "He wants something and he's softening us up for whatever it is by holding those damned interminable hearings—"

"Mr. Porter on 208," Barbara's voice says through the intercom.

Paul Brasher gets up and crosses the room to the President's desk. He turns on a switch, punches a blinking button, and picks up the telephone. "Hello, Mr. Porter?"

"This is Frederick Porter," says a low, slightly hoarse voice through the speaker on the desk.

"This is Paul Brasher," Paul says. "I believe we met briefly when you were here last Saturday to see the President. I'm his appointments secretary."

"Oh. Oh, yes, Mr. Brasher. I remember you."

"I'm sorry to call you so late, sir, but the matter is somewhat urgent and we thought you might be willing to help us."

"I'll try. I think I know what you have in mind."

"There's apparently been some sort of misunderstanding about your conversation with the President," Paul says. "Congressman Hatfield—"

"Yes," Porter says. "I know all about it. I saw it on the news earlier this evening. Randy called me about half an hour ago."

"Oh?" Paul says, looking at the President.

"Between you and me, Mr. Brasher, Randy didn't make much sense. He was drunk."

"I'm sorry to hear it," Brasher says. "It really isn't his fault, you know. He had that terrible family tragedy a year or so ago."

"Good," the President says quietly.

"Yes, I know that," Porter answers. "I sympathize. I knew young Benny Hatfield. But Randy has his public responsibilities too. I don't understand all the ins and outs of this thing, Mr. Brasher. But if Randy is referring to our conversation with the President when he accuses the President of threatening the Speaker of the House, then he's talking absolute nonsense."

Keith Bernstein raises his hands above his head, clasps them, and shakes them in a victory gesture.

"We think that the conversation that you took part in is the basis of what Randy said," Brasher replies. "We're mainly anxious to set the record straight if we can. Would you be willing to help us?"

Out in the dark night of Ohio, Frederick Porter is silent for a moment. "Well," he says. Then he pauses again. "You put me in a difficult position, Mr. Brasher. I am a friend of Randy's and —I must tell you quite candidly that I didn't vote for the President and I don't go along with a lot of his policies."

"Of course," Paul says. "What we had hoped you might do would be to meet with whatever reporters call you and just give your own factual account of what happened last Saturday. To cover yourself I think you ought to say that you didn't vote for us and find yourself in disagreement with many or all of our policies. That would be honest and would leave you in the clear."

Bernstein leans over to Saterlee. "Our boy Paul's an absolute genius," he whispers loudly.

Porter is silent.

"What is involved here," says Paul quietly, "is the integrity of the President, of the presidency itself. We have no desire to attack Randy. Please understand that. What we're concerned with is the constitutional issues that would be raised if what Randy said were true."

"Well," Porter says hesitantly. Again he pauses. "For all I know, the President might have threatened the Speaker on some other occasion—"

"All we want you to do is to discuss the one conversation you heard," Brasher says patiently.

"Randy called me, as I said," Porter replies. "As well as being drunk he sounded frightened. He tried to get me to agree that the President had made a threat. I couldn't, of course."

"Then would you—"

"Are you asking me in the name of the President?" Porter says.

"No," Paul says. "I really can't say that I am. I'm asking you as myself—perhaps a little bit in the name of history."

"All right," Porter says. "I'll do what you want. You can give any reporters who ask this number and I'll be at my office in Cincinnati after 9:30 tomorrow morning. I'll be there all day. Any reporters who wish to see me can."

"Thank you," Paul says. "I know this will help. You'll be hearing from us."

"Oh, one more thing," Porter says. "When I was talking with the President he mentioned his fondness for fishing. You might remind him that I have a place on Gaspee peninsula with some of the best salmon fishing he'll ever find anywhere. It's his for the asking."

"Any trout around there?" Brasher asks.

"Oh, plenty. Good trout fishing," Porter says with a small laugh.

"Then we might both take you up on it," Brasher says, smiling his serene smile. "I'm a trout man myself."

"Anytime, Mr. Brasher."

"Thank you, Mr. Porter."

"Thank you, Mr. Brasher. My regards to the President."

Paul hangs up.

"We've won," he says. "Ben, we'll give you some stuff to use on your backgrounder, statistics on riots and clashes and other data to show the urgency of the situation and why we need the bills."

"Okay," Ben says.

For the first time since the conference started after the Cronkite show, the President smiles broadly.

It is 11:55. Before one o'clock in the morning, Keith Bernstein and Peter have called the Washington bureau chiefs of the two wire services and have given them Porter's telephone number. The same data is transmitted to the bureau chiefs of the three television networks. Thirteen Washington correspondents and columnists—nine of them regular White House men, the others generalists with wide circulation or columnists like Willy Dern—have been invited to a backgrounder with Ben Saterlee at eight in the morning. The Attorney General's special assistant for public affairs has been told to release the two FBI reports on Friday night to *The New York Times,* and the Los Angeles *Times,* the Washington *Post,* the Chicago *Tribune,* and *Time* and *Newsweek.* At 1:15 Keith calls the overnight desk man at the Associated Press bureau and tells him that Congressman Hatfield is going to be interviewed at CBS at ten in the morning. Bernstein suggests that the AP and other organizations send reporters to hear what Hatfield says, or at least to see if he shows up. The suggestion is telephoned to five other bureaus or their chiefs. Peter has dealt with a girl who books guests for *Meet the Press;* he promises to try for Ben Saterlee for Sunday but warns that the White House is more interested in talking about its New Partnership program than in commenting on the squabble with the Majority Leader. The girl says that will be fine.

Keith goes home. At 3:15 the telephone rings in his bedroom. Wearily, he switches on the light and answers it. "Yeah?"

"This is John Crawford of *The New York Times*," says a voice through the slight crackle of long distance. "I wanted you to know that in our Saturday paper we're running a report, or a story based on a report, that we got from somebody in the National Institutes of Mental Health. They've been treating Congressman Hatfield since last August."

"What?" Keith says loudly.

His wife wakes up and says, "Keith, what's going on?"

"I can't say how we got it," Crawford continues, "but we will say that Congressman Hatfield has been under treatment for anxiety and depression since last summer—"

"Don't use that!" Keith says. "Jesus, man, people will think we gave it to you!"

"We wanted to know if you had any comment."

"Look," Keith says, "call me in the morning. But please, for God's sake, can't you make it clear you didn't get it from the White House?"

"I was asked to call now because we're putting this together for—"

Keith hangs up. He flops back on his bed and looks at the ceiling. "Oh God," he says, "goddamn . . ."

At 9:30 in the morning Willy Dern comes back from the White House, climbs the steps leading up to his house, unlocks the front door, goes through the hall and the living room, and enters the dining room, where his wife sits reading the Washington *Post*. Sally Dern looks up, her red hair falling back from her face. She is wearing a flower-print robe that is tied with a black ribbon at her throat. "Hi, darling." She smiles. "They got you up too early."

Willy kisses her and sits down at the table.

"Want some eggs?"

Willy shakes his head. "No, they gave us something at the White House. Just coffee."

She pours from a china pot and puts a cup and saucer before him. "How was it?"

"They're doing pretty well," Willy says. "They aren't beating on Randy but, you know, sort of stressing the program. They think this all started with a session Randy had last Saturday in the President's office. Some guy from Ohio was in with him. The President was sort of kidding Randy about being the next Speaker."

"But how did Randy get"—Sally waves a slender hand toward the front page of the *Post*—all *that* from that?"

Willy shrugs and picks up his coffee cup. "There was also something said when Donald Sherborne and Colin Maitland were over from London."

"Yes," Sally says. "Oh sure, remember when we saw them at the Markses'? They said they'd been in with the President."

Willy nods. "That coffee's hot," he says.

"What about the man from Ohio?"

"The AP's running a long piece in which he denies that the President ever threatened, claims that he was just joking when he said Randy ought to be Speaker," Willy says.

"Poor Randy. It's kind of crazy, isn't it?" Sally asks. "Or have I got it wrong?"

"No," Willy says, "you've got it right. Randy Hatfield's going to fall on his face because it is crazy."

"I wonder if I ought to call Dorothy and just try to be nice," Sally says.

"You should," he tells her. "Whatever bad time they've had is now going to get worse." He gets up. "I've got to write."

She looks up, her face is sad. She smiles. "Be kind to him," she says.

"Randy isn't important," Willy says. "He's not even the issue anymore." He kisses her and goes downstairs. Sally pours herself another cup of coffee and goes upstairs to call Dorothy Hatfield.

In his basement office Willy reads a few letters from the morning mail, dictates two answers to his secretary, and telephones to confirm a lunch date at the Sans Souci. Then he reads the rest of the *Post* coverage of the Hatfield affair and folds open *The New York Times* to the inside page on which it finishes its lead and adds sidebars. He opens his notebook and goes back over conversations he had the previous afternoon with Peter, Paul

Brasher, a legislative scholar at the Brookings Institute, and a friend at Harvard Law he talked to by telephone. At the end of a long evening with John Stermas he made a few more notes.

He turns to the typewriter, inserts two sheets, and pushes his office door closed with his foot. When his secretary, sitting in her own office, hears the typewriter start she will deflect all telephone calls. It usually takes Willy two hours to finish three drafts.

"Whatever the final reality behind the brouhaha between the President and the Speaker of the House," he writes, "the quarrel itself is neither novel nor particularly surprising. Theodore Roosevelt and Speaker Joseph G. Cannon despised each other, so did Woodrow Wilson and Champ Clark. In both cases, as in the present one, the Speaker and the President were of the same party.

"What is at issue is neither party nor personalities but two incompatible sets of imperatives, the unique pressures of two different political universes, one with the President at its center, the other revolving around the Speaker.

"Within these two universes political facts are seen in different ways. The fact in dispute here is the President's New Partnership program, symbolized by two bills presently in the House. From the center of his universe the President sees them as national necessities. From the center of his, the Speaker sees the difficulties the bills present to a clogged legislative system in which power is too dispersed . . ."

By 9:50 in the morning the sun has hoisted itself to its murder meridian in the sky and Keith Bernstein is having a screaming row with an editor of *The New York Times* by long-distance telephone. On Capitol Hill the Speaker is in his office talking to a House reporter for the Washington *Post*. "You know Washington," he says, smiling but not with his heavy eyes. "Gossipy town. Chatty town. Now I want you boys to be quite clear on this fictional feud between me and the President."

"Fictional?" the reporter asks.

"Oh hell, yes, of course it's fictional," the Speaker answers. "It's all in poor old Randy's head." He takes a slender, twisted Philippine cigar from a box on his desk, snips the end off, and looks at the reporter again. "Randy's had a lot of trouble, you know. I'm afraid he drinks a bit too."

"But he did come to you saying that the President had threatened him, didn't he?"

"Yes, he did. Of course, I never believed most of his nonsense. I was downright shocked when he started talking yesterday," the Speaker says.

"You never believed him?" the reporter says. "Can I quote you on that?"

"Of course you can. Have you seen the news wires this morning? There's a story about a man out in Ohio who was present when Randy saw the President last Saturday. He says it was all bosh. Joking, that's all."

"If you didn't believe him," the reporter says, "why didn't you say something yesterday when Randy started all this?"

The Speaker smiles again. "Why, young man, you know the answer to that as well as I do. Do you think I'm going to come and and call my dear friend and number-one colleague a liar? Why, CBS was in here last evening trying the hardest way to get me to go on the television. I didn't."

"Mr. Speaker," says the reporter, trying to keep his anger down, "isn't it true that you've been on bad terms with the President for some weeks now?"

"Prove it," the Speaker answers, his voice grained with hostility. "Why, next thing you boys will be accusing me of putting Randy up to this . . ."

At the CBS bureau on M Street the taping session is in its seventh minute. The bureau chief stands in the control room watching a monitor. He is still tense from a quarrel he had with four reporters who wanted to come up and watch the taping session.

"Let's go back to the beginning," the congressional correspondent says to Hatfield. "The story that came out on Thursday evening quoted you as saying that you had had three meetings with the President."

The director, speaking through his intercom, has been ordering camera number one to move in for a close-up of Hatfield.

On another monitor that close-up holds. The director calls for it. The close-up fills the main monitor.

"I don't care what I was quoted as saying," Hatfield answers, "I didn't say that I had three meetings with the President. I said that the President had discussed this matter three times to my knowledge."

"Take two," the director says.

A close-up of the congressional correspondent fills the main monitor. "That you should replace the Speaker?"

"That the Speaker should be replaced," Hatfield's voice says offscreen.

"Wait a minute," the correspondent says. "When I talked to you on Thursday afternoon you said that the President had offered to back you for the speakership in the 95th Congress."

"Take three," the director says.

A medium shot of both Hatfield and the correspondent flashes onto the monitor, "That's right. Last Saturday was what I had in mind," Hatfield answers.

"But Mr. Porter, who was there, says it was all a joke."

Hatfield shifts in his chair and lowers his chin. "Fred Porter can put whatever interpretation on it he likes," the Majority Leader says. "I put my own on it."

"Take two," the director says. Hatfield again fills the main monitor. He is perspiring and a muscle on his cheek appears to be twitching.

"Okay, Congressman," says the correspondent's voice. "When were the other two times?"

Hatfield takes a deep breath. With two fingers he wipes perspiration from his forehead. "Several weeks ago two members of the British Parliament were in the President's office and I am reliably informed that this matter was discussed."

"That you should replace the Speaker?"

"Take one," the director says.

The medium shot of Hatfield and the correspondent appears on the monitor.

Hatfield raises a clenched fist and brings it softly down on the chair arm. "No!" he says loudly. "I never said that! They were told by the President that the Speaker should be replaced!"

"But you said the President had offered three times to back you."

"Take two," says the director. "Jesus, this is pathetic."

"What I said," Hatfield begins loudly, impatiently," was that—"

The bureau chief leans forward and pushes a button under a microphone that communicates with the studio floor. "Thank you, Congressman," he says, "I don't think we'll want any more."

On the camera monitor both Hatfield and the correspondent look up at the control room.

"Cut," says the director.

7: The Lobbyists

> The host of contractors, speculators, stock jobbers and lobby members which haunts the halls of Congress, all desirous . . . on any and every pretext to get their arms into the public treasury, are sufficient to alarm every friend of the country. Their progress must be arrested.
>
> James Buchanan, 1852

> Because our congressional representation is based on geographic boundaries, the lobbyists who speak for various economic, commercial and other functional interests of this country serve a very useful purpose and have assumed an important role in the legislative process.
>
> John F. Kennedy, 1955

Washington is an island of self-contemplating expertise in a sea of inchoate humanity. Washington can run farm price support programs but it doesn't feel the despair of a rancher confronted with anthrax. Washington can negotiate diplomatic relations with Albania but it has no way of feeling the reaction of Albanian-Americans. Washington can do the multiple calculations necessary to keep a war going but it hasn't any means of gauging when or if the families of Americans held prisoner will stop being anxious and start demanding. Washington, in other words, knows how to make policies and forecast their results in the abstract but it isn't very good at subjectively feeling the infinite multiplicity of human and institutional hopes, needs and fears that are the festering reality of the country.

Receiving and feeling those hopes, needs and fears is a supreme problem for Washington because the political system of the

United States professes to be based on the will of the people. Yet the President is driven into isolation and the House of Representatives doesn't represent the people in the full dimension of their being and, indeed, that dimension of human being is only part of what the nation is. The people themselves coalesce into armies, Polish-American societies, trade unions and The Sons of I Will Arise and each of them is riddled with hopes, fears and needs. As well as being human the country is also vast; it is composed of institutions of an amazing variety—from cancer research labs to state prisons, from universities to banks, zoos, think tanks and asylums for the lost, deranged or deformed—all of them attuned in various ways to the cadences of Washington's arcane being. They all hope, they all fear and they all need. They all have to tell Washington about themselves.

When they cannot tell, or when Washington fails to hear and understand, two extreme phenomena occur. There is a suffocating pall of public apathy which results in political chaos or political mediocrity. Or, portions of the population erupt into attention-clamoring demonstrations of their will or grievance.

There are two channels through which at least some expression of the nation pours into this city. Both are more or less uncontrollable, unfashionable, often unattractive and frequently misunderstood and, therefore, despised. One of the national channels of expression is almost as old as the nation itself. The other is a mysterious new phenomenon whose precise origin, cause and anatomy is not yet fully understood. The old channel is the lobbying system. The new one is the spontaneous, mass movement.

Sometimes the two can join together to pressure Washington into action and decision. The 1964 Civil Rights Act was the most sweeping piece of legislation of its kind passed in this century. It came about in large part because a spontaneous, mass movement for civil rights created the proper climate in the country and because a task force of lobbyists from seventy-nine different groups helped to design strategy and then exerted the pressures needed for the bill's passage.

When discussing these two forces one has to define the terms carefully. "Lobbyist" means a Washington agent or representative for some entity in the country. The agent or representative may be a free-lance lobbyist willing to work for anyone. He may be registered or unregistered. Or, he may be the staff employee of an association, a business, an organization or an interest. He (and often she) might be a Washington lawyer with extensive knowledge of and contacts in the federal establishment. The executive branch of that establishment has its own lob· byists—usually called "congressional liaison staff"—who push for programs on Capitol Hill on behalf of the White House, the Pentagon, the Interior Department, Treasury, Health, Education and Welfare, and other departments and agencies. The Washington lobbyist may be as sleazy as one man with bad taste in neckties and a profound realization that business is terribly naive about government. Or he may be an evangelical visionary, disinterested in personal gain, obsessed with an idea and blessed with an understanding of, and a gift for, working with the Congress and the rest of the government.

The entity in the nation which employs lobbyists may be a plastics manufacturer, a labor union, a whole industry, a conservation group, an association of professional liberal or professional conservatives, an industrial conglomerate, a foreign government, a maritime association, a cause, a complaint, left- or right-wing nuts or a slightly deranged man in Idaho who thinks he knows how to use solar energy as a birth control device.

There are blatantly dishonest lobbyists and ruthlessly honest ones. A celebrated fringe operator in this city is known for getting friends in Congress to introduce bills that work against the interests of his clients. The bill has no chance of passage but the lobbyist puts on a ferocious display of fighting it. When the bill dies the lobbyist sends a triumphant telegram to his employer and collects a big bonus. At the other extreme there is Clark Clifford, Washington's most prestigious lawyer. He has a little speech for new clients: "There is one point I wish to make clear. This firm has no influence of any kind in Washington. If you want to employ someone who has influence, you will have to go somewhere else. First, because I am not sure what the term 'influence' means and second, because whatever it is, we don't have

it. What we do have is a record of working with the various departments and agencies of government and we have their respect
and confidence and that we consider a valuable asset."

The lobbyist may work on the offensive or he may take a defensive stance on behalf of his clients. One of the great offensive
operations of recent memory is the passage of the Merchant
Marine Act of 1970. It was an impressive feat (it is still called
"the miracle of the 91st Congress") because a history of lethargy
and disinterest preceded it. For years the American merchant
marine fleet had been decaying. Congress had, for years, either
ignored the fact or studied it to death. A coalition of lobbyists
from the shipbuilding business and unions and other groups in
the maritime industry was put together. The ultimate result was
the passage of an administration bill which provided for the
building of 300 new ships over a ten-year period. The cost was
$5 billion and the act provided for two-fifths payment by the
federal government. It was regarded as a victory for a group of
dedicated lobbyists.

The defensive lobbyist works to preserve some status quo.
The large, well-heeled Washington oil lobby operates through
such innocuous-sounding fronts as the American Petroleum Institute and the Independent Petroleum Association of America.
("Institute" is a relatively new term for lobbying fronts. It is designed to drape the endeavors of special interest groups with a
mantle of quasi-academic respectability.) The oil lobby devotes
its life, blood and sacred honor to keeping the oil-depletion allowance alive and the oil quota system in operation. The deple-
tion allowance is a wrinkle in the tax law which permits the oil
industry to deduct a large percentage of its gross income from its
taxable income. The amount used to be 27.5 percent. It was cut
to 22 percent in the Tax Reform Act of 1969. But the fact that
the allowance survives at all is a monument to the defensive
skill of the oil lobby and to the durability of the mysterious love
affair between some politicans and the oil business.

If, by "influence" one means something infallible and absolute,
then Clark Clifford is right. No lobbyist has total influence; being a lobbyist is a game of chance and skill and therein lies its

fascination for many of its practitioners. You never know if the view or interest you are pushing will be wholly successful, partially successful or whether it will be completely ignored in the making, defining or carrying out of the law.

In trying to win the lobbyist has a wide range of techniques at his disposal. They range from personal contact with members of Congress, their staffs or committee staffs, to grass roots and press campaigns, preparing and presenting research, testimony before congressional committees and efforts to defeat or elect candidates who oppose or favor the lobbyist's cause. No special onus or virtue clings to any of the legitimate techniques. The National Rifle Association which is the mortal enemy of gun-control legislation uses grass-roots campaigns. One of its executives told Congressional Quarterly, the Washington research organization, that he guessed that the N.R.A. could whip up half a million letters against something it disapproved of. Common Cause, the public interest lobbying group headed by John Gardner, also uses grass-roots campaigning. It has a system of telephone "trees." Somebody from the Washington office of Common Cause calls key members of local chapters, each of whom calls five other members who each call ten more. A few days later Congress may be deluged with letters, telegrams and phone calls on behalf of something Common Cause is pushing.

The gathering and use of research is a very sophisticated lobbying technique. The Pentagon uses carefully researched analyses of weapons gaps between this country and the Soviet Union in its annual battle for the military budget (since a lot of the information used in the research is or has been classified, few people can dispute the conclusions arrived at by military lobbyists). Ralph Nader is a skillful user of two techniques combined—research and grass-roots pressure. Nader's complex of consumer, law, public service and blue-collar action groups also uses testimony before congressional committees as a key device to push their campaigns for consumerism or government and law reform. But the basis of the Nader operation is research—his celebrated and controversial reports on pollution of the Savannah River, the DuPont Corporation, the use of farm land in California, the automobile industry and the First National City Bank of New

York. Nader has also touched a responsive public nerve. His operation, wrote Louis Harris, the poll man, "seems to fit the public mood for a new pattern of political action." Having seized that mood, which amounts to a spontaneous, mass movement, Nader has a weapon that turns other lobbyists green with envy.

The law prohibits unions or corporations from using their own funds in political campaigns. But there's a no law against setting up committees to funnel contributions from workers, corporation executives and associations into political campaigns. The AFL-CIO's Committee On Political Education (COPE) and the American Medical Political Action Committe (AMPAC) do just that.

There is a certain lurid charm but not much accuracy in the public's vague impression of the lobbyist as a slick character doing the rounds of Capitol Hill, dropping off envelopes full of money in return for votes. Most of the understandings between lobbyists and legislators are implicit. A senator who votes against labor's interests doesn't need to have a labor lobbyist tell him that he won't be getting union support the next time he's up for re-election. Direct bribery is considered crass and only small-timers try it (but some businesses operating without lobbyists *do* try).

Their are always a few members of Congress who want rewards for their votes. Most don't and most good lobbyists have contempt for those who do. But a Congressman so motivated is usually accommodated if that's the only way to get him on some important bill. The seal system of rewards is rather blurry, its lines stretching to the absolutes of right and wrong are indistinct, decipherable only in terms of atmospheres. The public may think that a reward practice is wrong. Washington is jaded enough to accept most of them with a shrug. A reward-seeking Congressman who has always treated the flyswatter industry kindly may, at the end of his service on Capitol Hill, be rewarded with a job as Executive Director of the American Fly Swatter Institute in Washington. He may, while still in Congress, be asked to make a speech "with honorarium and expenses" to the annual convention of the Fly Swatter Manufacturers Association. His otherwise unemployable nephew may be given a job in the flyswatter game. Which is illegal? None of them. But, if done consistently, stupidly or voraciously, such actions are immoral at worst and, at best, not exactly designed to inspire confidence in the Congressman's integrity.

In recent years various members of Congress or their staffs have been accused of bribery and some have been convicted.

John Dowdy, a solemn little Congressman from Texas, was convicted of taking a bribe in the late winter of 1972. Former Senator Daniel B. Brewster of Maryland was indicted but not convicted of accepting a payoff from a Chicago mail-order house. Martin Sweig, an aide to former House Speaker John McCormack, was convicted of perjury after testifying to his relationship with Nathan Voloshen, a New York lawyer and influence-peddler of unsanitary reputation. Brewster was later convicted of accepting a bribe. Bobby Baker, former secretary to the Senate Democratic Majority, went to prison for using his official position to help his business interests.

The temptations presented by an immense government dealing in billions of dollars and uncountable pressures and promises that influence national life, are terrifying. What is remarkable is that there isn't wholesale bribery and graft as there was in the late nineteenth century. What sometimes causes despair in Washington is that jaded atmosphere which seems to go with power. Is it, for example, a direct bribe when the Ford Motor Company offers important members of Congress cheap leases on fully insured Lincoln Continental cars? Who can precisely nail down specific benefits reaped by the American President Lines Inc. and Pacific Far East Lines Inc. of San Francisco when they made illegal campaign contributions to 16 Senators and Representatives including the chairmen of two committees which control federal subsidies to shipping lines? The amounts involved in the contributions weren't large (but the fines slapped on the companies were). No specific favor can be traced to most of the remodeling jobs done on Congressmen's homes at cut rates by construction companies.

What is involved in these crummy *quids pro quo* is the creation of atmospherics. They are the recognition of power by money and of money by power in the hands of people who aren't mature enough to handle either. The atmosphere created is based on contempt for the public and the Process; it is an assumption of superiority on the part of the participants, a superiority not based on any natural endowments but on their possession of money or their proximity to power. The atmosphere creates, for its political insiders, the illusion that the power they wield belongs to them and not to the Process. If not blatantly dishonest in the legal sense, the atmosphere presupposes that what the rest of the world doesn't know won't hurt it, that the normal rules of decent behavior are inapplicable to those who have the money or the power to veto them.

Congress has, over the years, made sporadic attempts to deal with the worst abuses of lobbying. But that is difficult to do for two reasons. First, much of the lobbying activity in Washington is crucial to the legislative process. And second, lobbying is implicitly sanctioned by the First Amendment's declared right of the people to "petition the Government for a redress of grievances."

Lobbying is almost as old as the Congress itself. The term was first applied to professional favor-seekers operating around the New York State legislature in 1829. Throughout the nineteenth century lobbyists employed by big business built their trade's onerous reputation. They were at the root of many of the scandals which periodically seared Washington from the end of the Civil War through the turn of the century. Some of the lobbyists of the period were relatively honest; the great Sam Ward, brother of Julia Ward Howe, was called "King of the Lobby" and he was one of the glittering social and intellectual figures of his time. But he was an exception in a period of general corruption.

Largely as a result of public nausea, Congress first cracked down hard on lobbying in 1907. It passed the laws that forbid corporations from making direct contributions to political campaigns. Congressional investigations of lobbyists periodically made headlines—the 1913 probe of the National Association of Manufacturers, investigations of the utilities, munitions and maritime lobbyists in the 1930s.

But the laws which have resulted from all of this activity are still inadequate. Under the Federal Registration of Lobbying Act passed as Title III of the Legislative Reorganization Act of 1946, a distinction is made between lobbyists for hire by anyone and those organizations which lobby for themselves. There is also a difference in the law between lobbyists who make direct contact with members of Congress and those who work through other means. Because of these distinctions, highly visible and active Washington organizations like the National Rifle Association and the National Association of Manufacturers don't have to register as lobbyists. Nor do they have to file quarterly financial reports with the Congress. Even the requirements for those who do have to file are shot full of loopholes. The lobbyists themselves define which part of their salaries and expenses go for lobbying as it is described by the law.

Some of the public good lobbying groups are extensions of direct-interest activities—the AFL-CIO spends as much of its time in coalitions working for education, civil rights and other public good bills as it does on legislation of direct interest to labor. More often, public good lobbying is done by groups set up especially for the purpose—either nonpartisan ones like the Nader operation and Common Cause or ideologically oriented associations like the liberal Americans for Democratic Action and the American Conservative Union. Some groups like the National Association for the Advancement of Colored People lobby for highly specific, noncommercial ends.

The new, nonpartisan lobby organizations in Washington are, essentially, an outgrowth of the second means of transmitting public needs, fears and hopes to Washington—the spontaneous, mass movements. For that reason they lean heavily on grass-roots pressures. Like all Washington lobbyists, the public good groups are in a perpetual state of flux, shifting in and out of coalitions of lobbying organizations brought together to work on particular bills. While it is entirely conceivable that A.D.A. and A.C.U. might find themselves on the same side in an issue, one group operates almost always alone: Liberty Lobby. It is a right-wing organization which defines legislation as "pro-American" or "anti-American" depending on how Liberty Lobby feels about it. Like most other lobbying operations, it tends to focus on those members of Congress who agree with the basic Liberty Lobby vision of the universe. Since there aren't too many of those, Liberty Lobby isn't very effective.

To be *effective,* a public good lobby has to connect with a large body of public feeling. Common Cause works on what it calls "structure and process" issues—the operations of government and matters like reform of campaign-spending laws. Nader has seized the tide of consumerism. The conservation lobby, picking up the widespread public passion for world-improvement, has had such an impact on Washington that it now fears environmental backlash. After the Environmental Defense Fund, Inc., won a temporary injunction against the Tennessee-Tombigbee Waterway, Senator James O. Eastland of Mississippi roared, "Everybody is in favor of protecting the enrvironment, but this business of yelling 'ecology' everytime we get ready for a new project has got to stop!" It was, in its way, a left-handed compliment to the success of the conservation lobby.

In the final analysis, lobbying is both a disreputable and an honorable profession and the difference can't be drawn simply in terms of who and what a lobbyist works for. Both the special interest lobbies and ones working for the public good are essential to the Process. No effective health care bill, for instance, can be drawn up without considering the views of the National Council of Senior Citizens, the American Public Health Association, the American Medical Association, American Hospital Association, National Association of Blue Shield Plans, child care groups, medical supply businesses, organizations and special pleaders involved in health care for any reason. That is not to say that the health care bill should favor any or all of the interests involved in such an array of witnesses. Rather, all of those organizations and groups and many others besides, are factors in American health care and they have viewpoints worth considering. They are part of the nation. If they have to live with the law, the law has to live with them. That's part of the bargain of democracy.

"Nigger lover!"

"Are you going to vote for the coons or for America?"

"*VOTE WHITE!! VOTE THE FLAG!! VOTE AMER-
ICAN!!*"

Tad Solomon lowers the handful of post cards reeking with
vilification and plastered with flag stickers. He looks at the
window. Waves of rain are smashing upon the panes. The sky
is black. He tosses the post cards back onto Representative Peter
Grimes' desk. Solomon's elongated face suddenly smiles. "Well,"
he says, "I guess they prove what such trash always has proved—
that there are some ugly people out there."

Grimes leans back in his chair. He is in the last stages of
youth. His belly is still flat, his blond hair is still thick and un-
ruly. His face is relatively unlined but it won't stay that way
long if the second district of Maine elects him to second and
third terms in the House. Grimes accentuates his particular sort
of New England youthfulness by the way he dresses—chino slacks
and sneakers, this stormy summer morning, and a seersucker
jacket draped over the back of his chair. "Yeah," he says. "But
damn, that sort of stuff really bugs me."

"Nobody in his right mind likes to be cursed," Solomon says.

Grimes looks up. "I mean, I heard a lot of irrational junk in
the campaign, but *that*—" He points at the pile of mail on his
desk. His face is twisted into an expression of angry exasperation. "Christ! You give up a lot of good things to come down
here and do a job for people and then stuff like *that* comes in
the mail—dumb, self-righteous stuff—and you tell yourself to
hell with them."

"The country doesn't deserve me," Tad says.

Grimes looks at him a moment, still scowling. Then he grins
and suddenly laughs. "Yeah, well—something like that."

"You're learning a new trade," Tad says. "Like anything else,
the lesson has its painful side."

Grimes, still grinning, swings around and puts one foot on
the edge of his desk. "Well, I suppose you get used to it." He
shoves at the mail pile with his foot. "You didn't come in here to
listen to my troubles. You've come about HR 1418, yes?"

Tad reaches into his jacket pocket and takes out a pipe. He is a small, slender man in his middle forties. His curly, black hair is still wet from the rain. Splotches of damp darken the shoulders and front of his gray, lightweight suit. He puts the pipe in his mouth and strikes a match. "In a way," he said. "We had a meeting in Mace's office last night—some of the leadership guys, Lou Howard and the departmental people, a few of us working for the lobbying coalition." He holds the match in his hand as he looks at Grimes. "We were going over the list of undecided members and wondering what we could do to persuade them. You were on the list. A few of the other guys had taken cracks at you so I volunteered this time. I've been looking for an excuse to come in and meet you."

"You'll burn your fingers," Grimes says.

Tad shakes out the match and drops it in an ashtray. "I'm going to burn my whole hand off doing that one of these days." He strikes another match and holds it over the bowl of his pipe.

"I've had a lot of guys in here on that bill," Grimes says. "I even had an Air Force captain. He said he could help out, maybe, if I was getting a lot of flack about the layoff of civilian workers from that air base in my district." Grimes grins again, his abrupt, awkward, kid grin.

"They aren't very subtle, are they?"

"It isn't a military virtue," Tad answers.

Grimes looks at him. "What's your pitch?"

Solomon sucks flame into the bowl of his pipe for a moment. The office is filled with that asthmatic noise and the slashing, wet sounds of the storm upon the windows. Tad shakes out the new match. "I really haven't got a pitch," he says, taking the pipe from his mouth. "Nobody knows why you're uncertain about this bill so I thought I'd come around and see if I couldn't get *you* to talk and I'd listen."

"You're with the United Auto Workers, aren't you?"

"AFL-CIO," Tad answers. "You probably know all the reasons why we're for the bill."

Grimes nods. "Yeah, I guess I do. They'd probably be my reasons, too. I mean, I instinctively agree with them—and that's the problem."

"Why?"

"Well, I'm not sure that I agree with what I assume are your arguments for the Youth Resources Development Act because I've thought the thing through or because they're the usual, standard, liberal reasons." Grimes takes his foot off the desk and leans forward, resting his elbows on the blotter before him. "When I ran for old Dan Cordeau's seat in the House, Dan kept accusing me of being a knee-jerk liberal, a guy who sort of mindlessly bought the liberal line on everything." He raises his head. "You know something? That really hit me. I got to thinking about it and, in a way, Dan was right. I came into politics right through that middle-class groove—master at a private school, guilty conscience, turned off by the left, fed up with the establishment, hipped on civil rights and ecology—Christ, my wife's on more committees than we have kids and we have five kids." He grins again. "We're sort of station wagon liberals all the way. So, anyway, I made up my mind that if I got elected I'd really try to think for myself in this place, at least on the important things. I've had my staff researching the hell out of this bill, I went to all the committee hearings I could and I've read the testimony from the sessions I couldn't get to. I've been over on the floor listening since the bill came out." He shakes his head. "I've tried to hear all sides. I even let those weirdos from Fredom Lobby come in and give their pitch. Jesus, those guys are really *crazy!*"

Tad nods. "They tend to think that most things are parts of a conspiracy against God, the flag and free enterprise."

"And themselves," Grimes adds.

Tad smiles. "So you've been wondering at what point you get enough information to make an independent judgment."

Grimes nods hard. "Yeah, exactly."

The lobbyist puts his pipe back in his mouth. "Well," he says slowly, "you never do. That's why there are orthodox liberal and conservative positions in politics, I think, because nothing is ever completely satisfactory." He listens to the rain on the windows for a moment. "Let me tell you something that better stay just between us."

"Okay."

"Well, *between* us, the AFL-CIO has some serious doubts about the whole New Partnership program. We really can't go along very happily with the tax credit angle."

"But that's the basis of the whole thing," Grimes says.

Tad nods. "Yes, it is. But we have this sort of instinctive, old-fashioned-liberal enmity toward big business. That's what organized labor was originally for. Sometimes it surfaces like in this thing. We don't want business having tax credits. We'd prefer to see a program like this financed out of the money you'd save by reforming the tax structure and closing some of the loopholes."

Grimes looks puzzled. "Then how come you're lobbying for it?"

"The President called Meany in last March," Tad says. "They had a big go-round. Finally the President said to Meany, 'I need you on this. I'm asking you as President of the United States. I understand your objections to the tax credit principle. I might even agree with you. But the whole object of the program is to show the taxpayers that they aren't getting soaked. I want you to help me.' " Tad takes his pipe from his mouth and shrugs. "What do you do?"

Grimes, who has been listening with fascination, says, "You go with the President."

"Exactly," Tad says quietly. "You give yourself *that* reason for going along with a thing. Did you see the news on television last night?"

Grimes leans back in his chair. "Yeah. Those street fights in Providence. That's up in *my* country. New England. Hell, I've been with this thing since the beginning. That's why I distrusted my feelings because it *is* so basically right."

"Have you heard any reason for being against it?" Tad asks. "Any persuasive argument?"

Grimes looks back at him and shakes his head. "No. All the reasons are for it. Besides, I owe Mace something. He got me a seat on Merchant Marine and Fisheries."

"Don't vote with him for that reason," Tad says. "He doesn't expect it on something as crucial as this."

Grimes shakes his head again. "No, I won't. Maybe I just

needed somebody like you to come in here and let me talk my thoughts out. You can tell Mace I'm with the leadership on this one."

Tad picks up his briefcase which has been leaning against a chair leg. He stands. "Don't give me a commitment unless you're sure."

Grimes rises. He is a shade over six feet two. "I'm sure."

"You tell Mace yourself," Tad says. "Call him this morning before the session. Do some good for yourself."

"I thought you said I shouldn't do things out of gratitude."

Tad smiles. "I did. But it won't hurt if Mace thinks he's the main reason why you're going with him. Get everything you can out of everything you do. I've got to go. Thanks for letting me in."

Grimes holds out his hand. "It was a pleasure, Mr. Solomon. It's kind of novel to find somebody around here who listens."

Tad tucks his briefcase under one arm and shakes hands. "I enjoyed it, Congressman."

"Peter," Grimes says.

"I'm usually called Tad," Solomon answers. "My aunt used to have a summer house on Deer Isle. I haven't been up there since I was a kid. It was great country."

"It still is," Grimes says. "Don't get yourself soaked out there in that storm."

"I won't," Tad says. " 'Bye."

He walks to the elevator enjoying the small, exultant feeling which is the periodic reward of the persuader. The devices of persuasion are many and varied on Capitol Hill. He has learned that listening is one of the best ones to use on the intelligent. He likes Grimes. Working with—or on—him in the future will be fun.

There is an episodic tempo to the House of Representatives. Each episode first stirs as a controversial bill begins its way through subcommittee hearings. The pace increases and the cast on the episode gathers as the bill goes into full committee; the opponents and proponents emerge, the flashpoints and lack of contention begin to show. Tad and sixteen other lobbyists representing over forty groups have been part of HR 1418's cast since it came to the two committees handling it—Public Works and Education and Labor.

During the committee stage a distinct leadership among the bill's supporters had also emerged. Mace Applegate, John Stermas and Hector Prince, chairman of the Education and Labor Committee, are the commanding generals within the House. Prince is the bill's floor manager. The coalition of lobbyists is led by Lou Howard for the executive branch and Bill Mitsawaka, a Japanese-American lobbyist for the American Association of University Professors. A temporary headquarters has been set up in a Capitol Hill hotel suite. As the bill moved to its climax in the Public Works and Education and Labor committees, it began to attract national attention. At that point the fight became the focus of a House episode. There was a skirmish in the Public Works Committee that beat down an amendment which would have permitted local contractors to hire kids from the camps for work on federal highways—at pay below the minimum wage. That was part of the opponents' strategy to turn the bill into a "Christmas tree" by loading it down with irrelevant or unacceptable amendments. Tad had devoted three days and several evenings to that one. Mace had bargained angrily. News articles described the men, forces and power sources ranged on both sides of the battle for HR 1418. The bill moved to Rules and its supporting coalition lost the struggle to send it to the floor under a closed Rule. Then the messy Randolph Hatfield episode broke forth and somewhere in the middle of it, for reasons that few outsiders understood, it was revealed that the Speaker had already scheduled the bill for floor action. Now, on this rainy morning, the floor fight was going into its third day, the House was obsessed, weary, and the lords and the barons were pushing for a vote.

Tad rides to the ground floor of the Longworth Building. He is tired. A strategy meeting in Mace's office had broken up at 10:30 the previous evening. He had been at the hotel headquarters until 1:45. This morning he had had breakfast with Hector Prince and John Stermas and had called on Dorothy Caulder of Oregon before seeing Grimes.

In the lobby of the office building, an aroma of wet is exuded by raincoats and folded umbrellas. This morning's first batch of tourists has come in from the rain. In the dim light, the patient, polite Capitol police give directions or sit chatting at their desks. Outside, the morning world of Washington is a montage of dark greens, gleaming black streets and the rain-streaked gray of buildings. The storm has exhausted its initial savagery. It now drums sullenly on the city.

Tad sees a taxi letting out passengers at the curb. He hurries across the lobby and through the revolving doors. Holding his briefcase over his head, he dashes across the sidewalk and jumps into the cab. He rides it three blocks to the hotel headquarters and goes up to the second floor.

The coalition of lobbyists working for HR 1418 has turned its three-room suite into a classic of the political organization scene. Metal banquet tables covered by green cloth are strewn with mimeographed forms, note pads, plates with the shriveled remnants of sandwiches upon them, telephones and cardboard coffee containers. On one wall a large chart lists every member of the House. Blue marks beside some names indicate that the member is for the bill. Red ones signify opposition. There is another chart of the three House office buildings, each building broken down by floors. On each floor the coalition has access to a telephone. When important amendments come up in the House chamber debate, a call from Mace Applegate's office warns the hotel suite. Calls then go out to coalition workers on every House building floor who scurry around urging Congressmen to go over and vote.

Women volunteers are seated at the tables, telephoning or talking. Lobbyists and hangers-on jam the suite. Harassed girls dash from one room to another.

Tad stands in the door, brushing the wet from his suit. A lobbyist from one of the business organizations working for the bill sees him and crosses the room. He is a tall man, impeccable and relaxed. "It only rains on the righteous," he says. "How about a cup of coffee?"

Tad smiles. "How about Peter Grimes? That righteous enough for you?"

The tall man raises his eyebrows. "You got him?"

Tad nods. "He'll telephone Mace this morning."

The business lobbyist turns and shouts into the room. "Hey, Betsy! Put down Grimes!"

A brown-haired girl named Betsy Niles, who works for the Sierra Club, gets up from a desk. She is holding a sheaf of papers in her right hand. A pencil is clenched in her teeth. She takes it out. "Who got Grimes?"

"Monsieur Organized Labor here!"

Betsy nods. "Okay." She turns and puts a blue mark beside Grimes' name on the master chart.

A telephone rings.

Somebody shouts. "Where's Bill?"

Betsy comes over to the door. She shuffles through her papers. "Goddamn it, Tad—congratulations on getting Grimes—"

"Thanks," Tad says.

"But Goddamn it, I wish you'd tell your pals not to call here." She shuffles the papers, drops two and yanks a slip from the batch. She shoves it at Tad. "This jerk's been on the phone four times already this morning. We need to keep these lines open. Okay? Tell your office not to give out this number. Okay?"

Tad takes the slip and looks at it. "Okay. Who is he?"

"Beats the crap out of me," Betsy says. "Just get him off my girls' backs, okay?"

"Okay," Tad repeats.

Bill Mitsawaka comes from an inner room. He is a stocky man in a white shirt. His sleeves are rolled up and his tie is loose. "Somebody said you got Grimes," he says to Tad.

"That's right."

"Great stuff," Mitsawaka says.

A telephone rings.

"Bill, for Chrissakes!" someone yells.

"Listen, Tad," Mitsawaka says, "you'd better get over to the floor before noon. Mace is feeling panicky this morning. Crockett's amendment is coming up first and Mace doesn't think he has the votes."

"Oh, Jesus," Tad says. "I wish he'd stop listening to his zone Whips and start listening to us. I told Hector and John Stermas at breakfast we have nothing to worry about on that."

"Bill, will you get the phone, please?" an anguished voice shouts.

"I'll go over," Tad says. "I've got forty five minutes yet."

"Go calm Mace but see me first," Mitsawaka says. He picks up a telephone, punches its blinking button. "Yeah?"

Tad goes into the next room. Two young men and a girl are sitting at a table, talking on telephones. Tad finds a hotel switchboard phone. He puts his briefcase down, takes the slip that Betsy gave him and asks the switchboard for the number. While he is waiting, he lights the first of his ten cigarettes of the day. He is trying to wean himself away from them and fully onto his pipe.

The telephone buzzes.

A man answers.

Tad looks at the slip. "Mr. Rengen?"

"Yeah. This is Ralph Rengen."

"Tad Solomon. You called me."

"Oh yeah. Hi Tad. I'm a friend of Guy Carroll. He said I should call you. I gotta problem."

"Do we know each other?" Tad asks.

"Nah. I'm a friend of Guy Carroll's."

"What can I do for you, Mr. Rengen?"

"Well look, Tad—Mr. Solomon. I work for the Bent Metals Institute."

"The what?"

"Bent Metals Institute," Rengen says. "I represent them here. There's this bill coming up—"

"What's the Bent Metals Institute?" Tad asks.

"We represent people in the bent metals business," Rengen says. "Like bobby pins, for instance."

"Okay," Tad says.

"There's this bill coming up—wait a minute." Paper rustles at the other end of the phone line. "It's H 2281."

"HR," Tad says. "That means it's a House bill."

"Yeah," Rengen answers. "Anyway, one of my clients wants to know about it. He's interested. Guy thought maybe you could help me find out something."

"Are you a registered lobbyist?" Tad asks.

"Yeah. Sure. For the Bent Metals Institute."

"Then why don't you just call somebody and find out?" Tad asks.

"I don't work the Hill," Rengen says. "I work downtown."

"You mean you don't know anybody on the Hill?" Tad asks.

"Well, not like you do, T—Mr. Solomon. Guy thought you could help me find out something."

"I'll do what I can," Tad says. "I'm pretty busy."

"Thanks, Mr. Solomon."

Tad hangs up and calls Henry Rutherford in Mace's office. HR 2281 is Randolph Hatfield's bill. It has to do with the insurance rates on certain categories of metal imports. It will come up on Friday and pass by a voice vote. Tad calls Rengen back and relays the information.

"Jesus," Rengen says. "That's fantastic the way you found out so quick."

"All in a day's work," Tad says. "You ought to get acquainted on the Hill and then you could do that yourself for your clients."

"Are you kidding?" Rengen says.

After a twenty-minute conference with Mitsawaka and two of the other lobbyists, Tad goes across to the Capitol. It is 12:45. The House chamber is half full. Maynard Crockett is in the well. Tad goes to the gallery to listen.

"There are federal guidelines for racial balance in our local schools," the Chairman of the Rules Committee is saying. "There are federally sanctioned definitions of racial balance. The school system of my state has lived with them for years. We believe them to be misguided, to be experiments in social tinkering. But we live with them. So have the school districts in all of our states. My amendment, Mr. Speaker, would simply extend those guidelines, those federally sanctioned definitions of racial balance to the educational establishments proposed by this bill. The existent guidelines are not mandatory. But they are powerful suggestions from a powerful executive speaking through its department of Health, Education and Welfare . . ."

Tad looks around the House floor below. Mace Applegate is sitting in his usual second row seat in the center of the chamber.

Stermas is on his left. Hector Prince, a heavy man in his early fifties, is on Mace's right. Prince is bent forward, his chin resting on one, clenched fist as he listens to Crockett. The Connecticut Congressman's eyes are intense behind his shell-rimmed glasses. Prince, a gutsy, power-savvy liberal, is floor manager of the bill. He is also Tad Solomon's closest friend in the Congress.

"Will the gentleman yield?" A short, white-haired Congressman rises from behind one of the committee tables set in a center row of the chamber.

"I yield one minute to the gentleman from Texas," Crockett replies.

The Texan swings a microphone toward himself. "Would the gentleman agree that this program must not be tainted with racism?" he asks solemnly.

Crockett makes a half nod, half bow. "I would certainly agree with the gentleman," he says. "That was one consideration I had in mind when I offered this amendment."

Tad's attention is captured by a movement in the center aisle. Hector Prince is looking up at him. Tad leans forward. Prince motions with his head.

The lobbyist leaves the gallery and starts down the marble staircase to the floor below.

He turns. A gray-haired woman wearing a seersucker skirt suit and carrying a briefcase is coming down the stairs behind him. "I've been looking all over for you," she says. "I hear you got Grimes."

"That's right."

They continued down the stairs together. "I've been working on that bastard Rollinsgate," she says. "I've tried everything except offering him my fair white body. I think we're going to have to build a small fire under Congressman Rollinsgate."

Tad smiles, "Like what?"

She stops. "Like he's eight weeks overdue on a ninety-day bank loan for—get this—*fifty six thousand bucks!* The dumb bastard's been horsing around with cotton futures again. Ninety-day loan. Due. And the banker likes this bill. How about them apples?"

"Don't do it," Tad says. "Never threaten. You may need Rollinsgate for something else next month."

"Oh *I'm* not going to mention the matter and neither is anybody else from the National Association of Corporation Executives. But old dumb-bunny Rollinsgate is going to get a telephone call from his friendly banker this afternoon. It's all fixed."

"I'm glad I'm not Calvin Rollinsgate," Tad says.

They reach the bottom of the stairs and walk around to an eastern corridor entrance to the House chamber. Hector Prince is standing by the window smoking a cigarette. He turns. His handsome, fleshy face erupts in an illuminating smile. "Hi, friend!"

"Hi," Tad says. "You know Margaret Sparkman, don't you?"

Prince puts his arms around her. *"Do I know Margaret Sparkman?* I was lusting after Margaret Sparkman when you were organizing your first sit-down strike in kindergarten, Solomon!"

Margaret laughs. "Let go, you letch. Professor Dunston'll see us and tell the Northern Baptist Convention."

Prince, still holding her at arm's length, looks down in mock wonder. "You lobbyin' for them folks now?"

She laughs again. "Shut up, Hector. We've got business."

Prince releases her. "Hey," he says to Tad. "Did you hear old Crockett and Joe Waters in there?"

Tad nods. "Pretty awful, isn't it? Those two lily-whiters pleading for racial justice."

"Y'know what Mace said?"

"No."

"Gah damn," Prince says in an imitation North Carolina accent. "Wouldn' that make a Gah damn goat puke? Sheee-*yit!*" He roars with laughter.

"When's Crockett's amendment coming to a vote?" Tad asks.

"Half hour," Prince says, suddenly serious. "I've lost count on it and so has Mace. I know it'll be close but I wanted to find out what you guys think."

"I don't know," Margaret says. "I've been over at the Cannon Building all morning. Tad?"

"I just came from the hotel," Tad says. "The coalition's done a new count. You're okay, Heck. It'll go down by about ten votes."

Prince looks out the window. Washington lies wet and glum beneath the rain and the low, gray sky. "Damn," he says. "I wish I could count on that." He turns back. "No offense, Tad, but, this, is a bad one. If Crockett fixes that racial balance thing on the bill, he castrates it. Most of the kids this program will help are black. And Crockett knows it."

"Yes," Margaret says, "and so do a lot of other people. It's as obvious as a stop light. Buck Turner, for instance. Buck doesn't like the bill and won't vote for it. But he also doesn't like Maynard Crockett and, as a good, conservative Southerner, he doesn't like Southerners beating things with sneakies. He'll vote against Crockett's amendment to keep his conscience clean. I know four or five like that. I agree with Tad. I think you're all right."

Prince nods. "I hope so. I don't want to use that alarm system of yours unless I have to, Tad. Guys get irritated at people dashing into their offices telling them to go vote."

"You don't need it this time," Tad says.

Prince suddenly grins. "Say, you two are great together. Why don't you get married?"

"Big business lobbyists aren't sexy," Tad says.

Hector Prince laughs. Then, in another abrupt change of mood, he is sober. "Maybe we beat Crockett's amendment this afternoon," he says. "What about tomorrow?"

"Final vote?" Tad says. "The bill?"

Hector nods.

Tad looks down at his feet. He frowns, "I think we're losing, Heck," he says after a moment.

Prince glances at Margaret.

"It depends upon a lot of vulnerable, mysterious or weak guys, Sweetie," she says.

"Are you going to get Rollinsgate?"

"Maybe," Margaret answers.

"Goddamn it," Hector says softly, looking out of the window. "When you think that something this big depends upon somebody like Jerry Cressap . . ."

They stand in momentary silence, a small man with his hands in his pockets looking at the floor, a heavy, tall man looking out at the rain, a middle-aged woman between them. "They're still fighting in Providence," Margaret says.

Hector nods. "The National Guard's being beefed up. The President's ordered paratroopers from Fort Bragg. It'll be announced in about an hour." Suddenly he grins again. "I love you both," he says, dropping his cigarette and crushing it out with his foot.

"C'mon, Thaddeus," Margaret says, "let's go back up and listen to Maynard Crockett save the world for racial brotherhood." She scowls at Prince. "God! I hate this damned do-gooding! I'd rather be back fixing postal rates."

The rain drums upon Washington, turning the dust of summer into little rivulets of mud. The trees bend and flash their branches in the storm's sudden gusts of wind. At 1:25 the House begins to vote on Representative Maynard Crockett's amendment to HR 1418, an act to establish a Federal Youth Resources Development Agency. The Amendment is defeated by nine votes. Margaret Sparkman, a lobbyist for the National Association of Corporation Executives is in the gallery watching along with D. Thaddeus Solomon, a lobbyist for the American Federation of Labor—Congress of Industrial Organizations. Congressman Jerome M. Cressap of New Jersey votes for the Crockett amendment. At 2:10 the White House announces that a battalion of the 82nd Airborne Division is being flown from Fort Bragg, North Carolina, to Providence, Rhode Island, to assist in the restoration of civil order in that city. Tad Solomon takes Margaret Sparkman to lunch in the House restaurant. The Potomac flows away from the capital of the United States, twisting its way past Alexandria and Mount Vernon, heading for the hills, the bay and the sea. . . .

In his dark, acute masterpiece, *The Revolt of the Masses*, José Ortega y Gasset looked out upon Europe in the 1930s and concluded that "the most radical division that it is possible to

make of humanity is that which splits it into two classes of creatures; those who make great demands upon themselves, piling
up difficulties and duties; and those who demand nothing special
of themselves, but for whom to live is to be every moment what
they really are, without imposing on themselves any effort toward perfection . . ."

For Ortega y Gasset this was not a formula of class division
but, rather, a definition of energies within masses. The self-demanding group is the genesis of new energy and the undemanding group is the mass which is shaped, pummeled and pushed
by the energy. It is a nasty, frightening and thoroughly realistic
description of the origin of modern politics. One cannot make
moral judgments upon the definition itself because, within itself,
it contains infinite possibilities. The self-demanding elite can
produce fascism as it did in Ortega y Gasset's native Spain, it
can produce a Communist system as it did in Russia and China.
It can be the strength of republicanism, the reinforcement of
monarchy, democracy's salvation or democracy's executioner. It
is a permanent formula for conflict because conflict is the permanent ignition of politics and movements.

For democracies, especially for American democracy, the division of humanity into undemanding masses and demanding
minorities is philosophically painful. Democracy conceives of itself—in the abstract—as a mass phenomenon, it believes, with
the eighteenth century, that the mass is capable of wisdom—or
so the politics of democracy keep saying. Democracy theoretically and traditionally despises elites.

Yet the reality of Ortega y Gasset's definition persists, even
in democracies. It keeps on saying that elites are the genesis of
politics and movements. An elite is a minority whose interests or
logic has succeeded in dominating its social surroundings. Elites
composed of demanding minorities have shoved America through
its history. The cycles of American political history could be described in terms of the rise of elites and the efforts to defeat them.

America's beginnings as an independent nation were overseen
and dominated by an elite composed of landed and intellectual
aristocrats. That elite lasted until the election of Andrew Jack-

son banished it from power. In succession, bankers and merchants, the robber barons of big business, visionaries and intellectuals whose logic was change, conservative businessmen and
liberal reformers all formed elites which dominated the United
States and its politics from 1836 to 1932. Thereafter the nation began to fragment into contending elites of liberals, conservatives, middle-class businessmen and Populist politicians.

All of these elitist groups—and that is only a sketchy outline
of them—exercised their dominance by manipulating the political
process and the undemanding majorities. All through American history the undemanding mass has moved and made itself
felt. But its movement has almost always been in response to
some elitist exhortation or in response to some need such as
that which prompted Coxey's veterans to march on Washington. Even then a mini-elitist identified the cause and suggested the course of action. The movements of the mass are
chiefly characterized by their lack of spontaneity.

But in the America of the middle 1960s and onward, a new
phenomenon began to appear—spontaneous mass movements.
These movements are not triggered by a guiding elitist but by
realizations widely shared. There was no single organizer of the
anti-war movement—it blossomed spontaneously all over the
country. Martin Luther King, Jr., became, for a while, the leader
of the civil rights movement. But he was its successful seizer, not
its originator. In the late sixties and seventies other mass movements proliferated, encouraged by the earlier ones, inspired by
a general atmosphere of challenge to official or accepted logic
. . . and by the realization that the challenge to official logic
can win. Women's Lib, the environmental movement, causes as
varied as consumerism and anti-bussing sprouted like cornflow-
ers in the aging social soil of America. Most of them were spontaneous—that is, not originally designed and raised by elitists.
Many were later captured by elitists as varied as Ralph Nader,
George Wallace and Gloria Steinem. But their uniqueness was
in the nature of their origins.

The movements did not involve a majority of the American
people. Mass movements never do. Indeed, the original, spontan-

eous mass movements of the early sixties frightened the majority
as well as official Washington simply because they *were* spontaneous. That was such an utterly unconventional idea that millions
of people refused to believe it. The early anti-war and civil rights
crusades were laid, in many minds, to some Communist plot. If
that sort of reasoning was glorious, conspiratorial hooey, it reflected the bewilderment of millions who couldn't believe in the
possibilities of American spontaneity.

For politicians and government the problem was and is more
acute. Politicians can handle pressure groups in one way or another as long as they know the location of the group's command structure or leverage point. But the spontaneous mass
movement has no command structure unless it is seized by someone. Its only leverage point is the fulfillment of its demands; end
the war and the anti-war groups will get off your back, ordain
full civil rights and equal access for minorities and the civil rights
movement will abate. These things are easier to demand than
they are to accomplish so the politician finds himself in an extremely difficult position when confronted by the movement.

In frustration, Washington sometimes adopts a form of the
conspiracy theory about such mass movements. Its investigative devices are turned loose, trying to find, in the movements' entrails, the guiding, motivating force. The army—under
orders from President Lyndon B. Johnson, it claimed—spent several years in an extraordinary snooping operation on the anti-war
and environmental movements. It watched demonstrators, people who attended Earth Day rallies, politicians and, according
to Senator Sam Ervin's Constitutional Rights Subcommittee, at
least one Justice of the Supreme Court. In a fascinating revelation, the then Acting Attorney General, Richard Kleindienst, told
the Senate Judiciary Committee on February 22, 1972, that a
lot of intelligence-gathering "is done without the thought of
prosecuting." It is, in other words, a form of federal anxiety over
what the hell is going on out there in the country.

The basic ingredients of spontaneous mass movements aren't
very difficult to figure out. The population of the United States
in the late 1960s and early 1970s is the best-educated population in the country's history. Millions of people are able to grasp

complicated issues and to relate those issues to themselves and to the general good. This is also the most affluent generation in American history. That means that millions of people have the leisure and, perhaps, the subliminal sense of guilt, which turns them to broad, public issues as matters of personal concern. The United States population of the 1970s is also bombarded by the greatest variety of signals and messages of any time in American history. Television and radio alert, shriek and explain, newspapers and magazines print descriptions and analyses of events. In the confluence of the ability to grasp issues, the leisure to consider and act upon them and the bombardment of the communications industry there is the genesis of the spontaneous mass movements.

That is not to say that the role of the elitist is over in American society or that masses of people are so enthralled by the possibilities of spontaneity that they no longer respond to the exhortations of leaders. When the feelings generated by the communications bombardment are not clear or cannot be precisely articulated or acted upon, then the exhortive leader can play a dynamic role in American society. George Corley Wallace was a classic example. In ways that no one (including Governor Wallace) fully understood, he articulated a massive sense of loss and exclusion among his followers. He was a Cassandra, backed by a vast and powerful following, who warned that the concepts and practices of an immense federal structure in Washington had become remote from the reality of ordinary lives. In a long discussion held in early 1972, Governor Wallace told me that the remoteness of government from the lives of his followers was "the abstract issue" upon which his campaigns were based. He was one step removed from the phenomenon of spontaneous mass movements in that he postulated for his followers what they could not postulate for themselves—that you *can* challenge official logic, that the challenge to official logic *can* win in some ways if not in ultimate ones. That is the meaning of Wallace's repeated claims that he makes traditional politicians adopt his particular viewpoints. He is the master of harnessing feelings to unspontaneous movements.

Since we do not fully understand the uses of his symbolism or

anyone else's in mass society, we cannot say with complete pre-
dictability which event will trigger what response in a significant
section of the public. Perhaps the vivid television portrayal of
the 1968 Tet offensive was the ignition of mass American revul-
sion with the war in Vietnam. Certainly photographs of marchers
in Selma, Alabama, being hosed by sheriff's deputies and savaged
by dogs created enormous sympathy for those who are black and
march and, thus, for the general civil rights movement. Again,
it is important to stress that such signals simultaneously received do not result in the same reaction on the part of everybody. They trigger similar feelings in a significant minority; a
minority of that minority reaches the same conclusion about an
event and a minority of *that* minority decides to act. In that way,
a spontaneous mass movement is born.

The movements are trying to catch Washington's attention.
But the politicians do not fully grasp what they are saying because the movements have created new definitions of self-inter-
est. It was predictable, for instance, that millions of middle-class
whites would feel threatened by the black march of civil rights.
What was *not* predictable was that millions of other, affluent
whites would identify their interests *with* blacks and would join
the civil rights movement. It was not predictable by traditional
political means that millions of women would become the impassioned core of the consumer and environmental movements.

Spontaneous mass movements often identify the interests of
their members with some other, unrelated group's interests
(whites in the civil rights movement for blacks), with causes
whose effect will be felt in the future (environment) or with an
end which the movement judges to be in the general interest of
the entire nation (anti-war). In these new definitions of self-in-
terest so mysterious to traditional politics, the infinite possibilities
of spontaneous mass movements exist—unpredictable, volatile, incapable of resolution by traditional political means. Washington, imprisoned in the patterns of traditional political thought,
often cannot grasp what the spontaneous mass movement is saying, and often cannot appease it. Therefore Washington fears and
sometimes hates the movements.

And well it should because the spontaneous mass movements

threaten traditional politics. As I write these words, it is an evening in March 1972. Frost leaves teeth marks around the edges of window panes and the presidential primaries are marching across the hills of New Hampshire again. But this year the New Hampshire campaign is a duller thing. It is a retreat from the aurora of bright promise that burned upon those hills four years ago. In March 1968 the children's crusade was alive, well and full of its driving visions. It had gathered itself upon one man whose followers knew he could win neither the Democratic nomination nor the presidency—and they didn't care. What was important to the children was the use of the American political system to bear witness to the inadequacy of the times, to display it as a means of redressing those inadequacies.

Eugene McCarthy didn't create the children's crusade. Indeed, by finding its symbols in him, the crusade created the candidate. Nor did McCarthy stand for much in American politics except the downfall of Lyndon B. Johnson because he was the commanding figure of a hateful war. Nor will that period in February and March 1968 live as an extraordinary time in our history because Eugene McCarthy was seen as virtuous and Lyndon Johnson thought evil—neither man was that simple. Rather, the significance and hope of the children's crusade was its immense belief in the American political system. Most of the spontaneous mass movements share that belief. What they ask is that the system give credence to the seriousness with which the movements believe in their goals and the faith they have invested in the politics of this country.

Power—the capacity to move men, money and ideas from one place to another—is the prize in politics. The great questions, now and forever, will concern where the power lies and who uses it for what ends. Children gathered upon the winter hills of New Hampshire, demonstrated, for a little while, that power can come from the most unexpected sources and can be used for the most unpredictable ends. The power of that spontaneous mass movement in March 1968 brought down a President who had been elevated, enshrined and protected by the traditional power devices of Washington.

The people are no purer than professional politicians, the

country is no more pristine than Washington, D.C., and power to the people is no absolute guarantee that virtuous things will be done. That wasn't the point of what happened in New Hampshire in March 1968. Rather, it was a graphic lesson by the children's crusade that power does not reside permanently in Washington, that the people have not lost the ability to seize it. Had intelligence prevailed in the political parties, in Washington and among other causists in the country that year, this might have been construed for what it was—a revitalizing of political power in America and a warning to those who usually use it that it is not theirs forever. But intelligence didn't prevail that year.

Lyndon Johnson, alone among the witnesses to the children's crusade, had the wit to understand what it meant. On March 31, 1968 he announced that he would not seek reelection. From then on, tragedy began to unfold through the months of what was the most terrible year of a decade. Robert Kennedy was murdered in June, an event that followed too closely upon the awful murder of Martin Luther King, Jr., to make believable any assertion that a terrible *Geist* had not been unloosed among the Americans. The Democratic convention in August turned into a brutal collision between two forces goaded to unreason by the ambiguity of the times—the Chicago police and the skeptical, radical fringe of the farther left. That left not only eschewed power but had an irresponsible, babyish contempt for it.

And so the children's crusade was betrayed—by orthodox Democratic politicians too limited to grasp that a spontaneous mass movement had opened rich new political possibilities for participatory democracy, by its fellow children on the outer left who were more interested in ego trips than in national salvation, by the power elite of Washington which simply could not understand what had happened because the happening was unorthodox, and, finally, by Eugene McCarthy himself who abdicated his own power by resigning his seat on the Senate Foreign Relations Committee and evaporating into a subjective nirvana. That was fine for him but it was unworthy of the Sam Browns, Jeremy Larners, Belle Huangs and other children of the crusade who, by investing in McCarthy's symbolism, had demonstrated a profoundly important new source of political power in America.

Despite the stupidity, arrogance and insensitivity of the reaction to the children's crusade, what it said about the system remains true. There is a new force out there in the enigmatic land, a force which Washington, as yet, cannot understand or deal with. It is a force set in motion not by the traditional means of political organization or exhortation; it erupts out of some mysterious, mass agreement on what a symbol or an event really means. It is a new dynamic whose purpose is to permit Washington to feel the United States in a better way, to improve Washington's grasp of the hopes, fears and needs of a people who have become, in large measure, a mystery to their government.

In our time we have seen Ortega y Gasset's self-demanding minorities produce horrid phenomena. Since this is an age of deep pessimism it is unfashionable to hope for—or even believe in the existence of—that which is basically good. The possibilities are precarious but, in these late American years, the new spontaneity of the country has thus far resulted in more that is good than bad. It is the sort of good which results from people broadening the definition of their own interests to include the interests of others or of the nation as a whole. But the power of the spontaneous mass movements could turn rancid if they continue to be ignored by conventional politics, misunderstood as to their true meaning or betrayed.

Maybe we will never again see children upon the cold hills saying that the times are inadequate. But once they were there and their echo remains. The mass is alive and moving—but to what end, nobody knows.

At last the hour arrives.

It is the terminus of a House mini-epoch, the point at which all the complexities attendant upon an event crash together and conclude in a simple resolution.

This particular terminus begins at 5:15 on a Wednesday afternoon. The debate on HR 1418 has carried through three days, eleven proposed amendments (two have carried), skirmishes, networks of pressure skillfully or bluntly applied, long nights of running strategy sessions, millions of words of oratory on the floor and millions more expended in that back stage which is Washington at work out of public sight. At 5:15 on this Wednesday, Lou Howard bolts out of the House gallery, dashes down a flight of stairs and runs into the outer office of the Speaker's suite. He telephones the President to report that, in the middle of a raucous and angry debate on a twelfth amendment, John Stermas suddenly got the chair's attention, moved the previous question—and his motion passed. Debate on HR 1418 is abruptly over. The vote will come shortly.

"How many votes did John's motion win by?" the President asks.

"Sixty six," Lou answers, "but it doesn't mean a thing. Everybody's sick of the damned thing, the amendment being debated wasn't going to pass and a lot of guys who'll vote against the bill voted to get the vote over with. They're just tired of it and the Speaker's passing the word that other bills can't wait any longer."

The President is standing at his desk with his back turned to the Oval Office. His middle-aged Vice President, the chairman of his Council of Economic Advisers and the Secretary of the Treasury occupy the two sofas by the fireplace. The President looks through the French doors to the rose garden. Trees, shrubs and borders are in full bloom and that, in a thousandth-of-a-second flash of irrelevancy, reminds him of someone he once loved who loved plants. A small pain sprints across the sub-surface of his mind and is gone. "Call me," he says.

"As soon as the vote's over," Lou says.

He puts down the phone and leaves the Speaker's office. Bells are sounding as he goes out into the corridor. Suddenly the whole place is permeated by excitement over the impending vote. Everyone in the House has known, from the opening of business hours earlier, that this would be the day that the HR 1418 epoch would end one way or another. Mace had gone into the well to make one of his rare speeches to the House. His brief oration was appealing in its jumbled syntax, awkwardness and dogged sincerity. He had been followed by Hector Prince, exhausted but eloquent. Oratory, parliamentary skirmishes and colloquies had erected an edifice of excitement as the afternoon wore on. The final duel which had climaxed in Stermas' sudden motion chopped the action. Now the decision will come.

At the door of the Speaker's lobby a tall, white-haired member from Louisiana is laughing with three colleagues. One is a wind-browned Oklahoman, another is a Jesuit priest and the third is a professorial-looking Congressman from Michigan. A family of tourists stands bewildered in the middle of the corridor. The woman wears a slightly askew hat and has her jacket folded over her arm, her husband is dressed in a short-sleeved sport shirt and two cameras; their small son in blue jeans is a scowling twelve-year-old with a crew cut. They came here wanting something, wanting to see something at the end of a long, hard day of seeing but, as the husband will later tell his friends in St. Paul, the whole goddamned place seems to be going crazy. Bells are clanging so loudly that you can't hear yourself think, the House doorkeepers are on their feet, cops are pushing other tourists aside as members come striding in through the doors that open on the Capitol's front steps. Two reporters hurry by, twisting themselves past the immobilized, bewildered family; they pursue a Congressman down the crowded hall.

Lou Howard moves into the excitement-charged human flow. Suddenly he is mentally blank. He can no longer focus his mind on all the fragments of hope, data, thought and speculation that have formed his alternating pessimism and optimism about the bill over the past few weeks. He can't catch hold of anything. Suddenly he doesn't know what's going to happen.

"Lou!"

He turns. Tad Solomon is coming up the hall. The tourist with the wife, nasty little boy and the cameras makes a sudden, impulsive move. He collides with Tad. Tad apologizes. The bewildered family bolts for the staircase.

Solomon is perspiring and agitated. "Goddamnit," he says to Lou, "Bob Marsh just told me he's switching. He's against us now."

"Oh God," Lou says wearily. "What's the matter with Bob?"

"He's had twenty-two hundred telegrams in the last thirty-six hours," Tad says, taking his pipe from his pocket. "All of them against the bill. I went over and looked at some of them. Half don't even come from his district. The wording is all the same. Pompous, hysterical."

"Freedom Lobby," Lou says. "The bastards saved it all up for the last minute."

Tad nods, puts his pipe in his mouth and lights a match. "I didn't even think about them. We goofed. We should have paid attention to them and warned the vulnerable guys that this might happen. I told Bob it was just the Freedom Lobby. But he's adamant . . ."

"You'll burn your fingers," Lou says.

Tad drops the match and puts his pipe back in his pocket. "What's Marsh so scared of?"

"He's just gotten a divorce," Lou says. "There are a lot of Catholics in his district. Mace has been worried about him all session."

They go up the staircase and into the gallery. "I've lost track of it," Lou says. "How're we going to do?"

"I can't feel it either," Tad says as they find seats. "We've been going over the list at the hotel since eight this morning. It's the closest damn thing I've seen in years."

Below them the House chamber is a swarm of temporarily disorganized political humanity. Members stand in the aisles, cluster as groups in the well, talk, wave papers at each other, gaze up at the galleries, argue or laugh. Maynard Crockett sits in one of the seats usually occupied by senior Southerners. He is reading. Jerry Cressap is alone at one of the rails in the back, looking out over the chamber but not seeing it. That morning his office received 857 telegrams not urging but demanding that he "vote the interests of the American majority" and informing him that "we the people are tired of giveaways to the corporations and the blacks." Jerry looks down the aisle to the well. Mace Applegate is standing like a fat, cigar-chomping Horatio at the bridge. Hector Prince and John Stermas are with him. They may be about to lose, Jerry thinks miserably, but they are *in* things, they are together. He thinks of the telegrams. The parking lot shimmers in his mind's fearful eye and he feels sick.

"Look at Jerry Cressap," Lou says. "That pathetic little twit could make the difference."

"Forget him," Tad says. "We lost him weeks ago. I should have given in to my worst instincts and gotten the local union guys to threaten the hell out of him."

Lou turns and looks at him. Solomon's long face is gray with fatigue. "You mean you *didn't?*" Howard says.

Tad shakes his head.

"Jesus God."

The gallery door opens and Margaret Sparkman comes in. She stands at the top of the aisle looking around.

Tad raises his hand. "Yoh," he says. "Over here."

She smiles, waves, comes down the aisle and sidles in to a seat next to Lou. "Hi troops," she says. "Guess who had a telephone call from his banker yesterday?"

"Rollinsgate," Tad says.

"You win the free trip to Milwaukee," she grins. "I just saw our boy and, after a day of deep brooding upon his patriotic duty, he tells me he's with us. Another bastion of the Old South has done fallen."

"Don't knock the South," Lou says. "We're doing pretty well there, all things considered. The National League of Cities guys got to a couple of mayors. We have some Georgia votes."

"Rollinsgate makes up for Bob Marsh," Tad says. "We're back where we started." He turns to Margaret. "Neither of us have any feeling for it any longer."

Margaret purses her lips, frowns and says, "Well, if I were a betting woman I'd take a small wager that we'll lose by—oh— three, perhaps two."

"That sounds about right," Tad says. "Look. There's Randy Hatfield."

The Majority Leader has appeared on the far side of the chamber, coming in through the Speaker's lobby. He stands at the edge of the well, hands in his jacket pockets, watching the members go up the aisles to their seats as the Speaker begins to gavel for order. Hatfield is dressed in a seersucker suit. He looks calm. He takes a hand from his pocket and waves.

Mace Applegate, sitting in his usual center seat beside Stermas, suddenly sees Hatfield. He heaves himself forward, gets up, goes down and crosses the well. "Harya, Randy!"

Hatfield smiles. "Hello, Mace. Looks like you've been keeping the boys amused."

Applegate grins. "Yassuh, Mistuh Leader. We've been havin' a time."

"Sorry I've been away," Hatfield says. "A touch of the summer flu."

"Aw, that's all right," Mace says. " 'Course, we're gonna lose this sumbitch, prob'ly. Takes a real leader t'get the fellers in line for one of theseyear bills." He looks up at the Speaker who is slowly rapping with his gavel. "And that feller, Randy, 'tween you 'n' me, hasn't been exactly bustin' his balls, either." He turns back. "Which is 'nother way of sayin' that we needed yawl around here."

Hatfield smiles again. "You're a good friend and a bad liar, Mace. By the way, I hope you have me down as being for the bill."

"Goddamn," Mace smiles. "That's fine. C'mon over with me 'n' John. Mights well show the folks that thisyear leadership's gonna take its beatin' together."

Hatfield hooks his arm through Mace's. They cross the well and go up the aisle. Stermas rises, smiles and shakes hands with Hatfield as they enter the row.

"Hey, Randy!"

Hatfield looks up.

At the committee table behind him, Hector Prince is on his feet, leaning over, extending his hand. "Hi, friend! Hey, welcome back!"

Hatfield, standing, shakes hands. "Many thanks, Heck. Good luck."

Prince laughs loudly. "We're going to need more than luck."

Hatfield sits down. "What're your chances?" he asks Mace.

"Somewhere between poor 'n' dreadful," Mace says. "It's a hard one t'figger. Got several fellers like Jerry Cressap who won't say what they're gonna do. The committed fellers come out 'bout even. We got one-two of the agins to stay away. We got some t'go away. Like our friends over T' B'nai Brith suddenly decided they just had to have old Fred Thompson make a paid speech out in Chicago t'day. But it still comes out 'bout even. I just dunno."

"Jerry Cressap?"

Mace nods, watching the Speaker.

The House is growing quiet.

"I think I understand Jerry," Hatfield murmurs.

The noise in the chamber has almost completely subsided. Mace looks up. The press and broadcasting galleries are full; reporters are leaning over the rails, looking down intently. The public galleries are jammed. As Mace looks across them he sees Lou Howard, Tad Solomon and Margaret Sparkman sitting together. More than forty other lobbyists and volunteer workers in the lobby coalition are scattered through the galleries to witness the final outcome of their work. Their presences are reminders, encouragements and subtle threats to the members the coalition has been working with.

The chamber is hushed. The two amendments which passed while the House was sitting as a Committee of the Whole are read and voted upon. Both pass the whole House. They are technical and relatively innocuous and don't hurt the main bill. Because the bill has been brought up on Stermas' notion to move the previous question, no further amendments are possible. Hunched over, scribbling the results of the amendment votes on a tally sheet, Mace still doesn't know what will happen.

The tension level in the chamber has risen like some emotional barometer. After a few minutes of cough, chat and buzz, the floor becomes quiet again. From his pinnacle the Speaker looks down at Hatfield almost directly in front of him. The Speaker's face is fixed in a curious, strained expression that is almost a smile. Hatfield looks back at him for a long moment and then turns and talks to John Stermas.

Below the Speaker's level, a clerk on the rostrum begins to read the bill title by title, the last formality before the final vote. His amplified voice barks across the stilled chamber, exaggerating syllables and vowels so that he cannot be misunderstood.

Around the wide arc of the House floor, some of the Congressmen who are both witnesses and participants in the climaxing drama, sit slouched in their seats, some lean forward to hear, some are rigid, eyes distant, others are bent together, still others are lost within themselves as the overly articulated words roll across the chamber, below the hushed galleries, below the plaques of Lycurgus, Pothier and the other priests, kings and sages of the ancient craft of lawmaking.

Slouched, legs awry as he sits between Stermas and Hatfield, Mace Applegate half listens. It is happening again, somewhere in his large body's hidden geography, the mind-fogging combination of dizziness and nausea is rising and a sharp, abdominal pain addresses his nerves. He closes his eyes. His fingers, wrapped around the chair arm, tighten. The brief spasm passes and his body gratefully receives its normal order again . . .

"Mr. Speaker!"

Maynard Crockett is on his feet as the clerk finishes the reading of Title IV.

A sigh, the sound of suddenly released tension, murmurs across the floor and galleries. The last joust is beginning.

Mace jerks up, opens his eyes and turns to look around the chamber. "Shee-*yit!*" he murmurs.

Hatfield lays a hand on his arm. "No," he says quietly. "You aren't going to lose it this way."

The Speaker leans forward. "The chair recognizes the gentleman from Mississippi."

"Mr. Speaker," Crockett says in his clear, thin voice, 'I offer a motion to recommit."

The Speaker leans back. The floor is rechurning in babble and mutters. "Ayes and noes," the Speaker says.

A call is made for all of those favoring Crockett's motion to return the bill to its committees thus effectively killing it. A barked chorus of "aye" booms in the chamber. The Speaker calls for those opposed. The volume of "no" is louder.

"The 'noes' carry," the Speaker says.

Another sighing ripple crosses the chamber and the galleries.

Stermas bends toward Mace. "That sounded interesting."

The Whip grins. His big body jigs with a short chuckle. "Well, you political science fellers are forever tellin' me that recommit votes are the true feelin's of this place."

"That's the theory," Stermas smiles.

Hands gripping the arms of his seat, Mace twists around to Stermas. "Okay, son. Now you tell me how you're gonna get these old boys t'vote their true feelin's on the goddamn bill because *that's* what thisyear game's all about!"

Stermas laughs. "You win."

Hatfield chuckles.

Above them, the Speaker is once again rapping for order. The chamber's prattle and mutter diminishes. The final vote is about to begin. Mace looks around the packed chamber. Over on the left George Stetson and the other, thirty-three members of the black caucus fill several rows. As Mace looks at him Stetson grins and raises his fist in a black power salute. Mace flaps a mock-reproving hand at him. Stetson laughs. Mace looks at Jerry Cressap but cannot catch his eye. The dapper New Jersey Congressman is bent slightly forward, hands clasped, looking at the floor. The Whip sees Peter Grimes who had telephoned him the previous morning to commit himself to the bill. Mace winks and Grimes grins.

Mace turns back to face the rostrum as the clerk begins the long polling process. "Mister *Ablock!*"

"Aye!" cries Herman Ablock of New York from the rear of the chamber.

"AY-*yee!*" repeats the clerk in his exaggerated, singsong repetition of the answer. "Mrs. *Acroyd!*"

"Aye," replies Helen Acroyd of Montana.

"AY-*yee!*" intones the clerk.

"You keep the list," Mace whispers to Stermas, shoving a tally sheet at him.

"Mister *Applegate!*"

"AYE!" Mace bellows, the exertion yanking that mysterious, abdominal pain alive again for a moment.

"AY-*yee!* Mister *Atchison!*"

"No!" shouts Paul Atchison of Nebraska.

"Noooooooooo," the clerk brays. "Mister *Atwell!*"

Dode Atwell of New Mexico cries, "Aye!"

"AY-*yee!*"

Within Randolph Hatfield there reigns a durable calm. It came upon him around one o'clock on the previous Sunday. He had been watching Dorothy as she sat on the sofa, legs tucked beneath her, reading the newspaper. Suddenly Randolph knew that what they had implicitly constructed over the years was finished. He had abdicated the last vestige of her original feeling for him. Now they would either continue together in a desert of mutual solitudes, find some new device to resume or, simply, consummate the evident barrenness and part for good. At that hour on that stilled Sunday afternoon, Randolph had found, within himself, the capacity to endure whatever happened. He still had the other half of his life to provide meaning and self-esteem. On Monday he had flown alone to Ohio for a checkup and some serious advice on drinking from his doctor. He had returned on Tuesday evening, knowing he would survive and even live again. It was a relief to be back in the House. He would have a hard time resuming the aura of leadership but the challenge of doing that excited him. It was good to be back and alive.

"Mister Crane!"

"No!" shouts Arnold Crane of Michigan.

"Noooooooooooo! Mister Cressap!"

There is a small, two-beat silence.

Jerry Cressap lifts his head. "No," he says, almost inaudibly.

"Bastard," Stermas mutters, marking the tally sheet.

"Noooooooooooo! Mister Crockett!"

"No!" cries Maynard Crockett.

It is 5:45. The last of the day's full blast of heat sears Washington. The Vice President, Chairman of the Council of Economic Advisers and the Secretary of the Treasury have left the President's office. The Secretary of Defense is in; he is a tall, gray-haired banker from Boston. At the moment he is talking on the telephone while the President sits on one of the sofas, reading a memorandum. Papers are piled on the cushions beside him. Ben Saterlee sits on the opposite sofa.

The Secretary of Defense is talking to General Morris Green in Providence. The evening is coming on and the vicious, complicated street fights have not abated. The paratroopers of the 82nd Airborne have not been able to get between the disorderly mobs of black and white rioters, snipers, rock-throwers and tossers of Molotov cocktails. The violence has widened, has become a matter of street-by-street encounters. Whole blocks are burning and, with the coming of darkness, it is going to get worse. Four Providence policemen, two National Guardsmen and three paratroopers have been killed, adding to the grand, grim total of forty-seven known dead since the fighting began seventy hours ago. General Green wants more paratroopers. A major confrontation is building just off the campus of Brown University. Caravans of cars are streaming out of Providence as frightened residents leave. General Green wants tanks. For the next hour the President, Saterlee and the Secretary of Defense will discuss strategy, wondering whether it is worse to spread alarm by bringing in more troops and equipment or whether General Green should be replaced by General Henry Platt, a specialist in street warfare. During the discussion the President will find himself consciously praying for his bill and, at the same time, wondering whether the passage of something so purely symbolic is enough anymore.

"Noooooooooo! Mister Massonetti!"

"Aye," says Luigi Massonetti of New York.

"AY-yee! Mister Moddell!"

"Aye!" calls Arnold Moddell of California.

"AY-yee! Mister Morowitz!"

"Aye!" says Abram Morowitz of Illinois.

"AY-yee! Mister Monk!"

"No," says Regis Monk, the fourteenth member of the black caucus to vote, the seventh to vote against HR 1418. Stetson has done slightly better than Mace thought he would.

"Noooooooooooo! Mister Musteus!"

Bent over his tally sheet, Tad Solomon checks the "no" column beside Larry Musteus' name and, vaguely, wonders, as he sometimes does when he is very tired, just what he is doing here. The choices of his life and the reasons for them have to do, in some way or other, with the durability of certain kinds of passion. The passion which drove Tad Solomon into liberal politics and the labor movement really came alive during his years at the University of Chicago. He had gone there as an underweight Jewish kid away, for the first time, from his home in Boston.

Through a girl he met in a political science class he was drawn into the university's loose liberal community. It was, to him, a world composed of sights, experiences, ideas and gradations. The Young Communists and Trotskyites were a dismal and hard extreme, puritanically righteous about their commitments to party. Tad found them unbearably arrogant and joyless. His own absorption was in Barbara Rolf and the aura that surrounded her. She was a tawny-haired, large-breasted New Yorker, afflicted with a combustible, loud humor and exquisite skill in bed. Tad had lost his virginity to her. They had roamed together through a twilight of parties in basements on Fifty-seventh Street, warm, wet spring nights prodding the leafy neighborhoods of south Chicago awake to another year, searches for places to make love, impassioned discussions of politics over bourbons and ginger ale at the University Tavern. They had made an assortment of friends and Barbara had taught Tad that the totality of being aware also embraced passions for Dostoevsky, the erratic works of Henry Miller, hard-held opinions on poetry as well as an enduring desire to remake the world for equality, brotherhood and anti-fascism. Now, thinking back, Tad receives the memory of those years as a blur of sensuality, awakening to the possibilities of the mind's world and the genesis of his own idealism.

Barbara wept when he was drafted in 1943 and swore fidelity to the edifice of intimacy and shared ideal they had built together. When he returned to Chicago in 1946, her tawny vigor had turned to a sort of blowsiness and her breasts were even bigger due to her nursing her twin daughters. She had married a Ph.D. candidate in physics and they lived in a messy apartment on Blackstone Avenue. Tad was relieved to be relieved of Barbara, but he was permanently rooted in the world she had opened to him. He got a job with the United Auto Workers and was sent to Georgia as an organizer. His Chicago-acquired vision of the world decreed that he would automatically hate and fear the South. But he came to love it deeply at the same time that he was becoming more interested in ideas and politics than in the life style that a particular set of ideas and politics offered. He began to wear coats and ties and married a girl from Atlanta. They moved to Washington when he joined the AFL-CIO. He still believes passionately in equality, brotherhood and, at least, a benign world. But now, too, he knows the Process and knows how much of that is possible.

"Mister Young!"

Tension clutches at the House and everyone in it like a seam of rivet, fixed upon the end of the roll call. Prentice Young is predictable.

"The vote is now even. No." says Young.

"Noooooooooooo. Mister Zerman!"

The world holds its breath. Mace is sitting upright, hands gripping the chair arms tightly. Randolph Hatfield is twisted around looking back. Stermas doesn't look. He keeps his eyes on the tally sheet, pen hanging upon Mike Zerman's name, the last name. Hector Prince leans on the table, his eyes closed. The Speaker is bent forward again, gavel in hand. The world holds its breath and watches Mike Zerman, a tall, sad-eyed Congressman from Ohio who has refused to see anyone about the bill, who has declined firmly to discuss it with the leadership. He is sitting in a middle row on the right side of the chamber, knowing now that it all flows to him.

"No," he says.

Pandemonium.

Two wire service men dash from the press gallery. Maynard Crockett is on his feet, actually laughing, but the sound is drowned out by the cries, splatters of applause, roars, the piercing yip of a rebel yell, people shouting in the galleries, paper flying in the air, crash of appalled and delighted talk as the Speaker cracks his gavel and Hector Prince, his amiability shattered and his face red, stands at the committee table cursing, close to tears. HR 1418 has been defeated by one vote.

On the left side of the chamber George Stetson is standing, fists clenched, looking at Mace. The noise grows louder. Members are standing in the aisles, gesturing, angry or delighted; others are coming into the well. The rapping of the Speaker's gavel is louder and more insistent. Lou Howard, Tad and Margaret are on their feet in the south gallery, Margaret is close to tears.

Mace remains in his seat, still clutching the arms. It has happened before, God knows it has happened lots of times, but not like this, not without reserve votes waiting to be changed if they are needed, not without members who have begged off their commitments and loyalties on the understanding that they will vote with the leadership if it is close. There aren't any now, goddamnit, because there isn't any leadership. His mind trying frantically to recover from the shock of the closeness and the cacophony of noise around him, Mace tries to think; he tries to bring names and faces into the forefront of his mind, trying to remember someone who can be changed, some debt that can be called, something, anything. But there isn't anything because everything has been pored over, tried and exhausted. Now, in the hour of the greatest need he has ever felt, Mace Appelegate is paralyzed and helpless.

Beside him, Randolph Hatfield has risen to his feet. He has turned, his back is to the well, and he is looking up the aisle to the rear of the chamber. His face, tranquil a few minutes before, is flushed and angry.

Suddenly Hatfield lunges for the aisle, tripping over Stermas' knees and colliding with an elderly Congressman from New York. Randy gains the aisle and begins to shout. "'Cressap!" he bellows. "You, Jerry Cressap!"

His voice carries over the chaos, deep, commanding and angry. In his seat at the back of the chamber, Jerry Cressap jerks up his head and stares. Randolph Hatfield is standing halfway down the aisle, pointing directly at him. "Cressap!" Hatfield bellows again. "Jerry Cressap, you get the hell down here and *change your vote!*"

Jerry half rises. Suddenly everyone is looking at him. Fear begins to surge in his mind, old fear, vague fear. But Randolph

Hatfield is coming up the aisle toward him, pushing people out of the way, shouting.

Jerry bolts. He scrambles across knees and seats into the far aisle and pushes his way down into the well. Gasping, he looks up. "Mister Speaker!" he cries, envigorated by immediate and real fear, "how am I listed?"

"Against," the Speaker says. His face is tight and unsmiling.

Jerry turns. In the chaos of the House, Randolph Hatfield is standing looking at him.

Jerry turns back. "I wish to change my vote to 'aye.' "

The Speaker nods.

The Clerk crosses out and re-marks his tally.

Applause ripples in the gallery. On the floor a few members cheer. Jerry walks across the well, shaking. Suddenly Randolph Hatfield is beside him, arm around his shoulders. "I won't forget this, Jerry," he says quietly. "None of us will forget what you've done."

Suddenly the fear is gone. For the first time since he has been in Washington, Jerry Cressap feels good.

The noise is subsiding as the realization of what has happened sinks in. The vote is now even and people look toward the Speaker. He, too, has been enigmatic as to his actual feelings about the bill. He is calculable by his hatred for the President. But how he will vote to break the tie is suddenly uncertain. Few people connected with the protracted battle for HR 1418 have even considered the possibility that is now before the House.

Hatfield releases Jerry Cressap and goes back up the aisle. The chamber is still filled with noise. Clusters of Congressmen are standing in the aisles arguing. Up in the galleries, most people have resumed their seats. The two wire service reporters return to the press gallery.

Stermas, Hector Prince and Mace Applegate are huddled together talking to Ben Conger, a zone Whip for the outer Middle West. Mace has his cold cigar jammed into one corner of his mouth, his mouth stretched around it, contributing to the expression of astonished disbelief in his eyes as he listens.

As Hatfield joins them, the Speaker begins to gavel again

and Mace takes the cigar from his mouth. Stermas is standing, looking toward a rear corner of the chamber.

"I'm telling you, it's true," Conger says excitedly.

"Yawl're standin' there tellin' me if I get Petey Willis on th' next Foreign Affairs trip to Paris, he'll switch?"

"That's *just* what I'm telling you!" Conger says. "C'mon Mace, what about it?"

Mace turns and looks. At the far end of the chamber a small man with soft brown hair and rimless glasses is sitting with his hands folded in his lap.

Mace turns back to Conger. *"What about it?* Why, goddamn-it, Ben, ole Petey there's on th' Post Office Committee an' I just remembered we gotta have a 'vestigation of how them folks in France send their letters. You bet your ass he's goin'!"

Conger straightens up, looks at Congressman Peter Willis and nods.

The Speaker is still gaveling as Willis goes to the well and changes his vote. It is 6:20 in the afternoon and the Youth Resources Development Act has just passed the United States House of Representatives by one vote.

Sometime later Tad Solomon is sitting in the nearly deserted hotel suite drinking warm bourbon from a paper cup and talking to Bill Mitsawaka. Betsy Niles, looking disheveled, tired and oddly pretty comes in from the next room. "There's a call for you, Tad. Get it in here, okay?"

"Okay," he says.

He puts down his cup and tilts back in his chair, stretching his arm until it touches a telephone. He punches the blinking light and picks up the receiver. "Tad Solomon," he says.

"Hi there, Tad? It's Ralph Rengen."

For a moment Solomon's dulled, relaxed brain doesn't register. "Who?"

"Ralph Rengen. You know. Bent Metals Institute."

"Oh," Tad says. "Yes, Mr. Rengen."

"Look, I feel kind of good about something and kind of bad, too."

"Okay," Tad says quietly. "Tell me."

It is dark outside; the lush shapes of trees and the domed elegance of the Capitol are outlined against the glow of Washington in the night sky.

"I got a bonus," Rengen says.

"That's nice," Tad answers. "Congratulations."

"I mean, I got it for finding out about the Hatfield bill that you found out about for me."

"Don't worry about it," Tad says.

"Well, I feel a little bad," Rengen answers. "So I thought, maybe, maybe my wife and me could take your wife and you out for dinner. How about it? We'd have a hell of a time. I know this place—"

Slowly, Tad sets the telephone on its cradle and tilts his chair forward. He picks up the cup of bourbon and smiles at Mitsawaka. For some inexplicable reason a line from T. S. Eliot learned long, long ago during a lush, Chicago spring, comes to his mind.

"Life," he says, "the last twist of the knife."

8: The Judiciary

No higher duty, no more solemn responsibility, rests upon this Court than that of translating into living law and maintaining this constitutional shield deliberately planned and inscribed for the benefit of every human being subject to our Constitution—of whatever race, creed, or persuasion.

Associate Justice Hugo L. Black

The Constitution is whatever the judges say it is.

Chief Justice Charles Evans Hughes

In a nation that proclaims its substance to be of laws, not men, somebody has to define the law. The power to do that is awesome; it draws the very perimeters within which the Process can operate. It is a negative power whose principal functions are to deny, to forbid, and to admonish. Throughout American history the power to define the law has struck down great presidential programs, killed the laboriously wrought works of Congress, humbled state governments, helped prepare the stage for war, given new shape to politics, and reprieved doomed men or recondemned them; it has even instructed Americans on the legal proprieties of public worship. Sometimes used brilliantly, at other times narrowly, the power to define the law has created both American heroes of durable reverence and national fools whose memory abides in the bitterness of the generations that lived after them. The power to define the law is the absolute of the Process; in the Washington world of shifting strengths, contested values, and transient victories or defeats, it states what absolutely is. Given the immense voltage of that power, it is one of the paradoxes of the Process that the law-defining function has been given to the smallest, the least democratic, and in some ways the most dependent of the triad of basic federal institutions—the Supreme Court.

Wreathed in its own mystique, misunderstood by a public more accustomed to openly political mechanisms of government, the Supreme Court sits at the pinnacle of the federal judiciary pyramid. Its nine Justices (the Constitution prescribes no particular number and there used to be only five) arrive at the Court with only the smallest bow to the niceties of democracy—they are appointed by an elected President and confirmed by an elected Senate. Unless impeached or forced into retirement by senility, illness, or an inability to do the work assigned them, the Justices can remain on the Court until they die—and more than half the modern ones have stayed that long.

Presidents and Congresses have constituencies to which they can appeal in the nation; they have traditional Process power with which to bargain, cajole, or threaten in order to achieve what they want. The Supreme Court has no constituency. It has only a few sentences in Article III of the Constitution and the moral authority derived of a mystique has grown slowly over the centuries as the means of imposing its will. Andrew Jackson, angry at his Chief Justice because of one of the rulings of the Court, snarled: "Well, John Marshall has made his decision; now let him enforce it." No modern President would think of openly defying the Supreme Court. He might prevaricate in giving substance to its rulings; he might apply the ruling in the narrowest sense. But he would never refuse to do what the Court ordered him to do. The mystique of that highest tribunal has become permanently enshrined in the pantheon of assumptions upon which the Process operates.

That doesn't mean that the Supreme Court is beloved. From the late-eighteenth-century controversies over its blatantly political rulings on the Alien and Sedition Acts through the venom heaped upon Chief Justice Roger Taney for the Dred Scott decision (which, by holding that Negroes weren't citizens, helped set the stage for the Civil War) down to the howls of contemporary right-wingers for the impeachment of former Chief Justice Earl Warren, the Court has been the lightning rod of controversy. "We are quiet here," said Mr. Justice Holmes, "but it is the quiet of a storm's center, as we all know."

Indeed, the mystique that surrounds the Court is sometimes fuel for the rage of people who hate it because it makes the Supreme Court appear untouchable. The Court seems to be above the brawling and calculating of the rest of the Process; it appears to dwell beyond politics and even beyond the normal prejudices to which most men are susceptible. The Supreme Court gathers about itself the appearance of a temple of serenity in which statute and Constitution slowly turn, casting the light of their reality upon wise and patient men whose every drawn breath is dedicated to the discovery of American truth. If that impression is a more romantic notion than a reflection of reality, it still endures.

Since all political systems require visible reasons for being, they are anchored in some absolute of principle, tradition, or theory. The anchor is supposed to keep the political system faithful to its original philosophical premises; it is a means of referring back to those premises as the system evolves.

Yet someone has to be in the constant business of checking present actions against the philosophic premises of the past to keep things on course. That, theoretically anyway, is what the Supreme Court is supposed to do.

The Constitution didn't give that role to the Supreme Court. The Court won it through a precedent that emerged from Chief Justice John Marshall's political skirmishings with President Jefferson. What the Court won in the celebrated case of *Marbury* v. *Madison* was judicial review—the right to rule on the constitutionality of presidential acts and congressional laws. The Supreme Court is thus the circuit breaker of the Process, periodically interrupting its flow in order to see if the present acts of government and Congress are in keeping with the intentions of the people who designed the government. Like Talmudic scholars poring over the Mishnah and the Gemara, the Justices of the Supreme Court endlessly search the nuances and phrases of the Constitution, bringing its meaning (or their opinions of its meaning) across the centuries, brandishing that meaning in the mainstream of the Process to make it pause, dismantle, or backtrack when it exceeds the intention of its authors.

The mystique of the Supreme Court and its actual role in the Process complement each other. The Court is considered awesome; therefore it can perform its awesome function. And because it performs its awesome function, it is considered awesome. Yet beneath that majestic exterior the Supreme Court can be just as political as any other institution in the Process.

As a body, it is acutely aware of the dangers stalking it if it pushes its law-defining power too far. When sufficiently aroused to wrath, Congress can limit the Court's appellate jurisdiction or it can pass laws that supersede the Court's decisions. *In extremis,* Congress can even impeach, convict, and remove a Justice from the Court, although the likelihood of that ever happening is remote. It was tried once, in 1804, on a particularly nasty and politically partisan Justice named Samuel Chase, and it didn't work.

The Supreme Court is also wary of Presidents who though capable of inflicting less practical damage than Congress can and will arouse public anger against the Justices. Alexis de Tocqueville identified this problem in 1832 when he warned the Justices that they would be "impotent against popular neglect or popular contempt."

Various Presidents have had their battles with the Supreme Court. Jefferson went to his grave muttering imprecations against Chief Justice John Marshall. Some Presidents have resorted to publicly vilifying the Court. In his 1968 campaign Richard Nixon portrayed himself as a big law-and-order man and as a "strict constructionist" of the Constitution. Yet he assaulted the highest legal authority on the Constitution by accusing it of "weakening the peace forces as against the criminal forces in our society."

To guard against the danger of such assaults or of congressional attacks upon it, the Supreme Court must have a healthy recognition of when to pull its punches. In 1937 the Hughes Court went through the bitter battle over President Roosevelt's appeal for authority to pack the highest bench with Justices more to his liking. Roosevelt had been enraged by twelve Supreme Court decisions invalidating legislative measures of the New Deal. As the court-packing fight proceeded, the Justices suddenly began upholding every New Deal measure that came before them, including some that were quite similar to previous invalidated measures. Contemporary wits cackled that this was "the switch in time that saved nine." Even the Warren Court, which made history in individual and civil rights opinions and took fearful abuse for them, finally backed off from the public and political uproar it had caused. Most of the criminal cases heard during the 1966–1967 term were decided in favor of broader police and prosecution powers. At other times in history the Supreme Court has refused, for reasons of prudence, to hear controversial cases.

It is fashionable nowadays to divide Justices into those who are judicial activists and those who favor judicial restraint. As practical descriptions or approaches to the law, the two phrases may not mean as much as they seem. An activist Justice concerned with individual rights in a mass society will claim that he is an apostle of restraint—that he wants the government restrained in its dealings with individual citizens. A justice who is considered a model of judicial restraint, who believes in the primacy of government power to regulate society, can become ferociously activist in pushing that concept of the Constitution.

What seems to divide the Justices are their views on the role of the Court in the Process and on what considerations should apply in the shaping of judicial opinions. Felix Frankfurter, a hero of judicial restraint, believed that the Supreme Court should limit itself to determining whether Congress stayed within the intent of the Constitution in passing laws. When in doubt, Frankfurter always deferred to Congress. He also believed that only the consideration of constitutional or congressional intent should apply in arriving at opinions. The moral or practical effects of the matter under consideration were not germaine as Frankfurter saw it. "It is not easy," he once wrote, "to disregard one's own strongly held view of what is wise. . . . But it is not the business of this Court to pronounce policy. It must observe a fastidious regard for limitations of its own power, and this precludes the Court's giving effect to its own notions of what is wise or politic." That view is widely revered by conservatives today. But in Frankfurter's own time its application in the Process infuriated the right. Frankfurter repeatedly upheld the constitutionality of laws passed by New Deal Congresses, not necessarily—as his critics charged—because he approved of the laws themselves but because he recognized the right of Congress to pass them. This is one of the Supreme Court's chronic public relations problems; outsiders keep mistaking its judicial opinions for political opinions.

A view that differed from Frankfurter's was held by an equally revered Justice, Oliver Wendell Holmes, Jr. Although he too denied the Court's right to make moral judgments or set policy, Holmes' great opinions and dissents like the great briefs of Louis Brandeis are riddled with arguments, theories, and interpretations that go beyond the horizons of the law. In dissenting from a majority opinion that barred naturalized citizenship to a Quaker woman who refused to swear that she would bear arms in the country's defense, Holmes wrote: "I would suggest that the Quakers have done their share to make the country what it is, that many citizens agree with the applicant's belief, and that I had not supposed hitherto that we had regretted our inability to expel them because they believe more than some of us do in the teachings of the Sermon on the Mount."

The Constitution does not reveal its inner meanings easily. It is not supposed to, because the men who designed it realized that the society whose government they were designing would evolve through epochs of changing social and political conditions. They phrased a good deal of their intent in that ambiguous generality that permits flexible interpretation.

Parts of the Constitution are, of course, explicit. When Article II, Section 1, says of the presidency "neither shall any person be eligible to that office who shall not have attained the age of thirty-five years," there can't be much argument about what is meant. But a thousand questions arise when Article I of the Bill of Rights declares that "Congress shall make no law respecting an establishment of religion, or prohibiting the free exercise thereof; or abridging the freedom of speech, or of the press; or the right of the people to peaceably assemble, and to petition the government for a redress of grievances." Does that mean that only the U.S. Congress is prohibited from making such laws? Or does Article I apply to state legislatures as well? Is there any limit to the freedom of speech? What does "peaceably assemble" mean? With or without shouting? With or without banners and posters? Are there any means of petitioning the government that are illegal (like threatening or insulting it)? Does a television station's refusal to sell time to an antiwar group abridge the freedom of speech of the press inherent in the First Amendment?

Divining and defining the ambiguities of the Constitution and other federal law is the Supreme Court's principal function in the Process. The Court does not speak with one voice. Its most embarrassing opinions are those rendered 5 to 4, which publicly display the Justices' disagreements with one another. Great Justices, whether liberal or conservative, spend their lives on the Court, as Hugo Black did, studying everything from the Federalist Papers to Greek law and reviewing the writings and times of thinkers as separated in history as Henry II, Edward Coke, and William Blackstone in a ceaseless effort to understand the minds and therefore the intentions of the men who wrote the Constitution.

Along with the fact that its Justices are not elected, the Suppreme Court makes another demand that goes against the American grain. It asks us to accept that there are men whose wisdom gives their opinions the binding force of law. We know that Chief Justice Hughes was right when he said: "The Constitution is whatever the judges say it is." But we find it hard at times to live with the fact when the opinions handed down create hardship or come into conflict with our own political opinions. Our principal act of faith in living with the Supreme Court must be exercised in the belief that its opinions are rooted in wisdom and in a more profound understanding of the Constitution than most of us can achieve.

But the American political system needs to be anchored in something, and the Constitution is the only anchor it has, the only rationale for almost everything else done in the Process. And somebody in a government of laws, not men, has to decide what the law is. Nuts, fanatics, and vigilantes would love the job, but the rest of us can't afford them.

Which leaves the Supreme Court.

Once upon a time Washington was more a town than a city on the river. It was a slow-paced community that wasn't very important to the rest of the nation. There was a settled order in Washington during the thirty years that finished the last century and began this one. Poor people were deserving if they behaved; black people were servants not people; and the visible world was made up of the important, the moneyed, and those connected with them in one way or another. Washington society was largely a reproduction of New York society. In that distant, era, families took long vacations together in the summer, horses bolted at the sight of automobiles, and there was a "season" between November and February marked by White House receptions, Christmas balls, and a rise in deaths from pneumonia and diphtheria. In those years Henry Adams went pessimistically to earth in his house on Lafayette Park and Senator James Wadsworth of New York had a house on Massachusetts Avenue where it comes into Dupont Circle.

Sitting in an upstairs drawing room of the Sulgrave Club Eleanor Hazard cannot help but think of how much has changed. When her father brought her down from Boston in the winter of 1915 there was a great dance somewhere and they had all come to the Wadsworths' for punch and cookies either before or afterward. She can remember herself in this room, just going on fourteen, her hands perspiring inside the short white gloves, wishing she were old enough for a long dress, wishing there were someone her own age to talk to, agonizing in awkward uncertainty over what to do with her mouth and her feet and where to look with her eyes. Everyone else was tall and confident, and she thought that she would die if any of them spoke to her.

She recalls meeting President Wilson. He was solemn, she had thought at the time, rather like somebody's grandmother. His breath smelled of something medicinal as he bent over to shake her hand and tell her that her father was a fine and useful man even if he did belong to the wrong political party. She also remembers crossing Dupont Circle one icy evening with another girl and the girl's governess. She remembers hearing the crunch of wheels on the snow and looking into the cars and carriages where gentlemen in tall hats and fashionable ladies were silhouetted against the cold lamplight. It was all staid and comfortable, and people were talking about the war in Europe. But that had little meaning for her then.

Now it is all changed. Almost everything has a new function within the old, remembered shells of house and place. Henry Adams' home has been replaced by the Hay-Adams Hotel. Senator Wadsworth's house is the Sulgrave Club, a private hotel for ladies who were children when the Wadsworths lived there (and a place where the National Gallery of Art gives luncheons and where dances are held by the Fivers and the Waltz Group). Out on the sun-baked benches of Dupont Circle young people in tattery clothes and headbands play guitars and tom-toms.

She doesn't mind change, even though she is often surprised by some of the things she finds herself doing in the flow of new circumstance. She still wears gloves when she goes out and she tends to judge the world in terms of taste. But now she is back in Washington, waiting for a man who is young enough to be her grandson, a man who professes to be a radical. He and she have been allies for the last three years, and that, she thinks, is somewhat unusual. Her father would have been amused.

She and Charles Marks became allies because of the Atomic Energy Commission. Seven years ago the commission announced plans to build a nuclear power plant at Jamestown, Rhode Island. She and several of her friends had strongly opposed the plant and had decided to fight it. Her original motives are not susceptible to precise explanation now. They had to do with a general desire to protect the island where her family had summered for five generations and where she has lived year round since her husband died in 1947. As the battle over the plant wore on and as she learned a great deal about atomic energy and the controversies surrounding it, she added more reasons to her instinctive objection to the plant—the fact that Narragansett Bay's water temperature might change, thereby damaging marine life; the possibility of contamination in water where her grandchildren swam and sailed in the summers. But these were all afterthoughts. She sometimes thinks that she is what her opponents accuse her of being—a reactionary old woman who doesn't want her life inconvenienced by change. At other times she knows that isn't true, that she is trying to hold on to some Jamestown quality that she loves and that is therefore lovable. She wants that quality preserved for other people. But she can't articulate it.

Anyway, it had all resulted in a lawsuit entitled *Eleanor Hazard, petitioner* v. *United States Atomic Energy Commission and United States of America, respondents*. But the suit to block construction of the power plant failed.

Then, after the plant was built, Mrs. Hazard and her friends started again. This time the number of plaintiffs was larger. Two environmental groups joined in the suit. One of them, the Jamestown Coordinating Committee, was made up of some decidedly strange people. There were angry young high school teachers, university students with odd life styles, and activists from Providence who were veterans of all sorts of protest movements. The other environmental organization was calmer, and its members tended to be a bit older than the unrelenting people of the Jamestown Coordinating Committee. That second group was called the Friends of Narragansett Bay. Mrs. Hazard joined it and paid founder's dues of $100 a year because she loved the bay.

The first suit had been very expensive. When the second one

began an environmental law firm in Washington offered to take the case on a *pro bono publico* (or public interest) basis. That was how Mrs. Hazard became allied with Charles Marks. He is a twenty-nine-year-old lawyer and the son of David Marks, the celebrated Washington attorney and adviser to Presidents. Charles is an interesting young man; he has long hair and a handlebar mustache and a very low-key manner. At first Mrs. Hazard thought he was hostile. Then she discovered that he was just very serious, very dedicated, and quite fascinating. They are light-years apart and have become very fond of each other.

The new suit claims that the Atomic Energy Commission hasn't complied with the National Environmental Protection Act of 1969, and that therefore the Jamestown plant should not go into operation. So far Mrs. Hazard and the other plaintiffs have kept the plant idle for almost a year. Their case has become something of a New England *cause célèbre*, with newspapers and politicians lined up on one side or the other. People whom Eleanor Hazard has known all her life warned her that she was getting mixed up with a lot of radicals and subversives, maybe even Communists. Later, when the U.S. Circuit Court of Appeals for the First District in Boston ruled in her favor and against the Atomic Energy Commission, a good many of those people stopped speaking to her. During the early summer riots in Providence the city suffered a power blackout that severely hampered the efforts of the police and the military to restore order. That started the mass of public opinion in its hard turn against the Jamestown plaintiffs. One of the state's leading newspapers focused its rage directly on Mrs. Hazard, accusing her and her colleagues in the suit as "either witting or unwitting allies of chaos and enemies of public order and human progress. The peevish objections of a rich, elderly Jamestown lady and her militant colleagues to a plant that would substantially increase the power capacities of this state have now, like the proverbial chickens, come home to roost upon the innocent people of Rhode Island." The editorial continued: "The Fort Getty power station may obstruct Mrs. Hazard's view of Narragansett Bay's west channel, but if the federal courts had an ounce of sense in them, that misfortune would have counted small against the real danger posed to lives, propety, and jobs by the chronic shortage of electric power in this area." That, she thought, was rather hysterical as well as inaccurate. Her house didn't have a view of the west channel of Narragansett Bay. The editorial also annoyed her.

During the long seven-year battle she has never been dismayed by the forces lined up against her—industry; the state government and its Governor of recent years, poor, dithering Leslie Wharton; the Atomic Energy Commission and the U.S. government. Eleanor Hazard is the daughter of a great Massachusetts corporation lawyer and the widow of another distinguished attorney who, she hesitates to remind the Governor of Rhode Island, not only persuaded Leslie Wharton to study law as a foundation for politics but financed his education as well. Her unpopularity at this point hurts, but the pain is surmounted by her strong if somewhat simplified view of the law, that *it* can decide the ultimate merit in all such matters. And in her second suit the appeals court has decided that she is right. That sustains her and makes the loss of some old friends and the ugliness of the attacks bearable.

But she knows it isn't over yet.

Thinking of all that while she does her needlepoint, she does not see Charles Marks come up the stairs. She is only aware of him as he drops onto a sofa beside her chair.

"Hi," he says in his soft voice.

She puts down her needlepoint and studies him for a moment. The sunlight glints on a St. Christopher medal dangling from her wrist just below the sleeve of her tweed suit. "You've lost weight," she says.

For a moment Charles looks back at her. Then he shakes his head.

"Yes, you have," Mrs. Hazard says. "Have you been eating properly?"

He shrugs. "Sure."

She picks up her needlepoint again. "Well, you don't look it. Is—" She pauses and raises her head. Suddenly she laughs.

"Isn't that the damnedest thing? I can never remember her name—"

"Lois," he says.

"Yes, Lois. I don't think she's feeding you properly."

"That's all over," he says. "We split. I'm living with my mother this summer."

"Oh," she says. "Well, then your mother isn't feeding you properly." She smiles at him. "But don't tell her I said so."

He grins back, his teeth showing beneath the scraggly fringes of his mustache. "Hey, I'm sorry to haul you all the way back from London. I really didn't mean for you to come back, just call me. Anyway, you're here. How was your granddaughter's wedding?"

"Very nice," she answers. "It was in Bromley last Saturday. I was ready to come back anyway. What's happened, Charles?"

He leans forward, clasping his hands between his knees. "Remember I told you that there have been an awful lot of suits like ours and that just enough of them were working to make the administration worried about the nuclear power plant program?"

Stitching, she nods.

"Well, they've decided that they need a very particular kind of test case to see if they can't put an end to all the cases. We're almost it. They want the Supreme Court to hand down a definitive ruling on the standards of the Environmental Protection Act because that's the basis for most of the suits."

"Why are we almost what they're looking for?"

Charles unclasps his hands and looks up at her. "Well, for a couple of reasons. First, because we brought our suit under Title 1, Section 102, of the act—the part that says that the federal government has to use 'all practical means and measures' to protect environmental values. The appeals court agreed with us that the AEC hadn't done that in the Jamestown case. Well, I'm told that the commission and the Justice Department think they have reasonable grounds for arguing that the AEC did conform to Section 102 despite what the appeals court said. So that's the basis for attacking the problem through us."

"But," Mrs. Hazard says, "you said we were almost a perfect test case."

He nods. "Yeah. Almost. The thing that's wrong with our case from their point of view is you."

She lowers her needlepoint. "Me?"

He nods and grins. "The White House had a staff meeting on this last week. They reviewed the whole thing. A guy named Ben Saterlee—have you heard of him?"

She raises her head. "Yes, I think so. I've probably read his name in the newspapers."

"He's one of the President's top people," Charles says. "Saterlee does a lot of political thinking for the administration. This is really his idea. If they win in the Supreme Court, they want it to be the right kind of victory for political reasons. They want to hit directly at what they call militant environmentalists. You aren't that. So they want you to bow out of the case and let the Jamestown Coordinating Committee and the Friends of Narragansett Bay be the main plaintiffs."

"I see." She begins stitching again. For a long moment she is silent. Then she smiles. "And, I imagine, they don't want to be in the position of attacking a little old lady. Even though I don't wear tennis shoes."

"That's right too. Wharton doesn't want you attacked either."

"Leslie has a guilty conscience," she says. "Let me ask you something."

"Go ahead."

"Did the President ask your father to ask you to ask me— if you follow me?"

"Yes," he says.

"Well, I don't want to create family difficulties for you." She thinks a moment. "You're my lawyer in this business. What do you advise me to do?"

"Tell them to go to hell," Charles answers, "and stay with it. We need you. If they want to fight somebody, make them fight you too. You got into this for your own good reasons."

"Not very popular reasons, I'm afraid."

"The courts don't judge popularity contests."

"All right," Mrs. Hazard says. "I don't think I'll tell the President to go to hell. But—" She nods. "Yes, I think I'll stay in until the end. When will it happen?"

"Oh, the Justice Department will probably petition the Court this afternoon or tomorrow morning. They'll ask to have the case expedited. That means arguments this week—if they do it that way—and a decision next week sometime."

"I think I'll stay in Washington until it's over," she says. "Do I have to write a letter to the President or Mr. Saterlee or someone?"

He stands. "No, I'll take care of it." He smiles down at her. "I'm glad you're sticking with it. You're pretty important in this thing. You're proof that even ordinary citizens get worked up about threats to the environment." He laughs. "I don't mean that you're really ordinary, Mrs. H. I mean you're not a causist or an environmentalist or anything like that. And you have that old Rhode Island name. That helps a lot too."

She looks up at him. "You know, suddenly I'm frightened. What if the Supreme Court rules against us? That would mean we've been wrong all along—"

"It isn't that simple." He shakes hands. "We'll do our damnedest and maybe we'll win again. If we do, it'll be the last time we need to win."

She smiles again. "Wouldn't Leslie Wharton be pleased if we lost? The newspapers would be happy too."

"So would a lot of other people," he says.

Forty-five minutes later a telephone call loops across Washington, connecting one law firm based in a two-room apartment on R Street with another that occupies the twelfth floor of a building on Connecticut Avenue just up from the White House. Mrs. Dunn, David Marks' secretary, presses an intercom button.

In his large office Marks turns away from a conversation with one of his younger partners and picks up his telephone.

"Yes, Mrs. Dunn?"

"Your son is on 27," she says.

"Which son?" Marks asks.

"Jesus Christ Superstar," she says.

Marks wishes to God that *someone* would make the woman stop that. He punches down a blinking button. "Hello, counselor."

"Hi," Charles says. "I've just had a talk with Mrs. Hazard. No go."

"You mean she will get off or she won't?"

"She won't."

"I see," Marks says. He pauses and looks across the room at his partner, a handsome, lean man with close-cropped black hair and a slightly cold manner. "If it wouldn't be violating the lawyer-client relationship—"

"I advised her to stick with it," Charles says.

"Because you need her," Marks replies.

"Maybe," Charles answers. "But also because she's got her own reasons for being in this thing."

"Yeah," Marks says. "Someday you'll have to explain them to me in words I can understand."

"I'll do that someday," Charles answers quietly. "Anyway, I told her that there's no reason for her to accommodate the enemy."

"I'll pass the word along to the enemy," David says.

"Don't give him my love," Charles answers. "If it wouldn't violate any of your complicated relationships, when is Justice going to petition the Court?"

Marks looks at his watch. "Oh, probably this afternoon. They're asking for a quick decision because of the power blackouts on the west side of Narragansett Bay."

"You've got somebody with you, haven't you?" Charles says.

"That's right."

"Well, I'll pick you up about 6:30. Okay?"

"Fine," Marks says. He hangs up. "Sorry about that," he says to his partner. "I'm also sorry to say that I have a rather private call to make now. Can your business wait?"

The partner stands. "I just dropped in to see if you and Lily could come out for Sunday lunch."

The image of an immense modern house in the Virginia

countryside flickers in Marks' mind like one frame of a movie film. The next frame is a picture of a wide stairway leading down into a living room the size of a sandlot baseball field. The third frame portrays people standing around in riding boots and dungarees drinking Bloody Marys and talking about horses as if they were naughty children. Marks hates horses. "Thanks," he says, "but I'm afraid we couldn't this Sunday."

When the door closes he picks up another telephone that is a direct outside line. He dials Ben Saterlee's private number in the White House. The secretary who answers says that Mr. Saterlee is in a meeting but that she will get him out.

While he waits, Marks leans his small body back in his big chair—Mrs. Dunn says he looks like a gray-haired kid in a stroller when he sits in that chair—and looks at the pattern the sun makes as it falls across his office wall. He is intrigued by its play upon the pictures hanging there—Adlai Stevenson sitting under a tree on his Illinois farm; Harry Truman looking into the camera, intransigent as a mule skinner; the tight, tragic features of James Forrestal; Lyndon Johnson in shirt sleeves, holding a telephone and stroking a dog; Dean Acheson. The pictures are variously inscribed: "To David Marks with gratitude . . . ," "To my wise and invaluable friend . . .," "To David with my deepest appreciation. . . ." All the inscriptions are meant; all have been earned. In the remorseless Process there is still room for the special affection that grows out of shared experience and admiration for the competence displayed in that experience.

Above these pictures are three others that are uninscribed. One is a 1936 campaign photograph of Franklin Roosevelt in a floppy, rain-splattered hat. He is grinning and the caption reads "Rain or Shine." On the left of Roosevelt there is a sepia-toned photograph of Louis Brandeis. An etching of Oliver Wendell Holmes, Jr., is on Roosevelt's right.

"Mr. Saterlee's coming, Mr. Marks."

"Okay," Marks grunts.

The phone clicks. "Hi, David."

"Ben. I'm afraid I've got bad news for you."

"Oh?"

"Charles just called. Mrs. Hazard has decided to remain a plaintiff in the Jamestown case. If you proceed you'll have to proceed against her too."

"Damn," Benjamin Saterlee mutters. "The President isn't going to like that. He's been personally concerned that she get out. Tenacious old bitch, isn't she?"

"It can't be helped," Marks says. "You aren't asking for my advice now, but I'll give it anyway. You'd better proceed on this one for two reasons. First because I think you can win it and second because if you don't, your whole power plant program's in trouble. There was an article in yesterday's *New York Times* about the suits pending—"

"I don't need the *Times* to tell me about them," Saterlee says. "Don't worry. We're going ahead with this one and I agree with you, I think we're going to win. I just wish we didn't have to win against old lady Hazard. Damn."

"Charles advised her to stay in," Marks says.

"You don't have much influence with your son, do you?" Saterlee asks.

"My son," Marks replies, "considers me and you and the President of the United States to be liberal fogeys and maybe he's right."

"Don't count on it," Saterlee says. "Anyway, thanks for trying on Mrs. Hazard."

Marks hangs up. The afternoon proceeds. A client in Waukegan is talked out of appealing a decision that went against him in the federal courts; an anxious friend comes in to discuss his divorce and Marks arranges for him to meet a lawyer who specializes in that sort of thing. Another friend, who is a member of the Senate, calls to discuss the propriety of buying into a bond issue for a project vaguely connected with the subcommittee that the Senator chairs. Marks advises against it. He spends the latter hours of the day with one of the firm's younger lawyers putting the finishing touches on a negotiation he will conduct on behalf of a client at the Federal Trade Commission in the morning. At six o'clock two of his senior partners come in for a drink. They exchange gossip for half an hour and then Marks goes downstairs. Charles is waiting at the curb in his square-bonneted, antique MG.

Marks picks up a folder lying on the empty seat and slides in. He closes the tiny door against his leg. The day's heat dangles upon the threshold of evening. Charles turns the car into the stream of traffic heading northwest on Connecticut Avenue.

"I had an interesting discussion with your young sister this morning," Marks says.

Charles smiles. "Did she get moral with you?"

"No. I got moral with her. That was my first mistake. The second was being logical about it." He turns and looks at his son. "Now that you've attained the age of twenty-nine I suppose you've forgotten that morality is the exclusive property of people nineteen years old or younger."

"It's been a long time," Charles says. "What was the issue this morning?"

Marks leans his head back and closes his eyes against the sun. "Sue was telling me about a new policy they've started at the People's Vegetarian Cafeteria. You'll recall that the purpose of the cafeteria is not to make money—that would be unforgivable. They want to serve the people good, low-cost vegetarian food."

"Okay," Charles says, taking the car around Kalorama Triangle and heading across the bridge.

"Sue said that bums have been wandering in looking for handouts. Under the new policy the bums will henceforth be thrown out. They bother the people, she says."

"And what did you say to that?"

"I asked her to define what the People's Vegetarian Cafeteria means by 'people.' "

"You did make a mistake."

"I did indeed. It seems that 'people' are freaks, hippies, students, and street children." He turns to look at Charles again. "I asked Sue why bums weren't people. That was a mistake, wasn't it?"

"It certainly was. What was Sue's reaction?"

Marks turns his face back to the sun. "I'd rather not describe it. Today has been a day of female triumphs over fathers and Presidents."

"Meaning my client," Charles says.

"Meaning your client."

"I take it you're still upset about that."

Marks shakes his head. "I've been in the practice of law too long to be either upset or surprised at anything. But I do resent the fact that the Supreme Court of the United States has to waste its time on what appears to be the petulance of an old woman. The environmentalists are one thing. A lot of them are misguided, but at least they think they're saving the world."

Charles swings the MG to the left and shifts gears as they go down Calvert Street past the Shoreham Hotel; he shifts again as they start up the long hill that leds to Reno Road and Cleveland Park. "Once you told me about a case you took, a murderer you knew was guilty. Remember that?"

Eyes still closed, Marks nods. "The Keiser case. You know what that's about. The murderer is unimportant. You take the case because you're trying to defend the rights he was denied."

"But you're still willing to take his miserable personal claim to court in order to do that?"

"Yes, of course."

"And his character, his acts, or his motives for his acts aren't important?"

Marks doesn't reply until they reach the turn into Reno Road. "Okay," he says, keeping his eyes closed. "You've made your point."

Charles grins. "I was hoping you wouldn't cave in so easily. I wanted to ask you if you knew a better place in the world for Mrs. Hazard to exercise her petulance than the Supreme Court of the United States."

Marks opens his eyes and straightens up. "I'm still interested in your motives, counselor. Why is it so important to you to have her stay in this case?"

Charles is silent for a moment. He drives looking straight ahead, the shadows of tree branches flitting across his face. "Your business has its politics," he says quietly. "So does mine.

The environmental movement's in hard times. We're winning court cases and losing public support. We need all the ordinary citizen suits we can get, people who aren't overtly committed to the environmental movement. We have to show that the ordinary, preferably respectable citizen is just as concerned as we are."

"And Mrs. Hazard's respectable. That's it?"

Charles nods. "Yeah. That's it. She's very respectable. In Rhode Island they don't come any more respectable."

"I thought you liked her."

"I do," Charles says, slowing the car to turn into Highland Place, "but if you held my feet to the fire I suppose I'd admit that I think her reasons for opposing the power plant are petulant crap."

"So you're using her," Marks says.

"Like you used Keiser," Charles answers.

They ride the last few blocks in silence. Charles stops in Highland Place in front of an old white frame house set among tall trees.

They go in. The big house murmurs with kitchen sounds in its dark, cool interior. Through open doors Marks can hear voices and splashing from the swimming pool.

It isn't until he is in his bedroom that he realizes that he is still holding Charles' folder. He sits down on the edge of his bed and opens it. There are papers, letters, and newspaper editorials inside. He pulls out one of the editorials. "The peevish objections of a rich, elderly Jamestown lady and her militant colleagues," he reads, ". . . have now, like the proverbial chickens, come home to roost upon the innocent people of Rhode Island." He reads the rest and then puts the editorial back and closes the folder.

He sits listening to the sound of his household below and out among the trees. David Marks always feels pleasure and a sense of gratitude when he comes home to this place so full of solidity, excitement, and love. But this evening that feeling is dulled by a persistent question about what the world and the law owe to Eleanor Hazard, whom he has never met but who seems to arouse such rage in so many people.

History hasn't much use for hysteria. Its principal value is to explain events or to illustrate the antithesis of greatness. A great man is often defined as one who keeps his head and sticks to his principles while everyone else is hysterical. In the 1950s and 1960s an extraordinary wave of hysteria rolled across the United States and crashed against the Supreme Court and its Chief Justice. Highways were plastered with ugly signs shrieking "Impeach Earl Warren," and the John Birch Society held contests to see who could write the best essay on why the impeachment would be a dandy, patriotic idea.

This nuttiness had been triggered by Supreme Court opinions of three kinds: the school desegregation decision of *Brown* v. *Board of Education of Topeka,* individual rights cases—such as the striking down of the Pentagon's industrial security program—and cases in which it seemed that the Court was trying to gather all governmental power to Washington. Like most waves of political hysteria in history, the one churned up against the Supreme Court was fueled by considerable ignorance of the subject that was causing all the emotion. The role of the Court in the American system of government appeared to be beyond the comprehension of the protesters. They seemed to think that it was supposed to hand down political opinions— preferably ones pleasing to the far right. The basis of the offending opinions was lost on the perpetrators of the hysteria; none of the anti-Warren Court pamphleteering of the period bothered to explain, for instance, that the industrial security program was struck down because it hadn't been authorized by either the President or Congress. Most curiously, the anti-Warren Court people didn't even have a schoolchild's knowledge of how the Supreme Court works. If they had, they would have changed their billboards to read "Impeach Earl Warren and Hugo L. Black and William O. Douglas and William J. Brennan and Maybe a Couple of Other Justices Too." The poor segregationists, superpatriots, and professional anti-Communists seemed to think that the Supreme Court was a sort of judicial soccer team whose captain, the Chief Justice, tells the other players what to do.

He doesn't, of course. In most ways the Chief Justice of the

Supreme Court is just another Justice, more often than not the junior Justice at the time of his appointment. He has only a few prerogatives not enjoyed by his brethren. Administrative duties add burdens upon the Chief Justice, but they do not enhance his influence over the other Justices. To exert that influence, the Chief Justice has to do what any other Process player must do in order to achieve power—he must exercise the few potentialities of his position to their utmost.

Cases come to the Supreme Court along three routes—appeals, petitions for certiorari, and original jurisdiction. In the area of original jurisdiction the Court sits as the only competent authority to judge what the Constitution describes as "all cases affecting ambassadors, other public ministers, and consuls, and those in which a state shall have party." Such cases are relatively rare. The principal avenue along which cases reach the Court involves petitions for certiorari, which can include all federal court cases and matters in the state courts that involve federal law. The Justices have a right to accept or reject petitions for certiorari; if four Justices vote to take a "petition for cert." Appeals from decisions based on any federal or state law that might be "repugnant to the Constitution" must be heard by the Supreme Court whether it wants to rule on them or not. The Justices can decide to hear appeals with or without oral arguments from lawyers. But every appeal must result in a lower court's decision being upheld, reversed, or remanded.

There are a good many reasons why the Supreme Court rejects cases that come to it in the form of petitions for certiorari. Some are turned down because they aren't important enough or symbolic enough, some because they arrive before the issues underlying them have reached full, national fruition. Others may be rejected for political reasons or because the Justices know that they would be unable to agree on a strong majority opinion. This selection process can be heartbreaking. The Court has time to take only a small fraction of the cases sent to it. Rejecting many may mean perpetuating some human misery, leaving someone in prison, denying someone money, property, rights, or even life. But pruning is absolutely essential. In its first term the Burger Court's dockets were loaded with 4,202 cases. The Justices were able to hand down only eight-eight signed opinions.

The nine Justices meet every Friday during term in a graceful, wood-paneled room lit by a crystal chandelier that hangs below a gilt-framed portrait of John Marshall. No one who is not a Justice has ever been present at the weekly conference. It is so secret that even messengers are not allowed in. The junior Justice goes to the door to take messages. In the weekly conference the Justices review about fifty cases, selecting a few for argument. Here the Chief Justice exercises several of his limited prerogatives. Before the conference he circulates a list of cases that he suggests not be taken. If no Justice disagrees with him, the listed cases aren't discussed.

During the conference the Court also rules on cases that were argued before it during the week. In these discussions, which are much longer and more detailed than the debates about admitting cases, the Chief Justice speaks first, setting the framework within which each case will be considered. After he has finished, the other Justices discuss the case in the order of their seniority. Then the Justices vote on the final disposition of the case in reverse order. The junior Justice, who has to speak last, must vote first. A few days after the case has been decided by vote, the Chief Justice assigns the writing of the majority opinion—if he is with the majority. If not, the senior Justice on the majority makes the assignment. The Justices in the minority decide who will write the dissent.

Obviously, this system gives the Chief Justice certain prerogatives not enjoyed by his brethren. On a close vote he can determine whether the Court will take a case or what the ultimate outcome of a case will be. If the Chief Justice disagrees with an opinion but sees that it is going to win, he can vote with the majority, assign himself the opinion, and then write it in a narrow way that is devoid of any sweeping implications. But aside from prerogatives of that sort, the Chief Justice is just another voice on the Court. His influence must arise from intellect or powers of persuasion—as with any other Justice.

How the Supreme Court ultimately rules on a case is also dependent to a large degree on the bargaining the Justices do between their personal visions and their philosophies of the law, and to a lesser degree on the role played by the usually brilliant young law clerks who assist them.

After the majority opinions and dissents on a case have been assigned, the Justices get down to the writing task. It is crucial, because the manner in which an opinion is written often determines its impact upon the Process and the country. A broad decision can cast doubt or reaffirmation on dozens of other laws and issues, while a narrow opinion is largely restricted to the matter under consideration. Phrases in opinions are crucial; the historic 1954 decision holding that separate but equal schools for black and white children were unconstitutional instructed the nation's educational systems to desegregate with "all deliberate speed." That meant there was time to work out the changes. The late Mr. Justice Black objected, seeking immediate desegregation to solve the problem in a single, searing jolt of time. As it was, the desegregation process took decades and involved many more suits and cases—including the political battle over bussing, which threatened some of the Court's sovereignty.

Aware that the phrasing of an opinion has a great deal to do with its applicability, the Justices bargain over wording. The author of a majority opinion circulates his first drafts among the other Justices. They return the drafts with suggestions for rewording and demands for changes in supportive arguments. The drafts are altered to meet objections and suggestions. If the writing Justice declines to change his draft, some of his colleagues may file separate concurring opinions or separate concurring dissents.

In all this the law clerks, fresh from leadership in their classes, play roles that vary with the characters of the Justices. The clerks, who serve for a year or sometimes two in this most honored of all legal apprenticeships, do research for their Justices, boil briefs down to manageable memos, and sometimes write parts or all of final opinions and dissents. Their writing, of course, is expository of their Justices' views. Some Justices use their clerks as sounding boards. Some rely on them a great deal, some not at all. And occasionally Justices will summon their clerks for extracurricular duty. Hugo Black's clerks were often required to fill in as fourths for tennis doubles at the Justice's handsome old house in Alexandria, Virginia.

Since 1935 the Supreme Court has been housed in a neo-Grecian temple on Capitol Hill. It stares through the branches of trees at the House and Senate located across a small park. Inside, the Court is a small world of its own. It has about 250 employees, who do everything from repairing furniture to serving as guards on the Court's own police force. The principal employee is the Marshall of the Supreme Court, who is its business manager and paymaster. He is also the man who utters the traditional cry: "Oyez! Oyez! Oyez! [an ancient Norman phrase meaning "hear ye"]. All persons having business before the Honorable, the Supreme Court of the United States, are admonished to draw near and give their attention, for the Court is now sitting. God save the United States and this Honorable Court!" Upon that cry, the Justices enter the courtroom on the first floor, sweeping through wine-colored drapes and taking their seats.

The courtroom is surprisingly small. The Justices' bench is low. Seats of highly polished wood, tables for lawyers, and a small press section take up the area before the bench. Lawyers argue their cases at a lectern directly facing and only a few feet from the Chief Justice. On the lectern there is a little light that blinks warnings when the arguing counsel's allotted half-hour time is almost up and when it has expired.

Beyond the courtroom the Supreme Court's home is a citadel of cool grace and that superb taste of which the U.S. government is capable when it really tries. The building is constructed around four inner courtyards, each equipped with a spraying fountain. The Justices' three-room suites are off main corridors of hushed, marbled simplicity—well, almost hushed almost all the time. The late Justice Felix Frankfurter used to bounce down the halls whistling "Yankee Doodle," and you could hear him all over the first floor. Nobody could do much about it. If

the Constitution is what Justices say it is, good behavior in the
building is whatever the Justices do.

The Supreme Court building has two law libraries on its
upper floors. Scattered through the halls and chambers is one of
the best collections of portraiture in Washington. From Rem-
brandt Peale's controversial porthole picture of John Marshall
to a dark, brooding portrait of Roger Taney radiating the particular animus of a man who senses that he is bucking fate, the
Supreme Court is a gallery of its own history.

The Supreme Court is a classic example of Process power—
it has power because everyone thinks it does. And its power
will endure only as long as everyone keeps thinking that way.
But unlike other Process institutions, the Court has no real way
of demonstrating its power; it must, for example, rely on the
executive branch to implement and enforce its rulings. One
way in which the Court maintains its power is to hand down
rulings whose validity remains evident over long periods of time.
Another way is to back off, refuse to hear controversial cases,
and sometimes even contradict itself when the controversies surrounding it become too heated.

James Madison once wrote that "in framing a government
which is to be administered by men over men, the great difficulty lies in this: you must first enable the government to control
the governed; and in the next place, oblige it to control itself."
By defining the law and keeping the system on its original philosophical tracks, the Supreme Court, at its best, permits those
two things to happen.

But the Court can do that only as long as two ideas persist
—the idea that the Constitution is the dominant rulebook for
the operation of government and law in this country and the
idea that the Supreme Court is the final and only really competent authority to say what the Constitution means. As long
as those two ideas are in popular force, the Process can tolerate
Supreme Court rulings that anger a great many people, perhaps even a majority of the people. The constitutional idea
presupposes that society's principles are more important than
any issue, problem, or desire of the moment and that their

preservation is more important than any inconvenience they may cause at the moment.

That, in effect, is what the American political idea is all about. It is what the Supreme Court is all about, too.

It was all absurdly brief. At one moment she and Charles were sitting in the small, high-ceilinged courtroom listening to Mr. Justice Caldwell drone through a long opinion on a grazing rights case (she thought that he really read quite badly). She had been looking at the friezes around the ceiling, trying to work out which figure represented what great lawgiver. Then, suddenly, she heard her name, and a few minutes later Mr. Justice Powell was saying: "But it remains to be seen how this legislation can be applied in balance with the other national priorities that it explicitly recognizes. Therein lies the judicial role. In these cases we must interpret the National Environment Protection Act of 1969 not only in the light of its own environmental standards and the adherence of the federal government to those standards by its declarations and practices, but against those other priorities and the legislation that created programs to deal with them. By that standard we conclude that in this case the commission's intent was within the requirements of the NEPA and that the operation of the power plant at Jamestown, Rhode Island, is necessary to other, recognized national priorities. Hence the ruling of the appeals court is reversed."

And that was all there was to it.

Charles had bent toward her. "You understand, don't you?"

"Why, yes," she replied, turning to look at him. "It means we've lost."

"This time anyway," he said.

Now they are sitting in a taxi that is stuck in the usual summer morning traffic jam on Fifteenth Street where it runs along the east entrance to the White House. Mrs. Hazard is looking at the long line of people waiting to go through the Executive Mansion on the morning tour. But her mind has its own visions, familiar ones; she thinks of the road leading across the narrows at Mackeral Cove in Jamestown, of Sidney Wright's old weathered farmhouse at the top of the hill. That house had always marked the limit of one's visible definition of that corner of the island. One knew that the decaying ruin of Fort Getty lay beyond the hill, between the hill and the west channel of the bay. The fort's old barracks were empty and peeling, the concrete bunkers were cracked and sprouting weeds, the barbed wire was rusted, snapped and coiling back in some places. That deadness, out of sight beyond the hill, had been a part of the known order of things ever since the end of World War II. Now it was all gone, and a great steel-tubed, brightly lit, metallic complex of machinery was waiting to come alive. The predictable order had been shattered. She had never quite figured out why that older order was so important to her. Perhaps she never quite dared work out the definition for fear that it would reveal something unpleasant about her, perhaps that selfishness which her critics claimed was her principal motive.

Now the long fight is over. She has lost, and suddenly it is important that she rearticulate to herself all her reasons for going into it in the first place. But she can't; the shock of losing is blossoming slowly in her, widening like a paralysis that bars her from thinking clearly. She grasps at fragments of phrases she used years ago to explain and argue the matter—the health of grandchildren who come here in the summer to swim and sail in the bay . . . keeping Jamestown as it always has been . . . the danger. . . . the swarms of technicians who will come. She can't fit the phrases into neat, logical arguments as she once did. It was all so long ago. She sits looking at the line of patient tourists and wonders if her pride in adapting to change hasn't been a false vanity. For the first time in years Eleanor Hazard feels herself disoriented by self-doubt.

The line of traffic creeps forward and the taxi begins to move. The movement brings her back to where she is and the fact that she isn't alone. She turns to Charles. "Let me ask you something."

He nods. "Sure." He is sitting at the opposite end of the seat. He wears a black suit today; his long hair is neatly combed.

His briefcase is in his lap and he has his arms wrapped around it.

"In the court you said we had lost this time. Surely this is the end, isn't it?"

He hugs his briefcase tighter and looks at the floor. "Well, Mrs. H., 'win' and 'lose' are really relative terms in the law— at least as I see it." He raises his head and looks at her. "If you mean—will we ever get to the point where the Atomic Energy Commission realizes that it can't operate that plant and agrees to take it away—no. In that sense, we've lost. But we're going back into court again."

She frowns. "But how—and *why?*"

"Well, we start in the state courts this time."

"But how?" she persists. "Doesn't the Supreme Court have the final say?"

"Oh, sure," he murmurs. "But we can find a new angle in the NEPA or in some state statute; we can start just the way we did this time, getting a restraining order out against the AEC." He smiles at her. "We can keep them tied up for, maybe years. That is, if it works."

The traffic jam has broken at Pennsylvania Avenue. They ride to Massachusetts and turn left. The heat of the day seems to dispel as they pass beneath the tall trees. The taxi slows to the next traffic jam in front of the Brookings Institution. Mrs. Hazard turns to Charles again. "Forgive me if I seem stupid," she says, "but wouldn't we lose again in the end?"

"Yeah, probably," he says. "But, you see, the value of this thing is just to keep on in litigation, keep them fighting us off."

The taxi moves forward again, crosses the lights, and turns into the short, curved drive in front of the Sulgrave Club.

Mrs. Hazard shakes her head. "Perhaps I'm terribly—oh, old-fashioned or something, but I don't see the sense in what you're proposing, Charles. *We've lost.*"

"Of course, but that isn't why we did this in the first place— I mean, winning wasn't the only thing. We wanted to hassle these guys. We can go on hassling them."

The taxi stops.

Charles gets out. "Wait," he says to the driver. He helps her out.

She lays her hand on his arm and looks up at him. "I don't think you're going to like this, Charles. But I'm afraid that none of what you've said makes any sense to me at all. If you want to go on—hassling, as you call it—you'll have to go on without me."

He runs his hand through his long hair. "Jesus, Mrs. H., you can't back out now. We need you."

She smiles and shakes her head. "Charles, dear, I did go into this to win. But I've lost. That, to me, is the end of it."

He tries to smile. The expression turns into a grimace of exasperation. "But doesn't that make you sore?"

"Why, of course it does. But I know when I'm beaten."

"*The object isn't to win, Mrs. H.!* At least not now."

"To me it was," she says. "And I didn't win. I'm afraid, simply, that you'll have to do without me if you really plan to go on."

He shakes his head. "Jesus, you really disappoint me."

"I'm sorry for that," she says. "I don't like to disappoint my friends."

He shakes his head again. "You don't try very hard to keep your friends, do you?"

"Oh, Charles," she says quietly. "How perfectly idiotic. You really don't mean that."

"The hell I don't, Mrs. Hazard. I thought you were a committed person."

"Charles," she says. "You're acting like a child. Now stop. Come in and have some lunch."

He holds out his hand. "Good-by, Mrs. Hazard. It was great working with you—for a while anyway."

She looks into his face and she knows the expression that is there. She knows it from dozens of confrontations with sons and grandsons who have been thwarted and who are caught in the cross-pulls of frustration, anger, and the embarrassment at being angry from which the young never seem to be able to retreat.

She takes his hand. "Good-by, Charles. Thank you for everything you've done."

She knows, as he releases her hand, that he would like to say something more, some last, wounding thing. But she knows that he won't. She also knows that much later, perhaps days or weeks from now, he will regret what he has said and will want to call or write and say that he is sorry. Knowing that hurts her the most, for some strange reason.

Charles gets into the taxi and it leaves. She stands alone for a moment, a small figure wearing a blue suit trimmed in white. The heat of noon is heavy and immense and the cicadas sing high in the foliage of the trees.

She turns and goes inside, telling herself what she told herself the night her husband died: there is so much to think about and so much of it painful that she won't think at all for a while. She lunches alone and the afternoon begins. She orders a taxi. The driver turns out to be a young man from Nigeria who is studying accounting at Howard University. He agrees to stay with her for the afternoon. They drive to a needlepoint shop on MacArthur Boulevard and then to the National Gallery. After she spends an hour and fifteen minutes looking at the collection of nineteenth-century French impressionists, they go to an airlines office, where she buys a ticket for a morning plane to Providence. By the time they return to the Sulgrave Club it is ten minutes to five; she has learned that the young man's name is Michael Kfawa, that he is twenty-six, has four little brothers, and is an Ibo tribesman, that his mother is dead and his father owns a Ford truck, that Michael hopes to work for the government as an inspector, and that he has been to Rome and London as well as Washington. She gives him $20, which he says is too much.

Elsewhere in Washington Ben Saterlee and Paul Brasher go into the Oval Office at four o'clock. The President is pleased about the Supreme Court's ruling on the Jamestown power plant, but he still has misgivings about the political value of the victory. At 4:30 David Marks calls Charles to commiserate over the Court's ruling. They talk for ten minutes. At 4:50

Mace Applegate leaves the House of Representatives and goes to Bethesda Naval Hospital for his annual checkup.

At 5:10 Eleanor Hazard is called by a friend in Jamestown who tells her that the evening papers and news broadcasts are headlining the Supreme Court decision. One Providence newspaper managed a quick editorial that concludes: "The genius of the American court system is often manifest in what it finally does rather than in the erratic decisions made en route to that final judgment. This newspaper has never doubted that the Supreme Court would, at the end of the day, rule for the public good and against the selfish campaign of Mrs. Hazard and her radical-militant backers." In the same newspaper a columnist who does political satire sarcastically thanks Mrs. Hazard for "clarifying several issues in this state: who runs it, who it is run for, and what is most important in it. If the Grand Duchess of Jamestown wants to do one more thing for us, there is one more thing she can do—move to Connecticut. With friends like her, as the saying goes, Rhode Island doesn't need any enemies." Having heard all that, Eleanor Hazard professes to be amused by it, chats a few more minutes with her friend, and then hangs up.

She takes a bath and turns on the television in her room to watch the six o'clock news. In Washington the Supreme Court's ruling on the Jamestown power plant isn't news at all. It isn't mentioned. She lies down for a nap before dressing for dinner. But she can't sleep, even though she is very tired. The thinking that she had earlier decided not to do now won't be denied.

Long ago, at a time lost to specific placing by date or circumstance, her father had told her that self-pity was the supreme enemy, that it was the worst thing she could do to herself. Because she loved her father very deeply and thought—and still thinks—that he was the wisest man she had ever known, she has done more than simply remember that advice. She has incorporated it into her character, eradicating any impulse to self-pity. When things have been bad she has made it a practice to immediately do something—garden ferociously, take a long walk, telephone a grandchild, turn to someone else's problems, embark upon a new project or plan. But now, for the first time in almost half a century, she finds herself unable to completely quell the rage and grief that are the parents of self-pity. Nor can she find open contempt for the people who now profess to despise her—the newspapers, the former friends, the politicians and officials. What makes this moment so awful, what propels her almost helplessly toward feeling dreadfully sorry for herself, is the wrenching, insistent feeling that they are right, that she has been selfish, that she had made a complete fool of herself. Once she had her reasons for fighting the power plant totally and clearly worked out. Fired by indignation, she had attached reasons to her indignation; she had developed complete arguments and logical persuasions. But now all she can remember are those wisps of phrases about the health of grandchildren and the condition of the bay. The fine, clear justifications have become muddled in the various episodes of the long fight; she can't regather that original logic any longer, not even to comfort and reassure herself. She lies looking at the ceiling, watching the patches of gold sunlight reflected there turn pale and then become smudges of light gray as late afternoon proceeds into evening. *Damn,* she says bitterly to herself, *it isn't fair!* The full knowledge of how alone she is breaks suddenly and savagely upon her, and she almost winces physically before the growing self-accusation that she has been a selfish old bitch. She wishes that she were the sort of person who wept easily. If she were, she would weep now.

The telephone beside her bed rings in a short burst.

Slowly, she sits up and reaches for it. "Yes?"

"Is this Mrs. Brooke Hazard?"

"This is Mrs. Hazard," she answers.

"Mrs. Hazard, we don't know each other," says the voice on the other end of the phone. "My name is David Marks. I'm an attorney. I believe you've been doing some business with my son Charles."

"Why yes, Mr. Marks. Charles has told me a great deal about you."

—but I sure as hell knew I'd been in a fight. He was a fine man. So was your father."

"How fascinating," she says. "You knew them both."

"The law tends to be a tight little community," Marks says. "At least among good lawyers. Brooke, your father, and I were all good." He leans back on the sofa as the barman brings their drinks. "Do you remember the Moffet divorce?" he asks.

Mrs. Hazard thinks a moment. "Oh, yes, Claire Moffet and—what was his name?"

"Same as mine," Marks says. "David."

"Yes, of course. Brooke represented Claire just because she was an old friend. He really didn't do that sort of thing."

"Neither do I," Marks says. "David was a friend of someone's." When the barman has left, Marks says, "If your father and husband were alive today they'd both give you hell for saying that you've been wasting lawyers' time. You were very opposed to that power plant, I understand."

She nods. "Very."

"All right," Marks says quietly. "Then that's what the law's for. To try to stop things you're opposed to or make happen those things you're for. It's a reasonable process, above everything else."

She tastes her drink. "At this point I have the feeling that I've been very unreasonable."

"No," Marks replies, "you haven't been. I might remind you that you won in the appeals court before you lost in the Supreme Court. That means that at least one very important judge thought you were reasonable."

She shakes her head, suddenly feeling that she is going to cry and wishing that she wouldn't. "Mr. Marks, I can't remember any longer all the reasons I started this. I—I feel as if I've been a damned old fool."

"Well," he says, looking at the ice cubes in the glass he holds in his lap, "there's a fundamental contradiction in there. You're being jumped on by the newspapers, and I understand that Leslie Wharton has made one of his predictably clumsy comments to the press. That means that what you tried to do was unpopular with a lot of people. But that doesn't mean it was unreasonable." He doesn't look up directly at her until she has wiped her eyes and put her handkerchief back in her small purse. "You know, Mrs. Hazard—I wonder if I might call you 'Eleanor'—"

She tires to smile. "Please do."

"I'm called either that son of a bitch who makes politicians do all the bad things they do or David," he says. "You know, Eleanor, I've been in the reasonable and unreasonable and popular and unpopular businesses for about forty years. I've learned a couple of things. First, there's a big difference being unreasonable and being unpopular. I've been around politics for a long time. I've seen men take courses that they strongly believe in at a certain time and have everybody screaming at them and jumping all over them. That doesn't mean they're unreasonable or wrong. It just means that they frighten or threaten a lot of people. That's what you did." He leans forward. "Now, I'm among the people who opposed you in this thing. I advised the White House to go to the Supreme Court and try to beat you. And I was the man who tried to get you off the case so that the administration could get a clear shot at the environmentalists. But just because I opposed you doesn't mean that I think you were selfish. Look, you say that you can't remember all the reasons you got into this fight with the Atomic Energy Commission. I suspect that what you really mean is that you can't remember all the arguments you used at the beginning. How long have you lived in Jamestown?"

"Oh, on and off, all my life," she says. "My mother and father bought the house I live in now in 1909."

"All right," he says quietly. "I suspect that the main reason was that you love that island and didn't want a great, ugly, and possibly dangerous piece of machinery moved onto it."

This time she can smile. "Yes, of course," she says.

"Well," he replies, "that's an excellent reason for going to law. There never will be a better one until somebody can prove that your desires are less important than those of any other citizen of this republic. You know, Eleanor, you belong to the last minority group that everyone feels safe sneering at—the well-off." He leans back in the sofa again. "I'm a Jew. We were fair game until Hitler made anti-Semitism unfashionable. There aren't many groups left to blame everything on. The rich, the well-born, whatever you want to call them, are a convenient and acceptable target for the same reason that Jews and blacks were once acceptable targets—nobody assumes that you have feelings, and in a funny way the acceptance that somebody has feelings is also the acceptance that he has rights. The rich don't have feelings because they're rich and can have anything they want."

She laughs. "I think you're right. I never thought of it that way. But I'm not even rich."

"You appear to be," he says. "Which is the same thing. You are different and therefore a target for public and editorial wrath."

She lifts her drink. "I don't know if you're right," she says. "But you do make me feel better."

"One more thing," Marks says. "I haven't argued with Charles about this because it isn't a father-son sort of issue. It's a lawyer's issue. But I believe that you were absolutely right when you refused to go back to court and start fighting all over again. The key to making the legal system work is the public's willingness to accept its decisions. That, it seems to me, is what you've done."

"I am sorry about that," she says. "Because I'm so fond of Charles and I know how desperately he believes—"

"Charles looks upon the law as a device for hassling the establishment or whatever he calls the system," Marks says. "I suppose that's legitimate. It's a very popular view just now. I look at it as a reasonable process for reaching decisions of one sort or another, in or out of court." He smiles. "Charles is fond of you. Very fond, I imagine. One of these days he'll re-assemble himself to the point where he can come tell you so himself."

The other drinkers are moving toward the dining room. The bar is almost empty. Marks takes out his watch and presses a button to spring its thin, gold lid. "It's 7:00," he says. He presses the lid down and puts the watch back in his vest pocket. "I have tickets for the D'Oyly Carte Company at the Kennedy Center tonight," he says. "If you have nothing better to do, I propose that we go. We can have dinner afterward and have another drink here to celebrate the federal government's victory over the forces of you and evil."

"That's awfully kind of you," she says. "But I wouldn't want to deprive Mrs. Marks of an evening at the theater."

"Mrs. Marks," he says, "is not easily deprived of anything. I happen to have three tickets, and the idea of dinner and the theater happens to have been Mrs. Marks' idea in the first place. She ought to be here any moment now."

"Then I accept with great pleasure," she says. "Thank you."

Marks raises his hand, catching the barman's attention. "Two more, please," he says. He turns back to Mrs. Hazard. "I imagine you'll think that this is pretty damned contrived," he says. "But you'll never guess what D'Oyly Carte's doing tonight."

She frowns. "Oh, wait a minute—something—ah, relevant?"

Marks nods.

She smiles. "Oh, I know, of course. *Trial by Jury.*"

"Yeah," he answers, grinning. "I'm corny and I'm proud of it. I like Gilbert and Sullivan."

"So do I," she says.

And so, she thinks, some things do remain after all. She looks at David Marks as he rises and smiles at his wife. Mrs. Marks is crossing the room, a slender gray-haired woman in a light summer print.

"You have had a day," Lily Marks says as they shake hands.

"But there's still an evening left," David says.

"And another day," Eleanor answers.

9: The Senate

[The Senate] is composed of eloquent advocates, distinguished generals, wise magistrates, and statesmen of note whose language would, at all times, do honor to the most remarkable parliamentary debates in Europe.

Alexis de Tocqueville, 1834

An honest politician is one who, when he is bought, will stay bought.

Senator Simon Cameron, 1875

The U. S. Senate is a political institution of a hundred human parts whose essence is contained both in the body as a whole and in each of its parts. It is the only elected element of the Process whose life never comes to an end. It is one of the two supreme trustees of the American national interest, and in the erratic political history of this country no institution has been more gloriously and foully various than the Senate. At different times it has served as an incubator of national greatness, a clubhouse for drunks, a commanding voice of the American conscience, and a school for thieves that made Fagin's look like a preacher's college by comparison.

In the second half of the nineteenth century William Ewart Gladstone, that most unflinchingly pious of British Prime Ministers, peered across the Atlantic and pronounced the U.S. Senate "the most remarkable of all the inventions of modern politics." He may have been right. The Senate had been remarkable in its early history and would be again, but it wasn't just then. During the twenty-six most important years of Mr. Gladstone's public life (1868–1894) the American institution that he adored was going through a period of such filthy depravity that Mark Twain was moved to his celebrated boast: "I think

406

I can say, and say with pride, that we have legislatures that
bring higher prices than any in the world." Twain was referring to the age of the spoilsmen, that greedy, corrupt, auda-
cious period from the 1870s to the early twentieth century
when the upper chamber of the U.S. Congress was publicly referred to as "the Senate of shame"—and didn't give a damn.
Seats were bought from state legislatures (which elected Senators until 1913); laws were made and bent for the benefit of
millionaire Senators; and a man's virtues were measured by how
much he could loot from the public process. By that standard
one of the most virtuous was Henry Gassaway Davis of West
Virginia, who amassed a huge fortune during his twelve years
in the Senate. He used to strut around waving a check for $8
million and bawling: "That there is the profit on just one of
my transactions!" The Senate was also known for its alcohol-
ism—"Whiskey is taken into the committee rooms in demi-
johns and comes out in demagogues," observed one Washington
wit. Some appalling creatures managed to get themselves into
what is sometimes called the world's greatest deliberative body.
Senator Roscoe Conkling was a horny, arrogant dandy from
New York who lingers in the memory of American history be
cause of his immense political power, his vicious feuds, his
penchant for sleeping with other men's wives, his superlative
oratory, and his pathological hatred of anything that smacked
of social or political reform. "When Doctor Johnson said that
patriotism was the last refuge of scoundrels," Conkling roared,
"he ignored the ee-normous possibilities of the word *REE-
FAWRRM!*" Then there was Senator Zachariah Chandler, an
illiterate manic-depressive from Michigan who alternately gave
lavish parties and prowled Washington at night with a revolver
moodily looking for newspaper reporters who had offended
him. (History doesn't record whether he ever shot any.) Marcus Alonzo Hanna of Ohio bought his way into the Senate in
the 1890s. He is remembered as a prince of the spoilsmen,
a cigar-chewing, flatulent millionaire who thought that reformers
and traitors were more or less the same thing. Hanna's principal
contribution to the accumulated wisdom of political science

was the ungrammatical observation that "all questions of government in a democracy are a question of money." He had come to the Senate in a search for respectability and culture. They eluded him. When asked once what he thought about Herman Melville, Hanna yanked his cigar from his mouth and snarled: "Who the hell is he? And what kind of job does he want?"

The late nineteenth century stands in special darkness because of its contrast with the periods of Senate history that preceded and followed it. In the years between 1829 and 1860 —a period of many weak, inconsequential Presidents—the Senate was peopled with giants. It was a time of rising national anguish over the cruel question of slavery. Men like Daniel Webster, John C. Calhoun, Thomas H. Benton, and their great colleagues were unable to save the country from civil war. But they did at least clarify the terrible issues propelling the country toward that crisis; they imprinted their principles on American history and provided the leadership that eight Presidents between Jackson and Lincoln were incapable of exerting.

Men's passions and practices need intellectual settings before they can be rationally debated. The Senate provided that setting during the middle period (1836–1860) of American history. During those years its real role in the Process emerged. The Senate is a collegiate body of national political figures who engage presidential power as their adversary or collaborator. In that role the Senate is, with the presidency, the alternate trustee of the national interest.

Unlike members of the House, all Senators are equal. Webster described the chamber in 1830 as a "Senate of equals, of men of individual honor and personal character, and of absolute independence. . . ." In the House all action is funneled through the committee chairmen and party leaders and in the process modified by their particular prejudices or incapabilities. In the Senate a challenge to presidential power can come from any member; the combined power of a Senate majority is awesome, as Presidents have learned to their sorrow. In contrast to the restrictive rules of the House, required because of its immense size, the Senate has no limit on debate except when imposed by unanimous consent or by cloture, a parliamentary device for cutting off debate. Cloture needs the agreement of sixteen Senators to be introduced and the approval of two-thirds of the Senate to be imposed. Between the time that cloture became a Senate practice in 1917 and March 1971, fifty-three attempts at imposing it were made and only eight succeeded. Debate in itself becomes a political weapon in the Senate. By launching a filibuster and defying cloture, a small group of members can tie up the Senate for weeks and talk a bill to death.

Because each of its members is recognized as a national figure, the Senate can reach beyond Washington and appeal for national support in its struggles to enact its own vision of the national interest against the President.

Before World War II only eleven Presidents had previously served in the Senate. (Garfield was elected to the upper chamber but never served there.) Since the war every President except Eisenhower has passed through the Senate on his way to the White House. Virtually every modern presidential candidate has come from there too.

Because it is limited to a hundred members, each of whom has to face reelection every six years, because of the laxness of its rules and the implicit national importance of each of its members, the Senate ranks after the White House as the greatest source of new ideas in the Process. From the Senate came the Missouri Compromise of 1820 and its annulment in the Kansas-Nebraska Act. The multiple measures of Reconstruction, including the Fourteenth Amendment, also had their origin in the Senate, as did the Sherman Antitrust Act, the defeat of the Versailles Treaty, the rejection of Roosevelt's court-packing scheme, the Taft-Hartley Act, the beginning and the end of the sordid McCarthy controversies, and dozens of other major policies upon which periods of history pivoted.

In theory, the Process works at its best when the Senate and the White House are in constant, vigorous competition and collaboration. But the commoner pattern in history has been for the Senate to exert itself forcefully over weak Presidents and then to retreat before strong Presidents—with occasional flares of defiance and rejection. Beginning with Franklin Roosevelt's first administration the United States has been increasingly dominated by presidential government—to the detriment of congressional power in general and Senate power in particular. The Eisenhower years were ones of collaboration between Senate and White House, but the period since has been a declining one for the Senate, especially in its constitutional share of the foreign policy and war-making powers.

Partially to assuage that loss, the Senate in the late 1960s and early 1970s hit back with strong use of its power over presidential appointments. A filibuster in 1968 frustrated President Johnson's efforts to appoint Abe Fortas Chief Justice of the Supreme Court. In 1969 the Senate rejected a Nixon Supreme Court appointee, Judge Clement Haynesworth, Jr. Again, in 1970, it blocked the appointment of G. Harrold Carswell. Stung by this Senate backlash President Nixon made the astounding claim that "it is the duty of the President to appoint and of the Senate to advise and consent. But if the Senate attempts to substitute its judgment as to who should be appointed, the traditional constitutional balance is in jeopardy and the duty of the President under the Constitution is impaired." That claim is astounding because it presupposes that the Senate's consent function is simply to give approval to whatever the President wants to do. However much its powers have diminished in the present era, the Senate cannot be a rubber stamp. Its role in the Process should be what Madison proposed for it in the Constitutional Convention of 1787: "a portion of enlightened citizens, whose limited number and firmness might reasonably interpose against impetuous counsels." The relationship between Senate power and presidential power in the matter of appointments is not what Mr. Nixon claimed it should be but what Theodore Roosevelt said it properly is: "I fully appreciate the right and duty of the Senate to reject or to confirm any appointment according to what its members conscientiously deem their duty to be; just as it is my business to make an appointment which I conscientiously think is a good one."

In that almost every other major Washington political institution derives from some source in British or colonial American experience, the Senate is the orphan of the Process. It has no true parent, not even in the legislatures of the American colonies. Thus from the outset its function was uncertain. Indeed, one essay upon its origins suggests that the history of the Senate over two centuries has been the story of its search for a role in the Process. Other theories hold that it found its role in the period 1829–1860. In the so-called grand compromise of the Constitutional Convention the Senate was created in part at least so that the states could participate in the national government. It was also a reassurance to the smaller, less populous states which feared that they would be shortchanged in the House, whose members were elected on a proportional representational basis. Each state, regardless of size, had two Senators elected not by the populace at large but by the method that Madison called "the most congenial with public opinion" —election by state legislatures. In the earliest period of Senate history its members liked to refer to themselves as "ambassadors" from their states to the national government.

There is evidence that the authors of the Constitution intended the Senate to be a somewhat aloof body, impervious to the pressures that governed the politics of the House. Jefferson, who apparently disliked the idea of a bicameral national legislature, argued his opposition to the Senate over breakfast with George Washington. At one point Jefferson poured coffee from his cup into his saucer. Washington asked him why he had done that. "To cool it, of course," Jefferson answered. "Just so," replied Washington. "We pour legislation into the senatorial saucer to cool it."

If the evolution of the United States and the Process of Washington have made leisured detachment impossible for the Senate, it is still capable, in the persons of its ablest members, of considerable deliberative genius. Some of the greatest Process debates of the early 1970s—on the antiballistic missile system, the supersonic transport, and Vietnam—arose because some Senators, thinking beyond the immediate implications of presidential policies, questioned those programs in terms of the more abstract issue of national priorities. In other debates of the same period, notably the one concerning school bussing in the spring of 1972, the Senate acted with all the measured deliberation of a coopful of chickens panicking at the approach of a summer storm. Still and all, the Senate's capacity for impact is far greater than that of the House, simply because fewer impediments stand between a Senator and his potential national audience. Visionary House members, smothered by repressive rules and dominated by old, conservative committee chairmen and party leaders, find it extremely difficult to command the attention of their own chamber, much less the nation.

In modern times the Senate is generally more liberal than the House in its votes and legislative products. There are two major reasons for this: the legislative process in the Senate is not so completely controlled by conservative committee chairmen as it is in the House, and the ideological instincts of the Senate majority are easier to express than those of the House majority. Political parties tend to elect to national office their ideological prototypes; if the Democratic party contains its own deep conservatives, it is on a national level more liberal than the Republican party. Since the Democrats controlled all but two Congresses between 1932 and 1972, the general tendency of Senate majorities in that forty-year period was toward the liberal end of the spectrum. House majorities probably leaned in that direction too. But the tendency was watered down by the old lords and barons who controlled the more populous chamber.

The Senate is unique in the Process because it is a perpetually continuing institution. The presidency is terminated and reborn every four years, the entire House every two years. The Senate never dies; a third of its members are up for re-election every two years. This continuity further enhances the Senate's national stature, allowing it to endure from one administration to the next as a trustee of the Process and the national interest.

In contrast to the sometimes raucous atmosphere of the House, the Senate is wreathed in a tradition of affable gentility.

Since each Senator is presumed to be an embodiment of the entire Senate's power and prestige, individual members tend to treat one another in public with rather sensitive courtesy. On the floor, amid the semicircle of polished Victorian desks that fill the small brightly lit chamber, formal flatteries dominate debate. To every Senator, every other Senator is "my distinguished friend," "my able colleague from Michigan." It wasn't always that nice. Senator Charles Sumner of Massachusetts once referred to Senator Stephen A. Douglas of Illinois as a "noisesome, squat, and nameless animal, who, switching his tail, filled the Senate with an offensive odor." There is one story, perhaps apocryphal, about a Senator who referred thus to a colleague: "I would not dream of impugning my illustrious friend, but I hope that when he goes home this evening his mother crawls out from under the front porch, wags her tail, and bites him on the leg." Off the floor first-naming is the general order of the day, although backbiting and bitchiness are as much a part of the U.S. Senate as of any other institution in which a large number of highly temperamental beings are confined in a small space. Much has been made of an inner Senate "club" composed of those members who, whatever their ideology, party, or particular passions, are accepted into a special realm of affection and influence because they possess certain senatorial virtues. The club does, in theory, still exist. But with the rise of a new breed of individualistic, issue-oriented Senators who care less about the body they serve than their capacity to achieve things through it, the club has become less important.

As in the House, the real work in the Senate is done in committees far from the floor and public debate. Senate committees, as political forces, tend to represent three things—regional interests, specialized economic interests, and ideology. Senators have an easier time getting the committee assignments they want than members of the House, especially new members of the House. A senator tends to veer toward those committees that reflect his ideology or his special or regional interests. Farm state Senators go to Agriculture; Southerners, particularly conservative ones, vie for places on the Judiciary Committee. This stacking of a Senate committee with members especially interested in or involved with the committee's specialty tends to be a source of political controversy. The liberals who drift toward the Senate Foreign Relations Committee come into conflict with the foreign and military policies of conservative administrations, while the conservative Judiciary Committee brawls with the more liberal Senate majority over matters of Supreme Court and Justice Department appointees named by the same conservative administrations.

The Senate has raised the function of the congressional committee to a political art form. As well as fulfilling the complex task of processing and preparing legislation, many of the Senate's sixteen full, one special, and three select committees and its swarm of subcommittees periodically use their power of investigation as a means of conducting public dialogue or debate with the executive branch or to address the nation at large. Only rarely does a House committee investigation exude the political voltage of a Senate investigation. Those inquiries have become the great open-ended dramas of the legislative process. The age of television was ushered in on the public spectacle of Senator Joseph R. McCarthy clawing and bullying his way to national prominence through the investigatory powers of a once minor Senate subcommittee. America's awareness of its problems with organized crime, the relationship between crime and some labor unions, the relationship between the Nixon Justice Department and the International Telephone and Telegraph Company, the multiple complexities and sorrows of Vietnam, the inefficiency of defense contractors, and dozens of other major controversies over the last twenty years began with Senate investigations. Such probes are powerful political weapons. They also serve another function: the congressional investigation is the only means of official public dialogue between members of the legislative branch and officials of the executive branch. Cabinet Secretaries who testify before Senate committees are doing more than just providing information upon which legislation can be based. They and their questioners are debating vital national issues before the bench of public opinion in the only open court available to them. The Senate is expressing its view of some national matter, and so, through his own spokesmen, is the President.

The fact that the Senate is a collegiate body doesn't mean that it is without individual leaders. The Senate is presided over by the Vice President of the United States, or in his absence by the President Pro Tempore, usually the oldest member of the Senate. In the absence of the latter figure, the man in the chair is usually a very junior Senator. Presiding is mostly a procedural task not sought after. But the presiding officer of the Senate, unlike the Speaker of the House, has little real power. Senate clout is vested in the Majority and Minority leaders, who head the two-party blocs in the chamber. But even their power is modest compared with the influence enjoyed by their opposite numbers in the House. The Senate Majority Leader schedules legislation (in collaboration with the Minority Leader and the Democratic and Republican steering committees) and tends to the desires, needs, and disputes of his party colleagues. Great Majority and Minority leaders (and there have been very few since the positions were created in 1911) become important in the same way that any other Process figure becomes important—by developing a reputation for being able to help and hurt, thereby stretching their Process positions to the limits. The Majority Leader enjoys the privilege of being instantly recognized by the chair when he wishes to speak; he is chairman of his party's caucus and its policy and steering committees. But it is his individual nature, his Process position, that determines how much power he will actually have. Senator Mike Mansfield of Montana, who is Majority Leader at this writing, is a decent man and a good politician, but he is not totally successful in his role. Mansfield is incapable of being a son of a bitch to anyone; therefore no one believes that he can hurt. He only helps. By contrast, his predecessor, Lyndon Johnson, was a master of the arts of Process power. Mary McCrory, the Washington columnist, described what it was like being persuaded by Johnson: "The full treatment is an incredibly potent mixture of persuasion, flattery, threats, reminders of past favors and future advantages." Only a human dynamo, a confident and ruthless one can really lead the Senate, where every member begins as a political if not human equal of every other and where each man embodies the Senate within himself. "The Senate," wrote Woodrow Wilson, "is merely a body of individual critics." Thus this endlessly perpetuating institution of the Process can only be finally understood in its ultimate role of alternate trustee of the national interest through the single Senator who personifies the whole.

Sometimes it is only a very slight thing that causes the pain, a gesture or a flicker of episode devoid of meaning to anyone but him—being made to wait in a White House anteroom; hearing conversation drift away from him as he talks to younger men; discovering by accident that important things are going on that he hasn't been told about. None of these things is meant as a slight, but each resurrects that reminding pain. *This is where it all ends, there is nothing after this.* He will go no further in the Process because he is no longer in the Senate, because he is no longer a powerful committee chairman, because he is sixty-nine years old, and because he is Vice President of the United States.

At the moment they are inflcting one of the small hurts and flattering him at the same time. At least he thinks they're flattering him. He no longer knows. There are times when they actually need him. But he can't tell whether this is one of them or not.

He is slightly offended by the fact that he isn't seeing the President alone. Lou Howard, a Missouri protégé of the Vice President and now White House chief of congressional liaison, is present at the meeting in the Oval Office. So is Ben Saterlee. There is something about Saterlee that the Vice President doesn't like. Saterlee is a professorial, theoretical politician, while the Vice President has always worked from the gut, defining things in abstract terms, mixing up his hunches, trundling style and experience distilled out of forty years in Congress. He knows that the feeling is reciprocated, that Saterlee disdains him as an old-school pol.

The President is smiling at him. "We won't hold you to your prediction, Ferdy," he says. "We just need one of those educated guesses you're so good at. You know the Senate better than any of us."

The Vice President scratches his chin. He is a short, heavy man with a large growth of gray hair and a face that he himself describes as resembling a coal scuttle turned upside down. There is lots of chin to scratch, a flat nose, and sharp blue eyes under bushy brows. Even though this is the hottest part of the year he wears his usual gray suit with a vest. A heavy gold watch chain is strung across his stomach. His Phi Beta Kappa key from Princeton dangles off the chain.

"Well," he says, the nasal Missouri accent coming out slowly. "You know how Jim Forrest is. Hell, all the committee chairmen are getting that way—more and more secretive as they mark up their bills." He turns to look at Howard, who is sitting on a chair just behind the sofa. "They've been at it, what? Six weeks now?"

Lou nods. "About that."

The Vice President turns back to the President, who is sitting on the opposite sofa. "I guess they'll have it out in another week or so. Maybe less. Jim knows you're in a hurry. The committee's friendly."

Saterlee, sitting beside the President, nods. "It's that friendliness we worry about. We're getting rumors that some of our liberal friends are trying to strengthen the bill. We don't want them adding things the House won't accept."

The Vice President leans forward and takes a cigarette from his jacket pocket. He carries them loose, which means that they are flaked out and flattened by the time he gets around to smoking them. "You've got a problem there. You're using this bill as a signal to the country. The Senate sees it as a program. I don't know what's going on up there. I haven't been around for ten days." He lights his cigarette.

"We've been keeping you too busy with other things," the President says. "Can you change your schedule so that you can stay around the Senate until the Youth Resources Development Act gets through?"

The Vice President nods. "You're the boss, boss."

"Until the bill's out of conference," Saterlee says. "We assume there's going to be no problem with Senate passage."

"That's probably safe," the Vice President says.

"But maybe problems in the conference with the House?"

The Vice President nods. "More than maybe if the Senate changes it much."

"We're going to need all the help you can give us," the President says. "I had to cancel my Western trip last month. I wanted to talk about the New Partnership and use the House passage of this bill to show that the Congress was with us. But I couldn't do it, not with the bill getting through the House on one vote." He shakes his head. "I want to make my trip by the end of September, Ferdy. We're working on the schedule now. Can we have a bill out of conference by September 1 or so?"

"That's when we'll have to have it," the Vice President says.

The talk moves on to other matters, things not directly involving him. He lights another cigarette and leans back on the sofa, one of his hands resting on an arm. He looks through the glass doors at the rose garden. It lies motionless and hushed in the late heat of the day. He has momentarily switched off from the talk around him. He glances around at the prints and pictures on the walls and the busts of the two Roosevelts. He can never spend much time in this room without wondering how he would have decorated it had things turned out differently at the last convention. Missouri's history isn't as old as New York State's, so perhaps the mixture of art, sculpture, and memorabilia wouldn't have been as rich as the present one. He might have had a painting or two by Thomas Hart Benton, busts of Mark Twain and Harry S. Truman. Certainly the room would have been dominated by a large portrait of his ancestor Aimé Mechin, who was present at Sault. Ste. Marie in 1671 when Daumont de Saint-Lusson claimed all of western North America

for France. The portrait of Aimé Mechin, a huge, round-shoul-
dered man wearing a frock coat and moccasins, hangs in the
living room of the Vice President's Washington house. But it
isn't going anywhere. Not now, not ever.

Abandoning the idea that one's life holds infinite possibilities
for further advancement comes hard to anyone. It has come
especially hard to Aimé's descendant, Fernand Adelore Mechin,
eleven-term Representative from Missouri, thrice U.S. Senator,
former chairman of the Senate Appropriations Committee, and
now Vice President of the United States. He is a child of another era in politics, a time when party really meant something—everything after one's duty to the country.

The President is nodding and saying "Right. Fine." He slaps
his hands on his upper thighs and rises, his signal that a conference is over. He holds out his hand to the Vice President and
smiles. "Don't forget my bill, Ferdy. We're counting on you."

Mechin nods. "We'll do our best, Mr. President."

Lou Howard walks him to the small elevator, another slightly patronizing gesture. He rides down to the basement and leaves
by the door leading onto West Executive Avenue. He gets into
his car still cross with the idea that they don't take him seriously. He wonders with a sudden dip of depression whether anyone
does. He sinks back on the rear seat and grasps the hanging
strap.

His driver, a red-haired man named Daniel, turns around.
"Where we going, sir?"

"Oh—" Mechin pauses. It is only 4:30 in the afternoon. He
hasn't anything to do for the rest of the day. But going home
is unthinkable; that would prove that he hadn't anything to do.
"Back up to the Senate, Daniel," he says. "Old Office Building.
Think I'll drop in on Senator Forrest."

"Yes, sir," the driver says. He glances into the rear-view mirror to be sure that the Secret Service car is ready. "Want me to
phone ahead that you're coming?"

"No," the Vice President says. "I'll surprise them."

He gets out at the side entrance to the Old Senate Office
Building. Followed by his Secret Service guard, he pauses to

chat with the Capitol policeman sitting at a desk just inside the door. Then he pushes the elevator button—three sharp jabs, the Senators' signal.

On the fourth floor, of the Old Senate Office Building he is stopped several times in the wide, marble-paved corridor as he walks toward Senator Forrest's office. Once it is by an old friend, twice by tourists who want his autograph. He has always been patient with people, giving time to all who want to shake his hand or chat, providing they are civil. But now he's a little afraid to give too much time. People might get the idea that he hasn't anything better to do.

Room 435 in the Old Senate Office Building has a photograph of a giant redwood tree on its door just below the nameplate, which reads "MR. FORREST—CALIFORNIA. WALK IN." With his Secret Service agent a few steps behind, the Vice President pushes open the door. The receptionist, a round-faced girl with bobbed blonde hair, looks up and smiles. "Why, Mr. Mechin!"

The Vice President nods. "Good afternoon, young lady."

"Why, sir, we didn't know—"

"I didn't know I was coming myself until a few minutes ago," he says. "Is the Senator busy?"

"Oh, I'm sure—wait a minute, sir." She punches a button on her telephone. "Shirley? The Vice President's here. Yes. Really! Okay." She hangs up. "Somebody'll be right out—oh, here she is."

A dark-haired woman comes across the small reception area. "Good afternoon, Mr. Vice President," she says. "Senator Forrest has Senator Crowe in his office. Would you care to go in?"

"If it wouldn't be an intrusion."

"Oh, I'm sure not."

He follows her back through a narrow hallway and into Forrest's office. It is a large cluttered room hung with Western paintings and photographs. A huge spread of longhorns hangs over the mantel. There is an autographed photo of Forrest with the President.

Behind his desk the Senator sits low, like a child at an adult's table. Grasping a short steel crutch in one hand, he wrenches himself into a standing position as Mechin crosses the room. Forrest's lower body has been withered by polio leaving him with huge shoulders and a powerful chest. He has black hair and piercing eyes behind steel-rimmed spectacles. "Just in time," he says, reaching across the desk to shake hands. "You may have saved someone from being killed."

Shaking hands, Mechin realizes that this isn't just one of Forrest's acerbic jokes. The room is heavy with tension. He can feel it exuding from Forrest and the three other people who have risen to greet him. "I've just been with the President and Saterlee," Mechin says. "They're mighty interested in your program on HR 1418."

"Interested, hell," Forrest says. "They're breathing down our goddamn necks."

The Vice President turns and shakes hands with a tall red-haired man in his middle forties. "Ed," he says, "what's going on here?" Ed Crowe is the junior Senator from Wyoming, a loner, and one of the Senate's most prominent liberals.

This afternoon Crowe's face is redder than usual and his mouth is frozen into a grim expression. "That depends," he says. "Jim thinks he's having problems with my amendment to the Youth Resources Development Act, and I think we're having trouble with Jim."

Mechin turns to a tall girl with long strawberry-blonde hair and delicately handsome features covered with a spray of freckles. He holds out his hand. "Fernand Mechin," he says.

Forrest reseats himself. "That's Daisy James of the Labor and Public Welfare Committee," he says.

"I had no idea," the Vice President says, shaking hands with her, "that the 'D. James' I see listed as staff director of that committee was—"

"A woman?" She smiles.

"Relax, child," Mechin answers. "I was going to say an attractive woman. I had a woman administrative assistant in the House before you were born."

The freckled face breaks into a new smile. "I know you did. I'm pleased to meet you, sir."

He pats her hand before releasing it and turns to a young man in shirt sleeves who is sporting a heavy handlebar mustache. "And what's your complaint this afternoon?" Mechin asks.

"Bill Brown," the young man answers. "I work for Senator Crowe. No complaints, Mr. Vice President."

Mechin lowers himself into an armchair. "The first thing I've got to do," he says, "is get a cigarette from one of you people. Then, if I can help, I will. If I can't, I'll choose sides and get mad too."

Daisy hands him a leather cigarette case. "Take half a dozen," she says.

"Thank you," the Vice President answers. "What's the problem, Jim?"

Forrest takes a typewritten sheet from his desk. "This is Ed's amendment to HR 1418," he says, peering at it. He tilts his head back. "This would add a program of Health services in the camps set up under the bill. It would"—his head goes back a little farther—"provide treament for skin diseases, drug rehabilitation, nutritional problems, counseling, etcetera, etcetera." He puts the paper back on his desk. "Daisy and her people have done a staff study, Ferdy. This program would add substantially to the per annum costs of the whole project."

"About $12 million," Daisy says. Mechin glances at her crossed legs. *Admirable,* he thinks. She is sitting at the end of the sofa, twirling her glasses in one hand. She wears a short, white, sleeveless dress.

Forrest leans over and peers at the paper again. "Counseling. I presume that means psychiatric care?"

"You know damn well what it means," Crowe answers. "Look, Jim—"

Forrest raises his head and looks at Mechin. "I can just see Jack Kotowski, who's got to administer this program, going to General Motors and saying, 'Sorry, the costs are going to be more than we anticipated. We have to hire 350 psychiatrists for the work-learning camps.' It's preposterous." His small face compresses into a wrinkled grimace of disgust.

"Goddamnit, Jim," Crowe says. "Have you read the testimony

that the Secretary of Health, Education, and Welfare gave before your committee? Were you interested enough to listen to him the day he—"

"Of course I've read it," Forrest snaps. "Have you?"

Neither of you have read it, Mechin thinks as he listens. *Your aides have read it and boiled it down to two paragraphs for you.*

"I've also read the support documents that HEW put into the record," Crowe continues, "including that two-year study of inner-city adolescents. All I'm saying, Jim, is that it isn't enough to take on these kids and send them to classes and put them to work. If this program's going to mean anything, it has to address itself to the basic problems of the youngsters it's designed for. That includes their health problems, physical *and* mental, even if you don't believe in mental problems."

"Or drug problems," Brown says.

"Exactly," Crowe answers.

Forrest leans back in his chair. "Let me give you some history, Ferdy." He takes off his glasses and draws a handkerchief out of his pocket. "When this bill came over from the House any idiot could have grasped the problems." He gives his glasses a quick polish and puts them on again. "The first problem was speed, getting it through here as fast as possible. The second problem was the closeness of the House vote. For both these reasons I decided that we'd better bypass the subcommittee stage and take up the bill directly in the main committee. That way we could keep the changes down to a minimum so that the damn thing wouldn't be killed in the House-Senate conference. Now Ed here is chairman of our Subcommittee on Children and Youth, as you know. I suspect that Ed's a bit piqued because he didn't get a crack at the bill first."

"Oh, nonsense!" Crowe retorts. "Jim, you're being paranoid. I've never had any objections to taking the bill up first in the main committee. All I'm trying to do is put in a sensible amendment that will strengthen the program."

"He's got a point there, Jim," Mechin says. "His amendment sounds pretty sensible to me. What do you say to that?"

"Our problem," Forrest says, turning back to Mechin, "is to report out a bill that the House can accept. That's why we haven't added much to it up to now. Or taken much out of it. We've had weeks of hearings here and out in the country. We've got four volumes of testimony and submissions, and we've had some pretty lively committee meetings. Up to this point we've got what the President wants—a good, politically sound bill."

"And a lousy program," Crowe retorts.

"Before you two break off diplomatic relations," the Vice President says, "let me make an observation. I think that what we've got here is two different ideas of what this bill's all about."

Behind his desk Forrest nods. "We sure as hell have."

"What we have," Crowe says, edging forward in his chair and closing his fist, "is two ideas of what the Senate should be doing. I know what the President's after. Who the hell doesn't? New Partnership, calm down the country, persuade the whites they aren't going to be socked with more taxes, and tell the blacks the programs are going to go on. I'm all for that. But this bill also institutes a new federal program, and I happen to think that it ought to be a good program. I'm not proposing that we change the bill all that much."

"A good program's no good if the House won't buy it," Forrest says angrily.

The Vice President turns to Crowe. "He's got something there, Ed."

"That's another thing," Crowe says. "I'm sick and tired of this body always having to give in to the House. Why in hell should we be limited by their limitations?"

"That's an opinion, not an answer," Mechin says.

"Senator," Daisy says to Crowe, "would you accept a rewording of your amendment?"

Crowe glares at her. "Making it vaguer and more innocuous-sounding, I suppose?"

"Well," she says, "if you'd let us prepare a draft we could try to phrase something that the House would accept in the conference."

Crowe looks at her for a moment before answering. In that

moment his face seems to get even redder. "No," he says finally. "No, Miss James. There's a principle at stake here." He turns to Forrest. "I'm tired of trying to reason with you, Jim. I'm going to propose this amendment in committee tomorrow. If it fails there—and I don't think it will—I've got the votes to attach it on the floor."

The Vice President leans forward and picks up an ashtray. "You know," he says, "everybody in this room's mad. That's the poorest damned condition I can think of for discussing legislation. I think you all ought to sleep on it."

Daisy turns to him. "You said we're all angry. Who are you angry at, Mr. Vice President?"

"Why, you, Miss James."

She raises her eyebrows. "What've I done?"

"You got yourself born forty years too late," he says. He stands and brushes ashes off his vest and jacket. "Jim, I'm ending your meeting. I want a word with you."

The others rise. Crowe turns to Forrest. "I'll see you in committee, Jim. Ten o'clock?"

"Ten-thirty," Forrest grunts as he pulls himself to his feet. "Try to break a leg getting there, will you?"

Crowe turns to leave by the hall door. Daisy puts her hand on Brown's arm. "Walk me back to the committee room, will you? I'd like to ask you something."

Brown looks at Crowe. "Senator?"

"I don't need you for anything," Crowe says. He leaves.

Forrest looks at Daisy. "I'll be on the floor until about seven. I promised Caldwell I'd go over and sit while some goddamn fool makes a speech."

She nods. "Okay. I'll be in my office."

When the door has closed behind Daisy and Brown, Forrest throws a pencil across the room in a violent gesture of rage. It hits a window and flies back, skidding across the mantel and clattering onto a table. "That goddamn pious son of a sea-bitch," he rasps. "He's going to wreck this thing if he can!"

Mechin sits down on the arm of his chair. He lights a fresh cigarette. "You sure this Crowe amendment's something the House won't buy?" he asks.

"With a one-vote passage?" Forrest snaps. "Are you kidding?"

"It's a sensible amendment," the Vice President says.

"Of course it's sensible! But it won't get through the conference, or if it does the House'll kill the whole goddamn bill. And where's your goddamn President going to be then? Looking like an ass who can't control his Congress, that's where!"

"Have you talked to Mace?"

"Mace is in the hospital," Forrest answers, sitting down again, slowly, bracing his arms.

"The hell he is," the Vice President says.

"The hell he isn't," Forrest says. "He went out to Bethesda for his checkup and they're holding him. Blood pressure or something."

"That's bad. He's too fat," Mechin says. "Jim, what's eating at Crowe?"

"He's off on another of his do-gooder kicks," Forrest says. "We had an executive session this morning and he brought up that damned health care amendment. It was late; he should have done it weeks ago. He put it in late just to be aggravating. I told him to hold it and come in and talk this afternoon." He grimaces and shrugs. "You saw what he was like. He came in mad, had his back up. I thought Daisy and I could talk him into dropping the thing or at least modifying it. He just yells about principle." Forrest sniffs. "He also keeps telling me he's got the votes to get his amendment included on the floor if we won't do it in committee. That's another way of telling me he's got the votes to kill the bill if it comes out of conference without his damn amendment." Forrest is silent for a moment, staring at the desk before him. "And he's right. He has got the votes. It wouldn't be the first time that Crowe and some of his liberal pals teamed up with the old guard to kill a bill."

"Now wait a minute," Mechin says. "He may have the votes to get his amendment into the bill. But he hasn't got enough to kill the bill if it comes out of conference without the amendment on it."

Forrest nods. "I guess you're right. God, I hate that son of a bitch."

Mechin exhales and looks at the tip of his cigarette. "What's really bugging Ed Crowe?" he asks.

"What's really bugging Ed Crowe," says Bill Brown as he and Daisy reach the door of the staff suite of the Labor and Public Welfare Committee on the third floor, "is Senator James Forrest of California."

Pausing before the door, Daisy frowns. "What do you mean?"

Brown reaches down and opens the door for her. "Crowe's a funny man," he says as they go in. "Everybody around this place thinks he's strong, intractable, adamant about matters of principle, and therefore selfless. He isn't."

The room they enter is small, an antechamber off the main committee room. The walls are lined with glass cases holding bound records of the committee's proceedings. There is a work table in the center of the room. At the opposite end, under a window, is Daisy's desk. It is surrounded by file cabinets; alongside is a typewriter on a stand. A pretty dark-haired girl looks up from the reception desk by the door. "Hi," she says. "Hi, Bill. Daisy, there are a couple of things—" She picks up a slip of paper. "Norm Porter's stuck in Salt Lake City. He missed his plane. He'll be in around noon tomorrow."

"Oh dear," Daisy says, quietly. "I needed to see him before the committee meeting in the morning. Did you take that copy of the Crowe amendment over to Congressman Prince?"

The girl nods. "Yeah. He called about half an hour ago. He'll call again. And you have an invitation."

Daisy smiles. "Is he rich?"

The girl giggles as she hands over a slip. "No. It's from Fletcher. They're having a seminar on the role of committee staffs in the Senate and in shaping legislation. Sounds heavy. They want you to come up for it."

Daisy looks at Bill and laughs. "God Almighty, I don't know if we should ever tell how we do it."

"I wouldn't," Brown answers. "I *like* running this place."

"I'll call them," Daisy says to the girl. "Be a love and go get us some coffee, will you?"

At her desk she looks through a packet of letters, opens one envelope, and reads its contents. Brown sits down beside the desk and looks out the window. "Okay," Daisy says, putting the letter back into its envelope and sitting down. "Tell me about Edward Crowe."

"Well," Brown says, "he's like most politicians only more so. Insecure. He's got principles—great, big, enormous ones. His father was an old outer Midwest Progressive, and Crowe's a true believer. But he's also got great, big, enormous complexes about himself. He's got Senate-itis."

"Oh my," Daisy says softly. She is sitting upright, arms on the desk and hands clasped together.

"Crowe," Brown says, "is more than just insecure. He really thinks he's a U.S. Senator and he thinks that people owe him all sorts of deference along with the love he wishes they'd give him." Brown smiles beneath the large mustache. "Crowe thinks he's the only U.S. Senator. He has to keep on asserting himself and his principles to get the deference. Don't get me wrong. I don't mean that the principles are just a device. He really believes in them. He really wants those kids to get all healthy and better in the camps. But Forrest bugs him."

Daisy shakes her head. "Amazing. I've been around Crowe for five years and I never paid much attention to him. He's always seemed to me to be"—she shrugs—"oh, just a reliable overly motivated liberal. A little hostile maybe. I suppose I don't really notice the committee members as a whole as much as I should. I'm pretty chairman-oriented, and I tend to assume that everyone gets along with Forrest—"

"Not Edward Crowe," Brown says. "Forrest bugs the be-Jesus out of him."

"Oh, Bill," she says. "Nobody takes Forrest's grouches seriously. Everybody knows that he's nasty because he's all twisted up and in pain a lot of the time. He doesn't mean it."

Brown strokes one side of his mustache with a crooked finger. "Not Crowe. Look, Daisy, what I'm trying to do is save you a lot of time if you're thinking of bargaining with Crowe or having Forrest try to persuade him to drop the amendment. It's personal, especially after this afternoon. Crowe himself may not know it, but he'll never drop the thing now, not after that row in Forrest's office."

She takes a deep breath. "I'm grateful for the advice, but where does that leave us?"

Brown shoves his hands in his pockets and leans back in his chair. "Look, there's something else you have to know about Crowe. He's a planner. He's got this thing on his amendment planned right past Senate passage and up to the conference and even *in* the conference." He looks at her. "And you know you can't keep him off that conference committee."

She nods. "I know."

Brown is silent for a moment. Then he says, "Interested in a deal?"

She looks at him curiously, a small crease furrowing her freckled forehead. "What're you up to, Bill Brown?"

He shrugs slightly. "Oh, a little of my own interests, a little of Crowe's. Want to hear?"

Daisy nods. "Sure. I'll listen to anything."

"I think Crowe's got a good amendment," Brown says. "But I think that passage of this bill's more important than the program it would start. I also know that this fight over the amendment isn't as important to Crowe as that day care bill of his, which Forrest has stuck in the committee and won't let go of—"

"Oh, now wait a minute," Daisy says. "You're beginning to sound like Crowe. We aren't holding that bill. It's stuck back there in the work load."

Brown nods. "Okay. You unstick it and get it up before the committee by, say, the fifteenth of September and I'll tell you something that'll help."

Daisy leans forward and flips over the pages of her desk calendar. "By the—fifteenth." She studies the calendar, bites her lower lip, shakes her head slightly, and then turns another page. "Crowe's subcommitee's all finished with it, yes?"

"June 4," Brown says.

Daisy looks at the calendar for another long moment. "How about the twentieth?"

"Get the day care bill up on the twentieth and have Forrest start work on it and you have yourself a deal," he says.

She nods. "Okay. I think I can get Forrest to do that." She leans back in her chair and folds her hands across her waist. "And if I do get the day care bill up, what do I get?"

Brown takes a deep breath. "Well, I hope that God forgives me now and that Crowe will forgive me if he ever finds out—I'm really doing this for him—but I'll tell you something he's planning."

"Tell me," Daisy says.

Brown tells her. In return, Daisy promises to persuade Senator Forrest to take up before the full Labor and Public Welfare Committee Senator Crowe's bill on expanded federal aid to rural and town day care centers. After a few more minutes of talk, Brown leaves, and Daisy James sits alone for a moment, hands clasped on her desk before her, thinking about what to do with the information she has just received. She calls Congressman Hector Prince, chairman of the House Education and Labor Committee.

"Hi, beautiful!" the ebullient Connecticut Representative shouts when he comes on the phone. "Have an indecent proposal for me?"

"Sort of," she says. "You might call it that. How are you?"

"Hot," he says, "fat, missing Mace Applegate, but not half as much as I miss you."

"What's the word on Mr. Applegate?" she asks. "I heard they found high blood pressure."

"Mace," says Prince, suddenly serious, "is a very sick man, a lot sicker than any of us who love him like to admit. High blood pressure, heart—"

"And just plain exhaustion, I imagine," Daisy adds.

"And that," Prince says. "You can do three guys' jobs just so long at his age and weight."

"I'm sorry," she says.

"We all are," Hector Prince says, "all the white hats over here anyway. Listen, Daisy, m'love, I called you because I've read Crowe's amendment. It's no go. It'll never be accepted over here. I personally think it's logical. But you aren't going to get this chamber to buy it. In the first place, as you know, most health legislation over here comes out of the Commerce Committee. Our old boys are fanatics for the rules. Commerce had nothing to do with this bill. So that's against the Crowe amendment. Then there's the cost—well, it just won't work over here if the bill comes out of conference with that amendment attached to it. The House'll kill the conference report and that's the ball game. Can't you stop it over there?"

"Not a chance," Daisy says. "It's complicated, but in the first place Crowe has the votes and in the second Crowe and Forrest have some personal problems with each other and—"

"Say no more," Prince interrupts. "You're stuck with it."

"We really are," Daisy says. "I wanted to ask you something."

"Be my guest."

"Am I right in thinking that the House will send some of the opponents of this bill to the conference?"

"We aren't supposed to do that," Prince says, "but I imagine we will. We haven't gotten around to appointing conferees yet. I'm going to be chairman, but I'll have to put some of the good old boys on."

"And am I right," Daisy continues, "in thinking that the opposition strategy will be to maybe approve the Senate version of the bill with the Crowe amendment in it knowing that if that happens the House will vote down the conference report?"

There is silence at Prince's end of the line for a moment. Then he says, "Yes. Yes, I could see something like that happening. It's sneaky but—yes, sure."

"I have an idea," Daisy says. "But it would mean fighting hard against Crowe's amendment and offering a compromise of your own that the House can accept. Can you do that?"

"No problem," Prince says. "I'm with the President. The country needs this damned bill—and fast."

"You've got your own health provision—"

"Well, it isn't much," Prince says. "Our version of the bill just presumes adequate health care in the camps. None of Crowe's counseling and stuff like that."

"But you'll fight for that over Crowe's amendment?"

"My pleasure," Prince says. "What's the rest of your idea?"

"I've got to talk to Forrest before I tell you," Daisy says. She listens as Prince replies. She begins to blush beneath the scatter of freckles. Then she starts to laugh. "Absolutely not!" she says loudly. "You ought to be ashamed of yourself!"

Prince's own roaring laughter is still flooding the telephone as she hangs up, grinning.

She makes a few more calls, dictates three letters, and then goes to the basement of the Old Senate Office Building. She rides the subway car through its gleaming tunnel to the Capitol. She walks to the Senate side, takes an elevator to the street level, crosses the hall, and goes up three steps. She pushes the ornate metal grillwork covering a glass-paneled door.

The Senate chamber is almost empty. On the far end of the majority side a young Senator stands behind a small lectern placed on top of his desk. He is reading his speech, lifting his head occasionally to ad-lib a phrase for emphasis. Roy Caldwell, the Senate Majority Leader, sits at his desk in the front row center of the curved half-oval of seats. His hands are folded and his head is tilted forward, chin almost resting on his chest. He appears to be asleep, but he is listening intently to his young colleague. Up on the dais, Vice President Mechin is presiding, leaning forward, one hand lying lightly on the gavel. Below him the parliamentarians sit in immobile attention, while below them, on the first tier of the rostrum, the shorthand reporter scribbles his transcript of the speech. Several other Senators are scattered around the chamber, some reading, some listening. Senator Forrest of California sits two rows behind the Majority Leader.

Up in the galleries several reporters listen and a few spectators watch. They see a blonde girl in a white sleeveless dress enter the chamber from a side door, go swiftly around the back and down the center aisle, and slide into the empty seat next to Senator Forrest. The Senator bends over to listen. She talks for seven minutes, gesturing slightly with her hands. Forrest nods, raises his hand, and signals a page. The boy, in white shirt and black tie and trousers leaps up from the bottom step of the rostrum and hurries up the aisle to Forrest's seat. He listens for a moment and then recrosses the chamber and goes up to Vice President Mechin. Mechin nods and says something. Again the boy goes onto the Senate floor, walks up a side aisle, and says something to a young Senator who has been sitting, chin on hand, listening to his colleague's speech. The young Senator nods and follows the page back to the rostrum. The Vice President hands him the gavel and leaves the chamber. At the same time Senator Forrest, arms stiff in his short steel crutches, is propelling himself toward a rear door. He and the blonde girl also leave the chamber.

The next morning at 10:30 the Senate Labor and Public Welfare Committee meets in executive session on the third floor of the Old Senate Office Building. Senator Forrest, the chairman, is in one of his rare pleasant moods. By 11:10 the committee has adopted the Crowe amendment as part of the Senate's version of the Youth Resources Development Act.

Seven working days later, under a rule waiver agreed to by the Majority and Minority Leaders, the U.S. Senate passes HR 1418 by a comfortable sixteen-vote margin. Nine Senators, including Edward Crowe, are appointed to the conference on the bill, which will meet the following Tuesday. Senator Forrest is chairman of the Senate conferees.

There are three ways to become a gentleman in the United States. The first is to act like one and hope that somebody will notice. The second is to get a commission in the Army. The third is to be elected to the U.S. Senate. Nowhere in the rules of traditions of the Senate is it made explicit that one attains the status of gentleman by being elevated to that body. Rather, it is implicit in the fact that the senate is a political aristocracy in Washington with most of the attributes of social aristocracies elsewhere. It is a small, exclusive neighborhood in the larger political community. Senators are forgiven behavior for which other, lesser men might be censured severely; they are due special deference in their ordinary dealings with other mortals; and like all aristocrats they are seen to be part of a mystique that is larger than themselves.

As with other aristocracies, the Senate is decaying and going slightly to seed in its traditions as the twentieth century proceeds toward its end. This is a bad time for aristocracies anyway. Some of the new sons of the old Senate peerage tend to be mavericks, impatient with the strictures of tradition and given to behavior in the Process that smacks of an indelicate and too open fondness for power and advancement. Indeed, more than a few modern Senators have been so crass as to look upon their aristocratic position as a mere stopping place en route to larger and more politically splendid destinations. An aristocracy ceases to be when its occupants stop regarding it as an end in itself.

The Senate has still another attribute of modern aristocracies: it isn't as much fun being a member as it used to be. The obligations are countless, the pressures constant, and the perils considerable. Because modern Presidents have plundered the Senate of so much of its constitutional power in war-making and foreign policy decisions, the Senate tends to overexert itself with the powers it retains, periodically disapproving presidential appointments or subjecting them to controversy, threatening presidential programs (especially ones involving foreign and military affairs), and appealing directly to the public in disputes over presidential policies. As a result, the contemporary Senate, as it has done periodically through history, maintains a bruised, breathless relationship with the White House—a relationship of guarded cordiality broken by periods of violent contention. Modern Presidents, swollen with power, tend to hit back at the Senate verbally and politically, accusing it of everything from a gutless lack of patriotism in the conduct of war to peculiar biases against Southerners. In 1970 two Senators who particularly displeased President Nixon found themselves running not only against their opponents but also against Vice President Agnew's velvet-wrapped crudities. Both lost.

The men and women who gain entrance to this troubled aristocracy are paid an annual salary of $42,500 a year plus generous allowances for help, telephone bills, travel, office expenses, and equipment. They have staffs that vary in size from twenty to fifty. (Senators get an annual allowance for staff on the basis of the size of the state they come from, and they can hire as many helpers as they can squeeze out of the allowance; if they want more, they must pay the salaries out of their own pockets.) Senators can expect to work hard. Congress is sometimes in session for eleven months of the year, and the workday tends to be long. They often begin with a breakfast meeting at the Capitol and end at the far, bleary remnant of an evening spent on some social or political necessity. (Senators estimate that if they accept a quarter of all the invitations sent to them in the course of an average Washington year they are out five to six evenings a week.) If the Senator comes from a state that is a great distance away, his travel home, which is an absolute and frequent necessity, becomes a nightmare of expense and exhaustion. West Coast Senators regale their East Coast colleagues with horror stories of rushing across the continent on Thursday nights and returning to Washington on Sunday nights aboard the red-eye special, arriving on Monday morning, shaking with fatigue, metabolism out of kilter, and stiff from spending five hours in an airline seat designed to accommodate underweight seven-year-old boys.

When working in the Senate or its environs, a member tends to spend close to 80 percent of his time on nonlegislative matters. These tasks involve answering mail (much of it demanding, some of it ignorant, some abusive, some all three), doing favors for constituents, and getting considerations for his state or keeping his state from losing them. Yet his legislative work is his greatest and hardest task, and it is ironic that most Senators feel they can spend only a minor amount of time on it. To compound the frustration, much of the legislation in the late twentieth century has been horribly complicated and technical; even trying to read a defense budget would drive the average intelligent layman round the bend, while the maze of considerations—chemical, political, economic, and moral—involved in the average piece of environmental legislation would reduce most of us to gibbering idiots. This means that Senators have come to rely more and more upon their staffs and assistants for help in grasping issues and formulating opinions on much of the business before the Senate and its committees.

From time to time, critics of Congress and Congress itself have professed to be shocked by the influence of unelected staff members upon the legislative process. Of the roughly 10,000 people on congressional payrolls, a few hundred or so—mostly one-time journalists, lawyers, former professors, and experts in some particular area of legislation—have authority so potent that it amounts to actual Process power. Lobbyists, other members of Congress, reporters, and various supplicants often prefer to deal with congressional aides because they believe that the aides can help or hurt them through their exercise of authority —in this case their power to make Senators do things. The Senate Foreign Relations Committee, increasingly frustrated in its dealings with the State Department, Pentagon, and White House, has developed a corps of investigators that discovered, among other things, the secret war in Laos, a clandestine agreement made between the Defense Department and the government of Thailand, and various CIA activities around the world that several administrations had neglected to mention to Congress. When Senator Karl Mundt of South Dakota was put out of action by a stroke in 1969, his staff kept his office running smoothly until the election of 1972. If provoked, congressional aides will turn on their masters. Senator Thomas Dodd of Connecticut was censured by the Senate and defeated for reelection because of financial hanky-panky revealed by two disgruntled aides. Senate staffers dream up legislation, write books, speeches, and articles for their Senators, tend to a myriad of back-home political problems, correct the *Congressional Record* to make their man's oratory sound better than it is, fend off pressuring friends, constituents, and campaign contributors, make deals with other Senators (through their aides) or with members of the House, answer much of the torrent of mail that comes to a Senate office every day, acquire a lot of the expertise for which their bosses take political credit, and absorb pressures in hundreds of ways.

"How else can a Senator from a major state operate?" asked Robert Sherrill in a *New York Times* Sunday magazine article.

> New York's Jacob Javits sits on seven committees and 19 subcommittees. He may be confronted with half a dozen hearings in a single morning, in which case he becomes a political wraith, floating from one to another, usually giving none of them more than 30 minutes. He makes the best of an impossible situation by assigning an aide to each of the hearings to keep tabs. When Javits arrives, the staff man greets him with a fast summary of what's been done. Javits tries to push in a question out of turn, to make the record reflect the presence of a body; then he is off to the next meeting.

If the U.S. Senator is thus an overworked, harried member of a declining political aristocracy whose works are likely to be the sum of his own thought and labor and those of his aides, what in the larger Process sense is he?

That is a question that political scientists love to build theories upon. The current fashion among them is to describe members of Congress as role players. In the role game the Senator is described, say, as the performer of six different functions—errand boy, advocate, administration loyalist, opposition spokesman, prosecutor, and representative. Good arguments can be made for the validity of that formula and of most of the other role-combination descriptions, even though the distinction between the roles may become somewhat blurred to the poor wretch galloping around in circles trying to perform all of them at once.

In the larger sense, the total national and Process sense, the Senator is that figure who acts as alternate trustee of the national interest.

National interest in this sense means that spectrum of plausible ideological viewpoints that is the driving force of congressional politics. Among its hundred members the Senate includes spokesmen for every operable position from left to right. In the sum of their views, they speak for the wide center area of the ideological spectrum and thereby for the totality of the national interest as it is represented in Congress. The history of the Senate is in part the history of individual men struggling for their own visions of the national interest—young Henry Clay harassing the nation toward the War of 1812; Calhoun passionately defending slavery, and Webster with equal passion fighting for the Union; Charles Sumner excoriating the supporters of the Kansas-Nebraska Act of 1854 (and taking a vicious physical beating on the floor of the Senate from Representative Preston S. Brooks of South Carolina); George Norris and Robert La Follette fighting for reform in the age of the spoilsmen; Arthur Vandenberg publicly repudiating his own isolationism and throwing himself into support of President Roosevelt's war policy; Robert Taft waging conservative war on the New Deal and the Fair Deal; Ralph Flanders attacking Joe McCarthy; William Proxmire fighting against the supersonic transport. All these historic moments in Senate history feature one man performing the classic trustee function—striving for the accomplishment of the national interest as he personally defines it. Many of these great Senate figures had allies; some managed eventually to recruit whole armies of congressional supporters to their points of view. But the struggles they waged were ignited by an individual vision of the national interest.

The fact that the Senate contains a number of views of the national interest is crucial to the Process. The other trustee of the national interest is the President. He has only one view. In its collegiate structure and internal fluidity, the Senate is capable of uniting behind one of its views of the national interest in order to prevail over the President or at least to temper his judgment. While doing that, the Senate keeps other views in reserve. They are ammunition for its power to challenge or work with the President.

Ideally that is what the Senate is supposed to do. Yet in recent years it has wavered and weakened as an alternate trustee, twitching in immense frustration as the power of presidential government grows. There are dozens of different reasons for that huge growth of executive power, but none of them offers much solace to a Senate that is steadily losing its own power—or for that matter to a people whose national interest depends more and more upon the White House's solitary view of that interest.

The long struggle over Vietnam is almost a casebook on how to lose power in the Process. From the first postwar financial aid program under President Truman and the first postwar dispatch of U.S. military personnel under President Eisenhower to the final, ignominious passage of the Gulf of Tonkin resolution in August 1964, the Senate lost perspective on Vietnam. It allowed itself to be swept up in the presidential logic that all this was somehow vital to American national interests; the Senate failed to unite in order to challenge presidential actions that, under a fairly strict interpretation, were of questionable constitutionality—Eisenhower's dispatch of technicians to Vietnam, Kennedy's declaration of March 23, 1961, that the United States had an obligation to defend Laos, Johnson's repeated escalations. In failing to oppose these moves and in numbly supporting others, the Senate simply lapsed in its role of alternate trustee of the American national interest. The other trustee, in the form of five Presidents, had its own way.

There were many things that the Senate could have done during the long years of blind, deepening involvement in Vietnam. The principal one was to have conducted full-scale debates early in the adventure so that the issues could have been laid as forcefully before the people as they were in the years of Webster and Calhoun. The Senate only raised its voice late in the involvement. Had it marshaled its capacity for investigation and consideration, it might have modified American commitments under the Southeast Asia Treaty Organization (SEATO) (which it ratified on February 1, 1955). It could have rejected that treaty, as it did eleven other treaties between 1844 and 1960. In 1969 a measure known as the National

Commitments Resolution passed the Senate by a vote of 70 to 16. It stated that no future dispatch of American troops to hostilities abroad should be made without "affirmative action" by the Congress. It was a weak lock on a barn from which the horse had long since been stolen. In the matter of Vietnam the Senate lacked internal coherence, prescience, perspective, and vision.

In that failure the Senate abdicated its role as Madison's group of "enlightened citizens whose limited number and firmness might reasonably interpose against impetuous counsels." Not only had the Senate abdicated as alternate trustee; it had also failed, as it fails in so many lesser matters, to take advantage of its own capacity for built-in detachment, its removal from hot national political pressures. All the foregoing is not to argue that Vietnam might never have happened. But it would have been better for the health of the Process if it had happened with the concurrence of the Senate or over the Senate's loud, clear objections rather than with its heedless acquiescence.

The Senate has been no more consistent in its Process role than any other major federal institution. The important thing about the Process is that its component parts keep their relationship to one another constantly in the forefront. For that reason the U.S. Senate is the one component part of the Process that simply must not change its role, as the other parts have done. As alternate trustee of the national interest it is a perpetual guarantee against an all-engulfing presidency. If there is a true tragedy in the Process today, it is the erosion of Senate power, often unwittingly concurred in by the Senate itself.

We huddle in the waning years of the American twentieth century bewailing the loss of national unity, the crumbling of honor, the slow disappearance of great leadership. As America peers through the dusk of her first two centuries and cries out to be led, it looks, by habit, to the White House. There is a threat of damnation in that. We seem to cry, in our sorrow, for one overwhelming vision of the national interest when in fact we should be crying for many such visions in vigorous contention with one another, for a revival of that creative conflict whose end is the synthesis of all interests from which wisdom begins. One man in full, unchallenged command of a nation might march it over a cliff. A nation in which many visions prevail, in which the Senate and the presidency endlessly contend for the supremacy of their separate visions, would never suffer such a fate.

Someone among the many would see the cliff.

Senator Don W. MacPherson of Iowa has stomach trouble. It manifests itself in a stinging, burning sensation that rises to a gripping, painful knot in his solar plexus. From there the pain spreads until it makes his eyes water and his back teeth ache. His wife Cynthia and the Senator's administrative assistant, Chuck De Suze, insist that it is all due to tension. Usually MacPherson denies the tension theory because it would imply that there is something psychological affecting him, and he is totally fed up with the fad of ascribing all of life's phenomena—from disarmament treaties to pimples on kids—to some Freudian cause. Yet he cannot deny that the present rising scorch in his stomach is intrinsically linked to the fact that his colleague Senator Edward Crowe of Wyoming is coming over for a talk.

Don MacPherson has mixed feelings about Crowe. They are both liberals and both are from the West. They frequently vote the same way. But they are not close. Nobody is very close to Crowe. He is an intense, touchy man who exudes a stringent sense of morality. Crowe seems to be constantly implying by his attitude that no other Senator cares as much for the national welfare as he does. He lacks a sense of humor; he is utterly incapable of the pleasantries of manner that characterize even the most casual of senatorial relationships. Crowe's only known diversion is tennis, but even that is approached with a grim sense of mission. If you ask Ed Crowe how the tennis game's coming along, he will reply, often as not, with a morose analysis of his backhand. It is now 9:45 A.M. In fifteen minutes MacPherson is due at an Armed Services Committee meeting, where there is to be an important vote. He has another committee meeting at 10:30. Following that, he has to catch up on a four-day accumulation of correspondence, have lunch with the

Vice President at one, and catch a plane for Chicago. This being the third Thursday of the month, he is on his way home to Iowa. He wishes that Crowe weren't coming. He hopes Crowe will be brief. He suspects that Crowe won't. His stomach hurts.

His secretary buzzes him. MacPherson picks up the phone. "Yes?"

"Senator Crowe's here."

"Okay, bring him in." MacPherson hangs up the speaker of his dictating machine, rises, and puts on his jacket. He cautions himself not to show irritation.

The side door opens. Crowe comes in, tall and unsmiling, his red hair combed straight back and his blue eyes moving as he crosses the room. He looks as if he suspects the presence of sin. "Don," he says, shaking hands.

"Good morning, Ed," MacPherson says. "Busy morning too. I'm about to leave for Armed Services."

"I came about the conference committee on the Youth Resources Development Act," Crowe says.

MacPherson gestures. "Sit down a moment, Ed."

Crowe lowers himself to the edge of a hard chair.

MacPherson sits down. "I'm not going to be able to make this afternoon's session of the conference committee," he says. "I have to fly out to the state."

"That's why I wanted to see you," Crowe says. "I wanted to have your proxy."

MacPherson leans back and folds his hands. "What's coming up in the conference today? Let's see. They've done about everything—the House amendment on the limitation of children in each camp, amendment on supply purchasing. The language differences are adjusted—"

"There's just my amendment," Crowe says.

MacPherson smiles. "They've been passing over that one, haven't they? Leaving it to the last."

"That's because Forrest and Prince are scared of it," Crowe says. "They'd rather have a bad bill than—"

"Oh, come on, Ed," MacPherson says. "It isn't as bad as all

that. I think that Heck Prince just wants to be sure he takes back a bill that the House can accept."

"Prince and Hatfield and Applegate can make the House accept the amendment if it's in the final version of the bill," Crowe answers. "The bill is ridiculous without it. We propose to take on damaged, ill, disturbed kids—"

MacPherson looks at his watch. It is five minutes to ten. He badly wants to be present for the vote in Armed Services.

"And we expect them to surmount their problems, be good children, and get on with their work when—"

"Okay, Ed," MacPherson says. "I guess I'm for your amendment. You can have the proxy." He picks up the telephone. "Susan, type up a proxy for Senator Crowe, will you? The usual form and put the time on it—ten o'clock this morning. Okay? Fine. Yes, I'll sign it when I come back from committee." He hangs up. "That okay, Ed? Can you have someone pick it up around noon?"

Crowe stands. "That'll be fine. You won't regret it. This bill either has to make some moral and social sense or—"

"You'll have to excuse me," MacPherson says. "I'm late now for my committee." He rises and moves toward the door. "Good luck, Ed."

On the way out Crowe pauses to speak to MacPherson's secretary. "The Vice President's giving a luncheon today," he says. "Will the Senator be going?"

The girl opens a desk diary. "Why yes, Senator. Perhaps you'll see him there."

"I'll send someone over for the proxy at about noon," Crowe says.

He leaves MacPherson's office and goes down the hall to make his next call. He hasn't been invited to the Vice President's luncheon. He heard about it accidentally. The fact that he wasn't invited could hurt if he let it. But he has devices for protecting himself. He can usually analyze the reason for some snub or rejection, putting it in political terms. Or, if that fails to soothe wounded feelings, he tells himself that he hasn't time for the fripperies and pleasantries of the Senate. He wasn't elected for the purpose of enjoying himself. If at times he feels shunned and friendless, he tells himself that he will be remembered in the legislative history of this period.

He visits the offices of two other Senators. Both have been appointed to the House-Senate conference on the Youth Resources Development Act. Neither can be present at what everyone assumes will be the final meeting of the conference committee this afternoon. At both offices Crowe gets proxies, one of them secured only after strenuous, protracted argument with the departing Senator. At both offices he discovers that these Senators too have been invited to the Vice President's luncheon. Both are from the liberal wing of the party. Since he is a prominent member of the liberal wing, that means that he is being snubbed. He walks back to his office thinking about the legislative history of this period.

In the substrata of the Senate this noon there is a sense of something impending. Twenty people are attuned to this sense. It arises from their own mental compilation of events. Two weeks ago it was common knowledge among aides, committee staffs, Senators, and reporters that Forrest and Crowe were having a bitter quarrel over the Crowe amendment to the Youth Resources Development Act. That quarrel abruptly ceased. The amendment was put into the bill. That, according to the Senate's conventional wisdom, was unusual, because Forrest doesn't give up that easily. Possibly he was planning some move against Crowe later on. But the bill came before the Senate and was passed with the Crowe amendment intact. Then the conference began and still Forrest did nothing. Today is the last day of the conference. All that is left to reconcile between the House and Senate versions of the bill is the Crowe amendment. All morning, according to gossip, Crowe has been in three Senate offices getting proxies. By something a little more than coincidence the Vice President is having lunch with the same three Senators that Crowe visited in the morning. Something is going on; somebody is doing something to somebody else; someone, before this day is over, is going to get hurt. But no one among the speculators on all this oddity can quite figure out what's happening or who its victim is going to be. The sense of something impending just hangs there in the heat of noon.

In her office on the third floor of the Old Senate Office Building Daisy James is taking a telephone call from Ward Burling, an administrative aide to the Vice President. "As far as I know everyone will definitely be there," she says. "I've just had the Senate conferees rechecked."

"That means six Senators present and voting," Burling says. "And Ed Crowe with three proxies. One of the six, Walsh, will vote with Crowe."

"You've got the same numbers I've got," Daisy says. "Crowe controls the majority of the Senate conferees."

"And we both know how he votes his proxies," Burling says.

Daisy leans back in her chair and picks up a pencil in her free hand. "If Crowe doesn't vote to keep his amendment in the bill," she answers, "and if the House doesn't reject the bill because the Crowe amendment is in it, then this isn't the U.S. Congress and I'm not Daisy L. James and—" She leans forward. "Oh, damn it, Ward, your boss has just got to do his stuff."

"He'll do his damnedest," Burling says.

"Is that enough?"

"He's a pretty shrewd old guy," Burling says.

"You're sure it wouldn't help if Forrest came to the luncheon?"

At his end of the line Burling shakes his head. He is a tall, handsome black man, lean and relaxed. Today he wears a blue-striped shirt, cavalry twill trousers, polished brown boots, and a black knit tie. "It wouldn't help at all," he says. "Listen, pet, you relax and leave it to us. You've hatched the strategy and made the deals. Now it's up to us. Confidence. Okay?"

"Okay," Daisy's voice says. She suddenly sounds very anxious.

"Confidence," Burling repeats. "Stop thinking about it for a few hours."

"Oh, Ward, I want this bill—"

"So do I," he answers. "Listen, Daisy James. Remember April 25, 1968?"

There is a pause. Burling leans forward and takes a cigarette from a silver box on his desk.

"I—no," Daisy says. "What happened on April 25, 1968?"

"You were the uptightest lady at Columbia Law School," he replies. "You just knew you were going to fail your finals. Remember that?"

"Oh," she says, "yes. I do remember that. And I also remember that some nice guy made me stop studying the night before and go swimming instead. And it worked."

"Go swimming, Daisy James. I'll call you when it's all over." He hangs up the phone, lifts the cigarette to his mouth, and then puts it back in the silver box. He gets up from his desk and goes into the Vice President's reception room. "Is he off the phone yet?" he asks.

"Just got off," the secretary says. "Go on in."

"Everything set for lunch?" he asks.

She nods. "I've told everybody it's been switched to the Whip's office in the Capitol."

"Okay," he says. "I'll go over and check after I've seen the boss." He goes into the inner office. The Vice President is at his desk, jacket off, his shirt sleeves bulging around the armholes of his vest.

"Anybody else we should be seeing?" Mechin asks.

"No, sir," Burling replies. "I've just talked to Miss James. Only MacPherson and the other two are going to be away."

Mechin nods. "I suppose they've already given their proxies to Crowe."

"Yes, sir."

"I suppose it's time to give Senator Crowe one last chance to be reasonable."

Burling looks at his watch. "Yes, sir. Lunch is in forty minutes."

"Okay," the Vice President says. He picks up his telephone. "Get me Senator Crowe, will you?"

He waits, hand cupped over the phone's speaker. "You

know," he says, "I hate doing this to anybody, even Ed Crowe."

"Life is hard," Burling says.

Mechin uncups his hand from the phone. "Hello? That you, Ed? Fernand Mechin here. Oh, fine. Fat and sassy as ever. Yes. Ed, I was calling about this afternoon's conference on HR 1418. I was wondering if you mightn't want to reconsider that amendment of yours. You know, the House just isn't going to take the bill if— Yes. Yes, I know that. We've all thought of that. But, Ed, the problem here really isn't the program that the bill will create. The problem—yes, let me put this to you if I may—the problem is the tension in the country, that man Leland and all the rest of it, and the sort of thing the President needs to do to get things calmed down. He needs this bill and the revision of the Revenue Act. Now, we're his party and we control the Congress and—" He listens. His heavy face flushes and then slumps into a grave expression. "Ed," he says, "let me tell you something. You could end up being awfully humiliated when this thing's over. I really mean that. Now look, young fella, I was in Congress for a long time and there's something I learned. A man owes it to himself to keep his standing in this place. You shouldn't humiliate yourself or put yourself in a position where you can be humiliated. Yes, I know you've got those proxies and I know that Nick Walsh is going to vote with you in the conference, but I also know a couple of things you don't know. Yes." He listens, the glum expression tinted more deeply by the red flush of anger spreading across his old, wide face. "All right, Ed," he says quietly. "I was hoping to give you a last chance to get on the team with the rest of us. Yes. Good-by." He puts the phone carefully onto its cradle and looks up. "Amend the record, Ward. Strike the part where I said I hated to do this to Ed Crowe. I'm going to enjoy every minute of it. Let's go."

The sun reaches its meridian and begins the long heat-tracked crawl toward late afternoon. On the floor of the Senate the chairman of the Armed Services Committee leans over to a colleague who sits beside him to complain that Don Mac-Pherson and the goddamn liberals have voted to hold up the

Military Air Transport Command's appropriation pending an investigation of who it's been carting around the world as part of its VIP services. A senator from Utah puts in a continuing resolution for the Veterans Administration because its budget hasn't been debated, authorized, and appropriated. Daisy James tells her secretary that she's going to take a long lunch. She leaves the Capitol and drives to David Marks' house in Cleveland Park, where she swims for fifty-five minutes. In a pleasant sunny office in the Capitol Vice President Mechin and his assistant, Ward Burling, entertain MacPherson and two other Senators at lunch. The Vice President is alternately eloquent, persuasive, and tough. When the luncheon is over he emerges, looking pleased with himself. He goes back to his Capitol Hill office and telephones Lou Howard at the White House. "We're in," Mechin says, "like Flynn."

Ward Burling leaves a message at Daisy James' office that reads simply, "We made it."

Senator Ed Crowe, who has no lunch date, decides to send out for something rather than be seen eating alone in the Senate dining room. At his desk he dictates letters and tries to read a biography of Robert La Follette, Jr. But his mind isn't on it. He feels guilty because he should be doing something useful rather than reading for pleasure. But he hasn't anything useful to do. The second reason Crowe's mind can't focus on Robert La Follette, Jr.'s, life and career is that it is choked in a thicket of thoughts and feelings. Resentment and hurt grow in coils around a hard stem of resolve; if the effect of his nature upon other men's natures dictates that he shall be forever alone, he shall at least be a victorious loner. Part of him is frightened by the coming showdown over the Youth Resources Development Act. What he is going to do in this afternoon's meeting of the conference committee—force the House and Senate to keep his amendment in the bill—will make his colleagues resent him even more than they do now. But part of Ed Crowe anticipates the conference with satisfaction. He has worked out his own definition of courage. It consists of swallowing his fear of censure, of deliberately denying himself the approval of his colleagues, daring to be outrageous. The reproving of courage

has become a necessity to Ed Crowe. It recharges his inner
will to continue. That is why a part of him anticipates the coming confrontation with Jim Forrest. Crowe is going to win again.
In the process of winning he is going to put down someone he
hates. That coming double pleasure almost wipes out the residue
of fear.

At 3:10 he closes his book, puts on his jacket, and goes into his private bathroom to brush back his straight red hair.
Then he goes to the basement and takes the subway over to the
Capitol. He goes to a small elevator hidden at the curve of a
corridor. He rides up to the third floor to the modern, window-
less suite of the Joint Committee on Atomic Energy. At the
end of a hallway the door to Conference Room S 407 is open.

In the large, paneled chamber Representatives, Senators, and their aides are standing around an oval table that is
fitted with microphones. Lobbyists and reporters are leaning
against the walls and against a large marble slab at the head
of the room. As Crowe comes in he sees Forrest seated at the
table with Daisy James beside him. Several colleagues are talking to the polio-crippled Senator. Forrest waves. *Again,* Crowe
thinks with a small spurt of apprehension, *that strange, affable
mood.* He goes over and shakes hands. "Jim. Hello, Miss
James."

Daisy looks up, nods, and smiles. "Senator."

"Only six of us here today, Jim," Crowe says.

Forrest nods. "We can still hold the bastards off."

Several Representatives standing nearby laugh.

"You know that I'm holding proxies for our three missing
members," Crowe says.

"So I hear," Forrest answers.

"No hard feelings?" Crowe asks.

"I never have hard feelings," Forrest replies. "I just hate everybody."

Again laughter.

Forrest twists himself around. "Where in hell's Hector Prince?
I want to get this goddamn thing over with."

Suddenly the doorway is filled with a burst of overweight
exuberance. Congressman Prince crosses the room, back-slap-

ping and rib-nudging. Grinning, he stops before Forrest but looks past him to Daisy James. "Hi, beautiful!" he cries.

Daisy's freckles scatter as she grins. "Hi, Mr. Chairman."

"Forrest, you bastard," Prince says. "It's just another example of the superior facilities offered to Senators. You've got the best-looking staff director on the Hill and all I get is"—he gestures toward a young man standing beside him—"Matt here. Kyuk!" He guffaws again.

Forrest looks up scowling. "If you can get your fly zipped back up, Hector, I'd like to get started, get finished, and get the hell out of here."

"Right," Prince says. He turns. "Oh. Hi Ed!" He shakes hands with Crowe. "Well, today's the day, eh, buddy? All we've got left is that amendment of yours."

"And you're going to go on having it," Crowe says.

Prince slaps him on the shoulder. "Magnificent! Let's make it quick, Jim. There's a 5:30 flight to Hartford and I've got to be on it. You ready?"

Forrest nods. "I've got six Senators and three proxies and we've been ready for fifteen minutes."

"I've got eleven guys and four proxies," Prince says. He walks around the table, dumps his briefcase beside a microphone, and sits down. His staff director takes the chair beside him.

"Okay, ladies and gentlemen," Prince says loudly. "We're going to start. Everybody who shouldn't be here—out."

The lobbyists and reporters move toward the door. Tad Solomon stops behind Prince's chair. "How's the stand-off?" he asks quietly.

Prince twists around and looks up at him. "Hi, friend! Keep calm. Something nice may happen."

"I hear Crowe's holding those three proxies and that Walsh is going to vote with him," Solomon says.

"Don't jump off a bridge until you see what happens," Prince says. "Now get out of here and have faith."

Solomon crosses the room, the last man out. One of the Senate aides closes the door and takes a seat against the wall.

"All right," Prince says, shuffling the papers before him.

"Everybody got copies of the bill as marked up to now?" He looks up. "Miss James?"

Daisy, sitting opposite him, nods. "Yes, Mr. Chairman."

"I think we've taken care of almost everything," Prince says, looking over his copy of the bill. "All the language adjustments. Anybody got any problems?"

Congressman Peter Grimes of Maine holds up his pencil. "Senator Crowe's amendment," he says.

"Yes," Prince says. "That's the remaining point. He folds his hands and looks around the table. "I've been bypassing this one until everything else was out of the way, gentlemen. This, obviously, is the tough one." He looks across at Forrest. "Jim, you want to say anything about Ed's amendment?"

"Only that our side's not unanimous on it and that we'll be caucusing alone before we reach our final position," Forrest says. "I'm not going to support it for the simple reason that I think you people over on the House side won't accept the bill with that amendment attached."

"I think you're right," Prince says.

Congressman Joe Waters of Texas leans forward. He is a tall white-haired man who was a bitter opponent of the Youth Resources Development Act in the House. "Now I haven't got that impression." He smiles. "I'm speaking for myself only, of course. But if the administration's bound and determined to go through with this program, why Senator Crowe's amendment strikes me as a reasonable addition to it." He leans back in his chair. "No, I've got no objections at all to this amendment. In fact, I congratulate the Senator for thinking of this useful provision."

Daisy raises her head and looks at Prince. He winks at her.

"With apologies, Joe," he says, "I've got to disagree with you. In the first place, Ed's amendment amounts to a whole new title of the bill. The various health programs proposed in the amendment add a whole new dimension to the act. It is way beyond the intent of the bill passed by the House. In the second place, the health program proposed by Senator Crowe would add substantially to the overall costs of the program, and I understand that those costs have been informally agreed upon by the corporations that will fund this program in the event that we enact it. I believe that Miss James has some figures on the added cost factor if anyone's interested. In the third place, health matters of this sort must go through the House Commerce Committee. That committee hasn't had a chance to consider this amendment at all." He pauses and looks around the table. Everyone is watching him. The committee and personal staff aides sitting along the walls on both sides of the room are making notes. "I've polled the House conferees," Prince says. "With the proxies I'm holding, I believe we have a majority on our side opposed to accepting Ed's amendment." He looks to his left and to his right. "Anybody want to contest that? Joe?"

Waters shakes his head. "I don't argue with your arithmetic, Hector. I just don't happen to agree with the majority sentiment. I think we could persuade the House—"

"So," Prince says quietly to Forrest, "I think we're in disagreement, Jim. Our bill," he says, opening the copy before him, "makes adequate provision for health care in the camps, Ed. Title 3, Section 2."

"You just mention health care," Crowe says. "You don't say anything about the special problems these kids will be bringing to the camps. Drugs, for instance. Look at the HEW figures!" He leans back, putting both hands on the arms of his chair.

"As I understand it," Prince says, "this program isn't the sort of thing that youngsters with drug problems should be getting into."

Crowe leans forward again. "Are you going to keep out any kid just because he has drug problems, Hector?" He is glaring across the table, face red and set in a grim expression. His head and shoulders tremble a little.

"I didn't say that," Prince replies quietly.

"You implied it," Crowe snaps. "I wonder what sorts of kids you think are eligible for this program."

"Oh, Ed, for Christ's sake," Prince says. "Stop being a Mormon bishop. We're all for poor kids, we're all for—"

"If they're black?" Crowe says loudly. "If they come from

some rotten slum? If they have pockmarks on their forearms?"

"We have provided for adequate health care in the camps," Prince answers. "That means all the facilities necessary to deal with all the normal—"

"It's your definition of 'normal' that worries me," Crowe shoots back.

"Hold it!" Forrest rasps.

"No," Crowe says, turning to look down the table at him. "I won't hold it. I came here to fight for—"

"You damned well will hold it," Forrest snaps. "You're putting the goddamn jackass before the cart. There's no point in getting into this brawl until we caucus and see if a majority of the Senate conferees want this amendment in the bill."

"Don't waste my time," Crowe snaps. "I'm for it, Nick Walsh here is for it, and I've got three proxies. That gives me five out of nine Senate votes. We're caucused."

"No we aren't," Forrest answers. "I want a private meeting."

"I'm afraid I won't change my vote, Jim," says Senator Walsh, a heavy gray-haired man sitting at the far right end on the Senate side of the table.

"I didn't say you would," Forrest replies. "I still want a private meeting."

Walsh looks down the table at Crowe. The Wyoming Senator shrugs. "I've got all day," he says.

Forrest struggles to his feet. "Won't be long, Hector. You kids play nice 'til we get back."

Despite his anger, Prince grins.

The five men on the Senate side rise and follow Forrest as he heaves himself on his crutches toward a door at the rear of the chamber. They follow him into a small, bare room. Crowe is the last to enter. "All right, Jim," he says as he closes the door. "What's this all about? You know you're licked."

Forrest turns and looks up at him. "I don't know any such goddamn thing. Let me see those proxies of yours."

"Don't tell me you're going to contest proxies!" Crowe says angrily.

"Just let me see 'em," Forrest answers.

Crowe reaches into his inside jacket pocket and pulls out a long white envelope.

"Give it to Nick," Forrest says.

Looking angry but puzzled, Crowe hands the envelope to Senator Walsh.

"Open it," Forrest says.

Walsh tears the end off the envelope and takes out three letters.

"Well?" Forrest demands.

Walsh glances over the letters in his hands. "They look all right to me," he says.

"Dated properly?" Forrest snaps.

Walsh looks at the letters again. He nods.

"What're the times on 'em?"

"Ten o'clock this morning," Walsh says looking at the first letter. He looks at the others. "10:45. 11:15."

Forrest props himself on one crutch and takes an envelope from his inside pocket. "Ferdy Mechin had lunch with your three proxies," he says to Crowe, ripping open the envelope. "He told 'em we couldn't afford to lose this bill because of you." He pulls out three letters. "Ferdy got three new proxies for me. The time on all of them is 1:30 this afternoon." He looks at Crowe. "You lose. I vote the proxies and they all vote no to your goddamn amendment."

Crowe looks at him for a long moment. He turns to Walsh and to the three other Senators standing by the door. Then he looks back at Forrest. He is suddenly calm. "You aren't very high on principle, are you, Jim?"

"There's principle and principle," Forrest says. "If this were any other bill—" He draws his other crutch back under his arm. "If it were any other bill, Ed, I'd be right there with you on your idea."

Crowe looks at him. He doesn't say anything.

"Goddamn it, man," Forrest says softly. "Do you think I liked doing it this way?"

Crowe shakes his head slightly. "No. You can be a bastard, Jim, but this isn't your style."

Forrest nods. "Well," he hunches himself onto his crutches. "I'm bringing up your day care bill on the twentieth. We'll get it out."

"I don't need deals," Crowe says.

"Somebody's already made one for you," Forrest answers.

"Who?" Crowe asks, frowning.

"Somebody who likes you," Forrest answers. "Come on, let's go back in. Hector's got a plane to catch."

The Senate conferees return to the room. The committee members from the House resume their seats. Forrest lowers himself into his chair beside Daisy. She looks at him and then at Crowe. Both men appear subdued.

Crowe leans forward. "We've voted, Hector," he says quietly. "I'm sorry for what I said."

"No problem, friend." Prince grins. "What was the vote?"

"The Senate is dropping the amendment," Crowe says. "A majority on our side is against it. We'll accept your health provision in Title 3, Section 2."

Prince looks around the table. "Well, ladies and gentlemen," he says, "it looks like the President has his bill."

The one thing he has always been bad at is doing nothing. That is why he has hated the evenings since his wife died, why Sunday afternoon has always seemed to him to be the most oppressive moment of the week. It contains nothing, and he is a man who is bad at doing nothing. He needs to feel the churn of events around him; he needs pressure and something to be always driving toward and a whole lot of people driving with him or trying to keep him from getting where he has to go

Sitting here in a cranked-up bed, wearing a green nightgown that doesn't even cover his indecencies, is just plain torment except for 7:30 to 9:00 in the evening, when people come to see him. Folks would come out during the daytime visiting hours, but who in the hell has time to go trundling all the way out to Bethesda in the middle of the day to pay a call on a sick, fat Congressman? Nobody. Anybody who did that would be out of his mind. There's too much to do. So the days are torment. He has books but he's never been much on reading books. Every evening Maude and Ruth bring him the *Congressional Record* so that he can see what's going on back at the House and over in the Senate. But that doesn't last more than an hour in the morning. Then there's the newspapers—The Washington *Post, The New York Times*, and the Baltimore *Sun*. He reads as much of them as he can stand, but he can't stand much. Just the main news. They offered to bring him the *Christian Science Monitor* but he said no, he didn't want that. He'd feel embarrassed reading a church newspaper when he didn't even have on enough clothes to cover his rear end. They laughed at that. And he gets magazines, *Time* and *Newsweek*. *Time* even had something about him in its Milestones column: "Ailing—Mace Applegate, 57, Majority Whip of the U.S. House of Representatives, in Bethesda Naval Hospital, Bethesda, Md., with heart and circulatory problems." But all the stuff he has to read, all he can read of it, lasts him until about noon, when those sailor boys bring him a U.S. Navy lunch, and goddamn, when he gets back to the House there's going to be the biggest investigation you ever saw of Navy lunches. The stuff they give you to eat—a hog wouldn't take his afternoon nap lying on it.

So that leaves him the afternoons with nothing else to do but think. But a man can't just sit in a room full of flowers looking out the window at the trees and think.

So instead of thinking he gets mad. There are two things to get mad at and he divides the afternoon between them. From 12:30 to 4:00 he gets mad at the goddamn doctors who tell him a lot of nonsensical crap and from 4:00 until 7:30 he gets mad at the President of the United States, who's been snubbing him.

This afternoon he sat with his beef propped up against the bed, the part they cranked up so he can sit, and he really gave the doctors hark from the tomb in his mind. Especially that tall doctor who looks about as cheerful as a preacher in a whorehouse; the fellow is a Navy captain and they say he knows more about hearts and blood vessels than anybody else, except some big-time doctor in New York. They brought *him* down to look Mace over too, and then the two of them sat in his room and gave him the glad tidings. The Navy captain did most of the talking. There was nothing to worry about, he said. Old Congressman Applegate could have a long and useful life ahead of him if he took things easy. Of course, that meant quitting his job, quitting the House, and going someplace where there was no stress and just being peaceful. So he told them that sounded to him like the biggest pile of shee-yit he'd ever heard, except for the time that old Congressman Baggs came reeling onto the House floor drunker than a Baptist owl and made a speech on how universal peace and brotherhood would be absolutely guaranteed by next Tuesday if the whole world switched to Greenwich Mean Time. That Navy captain with the long face—Mace calls him Admiral Giggles to the lady nurses and they all just about jump out of the windows for laughing—told Mace that the choice was up to him. He could go back to work and take his chances or he could retire and have that long and useful life. Mace told him he didn't think that a full-time career making porch boards creak with a rocking chair was a very useful life—long maybe, but not useful. Then he asked Admiral Giggles how long the doctors suspected he'd live if he went back to work. Admiral Giggles looked at the fancy doctor from New York and they both shrugged and the fancy doctor said it could be a month or it could be a year but the prognosis wasn't good. For a couple of days afterward that depressed Mace, and then it made him mad. Twice now in the last week Admiral Giggles dropped in to ask how Congressman Applegate's thoughts were going, and Mace had told him they were mostly dirty.

Getting mad at the President is a better mad because it deals with the here and the right now and not with some sort of God-awful choice that no man should be expected to make. Mace had sweated a couple of tons of lard off his ass getting that goddamn Youth Resources Development Act passed in the House. They hadn't had such bad times with it over on the Senate side, nothing like the troubles they'd had in the House.

Well, the President had his goddamn bill and Mace had busted his ass to get it for him. He didn't mind not being in on the signing ceremony, but he did mind being ignored. Every evening when Ruth and Maude came out he asked if there was anything from the White House and they said no. They looked at him like they were wondering what he was expecting. Well, he was expecting a pen from that signing ceremony. He deserved one; he was one of the old boys who got that bill for the President, and ever since the sumbitch had ignored him.

He could stay mad about that for hours. Sometimes he even rearranged his schedule and started in on his President mad early in the afternoon because it was easier than the other one.

He sits in bed looking at the blank wall and seeing upon it all the things he loves: the great, gloomy chamber, the narrow corridors, the restaurant full at lunchtime, the Whip's office crowded with the fellers planning something or trying to figure out something. He remembers the smells: the oiled stone smell of the corridors, the cigar smoke, the old, good musty smell of the chairs in the Speaker's lobby. All, everything, every part of the Capitol and the city he loves.

Goddamn, he thinks. *A man shouldn't have to—*

There is a short, sharp knock on the door.

Mace turns his head. "Come in!" he yells.

The door pushes open and John Stermas' head comes around it. "Hi, boss," he says.

"Hey, John! C'mon in here!"

Stermas comes into the room. "Brought a friend to see you," he says.

"That's good." Mace grins. "A feller can use all the friends he's got in thisyear penitentiary. Who's there?"

Randolph Hatfield comes in behind Stermas and closes the door. "Hello, Mace," he says.

"Goddamn. Mistuh Leader! Harya, Randy?"

Hatfield holds out his hand. "Well, I'm a little better for seeing you, old friend."

Mace takes Hatfield's hand. It grips firmly. "Well, it's mighty good to see yawl too, Randy. How're all the fellers?"

"Missing you," John says.

"Well, you tell 'em I'll be back 'fore they can steal the spittoons."

Stermas smiles. "You bet you will," he says, sitting down on the end of the bed.

Mace looks at him. *He knows,* he thinks. *He's been talking to Giggles.* "Don't believe everything y'hear, John," he says. "Randy, how's everything at home?"

Hatfield smiles. "All right," he says. "Dorothy and I have decided to call it a day."

"Aw, Randy, I'm—"

Hatfield lays his hand on Mace's shoulder. "No, really, it's all right. It's best."

"Well what're you gonna do, Randy?"

"I imagine I'll take a house closer to work," he says. "Dorothy's going back to Ohio, but at least one of the boys will be staying with me here."

"Aw, that's nice."

"And wherever we're going to be," says Hatfield, "that's where you're going to be when they let you out of this place to get better."

"You're on," Mace says. "That's gonna be great."

Stermas reaches into the pocket of his seersucker jacket. "Maude and Ruth aren't coming out tonight, Mace. They're going on a boat trip down the river."

Mace nods. "Good. Henry comin'?"

"No," Stermas says. "I checked both offices. There wasn't much of anything to bother you with." He draws out an envelope. "Just this one letter. It came by messenger."

Mace reaches for it and lays it in his lap. "I 'preciate you takin' the trouble, John. Randy, I hear that ole—"

"Mace," says Hatfield, "read the letter. Or at least look at it."

Mace picks up the envelope from his lap. On the upper left-hand side it says in stark, plain type: "The White House." He looks at Hatfield and then at Stermas. "What the hell's this all about?"

"Read it," Stermas says.

Mace rips open the envelope and takes out a two-page letter on heavy stationery. He looks at the bottom of the second page. The President's signature is there in a heavy black scrawl.

Dear Congressman Applegate:

    As you know, I signed the Youth Resources Development Act into law on Monday, August 30. I wish you could have been there, but I understand that you were unavoidably detained.

Since signing the bill I have been thinking about our first meeting so many years ago when I entered the House as a very uncertain freshman Congressman from New York. I had, in my first few months, very little knowledge of how the House of Representatives worked and even less about how, in its totality, the United States Government worked. In response to my anxieties, my new colleagues simply said, "Talk to Mace about it." I did. Perhaps you have forgotten the long lunch we had together in the October of that year. But I haven't. It was the beginning of my political education.

Now, these twelve years later, I have moved to my present job and you have remained where you were, as Representative for the Second District of North Carolina. Those who do not grasp the true nature of our Federal Government would say that I have progressed and that you have remained behind. The history of our country is, unfortunately, written primarily in terms of men who were prominent upon its peaks. The truth of history is that much of it is made by men and women who labor in the valleys of the system.

Now that it is public law, the United States owes you the credit for the Youth Resources Development Act, not me. It is my prayer and hope that this act, through symbolizing our Government's intent, will help to refocus the fears and anxieties of our people and will, in that way, assist in the healing of this nation. If that proves to be the case—and I think it will—the American people now and in history will owe you a debt that is beyond payment.

I would like to claim credit for the Youth Resources Development Act, but I cannot. To make clear the fact that the credit is yours I hope that you will permit the White House to release the text of this letter to the press. And, of course, a copy will remain in the archives of this administration so that the history of this time can be accurately written.

Sincerely yours,

Mace lowers the letter onto his lap and looks for a moment at the wall on the other side of the room. There for an instant he sees the boy sitting on the porch, watching the rain gush down the front walk, watching so that he won't feel the pain and ugliness in the house behind him. The boy is playing look-ing-straight-ahead-and-not-seeing-anything-else. *North Carolina.*

He looks at John Stermas, lifts the letter slightly, and shakes his head. "How about that?" he says.

Epilogue

The private citizen today has come to feel rather like a deaf spectator in the back row, who ought to keep his mind on the mystery off there, but cannot quite manage to keep awake. He knows he is somehow affected by what is going on. Rules and regulations continually, taxes annually and wars occasionally, remind him that he is being swept along by great drifts of circumstance . . . As a private person he does not know for certain what is going on, or who is doing it, or where he is being carried. No newspaper reports his environment so he can grasp it; no school has taught him how to imagine it; his ideals, often, do not fit with it; listening to speeches, uttering opinions and voting do not, he finds, enable him to govern it. He lives in a world which he cannot see, does not understand, and is unable to direct.

Walter Lippmann, "The Phantom Public"

Two visions of God haunt the restless sleep of the Americans, a people who dream alternately of perdition and hope, of the Judaic judge of men's sins and of God the giver of Eden and forgiveness. Depending upon the time and the climate of history, one dream or the other rises from the hidden chambers of the American unconscious, coloring deed, thought, and habit. Our course from our origins upon the curved, gray-sand beaches of Massachusetts and in the tidewater country of Virginia has been marked by interchanging visions of pessimistic doubt and ungovernable optimism. On the voyage to the New World, John Winthrop told his fellow Anglican Puritans that they had entered into a covenant with God. "The Lord," said the noble but bleak man "hath given us leave to draw our own Articles."

463

It was a breathtaking assumption and it could mean any number of things. What it ultimately meant was a fulfillment of the Puritan dream of Bible and life style harnessed together. The interpretation of God's will was so dire in its abjurations of all pleasure and its dictates of an almost impossible salvation attained through work, prayer, pain, and denial that it still grips the American marrow.

We were founded in a pessimism that still echoes in the words of Winthrop and those of the hill and marshland preachers of Essex, Ipswich, Gloucester, and Salem. That pessimism was so deep that it doubted man's very worthiness to be, much less his capacity to win God's grace and salvation. Transmitted through the next two centuries in many evolving forms, native pessimism even haunted the council chamber and boarding house sitting rooms in which the Constitution was conceived out of conflicting necessities and written with a deliberate vagueness.

Yet it is a miraculous paradox that the result of the Constitution was a nineteenth century born and lived through, for the most part, in an optimism that was equally stringent in its demands upon American society and the American nature. "Until American idealism had been safely buried in Flanders' fields," wrote Ellen Glasgow, "a belief in the happy end was as imperative in philosophy as it was essential in fiction."

Given the profundity of these pulls of pessimism and optimism in the American nature, it is remarkable that basic social and political assumptions have remained embedded in the American intellect, undisturbed by alternating visions of the world. The very coherence of our history between 1787 and the present is a tribute to the capacity of Americans to cling to basic assumptions about the principles of government and political life.

History is a cyclical process. Its periods are defined by the systems of logic which dominate them. Systems of logic, in turn, are based on assumptions. A period of history lasts as long as the validity of the assumptions upon which its system of logic is based. When a majority or even a significant minority of a culture's people begin to doubt the assumptions, the system

of logic frays and a period of history comes to an end. An interregnum follows, usually a chaotic and unsettling time, in which
new assumptions are born. Once they are given life through
their acceptance by a majority or a significant minority, a new
system of logic develops and a new period of history begins.

This process is neither uniform nor neat. Great periods of
history contain overlapping mini-epochs within themselves
which, when dying, threaten the great period itself and sometimes even destroy it. This is what is happening to the United
States in the 1970s; a mini-epoch born out of the assumptions
of the Jackson era is coming to an end. The question is whether
a great period of American history is going to die with it.

The great period began with the re-forming of the American
central government after the failure of the Confederate experi-
ment. The assumptions which underlay the Constitution were
mostly mechanistic. They involved systems of control and the
diffusion of power. The assumption was that the best way to
govern a diverse, growing nation was to divide authority between a federal government and the state governments. Within
itself, the federal government had separated repositories of power. They coexisted in creative tension. To the authors of the
Constitution the maximum evil of government was concentrated
power. When the Tenth Amendment declared that "The powers
not delegated to the United States by the Constitution, nor
prohibited by it to the States, are reserved to the States respec-
tively, or to the people," the Constitution was assumed to be
good, efficient and safe because it achieved a system of governing without undue concentrations of power.

Through nearly two centuries of usage the meaning of the
Constitution and the operations of government under it have
changed enormously as men and institutions discovered or
made up new interpretations of their roles to meet new problems and new conditions of governing. But a majority of Americans clung to the assumption that the system of government
created by the Constitution was the safest, most efficient and just.
The reasons for this enduring belief were not always noble; for
much of the nineteenth century the Constitution was regarded

as a document having more to do with the protection of property than the upholding of human rights. It became, in the sardonic words of Vernon Parrington, "the judicious expression of substantial eighteenth-century realism that accepted the property basis of political action, was skeptical of romantic idealism and was more careful to protect title-deeds to legal holdings than to claim unsurveyed principalities in Utopia." Perhaps the ultimate genius of the Constitution is that it can mean almost anything that any age or individual wants it to mean while still preserving a basic form and system of government which, as the preceding pages of this book have tried to illustrate, works badly at times and better at other times, but keeps on working.

While the great period of American history sustained by continuing belief in the Constitution and its federal system proceeded, mini-epochs rose and fell within it, crossing and coinciding with one another. The most durable of them began with the election of Andrew Jackson in 1828. There were a lot of things wrong with the Jacksonian period—government was corrupt and tended to reward mediocrity—but, as an exercise in political symbolism, it was crucial to the present formation of this country. The arrival of Andrew Jackson at the White House signaled the entry of the Common American Man into the mainstream of politics and, by inference, into the realm of other, infinite possibilities. The new egalitarianism, as Alexis de Tocqueville observed, produced two new assumptions; every man (every white man, that is) had a right to share in political decision making and he also had a right to as much of the national wealth as he could legally get his hands on. Beneath this latter assumption lay the fundamental declaration of American materialism: the possession of things can make you happy and when everybody has enough things, everybody *will* be happy. It was that simple and that complicated.

The vision of affluence churned up by this crucial new moment in history was the ultimate fulfillment of the new egalitarianism. It explained why Americans tolerated so many awful things in subsequent history—the blatant corruption of the Gilded Age was justified by reassuring everyone that big business was doing well and that the rest of society would profit from the trickle-down. The egalitarian vision of affluence for the common man explains the American reverence for the free enterprise system (which has been worshiped for generations as a Heaven-sent gift coequal with the Constitution), the eagerness of otherwise intelligent people to embrace the claptrap of Social Darwinism and how an appealing boob like Warren G. Harding could be elected President. The industrial values sustained by mass dreams of public affluence, of an eventual payoff, made all this possible.

Like many other long-held expectations, this one was murdered in its fulfilling. Mass affluence finally did arrive in the 1950s. But instead of making its recipients happy, it created mass misery, some understandable, some still mysterious. Blacks, who had mostly been excluded from the new prosperity, mounted a militant campaign for equal opportunities and sufficient social justice to get their share. So-called ethnics, trapped between the black inner city and the prosperous, upper-middle-class suburb, tied to mass union contracts and despised by liberal reformers, grew truculent, right-wing and militant in their fears and their adherence to the old Jacksonian assumptions. Moving in the opposite direction, the children of the newly affluent pondered the neurosis and purposelessness of that portion of society which, in the acquisition of things, had acquired nothing satisfactory; they proclaimed the goal of material enrichment unworthy of the terrible struggle to achieve it. One hot, July afternoon in 1968, a young man took me out to a new suburb lying heat-baked and hushed on the edge of a Texas city. He pointed down a treeless street upon which no bird sang, past the ugly little houses clutching car ports to their sides and plaster flamingos on the withered grass of little lawns and said, "Down there, in the last house, the one with the plastic swimming pool in the back, that's where I live." He paused a moment, hands shoved in the back pockets of his blue jeans as he stared at the dullness. Then he said, "The American dream has got to amount to more than two cars, three television sets, a mortgage and my Mom's monthly bill from the psychiatrist."

In saying that, he implied two things that were wrong. The dream that was first flashed on the walls of the American imagination in the Jacksonian era was too attainable. And, once attained, it was unsatisfactory. The belief that the common man could be very prosperous was too finite to be a principle. In the pursuit of principle we are always in the process of becoming, never finally arriving. When the great rewards of material society finally arrived for many millions of Americans, even the most belligerent defender of acquisition as an American art form must have sat amid the clutter that represented the strivings of a lifetime and, like the children at the end of Christmas morning when all the packages have been opened, asked himself the lamenting question, "Is that all? Doesn't it all amount to something more?" America, at that critical point, was undergoing a severe sense of loss. What had so cruelly disappeared for so many was a great sense of purpose. That sense had linked the dreams of individual men and the objectives of government together—the former desiring secure jobs, houses of their own, automobiles and pleasure objects while the latter sought power in the world and movement in the nation and each supported the other—outwardly anyway—with gestures and symbols. For the individual American, patriotism was a simple, emotive thing, wars were to be supported with pride (even unjust ones like the Mexican and Spanish-American conflicts) and, in return, the individual American got the eternal promise and prediction of his leaders that prosperity, if not always right around the corner, was out there somewhere nearby. This was the American form of the democratic bargain between the governed and their governors for many generations. When the payoff came for millions of those loyal, believing individual Americans, the things accumulated and became junk, the landscape was suddenly gashed by concrete highways and the old, soft towns went brilliantly garish and ugly with shopping centers, MacDonald's hamburger arches and Poor Boy Bar-B-Q's and it was unlovely. But, worst of all, the great sense of purpose was gone. Begrudgingly, the average American came finally to admit that the latest war was a violation of a great many things that America had always said it believed in and that emotive patriotism was embarrassing because it had become the property of right-wing politics. On top of that, the things which hadn't brought happiness after all, were threatened by crime, racial violence and revolutionary uproar.

Out of this crushing sense of loss, millions of people sought new purpose in reexamining the cost, effectiveness and soundness of the accepted American definition of progress. They discovered vast waste, the spoilage of land and waters, apocalyptic prophesies of nature's impending death, the rot of children's minds in trashy city ghettos and new afflictions of affluence itself—food reduced in nutritional value through the chemical processing of its big business producers, mind-crunching drugs to obliterate the intolerable contradictions of life, orgies of crime and a thousand other proofs that the good life promised for so long came at a horrid cost. From this emerged a new humanism, new passions for justice, new identifications of masses of people as yet unrewarded. Something else emerged, too—a clear signal that a significant minority of the Americans had begun to reject the assumptions that the nation had lived by since the age of Jackson. A mini-epoch was dying in great thrashings and convulsions of social turmoil.

In the anguished and strident questioning of everything from industrial values to sexual mores—and in the equally anguished and strident defense of them—it has not yet been concluded by either the significant minority or the defensive majority that the federal system itself is inadequate. Judgment upon it still waits in America because the old habit of accepting the constitutional values and assumptions lies deep and, for most Americans, any alternative is too frightening to seriously consider for long. For the moment, anyway, the great period of American history continues.

Yet the federal system has developed within itself a flaw which could bring down the condemnation of Americans; Washington has lost the capacity to clearly perceive the people it governs. It sits like some near-sighted, self-absorbed colossus, parsing time and events and calculating outcomes by definitions and standards of its own making. All around it there are conflicting demands, cries of rage and pain, pleas for reassurance and proclamations of public grievance. The colossus hears the sounds, reacts when they threaten its political continuity, but cannot grasp their inner meanings. Washington is an astonishingly unprophetic city. When a ghetto goes up in flames, farmers revolt against the price structure or masses of people descend upon the capital to protest, the federal establishment reacts. But it cannot forecast these and other events which, with prescient observation and a little thought about the meaning of things seen, could be predicted and prevented. The Process is reasonably good at binding up the wounds of its people once blood begins to flow, but it has a dreadful inability to keep them from hurting themselves in the first place.

As the intimate quality of political and bureaucratic life thickens in this city, as the federal vision turns inward upon concepts operated long past the existence of the conditions which prompted them, the sensors by which Washington could feel its people grow dulled and inoperative. The federal government has, literally, few ways of knowing what's going on beneath the public surface. Congressmen return frequently to their states and districts. But they are often so preoccupied by the minutia of people's individual problems and the distorted perspectives of local politics that they are unable to get an overview of what is going on. And when they do get it, they don't discuss their findings with the executive branch.

The executive branch hasn't many conduits into the hinterlands and provinces through which it could discern what is happening and the meaning of what is happening. The permanent representatives of the federal government out in the country are county agricultural agents, Treasury agents, F.B.I. agents, workers in the branch offices of executive departments, agencies and commissions and mailmen. There is something almost grotesque about the infrequent royal progresses of American Presidents through the countryside. They fly to a particular area, roar off to a reception center in a bubble-top limousine surrounded by Secret Service agents. There are meetings with local dignitaries, publishers and the grand sachems of the President's party. The Chief Executive has his picture taken pressing the flesh with roadside crowds while his bodyguards glower, makes a speech and hurries back to Washington. Later, in a speech or a press conference, he will say, "In my travels around the country I talk to our people and I know that they believe in—" whatever the President is selling that week. He doesn't talk to them. He can't. The grievance and instability caused, in part, by his remoteness from them, are so great that he doesn't dare get too close to the people. If they can't shoot him, he can't listen to them. The problem perpetuates itself.

Even when it does listen to the country in its own way, Washington doesn't hear the right things. The federal government is oriented toward and best equipped to deal with problems that are either noisy, statistical, political or threatening of the national security. It has no feel for the irrational stirrings and nuances that often reveal the real business of the human spirit. If you can't display a problem on a chart, by numbers or in terms of its threat to some political career, Washington has a hard time grasping what it's all about. The federal establishment can whip up a tax program, disaster relief or free hot lunches for little kids but there is no federal program for feelings of loss or for conflicts between old values and new realizations.

Theresa of Avila, that joyous and most lovable of all the figures in the otherwise stern pantheon of Christian saints, once observed that prayer gets us what we need, not, necessarily, what we want. God knows the difference and so should competent kings and governors. A people crying out in great cacophonous sound for a variety of things wanted, may need something far different—indeed, they may all need the same thing. But unless they are properly perceived by their governors, what they want is the only message that gets through. Washington knows what Americans want—all the many, varied and conflicting desires—but it is not finely tuned enough to the deeper voices and symbolisms coming through the public demands to know what the Americans need.

This institutional half-deafness is becoming worse and, from time to time various political solutions to the problem are proposed. The current one in fashion is for a rebirth of late-nineteenth-century populism. It is a thesis that doesn't hold up under close scrutiny. The political styles of George Wallace, George McGovern, Fred Harris, and Spiro T. Agnew may bear a passing resemblance to those of old populists like Calamity Weller, James Weaver, and Sockless Jerry Simpson. But the American people of the late twentieth century don't bear much resemblance to the American people grouped into the Farmer's Alliance or the Greenback, Single Tax and Knights of Labor movements. The American population of the late nineteenth century was smaller, divided into simpler economic classes and millions of people could gather together in a bloc made coherent by the fact that they all wanted the same thing. Today America is fractionalized into hundreds of competing, disagreeing groups. In its own day, populism tried to break the traditional pattern of American coalition politics and couldn't. It couldn't now.

Rediscovering old political forms or inventing new ones is not the solution to the problem of government's remoteness from the people. The problem isn't the politicians of Washington. It is the habits and institutions of Washington. The solution must be mechanical, not political. There isn't a lack of will to listen in this city, there is a lack of means.

Just as America discovered that it needed a domestic Peace Corps after establishing one for other countries, so now, it needs a domestic diplomatic corps similar to the one that operates in the American interest around the world. The domestic one would act in the same way—combining specialists in embassy-like establishments accredited to each state. A labor attaché in Georgia would do what a labor attaché in Belgium does, familiarize himself with local labor problems and movements, become acquainted with labor leaders, report back to Washington on the meaning to labor of any major federal decision affecting Georgia. Political attachés in Massachusetts would cover the state legislature as their counterparts cover the House of Commons in London. They would watch, analyze and report on the flow of legislation, try to grasp those human problems and movements of the state which are expressed in politics. Commerce and Agriculture department attachés assigned to California, would study and analyze the economy, working with the farmers of the Imperial Valley while black attachés, acting as emissaries to the black community of Los Angeles listened, answered questions and helped. All of this would be a civil service, not political function. All reporting would be back to some new Department of Internal Affairs which, in turn, would advise other departments, including the White House, of the multiple meanings of problems, of whispers and cries heard, of the impact that policy is likely to have on the more obscure and unnoticed elements of various communities—those obscure and unnoticed human pockets which are often the precursors of immense social movement.

The other function of the federal embassies in the states would be to provide a familiar place to which people could come with their problems that involved the federal government. New and simplified systems of dealing with problems and identifying the correct part of the federal government to talk with could be designed. If this would be one of the many aspects of the idea which would draw the wrath of Congress, it would, in the end, relieve Congressmen and Senators of some of the errand-boy function which absorbs an inordinate amount of their time and energies.

The idea of an internal diplomatic corps would be highly controversial. Congress would object because, in being relieved of a burdensome function, its members would also be deprived of a politically important source of public gratitude. The states, already wary of losing power to the federal establishment, would see the embassies as a further encroachment. The public, too well trained in the cliché that Washington already has too many bureaucrats, would suspect that this was just a device for creating more of them.

Yet this notion or something very much like it is going to become a necessity soon if it isn't already. The particular dialogue which expresses the bargain between Americans and their government is becoming choked. Both sides tend to talk past each other, neither sufficiently understands the other. Out there in the destroyed neighborhoods of cities that were once useful, in the suburban towns that have lost the American sense of village, in the increasingly abandoned countryside, the old assumptions of the Jackson era are crumbling—a logical if painful process because they no longer serve the present American condition. A new interregnum is beginning. In the depths of the American nature, now gone to pessimism once again, new assumptions are gathering. The larger question concerning the great period of American history is still unanswered. The city on the river is still capable of curing and illuminating the Americans. But they are no longer sure of that.

And so we wait.

RODERICK MACLEISH was born in 1926. He studied at St. George's School in Newport, Rhode Island, and at the University of Chicago. A radio and television commentator for the Westinghouse Broadcasting Company, Mr. MacLeish lived in London for seven years and has covered politics there, in Paris, and in Washington. He has also covered wars in Southeast Asia and the Middle East. *A City on the River* is his fourth book.

A CITY ON THE RIVER

RODERICK MacLEISH

Almost two hundred years old, the once sparse and modest federal government of the United States is a vast, sprawling enterprise that touches every corner of the world, whose programs brush almost all American lives; it is a colossus, a bewildering patchwork of the layons of history. Above all, it is unknown and mysterious to the people it governs. They *think* they know what it ought to do, but they don't grasp how difficult the doing is or how it is done.

A *City on the River* is a book about the central mechanisms of the federal government—the presidency, the foreign relations establishment, the House of Representatives, the press, lobbyists and mass movements, power brokers (outside advisors to presidents), the courts, the Senate; it attempts to explain the realities in which they operate, their limitations, failures and successes. Several hundred interviews, over sixty books about government and history, the work of seven researchers, the assistance of a vast range of experts and specialists from academics in Washington, Cambridge, Massachusetts and elsewhere, the private revelations of celebrated men and the descriptions of staff aides of two administrations have gone into this book.

Perhaps the most important words in Washington are power and politics—words often used but rarely explained. Power is